MW01178897

A Three-Day Event

Barbara Kay

Also by Barbara Kay

Unworthy Creature:
A Punjabi Daughter's Memoir of Honour, Shame and Love.

ACKNOWLEDGEMENTS:
A cultural memoir and other essays

A Three Day Event

Barbara Kay

A THREE DAY EVENT

Copyright ©2015
Published by
Peloton Press

Peloton Press
320 Kensington Ave
Westmount, QC
Canada
H3Z 2H3

Printed in the USA

ISBN: 978-0-9947632-2-8

Library and Archives Canada Cataloguing in Publication

Kay, Barbara, 1942-, author

A three day event / Barbara Kay.

ISBN 978-0-9947632-2-8 (paperback)

I. Title.

PS8621.A783T57 2015   C813'.6   C2015-908358-3

For Susan Robertson, a horse sport journalist
who paid a price for her investigative integrity

Acknowledgements:

I owe special thanks to Kathleen Delaney, DVM, for her technical advice on horse injuries and medication, and to former gamekeeper Bill Roberts for his deep knowledge on all things relating to that profession.

I also want to thank my son-in-law Matt Graham, for his help regarding aquarium life.

I am indebted to the following family members and friends, who read this novel in part or in whole, and either encouraged me or offered constructive advice: Rosalie Abella, Stanley Blicker, Naomi Caruso, Miriam Carver, Sandra Feldman, Ron Feldman, Anne Golden, Karen Goldenberg, Mark Goldman, Elaine Goldstein, Pauline Good, Naomi Goodz, Joan Graham, the late Geoff Graham, William Hart, Bruce Henry, Barbara Kalman, Ronny Kay, Joanne Kay, Jonathan Kay, Nancy Kumer, Christine Leibich, Jack Mendelson, Lola Mendelson, Sheila Moore, Terrye Perlman, Irv Perlman, Randi Perlman, Delores Rosen, David Saunders, Marilyn Sims, Zipporah Shnay, Patti Starr, and Lynn Walden.

GLOSSARY OF TERMS

LES CHAMPIONNATS CANADIENS POUR JEUNES CAVALIERS 1992:

A Short Guide to Equestrian Disciplines at the All-Canada Young Riders Championships

DRESSAGE:–*Rider and Horse Moving As One*

Description:

The most artistic of the equestrian disciplines, as elegant and precise as ballet or the compulsory figures of skating. The horse moves through all gaits and actions in energetic, but relaxed submission to the "aids", the physical commands of the rider, without any visible cues to the spectator.

Horse and Rider:

The horse–almost always a European warmblood breed, such as Westphalian, Oldenburg or Hanoverian–must exhibit precise and fluid gaits, articulate and "big" movement with superior balance and rhythm. The outstanding dressage horse must have patience for many years of intense, repetitious technical training. Taller horses (over sixteen hands) with beautiful conformation are the norm.

The rider is usually of a quiet, perfectionist temperament, disciplined, somewhat austere, and sensitive.

The Test:

Ten minutes in an arena of prescribed dimensions. Each horse–rider combination performs the same pattern of compulsory movements, which are graded by judges stationed at different points around the ring. There are individual and team competitions. The top competitors qualify for the championship rounds. The rest are eligible to compete in a consolation round.

THREE–DAY EVENTING–Endurance and Heart

Description:

Comparable to a triathlon, the Three–Day Event combines Dressage, Cross–Country Jumping over fixed and natural obstacles, and Stadium Jumping. The competition, originally a means of assessing the fitness and courage of cavalry horses who would be riding into enemy fire, tests the stamina, intelligence, speed, heart, and trust between horse and rider.

Horse and Rider:

The horse is almost invariably a "hotblood", an American, English or Irish Thoroughbred. Aside from good gaits and natural jumping ability, the horse must have superior boldness, heart and intelligence, so that it will willingly "go the extra mile" when fatigued. Event horses are the least expensive of the disciplines. The "mutts" of the horse world often perform surprisingly well in this discipline.

Good Eventing riders are risk–oriented ("extreme" in New Sport parlance), independent, fun–loving, and of all the disciplines, the most emotionally attached to their courageous horses, as well as the least likely to take themselves seriously.

The Test:

The three days of competition begin with Dressage, but less expertise is expected than in the "real" Dressage discipline. Judges look for a horse that is super–fit from endurance training and used to unrestrained galloping that will nevertheless demonstrate submission, suppleness and precision in the ring.

The second day is devoted to the Endurance phase. Two warm–up trotting sessions (Roads and Tracks) separate an all–out gallop over brush jumps on the Steeplechase and the hugely important Cross-Country obstacle race.

Veterinarians rigorously inspect the horse in the "Vet Box" before the Cross–Country phase. Many horses are "spun" (eliminated) at this juncture. The Cross–Country is the heart of the discipline with a strenuous gallop over varying terrain with a variety of jumps and water obstacles. These big, intimidating jumps involve "leaps of faith" on the horse's part, although the rider will have "walked the course" several times and planned his or her strategy in advance. Points are deducted for exceeding time constraints as well as for refusals or falls. The lowest score wins this–and all–phases.

Stadium jumping is the final test on the third day. Any horse that is lame, over–stiff or sore from the previous day's Endurance phase is "spun" in the vet check that precedes this phase. While this Jumping phase in no way rivals the "real" Jumper discipline for height or difficulty, it remains a challenge for a weary horse to show that, even after two extremely fatiguing days of competition, he retains the will, the 'honesty' and the heart to "finish the job".

SHOW JUMPING–Precision, Speed, Power

Description:

Like gymnastics or Giant Slalom in skiing, Show Jumping makes for a breath–taking exhibition. Horse and rider negotiate a variety of fences and obstacles at speed over a tight, confined course. Always popular, it is the last Olympic event, held just before the final ceremonies.

Horse and Rider:

The horse can be any breed, but escalating scales of difficulty usually demand a powerful European warmblood, such as those from Holland, Belgium or France, bred especially for Jumping. Good Jumper horses have power, balance, speed, competitiveness, and suppleness– but they must also have the insensitivity to submit to long hours of rigorous training without complaint.

Good Jumper riders are systematic, intense, focused, patient, unflappable under pressure, courageous, and possessed of blazing ambition.

The Test:

Show Jumping takes place in a fenced ring. The course demands shortening and lengthening of stride, tight turns and nerve–testing combinations of verticals, oxers (spread–out jumps), double and triple combinations, and water jumps. The jumps are high and the rails fall at a touch. Downed rails, stops, slowness, falls and refusals determine penalties.

CAST OF CHARACTERS

Principal Characters (in alphabetical order)

Thea Ankstrom	Coordinating Chairman of Young Riders' horse show
Jocelyne Bastien	Groom for Michel Laurin
Eva Briquemont	Wife of Fran Briquemont
Fran Briquemont	Dressage trainer at *Le Centre Equestre de L'Estrie*
Nathalie Chouinard	Wife of Polo Poisson
Ruthie (Jacobson) Cooper	Sister of Hy Jacobson. Daughter of (the late) Morrie Jacobson. Friend from childhood of Polo Poisson
Benoit Desrochers	Stable hand at *Le Centre Equestre de L'Estrie*
Guy Gilbert	Veterinarian. Housemate of Bridget Pendunnin
Clarice Jacobson	Mother of Hy and Ruthie, wife of late Morrie Jacobson
Hy Jacobson	Owner of *Le Centre Equestre.* President of *Tissus Clar–Mor*. Brother of Ruthie
Manon (Desrochers) Jacobson	Wife of Hy Jacobson
Michel Laurin	International Jumper rider. Son of Roch Laurin.
Roch Laurin	Manager and Head Trainer of *Le Centre Equestre de L'Estrie*
Gilles Lefebvre	Employee at *Le Centre Equestre* . Nephew of Roch Laurin
Liam O'Hagan	Head stable boy at *Le Centre Equestre*
Sue Parker	Toronto journalist covering Young Riders' Championships at *Le Centre Equestre*
Bridget Pendunnin	Three–Day Event trainer at *Le Centre Equestre*
Polo Poisson	Former Jumper champion. Friend of Jacobson family. Co–chair, Jumper discipline at Young Riders' Championships at *Le Centre Equestre*

Secondary Characters

Lord Fairclough	Father of Philip, neighbor to the Pendunnin family
Philip Fairclough	Partner (in England) of Bridget Pendunnin
Caroline Laurin	Owner of restaurant at *Le Centre Equestre*
Marie–France	Secretary to Roch Laurin
Denise Girandoux	Representative of C–FES Quebec Region on Young Riders' Committee
Stuart Jessop	Executive Director of C–FES
Barbara Lumb	Member of C–FES Young Riders Committee
Marion Smy	Chairman of C–FES Young Riders show
Bill Sutherland	Technical Director, Member of C–FES Young Riders Committee. Liaison to *Fédération Equestre Internationale*

PROLOGUE

September, 1981

BRIDGET PENDUNNIN PERCHED ON THE EDGE OF A TACK BOX outside her horse's stall and stared gloomily down at her mismatched legs. The left was its usual long, slim and shapely self: pale, a rider's sun–deprived limb. The right was an elephantine mass from ankle to knee, swaddled in an ugly cocoon of foam rubber, steel supports and rough webbing. It throbbed unbearably, and she regretted having left her vial of codeine tablets at the house. But it was not worth the trek back, not yet, she thought, scowling at the clumsy crutches propped against the wall beside her. She squinted down the bright, treed avenue, wondering when Lord Fairclough would arrive with the proposition she was both curious and fearful to hear.

From the open top half of the loose box Dudley pushed his snout amiably through her tumbling mass of russet curls, as if to say he bore her no ill will. Bridget thought about the accident at the Killinghurst Trials ten days ago. Up to now single–minded in her ambitions, Bridget was by no means a stupid person, and she was not slow to appreciate the implications of the fall that had almost killed her.

For one thing her leg would never be the same. She would never have the same flexion or strength where she needed it. Clearly her ability to ride again at the elite levels of the Three–Day Event was in grave doubt.

And for this blessing she almost cried with relief.

For Bridget knew that she could never again face the prospect of the Advanced, the highest and most risky level of eventing, in any case, and the excuse of a bad leg would henceforth be a godsend. The calamity had been completely her fault. She had frozen at the crucial moment, taken back with the reins when she should have given, and cost Dudley the impetus he needed to clear it safely. Thankfully, no one had been close enough to see. True, the footing had been greasy, and other horses had come to grief at the same fence. But she knew why brave, honest Dudley had faltered.

She had been terrified. That endless fall into the void she knew she would re–live in nightmare for the rest of her life. It was a miracle that the horse had escaped with nothing more than a badly knocked stifle. He might just as easily have broken a leg. She might have killed him. There was no use wringing her hands in futile penitence or in vowing to surmount her fears in future. Because they never would be overcome. You had it or you didn't in eventing. If you didn't, you were lucky to find out without ending up a paraplegic. She counted herself lucky. In her mind it was settled. She would never compete again at Advanced. And therefore she would never compete again.

But her sorrow was a luxury to be shared with Dudley alone. A lifetime of emotional solitude had armoured her with an impregnable public air of reason, amiability and traditionally English good sense. Outwardly she would slip gracefully into whatever new role life called upon her to play. She had already accepted with stoicism certain deprivations in her young lifetime.

But not to compete? Saying the words to herself caused a torment she was powerless to control as yet. And if one could not compete, then why bother with riding? And if the world knew what a coward she really was, why bother with life? The grim syllogism shimmered before her.

For she knew what *she* meant by life. Life was horses. It was hunting and eventing; it was breeding the perfect sport horse, it was 'making' a young prospect and riding it to victory; it was sharing it all with other people who cared as much as she did. What life was *not* was pushing papers round a desk, going to school, filling out tax forms, passing exams, balancing cheque books, wearing frocks and sipping cocktails, or living in cities.

She had never thought about the trajectory of her young adulthood as anything but a steady climb as a rider to the elite ranks, an eventual spot on the Team–that was the best case scenario–or a steady career near the top at worst. Then on to coaching, course designing, show organizing, breeding, importing and exporting–there were so many possibilities. But that was all finished now. Without credibility as a rider, without the will and courage to win–well, what was left? Where could she turn to make sense of living at all?

As if these desperate realities were not enough to bear, along with the pain in her leg, and now a splitting headache as well, Philip Fairclough's call this morning had crushed whatever remained of her shaken self-esteem. Philip, known in the Three–Day world as 'Fig'–because he didn't care for anyone or anything except his own magnificent self–had been Bridget's love–hate companion from earliest youth, living so close to each other as they did, and joined in their passion for horses. They were temperamentally similar and therefore usually at odds, but like two competitive siblings doomed to share the same space and resources, they had learned to cooperate and support each other for their mutual self–interest in the sport.

Fig was one of the great ones; there was no gainsaying it. A brilliant, fearless rider, he was a natural at coaching as well. He had been on the British Team twice now, and was a strong contender for Leading Rider of the Year. He was too good for Bridget to envy. She humbly accepted his superiority and was grateful for the advice and encouragement he was sometimes capable of extending. Most of the time, though, he was an insufferable, arrogant throwback to an England now largely confined to anachronistic, class–conflict driven novels.

Well, she reflected bitterly, he had as good a right as any to live by old-fashioned rules. It had paid off. He was engaged to be married–to a Royal, an amateur eventer bred in the inner circles of 'The Firm,' and Fig's adoring groupie. One of hundreds, if she only knew it, Bridget reflected wryly. Life was rich with irony in riding circles. Her heart beat faster as she recalled the morning's conversation.

–*Budgie, we have to have a rather serious heart–to–heart, old thing. There's been a bit of a balls–up at this end over that little tryst of ours in the tack room after my engagement party last month. Fa's got the wind up rather over it.*

–*Oh, was that a tryst, you bastard? And if there were four of you, would that have been a gang–tryst? You raped me, you little shit!*

–*Steady on, chaps! That's such an ugly word! I only had it in mind to set you free, little budgie bird. You should be flattered. I chose you for my 'hail and farewell' to bachelorhood.*

–*You only wanted to make sure you had screwed every single rider in England before taking a few months off–if that long. Does Her Highness know about Your Lowness? Maybe I should tell her.*

–*Dear me, I shouldn't think you'd be telling anything to anyone, Budgie. Fact is, someone else has already done some telling on you.*

–*What the hell are you on about…?*

–*Oh dear, patience, luv. Do you recall the little 'do' we had the other night to celebrate your coming out of hospital?*

–*Yes, of course. I don't remember much, because I took all those painkillers and then drank all that champagne you kept shoving at me.*

–*Mm. So I don't suppose you remember that rather hilarious take you did on your Israelitish surgeon, the hirsute and beak-nosed Mr. Goldstein from Golders Green. I mean, it really was a bit over the Fagin-like top even to my admittedly Buchanesque eyes. And more than a little unkind, do admit, considering the poor man put your shattered limb back together.*

–*Well what of it? I do hilarious takes on everyone. I mean, no one complained about my Irish bit, or my Paki number or any of the others. It's just for fun when I'm drunk. What's this all got to do with that fucking tryst anyway?*

–*Sorry, darling. One knows of course that you're an equal-oppor-*

tunity bigot. It's rather complex is all. Only it seems that the head lad was there, Davey Brown, who is to our stables as Mary Poppins was to the Banks family. Well, what do you think! Our Davey has a Jewish mum! Oy vay! And he wasn't best pleased by your panto, not one little bit. And what this all has to do with our little tryst–I'm so glad you're coming 'round to my own view, by the way, such a fine line don't you know, and don't deny you were just the teensiest bit cooperative towards the end–is that Davey was by heavy-handed coincidence a quite accidental witness to our two-backed beastliness last month. In the normal course of events, bein' a loyal and faithful servant to his betters, what, he'd've kept silent. But, alas, Budgie, Budgie, atavistic tribal loyalties seem to have gained the upper hand. In short, he wants revenge upon you for his humiliation, and I'm afraid he has taken it, m'dear. He's gone to the Pater and told all!

–And let me guess–you told daddy that it was all my fault, that you were drunk and I seduced you–

–I see that my mind is but a windscreen to your gimlet gaze. But as they say, tout savoir, c'est tout pardonner. *Do you know what that means? As I recall, foreign languages were never your strong suit, more's the pity now.*

–What the hell do you mean by that?

–Fa is riding over this afternoon, poppet, and he will explain all. I must say I was rather taken aback by his–well, he went rather ballistic over it all–I daresay Davey's thinly veiled threats to go to the paparazzi with this juicy tidbit would put any potential Royal-in-law off his feed. Either that or he can't bear the thought of losing a top stable lad. In any event, listen very closely to his proposal, and my advice is: say yes! Because we can help each other, darling. There's a fortune to be made from North American eventers, they're on the cusp of getting serious, but they haven't got a clue, they'll pay the moon for an English horse.

–What are you talking about?

–Oh dear. I wanted Fa to explain. It seems you're going to be a Remittance Man–or is that Remittance Person–m'dear! Dig out your O-levels Bescherelle, put on your most pukka Brit-speak at all times, never lose that accent, that's critical, and don't stay cross, you'll see, ever the best of friends, much the best way…

–What a craven little shit you are, Fig!

–Language, Budgie! What would Nanny say? And I'm not such a coward as all that, darling: taken all in all I'd say I'm just your average rider.

Shading her eyes, and straightening her slim back, Bridget looked defiantly down to the gate. Faintly she heard the delicate clip–clop of Lord Fairclough's black mare. In spite of her agitation, Bridget could not suppress the swell of admiration she always felt at this man's approach. It was not his virile good looks or the air of power he wore so carelessly–or not these alone. Rather it was a feeling of special kinship she had secretly felt with him since the earliest days of her childhood friendship with Fig. She had worshipped him as Master of the Hunt, as lord of his ancestral estate. He was bred to dominate, bred to lead, bred to decide the fate of others. She had sometimes even fantasized that *she* was the chatelaine of that magnificent estate.

As if this guilty secret thought had conjured up his presence, Bridget's father stepped out of a copse of beeches, surrounded by the inevitable trio of panting Labradors. Lord Fairclough hailed him, and slipped off his horse to chat a moment. Bridget watched their body language tensely. Of course he would not dream–he was a gentleman, he could not think of telling. But it was clear from their sweeping, pointing gestures and animated expressions that they were discoursing on one of the subjects dear to both their hearts: the prospects for good shooting later that fall.

Bridget's father was frail and somewhat stooped beside his robust friend. Although a discussion about shooting could engage him briefly, he normally bore the detached, ascetic look of the reader and solitary nature–lover. He was peculiarly un–English, Bridget reflected sadly, in his indifference to horses. If she could have ridden with him, perhaps she would not have spent so much time with Fig and his father, perhaps she would not have crossed that line.

And now here Lord Fairclough was, having walked the rest of the way, leading the prancing mare, looking back to make sure that Bridget's father had disappeared into the wood. His face was now cold and formal, thin lips a slash in a pale mask of anger. And something beyond anger. A kind of fear or disgust, it seemed to Bridget, which frightened her more than any degree of rage could have. She straightened and, in unconscious mimicry of an expression she had taken from him, lifted a proud chin to meet his gaze. His eyes swept over her, taking her measure in a new way. Bridget felt exposed under his gaze, and wrapped her arms tightly about herself.

Then the blow fell.

But it was not a blow! It was deliverance! Five minutes later, having rapidly delivered an obviously rehearsed speech in a low, hoarse voice, lifting a hand that gripped his crop with whitened knuckles against any interruption, he turned and, swinging lightly into the saddle, cantered down the avenue and was gone forever from Bridget's life.

She felt elated. How odd that her desperate need should have coincided with Lord Fairclough's rage against her. And it *was* rage. The timing must have been a factor, in this season of Fig's greatest competitive triumph. Yes, she could understand it in the light of his ambitions for his son. If *she* had a child, she would do anything to protect his interests. That's what being a parent was. Or should be.

Philip is going to be named the leading rider of the year. He's on the verge of signing for a sponsorship with Land Rover. And his engagement … I won't have it all wrecked by your selfishness. You're beautiful, yes, and that's a gift, but you have no understanding of beauty's power. You're a cool one, Bridget, you always were. Looking back, I blame myself. You were too close, even as children. I should have seen…you took advantage of his friendship…you could have ruined everything…

That last bit was of course brutally unfair. Fig had spun a face-saving tale. But his guv was offering her something quite amazing, and she could afford to swallow her pride against the injustice. Let him think his precious Philip was a wide-eyed innocent. What was that to the chance of starting over, a life in horses where no one knew that she was anything but a winner, a leader, confident, in control, and slated to be a Somebody in the world of eventing, even if she had to be stuck somewhere in the back of beyond of Canada to do it. She would have to learn to speak French. God, how horrible. She was useless at foreign languages.

Never mind, there was a lot to be said for being a big fish, something she could never be here in England, where eventers were falling over themselves, and the sport was glutted with breeders, coaches and sales agents.

Of course it would be sad to leave her father. He was struggling to accept Mummy's death only six months before. It would have been so perfect if Mummy had lived, so she could leave them both entirely without guilt. For there would have been no guilt at all in leaving Mummy, beautiful, distant, cold, cold Mummy. Better that she hadn't been there for the accident. Not for the usual reason, not because of the distress a mother would normally feel for a child in pain. No, better not to have had to face up to her amused indifference.

Would it be sad to leave Fig in spite of everything? She could not sort out her feelings yet. Fig was courageous on a horse, but not in friendship. Fig had said it himself. *...just your average rider...* and she had accepted long ago this odd juxtaposition of character in the people she knew most intimately. In general riders were not nice people. In fact, she did not exempt herself from this general rule.

So she could not be surprised at Fig's facile re-creation of events. But she could be forearmed in future. There was no point in burning her bridges, either. As a Royal Appendage, Fig could indeed be useful to her at a distance. They might very well do business together some day across the Atlantic. So there would be no recriminatory letters, no wearing of sackcloth.

She had learned a valuable lesson. From now on *she* would be in control of her relationships. And she did not think she would want to be close to another human being for a very long time. Nor would she ever again leave it to a stable lad to determine her fate.

Setting the crutches under her arms, she lurched slowly towards the house. She would take her tablets, make herself a pot of tea, and pull out her father's well-thumbed atlas. She hadn't a clue as to what Saint Armand, Quebec was like to live in. But it had a beautiful cross-country course, which she remembered from the televised games, when all of England and a good part of the rest of the world had watched the Queen watch her daughter fail to finish her cross–country phase of the Olympic Three Day Event. How awful to 'crash and burn' in front of so many people. She shuddered. Thank God she would never have to worry about that again.

CHAPTER ONE

March, 1992, Ottawa

MEETINGS OF THE CANADIAN FEDERATION OF EQUESTRIAN Sport (C–FES) were held in rooms of escalating charm and comfort, according to their designated importance in the roster of annual competitions. Today's committee had been assigned the best venue, the fading, but still elegant boardroom. Once it had been the parlour of Sir Lionel Creech–founding Chairman of C–FES–who, heirless and a lifelong devotee of horse sport, had bequeathed his magnificent Ottawa mansion overlooking the Rideau Canal to the Federation.

Stuart Jessop, executive director of C–FES, smoothed his already neatly slicked–back hair and surveyed the burnished oval with an inner flutter of nervous apprehension. Some, but not all, of the committee members were installing themselves at the table, pulling out notes and reading glasses, chatting, pouring coffee from the large sideboard urn, and settling themselves in for what had been forecast as a longish agenda.

Thea Ankstrom, naturally, had arrived spot on time and was sitting halfway down the table, materials neatly arranged, her composed, sphinx–like expression directed at nothing and everything. The politically neutral end seat facing the chairman–in case alliances took on logistical form–had been quietly appropriated by Denise Girandoux, chairman of Quebec region (*Fédération Equestre/Région du Québec*). Denise was a tall, modish brunette with a pleasant, straightforward manner belying a deep political savvy accumulated over years of collaboration with her anglophone peers. She smiled a polite general greeting and immersed herself in the papers before her.

Tottering slowly towards the table Barbara Lumb cradled her coffee cup and saucer in both arthritic hands. She descended heavily and gratefully into the chair beside Thea. Fairly deaf now and reputedly scattier than ever, she was one of Stuart's "Biddy Brigade," and Marion Smy, now noisily approaching the chairman's place, was another. As Marion and Barbara greeted each other with loud and hearty yelps of friendship and excitement–these meetings provoked intense animation in both of them–Marion set down her files and fussed over the pile of documents that pointed to her indispensability and importance in the forthcoming discussions.

Bill Sutherland, liaison to the *Fédération Equestre Internationale* and general reference on all matters technical and regulatory, slipped quietly into place beside Denise. Lightly caressing his nondescript tie, crossing his legs and settling his impartial face into the requisite air of attentiveness, he set his mind free to wander where it would for the next three hours. If there were a question that required his encyclopedic knowledge of technical minutiae, he would be called upon. Otherwise he had no interest in this particular competition. His thoughts roamed onto World Championship and Olympian planes of regulatory challenge.

"Where is Bridget, Marion?" Barbara demanded. " Is she coming up with Roch and the other man?"

"Oh, my dear, didn't I *tell* you!" Marion's feigned shock at her lapse did not conceal the triumph due the bearer of interesting bad news. "Bridget's father died rather suddenly last week. Actually, I was there in Saint Armand when she got the news. It was a shock.

There we all were in the restaurant. She had a message to call England, and she used the payphone there, so she got the bad news right there in front of us. Poor thing. She was quite overcome. She had to leave for England and she'll be there for a bit settling up the estate. But she'll be back well in time to prepare the course and look after the Three–Day end of the show."

"Such a lovely girl!" Barbara exclaimed loudly to the room. "And *very well connected,* you know. *Best friends with Viscount Fairclough*! Lucky to have her!" she concluded aggressively, although no one had implied that they weren't. Then, thinking things through a bit, she brayed, "That makes rather a lot of tragedies this year, doesn't it, Marion. Your Gordon, of course, and now Bridget's father and, oh dear, poor Thea's–"

"*Please!* Please, Barbara, I'd rather–really, I'd just as soon you didn't"–Thea's voice trembled slightly and she faltered a second, then pointedly changed the subject in her normal voice, with its rich, musical timbre–"I'm really not at all sure that Bridget can pull it off on her own. She knows what she wants done, but she's not the most organized person or the best at delegation. Apparently she actually forgot to order ice last summer at her own Three–Day in Saint Armand, and if one of the rider's mothers hadn't dashed out to the gas station and bought out their whole supply, the vet box would have been a disaster area. She wants supervision."

"Careless on regulatory issues. Works too close to a deadline. Not a good thing in my opinion," offered Bill Sutherland with an air of shedding largesse to the needy.

"Which is why we are so happy that you've agreed to be project manager, Thea dear," Marion burbled warmly. "Between your computer and your genius for organization, we know we can have total confidence, and we are *particularly* thankful under the circumstances. One would imagine that Bridget would be the last person you'd ever want to *see* again, let alone help–"

"Marion, can we please keep to the issues at hand. I know you mean well, but"–

"Oh very well. I'm sure I didn't mean to hurt your feelings, Thea. Some people appreciate sympathy and others don't. That's what makes horse racing, isn't it?" She smiled brightly at the aptness of her analogy, and Thea busied herself making notes, an angry spot of colour high on her cheeks the only sign of discomposure.

There were two very important members still to come. Marion held her wristwatch up ostentatiously and commented, loudly, in the peculiarly carrying tone of women who are in the habit of conversing at ringside over the competing sounds of a busy horse show, "You *might* think that the owner and general manager of a stable where a *major* event is going to take place would make an effort to appear at the plenary planning committee on time!" She then frowned, sniffed and shuffled papers in what she assumed was the manner of a much put-upon CEO of a large corporation.

Jessop sighed and ran his finger round the inside of a too-tight collar. He wished that Ronald March, the president of C-FES, had been able to attend. The blizzard in Calgary had been a piece of hard luck. Without his authoritative presence to subdue her, Marion would be almost impossible to channel. Stuart would do his diplomatic best, of course, but a staff person could only impose himself so far; Marion was in her 'confrontational' mode, and it was clearly going to be rough sledding.

Glumly he considered how he might have passed her over for the chairmanship. There really had been no option. First of all, she had paid her dues in the Young Riders category for more years than anyone could remember. She was *owed* the chairmanship, which was how things worked amongst the volunteers in equestrian sport. Then there was the sympathy factor over the death of her husband, Gordon, longtime president of the Don Valley Hunt Club, where this competition had been supposed to take place.

When the club went suddenly bankrupt, and Gordon Smy's role in the mismanagement fiasco leading up to it had been revealed…well, it was almost a blessing that he'd not had to face the consequences. And of course, Jessop wryly reflected, everyone in the sport, instead of using the debacle as a case study to make sure it never happened again, blamed the economy, heartless banks, sinister outside influences, and plain bad luck. Anything but censure one of their own, not this set, Jessop thought. Just rally round, circle the wagons and–

The sound of feet striding briskly down the hall broke off his reverie and the desultory chatter of the other members. Roch Laurin and Hy Jacobson entered the room murmuring apologetic explanations concerning construction tie–ups on the Champlain bridge and an accident on Highway 417 as they flung off their coats and took their places, Roch heading instinctively down to Denise's end, as far from authority as he could get, Hy unconsciously choosing a chair as close to the head of the table as possible, where he felt quite at home.

The meeting began. Marion had agreed to allow Stuart a preamble in which he would introduce Hy Jacobsen to the membership–everyone else knew each other intimately–and speak about the goals the Federation hoped to accomplish in the competition.

"Good morning, everyone, and–er–thank you, Marion, for giving me this opportunity to formally inaugurate the All–Canada Young Rider Championships Committee.

"As we all know, the All–Canada games, if I may so designate them, as they are in every way but level of difficulty a model of the Olympic equestrian games, will take place throughout the fourth week of June at *Le Centre Equestre de L'Estrie*–" he nodded somewhat obsequiously in Hy Jacobson's direction–"thanks to the timely and very generous offer of Mr. Hyman Jacobson to make use of his site. The games were in jeopardy and would have been cancelled without this intervention. I am sure we are all most grateful..."

As Jessop continued to pour out the Federation's gratitude, Hy settled back and watched his fellow members' reactions to this pretty speech. Marion Smy, whom he had met when she came down to Saint Armand for a site inspection with Jessop last week, did not look the tiniest bit grateful, as far as Hy could see. She looked downright pissed off, in fact, that the show which was supposed to have been in her back yard was now in his.

Marion was a possible future thorn in his side, that at least had been Hy's first strong impression back in Saint Armand. And there was something laughable about her too–long (horsy, no other word came to mind) face, brassy, crimped hair and superannuated felinity. He couldn't take seriously a woman so heavily made up at–he guessed mid–60s–who dressed in figure–hugging clothes cut and designed for a former size and decade.

The older woman beside Marion, Barbara Lumb, he guessed, her face screwed up in concentration, was obviously straining to hear. The yellowish streaks in her unkempt aureole of white hair reminded Hy of childish jokes about eating yellow snow. She looked very anxious, as if Jessop were about to announce the abolition of horse sport in Canada. She, too, did not look grateful.

Nobody did, nor did he expect them to. The committee process was a universal phenomenon. Hy had served on enough community projects to know the routine intimately. This was one of those little bonding formalities that were meant to put people into the mood for work on a common undertaking. It was the right thing to do, and everyone was waiting patiently for it to be over.

The woman at the end was very pretty. He admired her high colour and expert grooming. Her suit was a light wool gabardine in a rich fuschia–a Simon Chang, he'd bet. Good taste. She didn't stint herself on quality. Hy liked that in a woman.

The beautiful suit turned Hy's thoughts to his new wife, Manon–he was only a year into a happy second marriage–and he smiled inwardly thinking of how difficult it still was for her to shop for expensive, elegant clothes. He had to go with her, drag her past *La Baie* and Eaton and into Holt Renfrew, or to the more interesting shops on Laurier Avenue, and then he had to physically stop her hand from reaching for the price tag before trying something on. Usually she let him choose. His taste was impeccable. And in spite of his teasing, he was delighted with her reluctance to acknowledge that she was now a wealthy woman.

His glance slid over a bored–looking, featureless man and settled on the enigmatic loveliness of the woman sitting across the table. She had dipped into her briefcase for a tube of hand cream, and as Jessop hit his stride with the glowing history of horse sport in Canada, and the noble work of C–FES in furthering its glorious purposes, she began slowly and rhythmically to stroke and massage the cream into her long, sensitive–looking fingers, an activity Hy found both fascinating and unaccountably disturbing.

She was a few years older than him, he reckoned, fifty–plus. Her hair, a soft brown lightly threaded with silver, was drawn back into a low–lying ponytail, which suited her oval face and madonna–like features. Her gray eyes radiated quiet intelligence, not unlike his sister Ruthie's, he thought. But no, on second thought, Ruthie's eyes were darker, more textured, like much–used pewter. All her feelings were open to the world's inspection. This woman's eyes were light and steely, giving nothing away. This woman was veiled in some way from those around her. She sat very straight, like a job applicant or like a good schoolgirl raised by nuns. There was certainly something–perhaps not religious–but otherworldly about her–perhaps the expression of complete detachment, neither sad nor happy, neither interested nor bored....

"...and I have not gone on at this length merely to sing the Federation's praises, but in order to counterbalance the climate of suspicion and the negative public exposure to which our sport has been subjected recently, and whose effects have no doubt damp-ened all our spirits. If you'll all look through your kits, you will find reprints of several articles that have appeared over the course of the last six months in *The Financial Gazette*."

Everyone dutifully brought the reprints to the top of their fold-ers. A bold headline read: LILIES THAT C–FES–TER... The article that followed was familiar to all of them. It was an investigative ac-count of equestrian sport from the vantage point of litigants pursu-ing prominent professionals in cases of alleged fraud, both civil and criminal, involving corrupt veterinarians, venal trainers and mer-cenary coaches, all preying on their gullible, usually very young, clients in order to palm off underachieving or unsound horses, of-ten at exorbitant prices.

A second reprint, an op–ed piece entitled ONCE NOBLE SPORT NEEDS MUCKING–OUT, chronicled the woes of the en-tire horse industry, citing C–FES as a logjam of "old, *really* old boys and girls whose purpose in life seems to be shielding their own professionals from censure or sanctions, even when they have been judged guilty in the Superior Courts of Ontario and Quebec."

The op ed went on to a heart–rending human interest story about a boy whose brilliant career hopes were dashed through the duplicity of his own trainer, who had brokered a sale of an unsound horse. Even after admitting having forged a vet's signature to make the sale, and losing the case in court, "C–FES has so far declined to strip her of her accrued professional stripes, and she continues as an official judge, steward and trainer to this day. In this self-contained and self-referring clique, the obsession with ethical behaviour characterizing the nineties everywhere else on the planet has gone completely unnoticed. Could somebody please stop the world and let these people get on?"

Barbara Lumb loudly demanded, tremulously indignant, "I do not understand why you have brought these vicious slanders to this table, Stuart! Why is this–this journalist person–this–" she peered closely at the byline–"this *Sue Parker* person *persecuting* our people like this? I call this very *disloyal* of you–"

"I couldn't agree more!" Marion rose from her seat, a hectic glow suffusing her puffy face and neck, "I did not realize that we would be subjected to a re-hashing of this–*garbage*–at a time when we must be thinking only the most *positive* of thoughts. I mean, after all, why is all this happening all of a sudden? Why are these people suddenly attacking our sport? I'll tell you why!"

She leaned forward on the table and lowered her head in furious prophecy, "*It's because there are people in the sport now who were never there before. Not our sort of people at all–*"

"*Marion!*" Stuart hissed, trying desperately to remind her of who was at the table, but she was beyond his counsel–

"*These people have no history in horses. They have no respect for our traditions. They have no loyalty to our institutions. These people–*"

Hy's inner alarm system was ringing at full volume. In a split second a surge of adrenaline had his heart beating frighteningly fast in a spasm of fight-or-flight paralysis.

He struggled with his options. If he interrupted her to accuse her of anti-Semitism–for there was no question but that her reference was to a lawsuit recently won by Syd and Shira Greenberg against their son's trainer in Hudson–she would indignantly deny any such suggestion and everyone at the table would be uncomfortable. If he said nothing, he would be seething inwardly for the rest of the meeting, and feel a fool to boot.

What did he need this aggravation for? This was supposed to be a kind of honeymoon *cum* sabbatical year for him. With his marriage and his new home in Saint Armand as priorities, he had turned the daily management of the *Tissus Clar-Mor* sprawl of stores and warehouses over to his children, and repudiated the can't-say-no syndrome that had characterized his last twenty years of fund-raising, task forces and community leadership work in Montreal.

His determination to put his own happiness first had been re-inforced by the minor, but chilling little caution his heart had received last fall. He heard his ex-wife's brother, his doctor, urging lightly, *I'm not minimizing it, Hy. But sometimes a tiny warning can be your best friend. Change your lifestyle. Eat right. Get rid of the stress. Enjoy yourself, it's better than any medicine I can give you.*

In the half-second of his hesitation, Stuart Jessop had seized the initiative and cut Marion off. "I don't believe Mr. Jacobsen has been properly introduced to everyone. Why don't we go round the table for a moment, and afterward I will explain why our sponsor"–he hovered worshipfully around the magic word–"for the games, the Royal Dominion Bank, asked me to include the subject at this meeting." He patted Marion's hand and leaned in to whisper something to her. She pressed her lips together and stared fixedly away from Hy.

This was a bad beginning. Hy was weighing up the consequences of walking out. Let them put on the goddam show without his cooperation. It must have showed in his face. A stagey cough erupted to his left. Hy looked down the table to find Roch Laurin catching his eye with a wink and a tiny shake of the head: *don't do anything yet.* Roch began to write furiously on the back of his agenda. He folded up his note and passed it down to Hy just as Thea Ankstrom was introducing herself. Hy took the note, but waited to hear Thea speak before opening it.

Thea's voice, low, vibrant and suffused with the promise of a passion that didn't touch her public face, fell hypnotically on Hy's ears. She was explaining the 'critical path' she meant to follow as project manager. She described the computer programs she had devised to accommodate the complex scoring patterns for all three disciplines of Dressage, Jumper and Three-Day Eventing, the most complicated system of all. All entrants' names, colour-coded in their disciplines, would have their scores, logistical accommodations and billing progressions embedded in the same programs. It was a genial scheme. Thea was famous for her organization, as Hy now learned from the appreciative comments around him. Denise laughingly called her our "computer goddess", and Roch joked about women who make men feel even stupider than usual.

When Bill Sutherland began to speak about regulatory constraints, Hy opened the note. Roch's English was only functional, but his modest vocabulary and imperfect grasp of the language's syntax had never been an impediment to him. He was a communicator, gregarious and rich in the confidence of a boy raised in the bosom of a large, close–knit family with many adoring and indulgent older sisters.

The note read, "*I know that what Marion said, her, thats piss you off. Me too. Don't listen to that shit. I been to these meetings 1000 times. They just talk. Let that they talk. You and me, were the ones whose going to do the work, and we do what the fuck we want. Believe me you, don't get mad. Ce n'est pas la peine. p.s. she is not crazy for pepsis non plus…*"

Hy grinned down the table at Roch who winked back. Roch's cornflower blue eyes, ruddy skin and cheeky smile lent his face a boyish charm that even increasing baldness and a small but evident paunch did nothing to diminish. Men and women alike were drawn to his energy and *joie de vivre*.

Hy had learned very quickly after buying *Le Centre* that Roch was its heart and soul. The lively, dynamic atmosphere there was a direct reflection of Roch's passion for the stable and its resources, and his total commitment to a life in horse and rider training. Hy calmed down and determined to take Roch's advice. Like many successful businessmen, he had learned to trust the instincts of whoever loved what they did and had the most experience at it. Roch had been putting on successful horse shows for 25 years. He hated committees and loved to work. Hy would go with his judgment.

"…and it was only early this morning that Mr. Cosgrove from the bank gave me word that they had finalized their decision. I can tell you that this publicity came very close to provoking a cancellation of their role in the show. I needn't remind you that without their $150,000, almost half our budget, the show could not go forward.

"And so their public relations department has struck a deal with this journalist, this–er–Miss Parker, to produce a *positive* documentary about young athletes in the sport. It appears that Miss Parker is a rather precocious and–er–spirited graduating student in the Communications/Journalism program at Ryerson Polytechnic University in Toronto.

"Apparently she is delighted at the opportunity to be involved in such a project and understands the... mandate, so to speak, of the Bank. So she will be coming down for a week in May on the site to do preliminary interviews, with many of you, no doubt, as the principals, and she will use these interviews–edited–as voice–overs for the show, which will be filmed as it happens. I hope I have made it clear that this is a non–negotiable clause of our sponsorship, and your cooperation with Miss Parker is–shall we say–*assumed*, as it were."

Silence reigned for a moment. Marion gazed off into the middle distance, and the agenda continued to unfold. Public relations would be handled by the people at the Château Saint Armand, again courtesy of Hy Jacobson (nod, smile), who held a partial interest there, tents and catering by *Evénements Ltée*. Videotaping by...

Hy began to daydream. His own meetings at the head office of *Tissus Clar–Mor* rarely took more than one hour. This agenda was a hodge–podge of important decisions that should have come up pre–discussed by the executive of the Federation with recommendations attached, and trivial details any sub–committee could have dealt with. There was no order of priority, and he could see large gaps in representation from involved parties.

He strolled over to the coffee urn and eyed the solitary muffin on the tray beside it. Lunch would be a while yet, he could see. Then imagining Manon's mock–reproachful caramel eyes reminding him of his determination to shed those last five pounds, he sighed and took just the coffee back to the table. He wished he were home with Manon right now, in the newly renovated, rambling country kitchen, watching her quick, skilled hands assembling a delicious salad, or stirring one of her aromatic chunky vegetable soups, as they chatted about their respective days, the progress her new Belgian mare was making in the working trot and shoulder-in, the plans for renovating the barn and building the indoor arena...

Hy frowned as thoughts of the arena brought a niggling question to mind. Polo had said he might come over to Saint Armand one day this week from St. Lazare if he could collect all three bids for the rough exterior work. Had he mentioned what day? Hy couldn't remember if he had told him he would be away all day today. *Damn.* It was unlike him to miss or forget to cancel an appointment of any kind. No, now that he thought of it, he was sure one of them had said to confirm first.

Hy sighed hugely and looked up to catch Thea Ankstrom's amused eye. He smiled back. He looked forward to telling Manon about this interesting woman, as he looked forward to telling Manon everything. It was a continuing wonder to him that happiness like this had been waiting in the wings for him. Manon often said the same. Their luck in finding each other was one of the great topics of their ongoing conversation.

What if the manager at the Granby *Tissus Clar-Mor* where she worked had been more competent and the year-end figures consistently inconspicuous? What if his behaviour–the manager's–had not become so erratic that Hy felt he must come to Granby in person to check things out? What if she–assistant manager–had been on her day off when Hy arrived and appropriated her to go over the books and question her about the operations?

Then Hy would never have noticed and exclaimed over the picture on her desk of herself and her daughter on horseback. He would not have found out that she had been a single mother for twenty lonely years. They would not have gone to dinner together at the Château Saint Armand. He would not have told her about the mistakes he had made in his own marriage and the resentment his children now felt over his impending divorce. They would not have fallen in love.

The committee was now on to Disciplines Chairmen. Dressage would be looked after by the resident Dressage trainer, Fran Briquemont, the native Belgian, but German-trained, classicist and perfectionist. His wife Eva and Manon Jacobson would assist him.

Manon would also oversee the landscaping and assume hostess duties for the show as a whole.

The Three–Day Event would naturally be under the supervision of Bridget Pendunnin. The physical preparations of the cross–country course would be carried out by stable hands and extra labour paid for by grants from the provincial government.

"And of course," Marion concluded, "Roch will be in charge of the Jumper division, but as you indicated some time ago, Roch, since you are also the General Director of the event, you will need a good deal of help–a co–chair. I have recently been in touch with Rob Taylor, who will be off the circuit for a few more months recovering from the wrist injury he suffered in Florida. And I have a surprise that I think will please you all very much."

She stopped to enjoy the swivel of curious faces in her direction. But Hy looked in puzzlement down the table to Roch. Had he not told her? The guilty expression in Roch's apologetic eyes gave him his answer.

CHAPTER TWO

March, 1992, Mt Armand

Liam O'Hagan was in charge of *Le Centre* for the whole day. He could not remember a time since his arrival there six months ago at the tail end of the show season when his boss, Roch Laurin, had left the stables for more than a few hours. And then there was always someone higher up in charge: Bridget or Fran, or Michel, Roch's son. True, Gilles Lefebvre, Roch's nephew, was here today, but he was junior to everyone. So was Benoit Desrochers, whose main job was to muck out mornings and afternoons and strip-clean the stalls on a rotational basis.

There was Jocelyne, who only looked after Michel's horses, though she was supposed to help in the barn if needed, and she was working today. Jocelyne didn't count either. But the others, the higher-ups, were all of them away, and Roch had seemed confident about Liam looking after things. He'd left early in the morning with the owner–the Jew Jacobson–for Ottawa, and would probably only be back late in the afternoon.

Of course there were no lessons scheduled to create additional hubbub and work, and few, if any, of the private clients would go out hacking in this bloody freezing weather, killing it was, he'd never get used to it. Not that he intended to. He gave this job another few months at most. *Until he'd fulfilled his mission.* Then he'd be off. To somewhere warm. Georgia, maybe. Bremen. There was activity there of the kind he was now addicted to. And horses, of course. Where there were horses, there was work for Liam O'Hagan.

Liam thought about what form his mission might take. It was a shame that it always came down to getting even, but there it was. In his earlier life, the word itself–revenge–had been charged with emotion, guilt and pain. Growing up in Belfast, seeing the wreckage and sometimes the bodies, feeling the suffering and anger of the grown–ups, hearing the gruesome stories, dreaming his own death night after night, he had used to think he would give anything to live in a world without conflict.

But it was terrible to be hated, a terrible thing. And not by one or two people, but by everyone around you. That's how it had been since he left Ireland. And it had been hard to bear. Hard to be mocked and ostracized by the English riders in the barns where he always found work. Equally hard to be ignored and isolated by the grooms and the other lads. They all thought they were so *superior*.

He'd been lucky to get away from Belfast and Ireland altogether. He was under suspicion by association, and could probably never go back. His brother Mick now, he'd been locked up for all these years, and who knew for how many more? For what? For nothing. For keeping a few bits and pieces in the cellar for his mates.

Liam looked up and down the 130 ft. main aisle. He patrolled it to make sure the horses were all finishing their lunch, water running free from the automatic dispensers, none of them off his feed or restless or lying down too long. All the horses here were boarders and school horses, except the two stalls facing each other at the very end under the window.

Those belonged to Rockin' Robin, Bridget's stallion, and his nine–year old get, Robin's Song, a gelding, owned by a Mrs. Ankstrom in Toronto. Jocelyne had told him the lady's daughter had died in a terrible fall riding him in a Three–Day Event last year. She had told him so he wouldn't ask dumb questions around Bridget. It was a sensitive point apparently, as the lady had never agreed to its being her daughter's fault, and Bridget would never accept that it wasn't.

Liam had listened to this explanation without comment, without mentioning that he knew all about the accident, because it had happened at Timberline Farm where he had been working at the time. He had helped to build the course where the girl had fallen and been crushed under the weight of the somersaulting horse. He had measured the excessive depth of the 'drop' jump while they were building it, and he knew whose error it was. Bridget's. No one else's.

He considered the unfairness of Bridget owning such a fine stallion as Rockin' Robin. Both Rockin' Robin and Robin's Song were chestnuts. The stallion was bigger, a deeper liver chestnut with a wide face blaze and both had four white socks up to the knee. Liam liked a lot of "chrome" on a horse, and these were Irish Thoroughbreds, so he was prejudiced in their favour over the other horses. Not that he gave them special treatment, or not much. But he enjoyed their surliness, the way they put their ears back if you walked in on them while they were at their oats, and he liked the way you had to nip out of the way of their back feet sometimes when you were grooming them and tickled them where they didn't like it.

Rockin' Robin was a biter, typical stallion stuff, and Robin's Song kicked the back wall like crazy if you didn't feed him first. Liam wasn't afraid of them and handled them with ease. He felt an almost proprietary interest in Robin's Song, because the gelding had a history of colic, usually in pretty mild form, but once he, Liam, had worked through the night with the vet to get him through a bad bout. That was a good memory. He had been exhausted by dawn when the horse passed normal manure, but Dr. Gilbert, the vet, had told Liam he was a first class assistant, and they might not have saved the horse without him. He felt physically warm just thinking about his collegial friendship with Dr. Gilbert.

He knew Bridget respected him for that, though grudgingly, because she didn't like anything else about him. The feeling was mutual. Her plummy Brit accent got across him, and he knew she played it up for his benefit, just as he found himself falling back in her presence on Irish folklorisms he'd left off long ago. But he had no problem separating his feelings about the horses from their owners.

He liked high performance horses like these two because they weren't pets to be fussed and slobbered over, as most of the boarders did with their horses. They were big, powerful brutes–animated tools–who did their jobs well, and took their licks when they didn't without complaining.

No one was allowed to ride either of them except Michel, or Roch if Michel was away at shows. Both Michel and Roch could be tough on a horse if he acted up, but Roch had more patience. When Michel rode them, Liam sometimes had to wash the blood out of the whip marks when he did the post–ride grooming. He disapproved strongly of this kind of thing, even though it was common practice amongst high–achieving competition riders. He wondered that Bridget didn't take Michel to task over it. She should protect her horses' interests better. It was one more of the many injustices he brooded over at night in his cubby–hole bedroom.

Liam now headed down to the 'round barn'–a circular bulge running off the main barn–which was lined with nineteen stalls. Here the stalls faced onto a 10 ft wide access corridor surrounding a small inner rotunda of pie slice–shaped cells, 18 ft wide at the outside end, 3 ft wide at the blunt 'point'. There were six cells: a tack room, a wash stall, the round 'filet' of a barn office, a tack box and storage room, and a spartan bedroom, where Liam slept. In daytime the rotunda received natural light through a dirty skylight.

In the round barn Liam made a slow circuit of the stalls, paying closer attention to the horses here. These horses belonged to Roch and Michel. Many of them were in transit, horses bought on spec for resale, some acquired in the hopes of high performance, quickly assessed and found wanting, and passed along as hunt horses, junior prospects or pleasure mounts. Like most horsemen Roch was a mixture of impulsiveness and astuteness in his purchases. He usually broke even or made a small profit at the end of the year. Occasionally he won big. He rarely lost big. The fun of it, the gamble, was as important as the money.

Three of the horses were extremely valuable. They were Michel's potential and current Grand Prix mounts. The youngest and rawest of them, Maestro, had recently been purchased in Switzerland for $50,000, not by Roch, of course, but by one of Michel's sponsors.

Beside Maestro were Aur, a bay stallion, and Amadeus, a glossy brown gelding, shaved in January to cope with the Florida heat, now thickly rugged to ward off the chill. They were owned by a consortium of businessmen, fiercely nationalistic, whose pride in Michel as a *québécois* sports hero had driven them to the outer fringes of speculative fever in the high stakes of modern equestrian one-upmanship. They had sent Michel and Roch to Europe-European warmbloods were as a rule the only serious contenders for international glory-on a *carte blanche* spending spree.

At a small stud farm near Aachen, the Laurins found one of what they were looking for: Aur, a nine-year old Hanoverian, winning consistently at Intermediate, considered a reasonable buy at $250,000. In France they found Amadeus, already a big Grand Prix winner, but difficult. His former owner, an amateur, had paid $1,000,000 for him, then found himself out of his depth. The horse developed a bad reputation for stopping, and the Laurins got him at the bargain basement price of $350,000. Relentless in his demands, Michel had brought the horse back to winning form, and had taken over $100,000 in prize money on the Palm Beach circuit, a promising beginning.

Liam checked on these horses compulsively whenever Michel and Jocelyne were away for more than a few hours. Today he only peeked in routinely. Jocelyne would be back after lunch. No problem. The three huge creatures, dwarfing the thoroughbreds around them, dozed quietly, gently puffing warm vapour through their pink-lined nostrils and humidifying the air, offering no hint of the dynamism and explosive power they could display under saddle.

The barn was clean. The overhead fans whirred gently, freshening the air. The cold gray concrete floor, installed to support the weight of steel-reinforced stalls and 1500 pound horses, as well as to repel moisture, had been watered down, was now swept and dry. The covering anti-slip rubber matting was washed and down again. No shavings crept out from under stall doors, no bits of hay, grain or manure. The blankets hanging on the outside bars of each stall were clean and uniformly folded. The wash stall hoses were coiled and stowed. The tack was scrubbed. Bridles hung neatly in the prescribed order, saddles were ranged on their racks, fragrant with saddle soap, supple and gleaming, stirrups tucked up and polished. Grooming gear was methodically tidied away.

Liam was satisfied. Roch liked his barn ship–shape. Michel, on the other hand, was meticulous in what Liam considered a fanatical degree. Neither would have anything to complain of today. That was important. If they were pleased with his work, they would not think about him, they would take him for granted. He would not be an object of suspicion.

Liam was hungry, but lunchtime was the only hour of the day when everyone else was out of the barn, including Roch's secretary, Marie–France. She generally took her lunch in the complex's restaurant, coyly named 'De Trot' (a play on words lost on the impenitently unilingual Liam). And she was a slave to routine. She would never enter the barn on her hour off. So now was when he was free to slip into his cubby, flip the hook and eye catch closed, pull his collection out from under his bed and dwell on it without interference. He liked to look at least once a day. At night he was usually too tired, and the light, a single sixty–watter overhead, was feeble.

There were texts, pamphlets mostly, and there were cartoons and comic books, which Liam liked better, all stowed under a camouflage layer of ordinary comic books scavenged from the clients' lounge. He found the long, written pieces, like *The Protocols of the Elders of Zion*, difficult to follow. Anyway, he knew what it all added up to and how to communicate its message to others now.

He hunched over one of his favourite cartoons, a picture of the planet Earth being straddled by a huge spidery Jew with an evil leer on his monstrous, beaked–nose face, his long, proboscis–like fingers digging deep into the soft tissues of the poor victim, Earth. Why bother with words at all? This sort of thing was just the ticket for fascinating new recruits and striking terror into the Enemy.

It had been a lucky break meeting that Canadian girl, Janie Jones, training in England at his rider's barn. She'd been friendly to him for the few weeks she was there, the only one who was, and he got the impression that Canada was a decent sort of place. She told him that if he ever went over, her dad, Brian Jones, might give him a job on his hobby farm north of Collingwood, Ontario where he was building up an eventing centre. It sounded peaceful and pretty in a rocky, wild sort of away. Romantic, like.

Timberline Farm was all of those good things plus the bonus that had changed his life forever. The farm was only five miles away from where he boarded, the little hole–in–the–wall village of Flesherton, which, it turned out, was the publishing capital of Canada for all the fascinating literature he now had spread around him.

Liam had found a cheap room in a small, dark house on the main street of the town. At first he had avoided the family who lived there, the Fressermanns. The father was blond, rubicund and beefy, and looked at him with suspicion. He was a printer by trade. The mother ran a little Sears catalogue outlet in the front room, and crept in and out of the kitchen all day with a frown and pinched lips. The daughter was sallow and thin. She wore the furtive look of a ferret and had tiny, sharp teeth. Liam was not sure what her occupation was, if any.

Then one day the daughter, Christine her name was, showed up at a horse trials. She saw the horses go for a while, but then she watched Liam at his work She hung around after the competitors all left, and took in how he organized the mess, and put the barn back to rights. He pretended not to notice her. Before leaving, she smiled shyly at him. This pleased him. She didn't seem so bad, Liam had thought. She seemed quite pretty in a quiet sort of way.

The next night Liam was invited to sit down for dinner with her family. He was quite moved by this gesture of hospitality. It was the first invitation to eat with a real family that he had received since leaving Ireland. They hardly spoke, but they ate off matching plates and there was plenty of hot food, the kind he liked but rarely got, thick slabs of long–cooked meat, potatoes and a lot of gravy.

Liam and Christine went to the movies in Collingwood on his next day off. They talked over a coke at the diner afterwards. He told her a bit about his life in England. He let on that he was lonely. They shared their views on life. She diffidently brought up the question of religion. Was he Catholic? He could tell from her tone that saying yes was not the right answer. He told her–it was true, anyway–that he wasn't any religion anymore, religion was nothing but trouble. She nodded as if she understood this only too well. She said she thought he might like to meet some friends of her family. There was going to be a rally soon. Maybe he would like to come. He said he would, although he was not sure what she meant by a rally.

And there, at the rally, and afterwards at the Fressermanns' home, he had met people who understood him. Who *liked* him. Tears pricked at his eyes as he relived the swell of emotion he had felt at the next rally, when the leader had called his name, welcomed him, and everyone had cheered. *Cheered*!

It was during that wonderful year that he learned why he had always been so unhappy. He learned that he was a self–hating person and a victim, always subject to the will and domination of other people. Most white people, he learned, were self–hating.

(Non–white people were not worth comparing himself to. They were inferior races. A lot of people were too cowardly to come out and just say it, but this was something he had known before he came to Flesherton. It was something he and Christine had agreed on from their first talk at the diner.

He had told her that was one of the things he liked about the horse world. Apart from the odd rich Korean or South American who came to train in England or the States, it was an all–white world. What other sport than riding could you say that about today? Except that it was changing. There were all kinds of people getting into it now…)

And why were most Christian white people self–hating? Because they did not appreciate their own worth. Why not? Because other people were struggling to take away the space, the jobs and the good, decent life that was rightfully theirs.

These other people were Communists, Freemasons, homosexuals, and of course the Jews, the worst because they were invisible–in spite of the illustrations and caricatures, Liam had by now met enough Jews who 'passed' to know this–the smartest and the most organized. All of these drains of society had access to money and powerful positions. They owned things: the banks, and newspapers and television, so they could control what you thought–that is, if you weren't vigilant, if you didn't struggle back. There were so few against so many.

Now he was no longer just an Irish Catholic–what a parochial, dead–end self–definition that had turned out to be. How wrong he had been to blame Protestants and the English for his anxiety and self–doubt. He was an Aryan. He was part of a huge Brotherhood. He had a purpose and a destiny. He was strong, self–determining and respected. He was a man with a mission!

Of course he hadn't done anything *major* yet, but he had begun. His little band of recruits–Gilles and Benoit, they were timid, they hadn't yet quite grasped the *essence* of what their task was. He believed it was something to do with them being French–Canadian. They didn't quite grasp the depth and malignancy of the problem. Their own gripes–being victims of English Canada and all the rest of that crap–were just pure chickenshit. They seemed to understand his *words*–their English was quite decent, really–but they didn't seem to have the requisite *spirit* for the mission. But it would come. It must…

He froze as he heard Fleur, Jocelyne's big yellow mongrel, start to bark and then the sound of footsteps in the corridor. Fleur knew all the regulars, she only barked at strangers. Quickly he swept his precious hoard together, stashing it back under the bed. Kneeling on the bed, he peered into the little square of mirror, awkwardly but strategically placed to cover the tiny hole in the wall emerging adjacent to the telephone in the inner office. Swiftly he retied his greasy black hair into a neat ponytail, smoothed his beloved sweat-shirt, and went out to investigate.

"Are you a vet?"

"Wha–a vet!–No, why would you be asking that, then?" Liam stared suspiciously at the visitor, a slim, blond, athletic–looking man in his forties with posh–looking glasses, wearing jeans and a worn bomber jacket. He was absently scratching Maestro's spackled gray nose, and his relaxed, easy air communicated a sense of comfort in his surroundings.

The man nodded laconically at Liam's sweatshirt, which of course boldly announced itself as a souvenir of *Tufts University School of Veterinary Medicine*. That was probably why he had spoken in English, for his accent, though almost imperceptible, identified him as a franco.

Liam felt a bit foolish, and bloody angry too. He knew a horseman when he saw one, and no horseman would take him for anything but one of the grooms. This bloke was having him on. He didn't like having the advantage grabbed by a total stranger, especially not when he was in charge. Well, he wasn't bound to explain that Dr. Gilbert, had given it to him. And for good reason, too.

"No, I'm head lad. Something I can do for you?" he said as rudely as he could without risking a complaint to Roch.

"The barn looks good. Organized. I like to see a clean barn," the man went on mildly, taking in the scope of Liam's labours at an appreciative glance. Liam was prepared to be mollified, and these words smoothed his hackles. The following words raised them right up again.

"I'm looking for a friend of mine, the owner actually. There's no one at the house. I thought he might be here."

A Jewlover! Be careful.

"Mr. Jacobson's up in Ottawa for the day, gone up with Roch," Liam said neutrally, "to some kind of meeting, I believe, for a show they'll be having here in June."

"Oh yeah, that's right." He shrugged. "My fault. I didn't phone. Too bad. I just picked up some information he needs, but I can't hang around too long. I guess I'll leave it with Marie–France." He drew a fat envelope out of the inner pocket of his jacket.

"She's on her lunch hour, probably in the restaurant." Liam eyed the envelope avidly. Knowledge was power, and he already knew a lot about the people at the barn. Secrets. And you found them in the strangest ways. You had to be on the lookout. "I could take it for you, if you like. She may be gone by the time he gets back, but I'm always here."

Polo hesitated and looked assessingly at Liam. It was true that if he left it with the secretary, Hy might not get it until tomorrow. "It's not particularly urgent, but he'll want to see it." He could see the eagerness in Liam's face. *This kid is going to steam it open if I don't tell him.* "It's the quotes for the construction of his arena–you can tell him I've attached comments to all three bids."

Polo thought this boring piece of news would extinguish the light of interest in the kid's eyes, but he seemed more fascinated than ever. "Mr. Jacobson is building a private arena, then? Beside his house that would be?"

"Yeah, a '60 by 120'. Heated. Attached to his barn. It'll be nice."

"When?"

Why is this guy so tense about something that doesn't concern him at all?

"Probably starting early May, when the ground's soft enough for a foundation. Why?"

"Oh, just wondering, that was all. Are you–like–in charge of it?"

"I guess you could say that. I'll be supervising its construction."

Liam tried to act nonchalant, but his thoughts were racing ahead. *This is it. This is my mission. In May…*

He licked his lips nervously. "Well, that's really fine news, isn't it just? That's great. I guess I'll be seeing you then…"

Fleur charged past them to the barn door, set between the round barn and the main corridor, and jumped up, tail wagging. The door opened and Jocelyne Bastien stepped in. She stopped abruptly in surprise, paying no attention to Fleur's frantic demands for attention. She glared in naked hostility at Liam, then turned to the visitor.

"*Bonjour, toué! Ça va?*"

"*Pas pire. Ça va, toi?*"

It was clear from the contempt for Liam she'd made no attempt to hide that Jocelyne would have no qualms about communicating it to this visitor. And it was obvious she wasn't going to speak English for Liam's benefit if he hung around. Liam slipped quietly away.

"It's been a long time, Polo," Jocelyne said warmly.

"Actually, I've been here at least twice since Hy bought the place, but you were on the circuit in Florida and before that on the Quebec tour. How's Michel? I get to a few of the shows, I was at the Royal for a day or two, but we didn't have time to talk much."

"He's okay, I guess," she shrugged.

"Look, I'm starving. I'm going to grab a sandwich in the *resto*. Are you eating?"

"Sure. Just let me check the boys–" she walked over to the stalls of the three warmbloods, glanced down to see if they'd finished their noon feed, counted and evaluated the texture of the droppings, assessed the water taken from their buckets (more work, but measurable where automatic dispensers were not), gave each one a quick nose rub and kiss, and hung her ski jacket on a hook in the tack room.

Near the window end of the main corridor a glass–paned door led out to the administration and restaurant corridor. This door was locked at night, but left open all day for free passage between the two sections. Jocelyne and Polo walked past the locker rooms (both had bathrooms and showers), the main office, still locked for Marie–France's lunch hour, and the clients' lounge. All these rooms were on their left.

The right of the corridor was a long panel of picture windows looking out on a courtyard, a quadrangle bounded by this administration wing and restaurant, the corridor of stalls, the feed, hay and machinery storage opposite and the huge indoor arena. In this enclosed square horses were turned out all year and beginners' classes held in good weather. At the moment the square was tenanted by Popote, Michel's first pony, now 28 years old and blind, and Daisy, a goat acquired as a retirement companion for her. They lived in the same stall, and Daisy guarded her from the advances of others, equine and human alike.

At the corner on the left, after the lounge, one could exit via the main door. Or, continuing across this passage one arrived at the restaurant, a cozily wood–panelled, pub–like room with a welcoming fireplace, with views to one side of the Jacobsons' beautiful home, grounds and pond, to the other the inner courtyard, where the antics of turned–out horses amused the watching diners.

There were few lunchtime customers left. Marie–France was paying her bill at the counter, and greeted Polo with affection. "Bad luck. You've come on the one day Roch is away! You know he's usually here seven days a week. Never mind, I understand we're going to have you with us for a month at least this spring." She waved and headed back to the office.

They sat down at the outside window, and Jocelyne slapped her pack of Export A's onto the table. Roch's sister–in–law Caroline, who leased the restaurant, came over to say hello and take their orders. Jocelyne had already eaten at her tiny flat in the village, and asked for a coffee. Polo was hungry and ordered a hamburger with fries and a coke.

While Jocelyne lit up, Polo took in her appearance. A fresh–faced girl of fifteen when she had started grooming for Michel, she had already shed her bloom at twenty–three. Too much sun, dust, junk food, beer, cigarettes, sleeplessness, tension, and indifference to the most fundamental cosmetic aids had robbed her hair and skin of vitality and colour. Her weather–lined face was pasty, her mousy pony tail lank and lifeless. She looked tense and unhappy as well.

"Michel's okay, I guess," she repeated, unprompted, after a long drag at her cigarette. "He's under a lot of pressure from his sponsors, those guys from Montreal, they're after him all the time for wins. And from… well, just everything, you know how it is," she shrugged.

Polo decided not to probe for what was bugging her. It would come out. Grooms were starved for someone to talk to about their problems. They spoke for a few minutes about neutral horse–related events and people.

"I may have a buyer for your young one, that Maestro horse," Polo finally said.

Her eyes widened. "How did you know Michel was thinking of getting rid of him? He hasn't said a word to anyone."

Polo smiled. "Nobody told me. I saw him go at the Royal. He's good, but he hasn't got the magic. I figured Michel would find out for sure on the Palm Beach circuit–and I guess I was right." Caroline set down his hamburger and coke and Jocelyn's coffee with a cheery '*bon appétit*'.

"*Maudit*! You always had the best eye, that's for sure. I'll tell him when he comes back from New York. He's meeting with…maybe a new sponsor. Roch arranged it. Really super–rich this time."

She sipped at her coffee and Polo attacked his burger. He ate and waited for Joc to get on with whatever it was. Had to be something to do with Michel, because she had no other life. She worked twelve hours a day six days a week, and seven, happily, when asked.

Everyone in the business knew about Jocelyne. Grooms as a group were known to become slavishly attached to their riders, the girl grooms to the male riders, that is, but Jocelyne was a legend even amongst her peers. Eight years of passionate servitude so far with no signs of burnout.

And no payoff either, Polo reckoned. There wasn't a hope in hell that a young man like Michel and she were sleeping together. Not that in general any of the (straight) male riders took up romantically with their grooms. Polo personally had never seen a love affair blossom between such a pair. Thinking of his own history, he immediately amended that thought. When love affairs did blossom, the grooming stopped. So it was the best way to lose a good groom, for one thing. Sex could be had with any number of people on the circuit, but good grooms were hard to find. He doubted if Michel– no, not Michel, who had his choice of anyone.

"I'm worried about Michel," she finally said flatly.

"Why?"

"He's unhappy. It's not just the sponsors, he can handle that, I mean he *does* win a lot and whatever is bugging him, it doesn't affect his riding. No, there's something else. He's been all torn up since Palm Beach, something's eating at him. I think it's something with his father.

"Michel's too old to still be here, you know," she confided in lowered tones, though no one was within earshot. "Roch still treats him like a kid. And *he* still acts like a kid when he's with him. He needs to get away from here, start his own barn. It would be so great, just a small, private barn…not here…maybe in North Carolina, Southern Pines is really pretty…"

And you'd run it together, just the two of you. Dream on, you poor kid.

"How do you get along with Roch?"

Shrug. "Okay. But I guess I see him different from everyone else. I mean, everyone thinks he's just this fun–loving, jolly guy who's good at running shows and training horses and riders."

"And in fact you see him as–?"

"Tough. **Very tough** on Michel. I think he's like–kind of living through him–like Michel is doing what *he* had to stop doing because he got married too young. You remember when he quit, don't you? He might have had a career like yours. Actually I always wondered why *you* quit when things were going so great for you. I don't know. Roch and I sort of stay out of each other's way."

She was fiddling with her mug, twisting it back and forth. And she smoked one cigarette after another. She evaded Polo's increasingly concerned gaze. He had never seen her so jumpy.

"Joc–what is it?" Then he remembered the searing glance she had directed at the stable boy. "Is there something else? Something to do with that creepy–looking kid with the fancy belt buckle?"

Her face sagged with released tension, and she shoved her hand through her uneven bangs. Looking anxiously around her, she leaned over the table and, in a strung–out whisper, said, "Polo, I don't know what the hell is going on here, but there's no one I can talk to about it. Ever since we got back from Florida–the tension here, you can cut it with a knife. And it's that Liam, for sure. He's scary. But Michel won't talk about it, and Roch tells me it's none of my business."

"I'm listening."

Jocelyne drew a deep breath, stubbed a cigarette out with a savage twist and immediately lit another.

"This guy has something on everyone here. I don't know what he's after, whether it's blackmail or just for kicks. But he follows people around, he knows what gets to them.

"Me, I found him once going through my purse–I always leave it on the floor of my car–he said he was looking for one of the horse's passports–as if I'd leave one there, he knows they're all together in the office. I mean, it was a really dumb excuse. But I had a few joints in my bag and now he probably knows it. Michel hates that shit, he's so squeaky clean with drugs, he'd be disgusted if he knew…I mean, it's only on days off, but he'd think I was garbage.

"Then one day I see him talking to Fran's wife Eva. Fran is the dressage instructor–he's from Europe, an old guy, a real military riding type, you know, strict, but knows his stuff. His wife is a really nice lady and she used to come all the time to watch Fran and help him set up *cavaletti* or whatever, and then I see Liam talking to her one day, like as if he had something really juicy she'd want to hear, and she's looking suddenly like she saw a ghost and she starts crying. And Fran runs over and starts to yell at him in German. And now Eva never comes here, and Fran looks at him like he wants to kill him…"

"But surely he must have said something to Roch?"

"No, that's the weird thing. He never said anything, I know he didn't. It's like he's afraid of Liam. *Nobody* complains to Roch, and Liam makes sure he sucks up to him to keep him happy. But he isn't a fool–Roch, I mean–and he knows there's *something* wrong. He's been snapping at everyone, usually it's Gilles, his nephew, who gets shit…"

"Go on."

"Liam and Bridget–she does the eventing side, she's from England–they're like cats and dogs all the time–like snarling, trying to see who can insult the other the most. And he's not all impressed with her the way most people are here. He keeps making these snide comments about the cross–country jumps and how they're not built right, and what if the people in Ottawa knew–and she just laughs and tells him to–what is it–*sod off*–is that it? Nobody else says it here…"

"I don't really know Bridget. Is she any good?"

Jocelyne shrugged. "She knows eventing stuff, I guess, and pretends to be an expert on everything. She spouts off all the time about what a big time rider she was in England before she had to give it up. I don't know that much about eventing. Michel and Roch think it's sort of a joke sport, like doing three different disciplines and none of them properly. It's for amateurs, they say…"

Polo smiled fleetingly and said nothing. He shared their view. When eventers joined the jumper circuit to improve that phase of their discipline, they were usually pretty hopeless, and he understood their dressage was laughed at in the same way by the fulltime dressagists. As for the cross–country jumping over solid barriers, it was known to be a high–risk thing, and in his time he'd heard some horror stories, both about riders and horses. Lately, he knew, the animal rights people had been on their case.

"Okay," Jocelyne continued, "so there's these two kids who work here. There's Gilles who I mentioned before, that's Roch's nephew from Brossard. He's like not a bad guy. Doesn't know squat about horses, still he's trying, but he makes a lot of goofy mistakes. And Benoit, who's in my opinion a jerk, thinks he's hot shit, Mr. Muscles, you know the type, always trying to cruise me–like as *if...* and any other girl who walks through the barn. I mean, really *cruises* them, even the clients.

"He's an asshole. I mean, Roch flirts with the girls, but everyone knows it's just a routine. He knows where the line is, and he knows who not to try it on with. But this guy is so thick...I'm sure some of the clients have said things to Roch, but I guess it's complicated... he's a Desrochers and that family and Roch's are close...I get the impression he thinks he has some big future here, maybe because his family used to own the place.

"Anyway, this Liam has them both, Gilles and Benoit, in some kind of weird..." she gestured with her hands, searching for a word, *club* or something. I mean, you see them all three talking all the time and you walk by and they stop and stare at you as if they were like spies or something..."

She sighed. "Do I sound like I'm crazy? Like what do they call people who think other people are after them or something?"

"You mean paranoid? No, you sound as if you're reacting to something real. But what about Michel? Why won't he talk to you about it?"

The girl bit her lip and looked down at the table. "I–I feel disloyal to talk about Michel."

"Joc–" Polo weighed his words, "Joc–if you think Michel is in some kind of trouble, it would be wrong not to try and help him." He paused. "It doesn't have to be me, but–" he waited for her to meet his eyes and added gently –"I think I've been as good a friend as he's likely to find in this business...and Roch and I used to compete together. I wouldn't want to see any harm come to either of them if I could help it."

Jocelyn blushed deeply and tears crept down her cheeks. *Calvaire, don't cry. Please don't cry.*

Taking a deep breath, Jocelyn said in a tremulous murmur, "Liam is trying to blackmail Michel, I think. He told me he knows

Michel is–he says Michel is"–she was trying but she couldn't say the word.

"Gay?"

She nodded dumbly, her head bent miserably down to the table.

"Is he?" Polo asked as delicately as he could.

"*No!*" she said firmly and her head snapped up so she could meet his eyes with all the defiance her love could command.

"Joc–" *Marde de la marde, this is a tough one–* "Joc, you've been in this business a long time. You know the guys–the riders–you know there's more gays than straights–it's probably like fifty, maybe sixty percent, at least on the east coast, so the kid, this Liam, may be taking a statistically good chance on spec. But on the other hand, if it were true–I'm not saying it is–but what's the difference? He's still Michel, nothing changes for you…"

"It's not true! You mustn't say it!" She hissed.

"Okay, Jocelyne, okay. I'll take your word… and you think he's blackmailing Michel and that's why he won't talk about it?"

"I don't know if it's for money, or just to get at him. He seems to hate him for other reasons. He's always mooning over those two Irish horses, Bridget's, that Michel rides. He thinks Michel's too tough on them and he tells him so, right to his face! I mean what a nerve, telling *Michel Laurin* how to train a horse…shit, I don't know why Michel hasn't whacked him one by now. I know I would have!

"And I know one thing, that if Roch knew Liam was saying these things, I mean about Michel being gay, he'd kill him. You know how macho Roch is, it's like a religion with him. Meanwhile, Roch's happy with the guy's work, which counts a lot with him, and I got to admit myself he's fantastic in the barn, and great with the horses. Guy thinks he's God's gift."

"Guy?"

"Yeah, Guy Gilbert–the vet–Liam's been here during some bad times–a tough colic, a horse almost died, and then when Aur cast himself, he got him turned around, not easy with such a monster horse–so that's another reason Roch doesn't want to know–he wants Guy to stay happy. He isn't like most vets. He doesn't have a practice or anything, so he's like always around. And Liam acts like he's the official assistant. It makes me crazy, he's like two different people."

"Do you want me to speak to Michel?"

"No!" she said sharply. "No, I can't stand…I think we got to let Michel work it out. But I really appreciate you listening to me. I feel better." She added wistfully, "I don't get to talk to anybody like you very often."

"Like me?" Polo was genuinely puzzled.

She squirmed self–consciously and twisted at a ring. "I mean, someone who–it's hard to explain–someone who's in horses, but isn't–like–doesn't need to suck up to anyone?" she ended on a note of query, as if asking him to substitute a more comprehensive and articulate thought.

Polo smiled sympathetically. "That's a nice thing to say, Joc. And I'm glad you think of me as independent. It's the answer to your question, by the way."

"My question?"

"You said before you always wondered why I quit the circuit when things were going so great."

"Oh. Yeah. I see what you mean." She nodded, frowning, trying to look smart.

No you don't, you poor sucker. You don't know what freedom is. You don't want to know, either.

She sighed. "Maybe I'll take a few days off to get my head to-gether. I should visit my parents, I haven't seen them in more than a year…"

"Where do they live, Chibougamou?"

"No," Jocelyn said morosely, "just in Valleyfield…"

Cristi! Just a two–hour drive away. And she's not the only one. They're like slaves, only they make their own chains…

On the way out, Polo passed a stocky young man mucking out stalls, who stood up at his approach and followed his progress from dark, hooded eyes. With his full, sensual lips, doughy baby face and carefully molded fifties'–style pompadour, he had the air of a youthful Elvis Presley. That must be the unsavoury Benoit, Polo thought to himself. Further on a bit, Liam was wheeling fresh shav-ings down the aisle. Polo nodded curtly to him.

"Hey, wait," Liam said as Polo moved briskly to the exit, "you didn't say who I should say was here."

"Tell him Polo was here," he said, his hand reaching for the door, "Polo Poisson."

CHAPTER THREE

"*POLO POISSON!*" EXCLAIMED MARION SMY INDIGNANTLY. "What do you mean you've asked Polo Poisson to be your co–chair! I just told you Rob Taylor has very graciously agreed to help us. You can't possibly imagine the committee would prefer to have Polo Poisson when *Rob Taylor* is willing to join us!" As she pronounced Rob Taylor's name, the internationally renowned nickname 'Canajun, eh?' seemed to tremble silently, reverentially, in the air beside her She glared fiercely at Roch, the unhappy sur-prise–spoiler.

Roch appealed mutely to Hy, who had leaned back and crossed his arms with satisfaction at having Marion's anger deflected onto someone else. And Roch deserved to twist in the wind a bit, Hy thought. Although overwhelmingly gregarious, Roch avoided "situations." Hy was starting to recognize this conflict–avoidance as characteristic of many people he was meeting in the sport. He couldn't help comparing horse people to businessmen–and women too, of course–for whom conflict came with the territory. In business you developed strategies for dealing with problems, and dealt with them. This lot wouldn't last a year if they were running a business, he mused.

In the end, exerting all of his considerable charm, Roch smoothed Marion's feathers, explaining that Polo was going to be on the site in any case as Hy's contractor, that Hy was footing the bill for his accommodation in the ski condos nearby (at which point Stuart murmured encouragingly to Marion), that he was more than competent in all the areas needed: jumper course design and building, logistical supervision–well, he appealed around the table, everyone knew there was no one in the horse business who had covered every base like Polo, so…

When it seemed as if Roch had suffered enough, Hy broke in with, "And Roch was also influenced by the fact that Polo is a personal friend of mine. I guess I felt that this was one perk I could assume as–" he made a little show of finding and adjusting his half-moon reading glasses and scanning the papers before him–"ah, yes, *honorary chairman* it says here, right…"

Marion unleashed fresh indignation in her return look, but Hy was by now fed up with the overlong meeting, determined to finish with this–to him–non–subject, eager to move on to lunch which they had committed to attend, and get going home, home, home, home…. he looked across to find Thea Ankstrom staring quite intensely at him. He moved firmly for adjournment.

There was a brief recess before luncheon was served. People clustered in pairs and groups to review their impressions of the meeting or cultivate personal contacts. Denise Girandoux and Roch slipped into the corridor for a smoke and a quick gossip about the Quebec show circuit. Stuart Jessop and Bill Sutherland disappeared into the offices, Bill to consult the massive FEI rulebooks concerning queries that had arisen during the meeting, although he knew his responses had been perfectly correct, Jessop to telephone Ronald March in Calgary who was awaiting news of this and other Federation business. The bathroom doors on the main floor swung briskly to and fro.

There was a private, more elegant Ladies Room on the second floor with an old–fashioned ante–room where female Federation mandarins could perch on red velvet demi–back chairs and shore up their fading charms in the flattering light of rose–tinted glass wall sconces. On one of these dainty thrones Thea Ankstrom was sitting, staring somberly into the sepia–tinted mirror, massaging hand cream into her fingers, when Marion Smy entered the room. Thea started and a barely audible hiss of annoyance escaped her lips.

"Aha! So this is where you're hiding!" Marion chirped enthusiastically. Seeing Thea move to sweep her lipstick and hand cream into her handbag with the obvious intention of leaving, Marion slipped quickly into the adjacent chair and laid an imperious hand on the younger woman's arm. Thea flinched imperceptibly, but acknowledged to herself the impossibility of any explicable withdrawal from Marion's normally tolerable presence. She screened her thoughts with her civil public face as she turned a passive and apparently receptive ear to whatever it was Marion wanted to say.

"Thea dear," Marion began, awkwardness creeping into her voice as she groped to frame her apology, "I really *am* sorry about that little *gaffe* I made in the meeting." Thea quickly murmured the appropriate pardon and put up a hand to forestall any further inroads on the privacy of her feelings, but Marion, intent on her mission, was blind to any and all emotional moats as she galloped heedlessly across the still open drawbridge of their longstanding friendship.

"My dear, you must know how terribly I–all of us in the Federation–feel about what happened to your beautiful, talented Stephanie. We all know what a brilliant student she was, and what a great veterinarian she would have been. I thought her professor from Tufts was so eloquent at the memorial service. Please believe me. Any riding accident is a tragedy, and when it happens at an official event, well of course it's that much worse, I'm sure you agree."

"Worse?" Pale and trembling slightly, Thea gazed steadily and inscrutably into Marion's exorbitant eyes. "You say it is worse that Stephanie died in an *official* way than if she had died out hacking, or training, for example? Worse for whom, Marion?" She spoke quietly, uninflectedly, but now it was Marion who shrank away.

"Oh, I see what you're saying, of course," Marion, pinkening, stammered hastily. "Nothing could be worse for *you*, no matter

where it happened. Oh yes, I see that. And it's true. A mother, well–
there it is. But you see–" she frowned and hesitated. The scene was
not playing itself out properly and she was not coming up with any
fresh themes. She cleared her throat and tried again.

"It's us, you see, the Federation," she began plangently with a
nervous smile. "We're under a lot of pressure, as you just heard.
Those articles, this horrible publicity, these disgusting lawsuits–"

Thea swivelled on the little chair and leaned towards the older
woman. In her rich, full–timbred tones she asked, "Marion, am I
to take it that the Federation–Stuart, Barbara and the others–have
sent you to find out if I'm considering taking action about what
happened? If I've thought of suing Bridget or the Federation for
negligence? Because I am sure Bill Sutherland has told you that any
event held under *official* Federation sanctions would, indeed, make
the Federation liable."

She turned back to the counter and sat very still for a moment,
recovering total control over her feelings and, locking Marion's
anxious eyes to her own in the mirror as she delicately applied the
palest of lipsticks, added with a kind of detached amusement, "Do
you know how much liability insurance C–FES carries for all of
Canada, Marion?"

Dumbly, slowly, as if hypnotized, Marion wagged her head neg-
atively.

"Well, I'll tell you, *my dear*," Thea said. "Three million dollars."
She shook her head in quiet amazement, as though hearing this
news for the first time. "Think of it, Marion. Why, I carry a million
dollars liability insurance on my horse, on my one horse. I'm sure
a lot of us do. And C–FES, in this riskiest of all sports, for *all of
Canada*"–she broke off and shook her head at herself in the mirror.
Marion's eyes widened with anxiety as she absorbed the obvious
fact that Thea had done her homework–as usual.

What did it mean for the Federation? Marion had thought she
knew Thea pretty well after so many years together in common
service to horse sport. Now she was not at all sure she knew anything at all about her. What with her divorce from Harold and then
Stephanie–well, Thea might even have come unhinged by what had
happened. That detached, really very cold look in her eyes...Any-
thing was possible.

Marion squirmed and opened her mouth, closed it, opened it again and blurted out, "Listen Thea, you can't blame us for being worried. Nobody denies it. The 'drop' on the cross–country course was deeper than it should have been. But that wasn't the cause of it. I mean, the horse *stopped* before he flipped over. It was a rider error. You can't blame the organizers for that."

"So I've been told," Thea answered coolly. "First by Bridget, who claims Stephanie lost her nerve in the approach to the drop, as well as by Brian Jones, whose precious Timberline Farm must at all cost be saved from bad publicity, and later by other parents and coaches and trainers who all say it's part of the sport, tragic, but there you are, that's horse sport."

Marion seemed relieved that Thea was helping her write the revised scenario, and nodded vigorously. "Yes," she went on eagerly, "that's it exactly. And who should understand that better than you, dear. After all," she smiled with genuine warmth and camaraderie, "you're one of us, Thea, you've been there all along. If you took against us, well, the whole thing could fall apart. I'm not being dramatic. It's a fact. We have to stick together, you know. Especially now," she concluded intimately and ominously.

"I understand exactly what you're saying," Thea responded evenly, facing her directly, "and I can assure you that my plans do not include any lawsuits at the moment." Turning back to the mirror, she met Marion's image, rosy and childlike in relief, with a slight but dismissive nod, which let even Marion know that the interview was over. Marion smiled, feeling she was back in control of the situation. She squeezed Thea's unresponding hand, stood tall in her famously no–nonsense way, flashed a V for victory salute, and swept out of the room.

Thea continued to stare fiercely into and beyond her austere reflection in the mirror.

You're one of us.

What had she and Marion, this foolish, bovine, boring woman in common?

You're one of us.

How had it happened that she had so willingly devoted so much time, half a lifetime, to a pursuit that now seemed so utterly meaningless?

You're one of us…

Thea covered her face with her lily-of-the-valley-scented hands, which so grotesquely twinned memories of her own bridal bouquet and the masses of funeral wreaths, and moaned quietly, "Oh Stephanie, you were always the brave one. I have been the coward. I'm the one who lost my nerve. But I'll find the way to avenge you, I promise. I failed you in life, but I won't fail your memory."

Lunch was served in the baronial dining hall across from the meeting room. Hy assessed its content with gloom: canned *consommé* with nothing but a sliver of julienned carrot to gladden the eye, thin sandwiches of pallid ham, stringy roast beef and American cheese on sliced white bread, and the whole depressing collation topped off with canned fruit cocktail and commercial shortbread cookies. Hy tried not to think about his usual noon fare.

Thea Ankstrom, weary-looking and later than the others, slipped in beside him. In a low, silky voice, she asked quietly, "You said you were a friend of Polo's?"

"Yes," Hy replied. "We go back more than thirty years now." He laughed. "I always feel old when I think of how long I've known him."

"Is your father's name Morrie?" Her voice was lower and slightly rougher to his ear now.

"Yes, it was."

"Was?"

" He died a few years ago, actually. But how do you"–

"Died?! Oh, I'm terribly sorry, very sorry." She bit her lip and rushed on to forestall Hy's natural curiosity. "You see, I met him once. Just the once. But I was–well–the circumstances were unusual–oh, dear, I'm not making much sense–but it's really not important about the circumstances. I just wanted to say that I thought he was a most–well, *extraordinary* person."

"We all thought he was. And thank you–I assume." There could only be one connection between this elegant Rosedale matron and his father. " I take it you must have met through Polo."

"Yes, in a way." She flushed slightly and looked down at her plate. "It was so long ago that I didn't twig to the coincidence of your names until Polo's name came up at the meeting. Did you say that Polo will be on the site all through May, then?"

"Yes, he will. As a matter of fact you'll be neighbours. We're taking over some of the ski condos, they're just down the road a bit from the barn, and that time of year we can have our pick. I think you'll be comfortable there, with plenty of room for your computers and stuff. Nice view of the mountain and the cross–country course. How long has it been since you've seen Polo?"

"Seen him? Oh, my dau–my interest was always more in eventing than in jumping, so I've seen him occasionally around the shows when he coaches or designs the course. But I've never actually spoken to him. It's just, well I knew that your father was his sponsor, and I rather got the impression that Polo was in some way a member of your fam–your household?"

Hy laughed and shook his head. "You know, I still haven't quite figured out how to answer that question. He was around our house so much he was *like* a member of the family, but–" Hy shook his head again–"his life was so different from ours, my sister's and mine, and he came and went so freely–" here he raised his hands in a gesture of surrender, "all I can tell you is that in spite of us having practically nothing in common, I consider him one of my oldest and best friends."

She nodded, then became her usual, sphinx–like self again. She turned to talk to Bill Sutherland, and Hy felt once again that curious mixture of fascination and unease she seemed to conjure in people as a matter of course.

It was at last time to leave. People were stowing papers in their briefcases, brushing crumbs away and congratulating each other on the morning's accomplishments. Hy was delighted that the moment had finally come, but something tugged at his memory. In the commotion over Polo's chairmanship, he had forgotten to mention a curious oversight in the agenda. Now he remembered, and prayed it wouldn't involve another battle with Marion.

"Look everybody, I'm sorry to delay you a few more minutes. I know we're all anxious to be off, but my people are going to have to order the T–shirts pretty soon from our suppliers, not to mention the banners and flyers and whatnot, so I'll have to know before the next meeting what the name of the show is."

The committee turned as one to stare at Hy in total bafflement. Except for Denise Girandoux whose sparkling eyes betrayed a cautious hope. "The name of the show?" she prompted demurely, encouragingly. "I was wondering about that myself."

"Whatever is Mr. Jacobson talking about, Marion?" brayed Barbara Lumb. "I'm quite sure Stuart mentioned it several times and it was right on the agenda!" She looked at Hy with undisguised scorn.

Patiently Hy explained. "I meant the official name, of course. The French name."

Bill Sutherland broke the stony silence following this statement with the first sign of animation he had shown that day. "An interesting point, actually. The FEI has standard regulatory names depending upon the host country's language. A nice ambiguity here, very nice indeed. I would be more than happy to explore the issue. I daresay it would be something like '*Les Championnats Equestres Canadiens pour Jeunes Cavaliers*' or some such"(his accent was execrable, but Hy gave him points for going public).

Stuart Jessop added hastily, "Well, I really don't think we ought to get into any *political* situations here. Most of our riders are coming from outside of Quebec. This is a *Canadian* event, after all. So why don't we just stick with the name we have. Of course, that's *not* to say–" smiling broadly at Denise –"that we shouldn't have a *bilingual* title. That might be in quite good taste, actually."

If Marion had left it at that…but no… "No, Stuart", she asserted loudly, "I call that *giving in* to the separatists. They've *had* their referendum, and they voted to stay *Canadian*. Our national events have *always* had English titles. We will have visiting dignitaries from the American federations, after all. There is no reason why we can't publish French–language flyers and schedules with a French name on them. But this business of *ramming* French down everyone's throats every time we put on an event in Quebec…"

Hy exchanged a speaking glance with Denise. He saw she was prepared to do the quick and dirty, but in these particular circumstances it would be better coming from a lay person, and even better, from an anglophone. Clearly he was the one anglophone in that room for whom this particular conflict was neither threatening nor unwelcome where a principle was at stake. Her eyes thanked him as he rose to the occasion.

✤ ✤ ✤

They were traveling in Roch's pick–up truck because he had to stop to get a magneto–therapy unit at an Ottawa tack store for use on the "boys," and Manon's car was in service, so she had needed Hy's Audi. Hy was tired and just as happy not to have to drive himself, but the heating unit was volatile and he felt cranky from the morning's irritations.

They spoke in French, because five hours of English had given Roch a headache, and because Hy didn't care, and was actually happy in this case to shake the Federation's dust from his heels. Normally Roch's rule of thumb was to speak the language of the person he perceived as higher up in the influential scheme of things: sponsors, owners, clients–it was a pre–Quiet Revolution habit he admitted to freely, but now it suited them both to achieve a distance from the committee.

"Is Ghislaine still visiting her parents in Quebec? Because Manon and I would he happy to have you join us for dinner" –

"Thanks, but I have to give *le maire* a nice time tonight at the resto. We're going to discuss how much the town is giving us for the show," Roch answered. "Ghislaine will be back soon, but I'm okay, there's always someone at the barn."

They rolled along freely. Traffic was light. Hy yawned. He wasn't used to getting up so early. Roch was up every day at six and in the barn by 7:45. Hy thought back to the final hassle of the day. They had ended with a French name, but there was by now no hope of reconciliation with Marion. The battle lines were drawn. What a collection they were. His mind unwillingly alighted on what his father would have said. *A bunch of goyische kopfen, Hymie.*

"You know, it didn't help when Marion asked your opinion and you said you didn't care if the name was Japanese, as long as the sponsors paid up," Hy grumbled.

"I'm sorry, but I get so damned fed up with this political shit," Roch answered. "It took me fifteen years to get the anglos to come to *le Centre*. Now I got them, business is good, and I don't want to fuck it up. I hate that at *le Centre*, all these local guys giving me the gears, dreaming of *les bons vieux temps* when it was a little private club. Let them pay the bills if they think it's so important everyone should only speak French there."

"You're very '*politiquement incorrect*'," Hy said, not sure at all if that was the proper way to express his thought or just an anglicism.

"*Comment?*"

"Never mind." He started to reach automatically for a non–existent car phone, then remembered where he was. "Listen, you need some gas, and I'd better call the office. Can we stop in a minute?"

"No problem."

At the gas station, Roch disappeared into the *dépanneur* to browse amongst the snack food while Hy telephoned.

"*Tissus Clar–Mor, bonjour.*"

"Hi, Debbie. S'me. Put me through to Howard."

"Oh, hi, Mr. J. Just a sec."

Howard gave him a fast run–down of the morning's offerings: burst pipes in the Ste. Agathe store with plenty of ruined fabric, he was waiting for the insurance company's call, no problem on a re–order of the fabric, a sudden resignation of the manager in the Pierrefonds store, no big deal, the assistant was an up–and–comer anyway, a screw–up at customs on the stuff from Dusseldorf, Denis was looking into it, a price error in the *La Presse* insert, they'd probably get half off… oh, and Elaine had just checked in from the airport after a good round of appointments in New York.

"She said to tell you she saw your manager's son on the plane coming back, whats–his–name, the gorgeous famous rider, she recognized him from all the posters, but he looked so pissed off at the world she didn't introduce herself."

"Really? Wonder why. Anyway, think you'll finally make it up to Saint Armand this weekend?"

"Gee, I don't know, dad. Judy's folks are expecting us in Stowe. It's probably one of the last really good ski weekends. And …I know it's taking a while…I hope you understand…I'm just not quite *there* yet with your new life. Don't get me wrong, it's not Manon, she's great, really, she's great, but…"

"It's okay, Howie, I get the drift. And don't worry about it. Anyway, I'll be home in two hours. Fax me if there's news on the insurance thing. Bye.'"

Roch was waiting in the truck, guiltlessly finishing off a May West, the chocolate-covered rondelle of cream-filled white cake sold uniquely in *la belle province*. Hy inhaled the sweet vanilla-charged aroma that represented the dominant snack fetish of his whole conscious life, and watched him pick off the lingering crumbs with covert envy. Sometimes he wished he were not so well-versed in the fat and cholesterol content of the foods he still craved but could no longer enjoy.

"Everything okay?" Roch started up and eased back out on the highway.

"About as usual. Nothing Howard can't handle."

"So it's working out okay? You don't mind not being in charge any more?" Roch glanced at Hy to see if he had taken this as criticism. "I mean, it's none of my business, but that's a hell of a responsibility for a kid his age to handle."

"I wouldn't say I've handed over all that much responsibility. I'm still the heavyweight in the big decisions–opening new stores, or acquiring real estate–but in the day-to-day stuff I'm sharing management with Howard–and with Elaine too. She's doing most of the buying for the bedroom and bath boutiques, and she's terrific. Both my kids really like the business. I'm lucky. They both have business degrees and Howard is taking this program Harvard University runs for family business transitions between generations. It's amazing how things can fall apart if you don't plan carefully. Well, look who I'm talking to–Michel is a *fifth* generation in the family business–we're '*bleuets*' compared to you guys."

Roch was uncharacteristically silent for a time. Hy hoped he hadn't offended him by praising his own kids' education and achievements. He didn't think so. Roch's sun and moon rose and set on Michel. As for achievements, in any horseman's eyes Michel had more than fulfilled a father's wildest ambitions.

"Elaine said she saw Michel on the plane home from New York today."

Shaking off whatever thoughts were preoccupying him, Roch enthused, "You bet. There's a guy there, he owns a phone company. The ones with no cords. Filthy rich. Panaiotti–you heard of him?"

"Yeah, as a matter of fact, I think I have. Got in on the ground floor of cellular phones."

"You got it! Well, he's crazy for Michel. He wants to sponsor him. They were talking today."

"Isn't it a little odd for an American to want to sponsor a Canadian rider?"

"Not for this guy. He has a daughter. She's a little on the skinny side, but pretty enough. Anyway, that's not the main thing. She's an amateur rider. Follows the circuit around. And she's got the hots for Michel. Get the picture?" He grinned happily at Hy.

"You mean Michel wants to marry her?"

"Sure he wants to. He's not a fool."

...but he looked so pissed off at the world that she didn't introduce herself.

"I mean, has he *said* he wants to?"

"Hy, you got to understand something. Michel, he has no education past CEGEP. He's a rider. That's all he knows. I spoiled him, I admit that. I always said, you just ride, I'll take care of everything else. It costs a fortune to compete. A lot of the riders come from rich families. Okay, you're pretty rich, Hy, but even you don't know what kind of money we're talking here. I'm not rich and I never will be.

"When he was young I scrounged money from everywhere for him to compete. From the Optimists Club. From my MP. From my MNA. Anywhere I could. It's never enough. He's never sure if he'll make the next season. Do you remember 'D'Artagnan', that horse he went to the Olympics on?"

What horse lover didn't remember Michel Laurin and D'Artagnan? At nineteen, a recognized prodigy in the sport, Michel had been the youngest rider in history to win both the World Championships and an Olympic medal on the same horse. The horse had been a national treasure, his name resonant with glory even to people who never followed equestrian sport. And Michel became a local god in the Quebec media.

"Of course I remember. They were amazing!"

"Well, maybe you don't remember what happened to that horse. The guys that owned him, all these *pure laine Québecois* who were so excited to see their *p'tit gars* get famous and make them so proud, after the Olympics these same guys grabbed the money when a big

American rider offered them a price they couldn't say no to. They didn't even tell Michel they were thinking about it. The same day he found out, this American guy's van pulls up at the barn, and they walk out with the horse." Roch's face was stony with memory.

"I didn't know that, Roch." Hy tried to imagine someone walking into Howard's office and asking him to leave, putting up a new sign on the door…

"Don't get me wrong. I'm not complaining about what they did. They paid $75,000 for that horse–Polo found him in Belgium–and they got offered $750,000 three years later–American dollars!" He shrugged. "You can't blame them."

There was a short silence. The morning's blowing snow had given way to bright afternoon sun, still high in the late March sky at three o'clock.

"So you see," Roch continued in ordinary tones, "I got no use for romance when it comes to Michel's future. These new guys who own the two big horses he has now, sure they're all over Michel, they love him like a son. But if he stops winning, or they get a really good offer, or one of them goes bankrupt and needs the money…" He hoisted his shoulders in a huge Gallic gesture of frustration.

"But Roch, if he marries this girl, he'll probably end up in the States. No rich girl from New York is going to want to live in Saint Armand."

Roch shrugged again. *"C'est la guerre, mon ami."*

"By the way, what happened to D'Artagnan? I never heard about him after Michel stopped riding him."

"The American rider–Gully Gray–he never won anything much on him. The horse was always a tough ride, but Michel made it look easy… anyway, the horse had surgery for something and–lucky for Gully–he died on the table…"

"You're not saying"–

"In this business nobody ever says anything. All I'm saying is that the guy couldn't ride him, and looked like a fool, and then the horse died. *C'est la vie, vieux…*"

'You have one message! Hi, Manon. Elaine. I just want to thank you for lunch yesterday. Sorry your daughter couldn't join us. I'm off

to New York for the day. I really appreciated our talk. I'm really okay with everything, and now that she and Jacques are a couple, I think my mom is too. I'd love to come out to Saint Armand, not this weekend, but probably next if that's okay. Love to daddy. Bye'.

Manon Jacobson smiled as she surveyed her table setting with approval and made a cursory circuit of dinner's progress in the kitchen before heading off to her bath. The meal would have to be something nice. Poor Hy would be exhausted after two three–hour drives and the kind of long meeting she knew he hated.

She had made the chicken soup yesterday, so she could skim the chilled fat off easily today. According to Hy she was actually approaching the standard for chicken soup by which all efforts must be judged–his mother's–and she was serving roast veal (de–fatted gravy) with steamed leeks, new potatoes and swiss chard. And on the side fresh baguette with roast garlic (instead of butter), already filling the kitchen with its aromatic presence. Mm. No dessert except paper–thin slices of sponge cake and chilled melon or sherbet, of course. But a nice burgundy, and decaf cappuccino *après*. Hy wouldn't suffer.

She turned towards the hall and the phone rang. Immediately she tensed. She let it ring twice more, then picked it up. She waited before speaking.

"Manon? Manon? *C'est toi, Manon?*"

"Oh, Ruthie, it's you, thank heavens. I'm sorry I didn't say anything, but…" her voice quivered with relief.

"Manon, what's wrong?"

"Oh, it's just that we've been getting some…*calls*, these nasty anonymous calls, and they say such awful things…"

"Obscene calls?" Ruthie asked with sympathetic indignation.

"Worse, really. These are directed at us personally–well, at Hy, actually, and it's just so upsetting…"

Ruthie was alarmed. "What are they saying?" she asked sharply.

"Oh, it's all about les *juifs*, how they control the banks and the media, how they have a plan to take over Quebec, how they were stealing property from *nous autres*, about the barn and this land, how it belongs to *nous autres*…really, it's just sick, and it makes me so nervous…"

"Do you have any idea who it is?"

"That's just it. I think I do. And–oh, Ruthie–it's one of my *relatives*. Or at least I think it is. He works for Roch at the stables. He's from the 'other' side of the family…"

Manon's family in Saint Armand was a sprawling network of the Desrochers clan. The Desrochers owned half the county one way or another: quarries, construction companies, the ski hill, an interest in the golf club, car dealerships…there was no corner of local industry that did not include some enterprising member of the tribe. But they were not a close or united family.

They had split politically in 1980 over the referendum. There was still very bad blood between Manon's father–he had campaigned for the *NON* side–and his brothers–staunch nationalists then and aggressive *souverainists* now.

Hy's acquisition of *Le Centre* had divided the family further. *Le Centre* had once been owned by Jean–Claude Desrochers, Manon's uncle. In the real estate mania of the eighties he had wanted to develop the 500 acres of the cross–country course, which would limit the competitive equestrian activity to Jumping and Dressage. Nobody had ever argued that Eventing was a lucrative corner of the business and he saw the issue strictly in financial terms.

But the town saw it differently. The exquisite, rolling parklands, dotted with tiny ponds and charming woods of diverse flora were an environmental jewel. The space was used for other activities now: triathlons and cross–country skiing, and for people who just liked to walk over them, picnic and enjoy the scenery. The townspeople were proud of it and wanted it to stay green space.

And they liked the annual Three–Day Events. They came out to wander the course and spectate in numbers. The events were an increasingly popular tourist attraction, drawing visitors from nearby Vermont towns and the spokes of Quebec villages surrounding Saint Armand.

There was a showdown between Jean–Claude Desrochers and the town council. Hy Jacobson married Manon at a crucial moment in the dispute. Both of them were amateur riders and loved horses, it was one of the things that had drawn them together. And he wanted to buy a wedding present magnificent enough to express his love for her.

So Hy made an offer to the town to safeguard the area from development and, in an uncharacteristic burst of courtly abandon, an offer to Desrochers no sane businessman could resist or refuse. Pressured on both sides, Desrochers walked away the richer for it, but not happy. Manon knew that she was considered by some to be a traitor to her family and her people, so it was not intra–family acrimony alone that influenced her suspicions.

"What does Hy say?" Ruthie was very uneasy and she felt very bad for her brother. The purchase of the house, the extensive renovations and decorating undertaken with such delight and pride, had been a symbol of happiness after a long period of misery for each of them in their former lives, and she was angry that there should be any blight on their contentment. They were so right together. There was no envy in her contemplation of their joy. Though nobody could have blamed Ruthie if she *were* envious. Her own husband had died only months ago.

"Ruthie, I haven't even told him about most of them. He was so upset I told him they had stopped."

Ruthie had shivered inwardly at Manon's news, but tried instinctively to minimize her sister–in–law's obvious fear. "Manon, I'm sure it's just meant as a prank. If it were serious, it would have gone farther by now. It's just name–calling, I wouldn't worry."

"Oh, do you really think so?" Ruthie heard in her voice the desperation to clutch at relief from the strain. "I hope so. Listen, do you want to come out this weekend? We'd love to see you. I already feel better just having told someone. It seems less horrible now, more like it *could* just be a bad joke."

"Yes, I will come. I'd like that. The girls are busy on the weekends and my married friends are all up north or busy with their families...*mon dieu*, do I sound self–pitying? Stop me quick!"

"Don't be silly. And even if you were, what's wrong with that? It hasn't been very long, after all. You're allowed to be sad, *chou*. By the way, Polo was here today while Hy was in Ottawa. He dropped off the bids for the new arena. But I missed seeing him."

"Gee, I haven't seen Polo in months. Not since the *shiva*. We barely spoke even then, there were so many people. Well, more to the point, you know, he has such a thing about women crying. I'm usually so upbeat and buffed, and there I was all teary and scruffy-looking. I think I spooked him, and he couldn't take it. I was sort of pissed off, in fact. Fair weather friends and all that, eh?"

"You'd better forgive him. You'll be seeing a lot of him if you come up for a long holiday in May. He's looking after the arena, and he's involved in the big Young Riders show we're putting on here in June."

"It'll be strange to see him alone. It's always been with mom and the girls or the whole family. I haven't been alone with Polo since–well, since I left home and married Marvin, I guess…it'll be strange…"

"Strange–unusual, or strange–uncomfortable?"

"I'm not sure…"

CHAPTER FOUR

G ILLES LEFEBVRE JERKED AWAKE AND STARED BLANKLY AT the alarm clock beside his narrow cot. *Five a.m.* He had slept for more than an hour! He must have missed it! He dashed the two steps to the light aluminum door of his little trailer, yanked it open and strained to see in the faint pre–dawn light. But surely he couldn't *not* see, if it had really happened. The sky would be ablaze with light from the flames. He looked to where the arena in progress stood, a tall skeleton of joists and timbers and roofs and partially filled–in walls. He saw its massive outline, high on the hill above him. Nothing had changed. They hadn't done it, after all. *What had gone wrong?*

He shivered in his thin T-shirt. The mornings were still chilly. It had been a cold spring so far. He retreated into the fuggy warmth of his home. The tiny 'silver bullet' trailer seemed claustrophobic to other people, but for Gilles, these last few months being the only time in his life he could remember having any privacy from the invasive presence of his six siblings–he was, like his Uncle Roch the youngest, the *benjamin,* of his family–and this the only space he could remember ever belonging to himself alone, the little nest was a royal retreat. Even the primitive outhouse and tiny hotplate could not dampen his pride of possession. He was allowed to shower in the men's locker room at the Centre and, all in all, he had been happy enough. Except for…*don't think about it yet.*

He had not been at all sure, when his uncle offered to take him on, that he would be happy at *Le Centre.* Gilles had never worked with horses or done heavy manual labour before. He thought of himself as a city person, even though he rarely made it into downtown Montreal from the south shore suburb where he lived.

His options had been limited, though. Having rebuffed his mother's pleadings to go on to CEGEP after high school, he was bound to get a job of some kind. With his father laid off from *Clar-Mor* and his mother's nurse's salary the family's sole, fragile hold on security, he needed something better than minimum wage at a fast food outlet, the best he could find in a depressed market without skills, good English or any decent experience.

He shrugged into a sweatshirt and thought about what he should do now. If things had gone as Liam said they would when he last saw him yesterday, Gilles would have shown up at eight o'clock this morning as usual, and appeared surprised at all the commotion. Liam had promised that in return for making duplicate keys to the administration entrance, Gilles could be totally uninvolved in the action. Gilles had thought this was preferable to them forcing the lock and ruining the door. Liam had promised that the office would only be messed up, but nothing would be damaged or stolen. There would be graffiti, of course, but that could easily be washed off.

How did I get mixed up in all this? Because Liam was so friendly to me, and nobody else but Polo ever paid any attention, except to complain when I made mistakes, or they were so busy falling all over Michel, and Uncle Roch thinks I'm worthless. I know I make mistakes, and I didn't mean to insult a client, why would I do that, I didn't even know what I said wrong, my English isn't so good, then Polo explained, but it was too late, Uncle Roch said she was so insulted she nearly went home to Toronto and he would have lost a whole season's money.

But I'm trying, and he thinks I'm a moron because I go to mass, what's wrong with that, why does everyone think religion is such a joke. I wish I could talk to Father Pascal about all this. It's so confusing. Or to Polo maybe. He's the only grown-up who gives me the time of day and tries to really teach me how to do things right. But how can I? He's a friend of...them.

And Benoit, it seemed right what he said about the Jews taking all the jobs and the land, it's really his family's house, his family's land, they think they can just come in with their money, they're so clever, they just take control of whatever they want, the newspapers and the banks, Liam says, and he must know. Papa says the same thing, it's why he has no job. Why should Mr. Jacobson have all this, and my father was doing his job at Clar-Mor, and just like that, laid off, and yet he's a real québecois, it's not right...

But Mr. Jacobson isn't the way Liam says they are, he doesn't seem so bad, he's very nice to me, how come... and how come papa always says if you're really sick and your doctor doesn't know, then go to the juif...How did I get into this? I couldn't back out, Liam said he would tell Uncle Roch and he would, I know it, he knows so much about everyone here, everyone is scared, even Michel...

Oh shit, that was terrible yesterday afternoon, what Liam said to him, and Michel, I thought he was going to kill him, but he walked away... and Jocelyne was in the feed room, I think she heard too, and she was crying, oh Seigneur, what a mess....

There was no point in even thinking of going back to sleep. He might as well make himself useful. His trailer was tucked into the corner of the field used for parking cars at the shows. It stood on a rise overlooking the stadium, the jumper and dressage arenas, and off to the right he had a good view of the steeplechase and the first few jumps of the cross-country course. Looking up and across the road, he could see the owner's property, partially obscured by woods, and *le Centre* beyond. He could walk to the barn in about eight minutes, but Roch let him take the pick-up home at night. Everybody borrowed the pick-up when they needed it, and left the keys in the ashtray.

What he thought might calm his jangled nerves was some hard physical work. At the corner of the jumper arena beside the stadium stood a huge mound of sand. The sand was to be the final layer on the re–worked foundation of the arena in preparation for the June show. It was time to re–do it in any case, that was what Polo had explained to him. An outdoor jumper arena needed continual updating or the footing grew uneven. No professional rider would jeopardize his horse's fragile feet and legs in a bad arena, so the good competition barns invested heavily in arenas with a deep base of layered gravel, earth and sand which drained evenly and quickly after rainstorms, and cushioned the horse's expensive hooves with just the right degree of 'give'. Too little, sore feet and ankles, too much, strained tendons. Too little was an irritant, too much could mean a long–term, even permanently debilitating injury.

The wheelbarrows and shovels were kept in a utility cell in the wing connecting the round barn to the indoor arena. Access could be gained from the interior corridor or from an outside door. He could pick up the gear without entering the barn and maybe waking Liam up. He didn't want to see him yet. And he wouldn't wait for coffee. He had already drunk too much trying to stay up all night.

He drove right up to the access door and slipped inside. Fleur had heard the truck and was upon him immediately, whining softly for affection. Gilles felt sorry for the dog. She was supposed to be Jocelyne's, but the girl never paid any attention to her. She got fed and she had as much exercise as she wanted, often following clients out on their hacks, but nobody except Gilles really cared about her, or petted her, or even talked to her. Lonely himself, never having owned a pet before, Gilles had taken the dog over.

Now the truck was loaded with what he needed. It was dawn. The dog pleaded to come with him. *Why not?* She hopped gaily into the front seat beside Gilles. He drove the long way down on the asphalt road. There was a short cut, a rough track between the paddocks, but it cut too close in front of the Jacobsons' house. He didn't want anyone asking what he was doing at that hour, unlikely as it was that someone from the house would be up and about. And there was an unfamiliar car in the driveway, a Lexus. Typical. All the Jews had nice cars. Must have come last night, because it wasn't there yesterday. Better to go around.

66

He parked on the far side of the mounded sand, where the truck would be invisible to passers–by and the stable people. What he thought he would do was to time how long it took to fill a wheelbarrow and assess how much ground each barrow–load covered. That way he could tell Polo how long it would take the two government grant workers who were supposed to come on Monday–it was Friday today–to finish the job. Uncle Roch might appreciate this initiative and lighten up on his criticisms.

He began to dig and very soon fell into a rhythm that began to soothe away some of the tension. He didn't know why his uncle was so short–tempered these days. In Gilles' youth Uncle Roch had always been his favourite of all his mother's many brothers and sisters. He was a joker. He loved parties. He *gave* great parties–his New Year's *réveillons* brought the combined relatives of their side and *tante* Ghislaine's together every year, over one hundred people at their small, cozy home a mile from the Centre. Everyone pitched in with cooking and baking. The kids swarmed over the house, the bedrooms, the rec room, everywhere. Uncle Roch hugged and kissed everybody, pressed food and wine and beer and Pepsi on them. Or he'd have his father's big work horses hitched up, pile all the kids in the sleigh and personally drive them through the woods, singing, laughing, shrieking as they plunged downhill and around the corner. But lately…

Fleur was suddenly barking frantically and digging madly in the sand twenty feet away. Maybe a mouse or a snake. Better shut her up, though, even though no one was in sight.

"*Tais–toi, Fleur, qu'as–tu là?*"

Beside her now, he saw the big paws scrabbling furiously, and he heard the clacking sound of nails meeting metal. He shivered and grabbed the cowboy–style bandanna Jocelyne tricked her out in, dragging her away so he could see.

Crisse de crisse de crisse!

He would know that belt buckle anywhere! It was plainly visible now, and a few inches of blue jeans beside and a square of white hairy skin where the T–shirt had rucked up and–

Gilles crossed himself with wild imprecision, turned and retched violently onto the grass. Nothing but coffee and bile came up. He retched again and again, he thought he would never stop. *Christi!* He sank to his knees, weakness spreading everywhere in his body, and started to cry. Fleur whined softly, licking frantically at his face. He pushed her away with a trembling arm and tried to think.

Think, think, think. O shit, o shit. Who? Maybe Benoit? They must have fought over what to do. Or Michel? O God, the way he looked yesterday. If it's Benoit, I'm fucked, he'll tell on me, or say it was me, I can't prove it wasn't, or if it was Michel, I got to do something, blood is thicker…or Jocelyne? No, a girl could never…and how? O God, now I have to find out how, I have to see. I have to touch him…

He retched again and he was still shaking as he gingerly shovelled the sand away, up the T–shirt and there was that goddam *Tufts* sweatshirt he always wore, and up some more, the hands all white and somehow inhuman, rubbery, pressed against his chest and then–o *Seigneur, strangled with wire still wrapped around, the thin wire they used on the fence posts and everywhere, I use it more than anyone, the face all bluish, tongue just sticking out a little, swollen, eyes half open and staring–and so–so dry–looking, like wood or plastic…*

"*Fleur! Non! Touche pas…*"

Think. Think. Think. To leave him here? They'll find him on Monday when the men come to…but how can I pretend til then? Okay, and if it was Benoit, that's the most–because Liam kept pushing him, and then if Benoit tells on me, says I was in on the whole thing, why should they think it was only Benoit…if I quit and go home and they find him, then I'm fucked for sure, they'll say for sure it was me… and if it was Michel, and what if it was true what Liam said, and then Michel would have to say why he was so angry.… oh God, Uncle Roch would die, just die, he thinks Michel is out every night with a different girl, it's so important to him…I got to protect my cousin, I know he doesn't even know I'm alive, but it's blood, it's family…I can't stand it…to know he's here and keep on working as if…I got to get him out of here…I can't stand it…

He thought it must be seven o'clock already, it felt like hours had passed, but he looked at his watch, and no, it was only five–thirty. And then he closed his eyes a minute to think, and then he opened them to see under the protective roof of the VIP section of the stadium bleachers a thick pile of cotton material, it must have been a metre high, all the bunting for the show, loosely wrapped in a huge rectangle of shiny paper, heavy store wrapping paper that he knew like he knew the bottom of his own pocket, and a plan unscrolled itself in his mind.

First he had to do what his whole body was screaming at him not to. He pulled the body out by the legs and laid it on the grass. *Don't think about it. Just do it.* He leaned into the back of the truck for the toolbox and found the wire cutters. He cut the coiled wire carefully without breaking any skin, picked it away with the tips of the cutters and dumped it into the big garbage drum beside the stadium. Once a week the garbage was collected. It was pretty full now and he pushed the wire down amongst the debris.

Still using the wire cutters, he cut off the ponytail. The hair was thin and it only took a few seconds to saw through it. This he scattered around the ground. It had the exact texture and colour of horsehair. It would blow around and would not be noticed. Now for the hard part.

Muttering a combination of oaths and hail Marys, the boy undid the belt, trying hard not to touch the actual body. He slid the belt through the loops and rolled it up, buckle and all. Then the really disgusting moment. He pulled the identifying sweatshirt over the horrible mask of a face and yanked it free, shuddering and retching up nothing. Thank God the T-shirt underneath sported only a generic *Expos* logo. The jeans and sneakers were standard issue. He forced himself to look for tags or felt-penned names on both pieces of clothing, seizing the material by the tips of thumb and forefinger, taking care not to touch the skin that looked like sausage casing. Nothing.

He leaped up into the stadium bleachers into the overhung area. Carefully he slid the big heavy rectangle of paper from under the bunting that he left stacked on the table. The wrapping paper, surprisingly heavy, was the size of a kingsize sheet. Jumping down, again shoving Fleur out of the way, he laid the paper on the ground beside Liam, then rolled the body onto the paper with the shovel. Tucking one end around the head and the other round the feet, he rolled the body and paper up together like a rug. Tying the ends with baling twine from the truck bed, the oblong bundle was neutralized, a thing only, could have been a rug, a floor lamp, mattress pads, anything at all really…

Gilles was fit and strengthened by months of hard work. Liam was skinny and smallish. It was no exertion swinging him into the back of the truck. There he lay. Gilles almost covered him with a loose horse blanket, but no, there mustn't be horsehair found on him. Anyway, why cover him? He might easily be mistaken now for any other package lately delivered from *Tissus Clar-Mor* whose name on the wrapping paper was boldly printed in purple and teal at regular intervals over a half tone background of the same name and font in miniature, endlessly inscribed in pale mauve on glossy white: *tissus clar-mor, tissus clar-mor, tissus clar-mor…*

It was six forty-five a.m. when he arrived at the Taschereau Blvd. mall. As he had anticipated, there was only light traffic on the arrow-straight autoroute linking Saint Armand to the Champlain Bridge. If he'd had to cross the bridge, he couldn't have predicted his timing. Construction cordons, accidents and commuter build-up near the bridge could complicate entry to the city, especially in the spring and summer. But his route took him out of the heavier lanes and onto the south shore shopping strip he knew intimately.

He hadn't passed any cars or people that he knew on the two-mile road into Saint Armand from the Centre. At six a.m. even Uncle Roch's spry little father wasn't bustling around the lower barns where the broodmares and workhorses lived. Only turning onto the town road a woman jogger passed close to the truck and glanced up at the cab, but he had never seen her, and she did not look at him with any sign of recognition. There were a lot of city people who had weekend houses near *le Centre*, tucked away in pseudo-rural pods around the golf course and ski hill. She was a city person, her stylish jogging outfit made that clear.

Now he pulled into the mall and headed directly towards the anchor store, *Tissus Clar-Mor*. The parking lot was enormous, and he knew, he'd been here recently, that it backed into a construction site for a mammoth new *Club Prix*. He headed for the far end. The only cars in the lot were clustered close to the stores, just a few.

Where he was headed, his truck would be assumed to be attached to the construction site, if in fact it was noticed at all. It was an '87 Chevrolet, a boring, gimmick–less beige and brown model. No special antennae, no dangling dice or splayed Garfields on the window. A workhorse. Gilles figured there must be 50,000 like it on the road in Quebec.

He dumped the body in a ditch–like depression on the edge of the site. Thankfully, just as he'd imagined and hoped, there was a mixture of earth, sand, gravel, grass and the usual construction detritus in the immediate area. Unless the police were motivated to compare the sand on the body with what was here–it was the same colour and texture to Gilles' eyes–they were bound to assume he'd been done right here. *Clar–Mor* was a hundred yards away. He would be thought to be an employee, then when that didn't work, an intruder or an employee's jealous lover, or something.

Gilles wondered what to do with the belt and the sweatshirt, though. He decided to keep them in his knapsack behind the seat for now. If anyone accused him, he would put them in a place where *they* would be implicated, and make damn sure they got found. They were insurance. He felt better.

Liam had often boasted about having no family here, making his own way in the world, a rolling stone and proud of it. Nobody would ask after him, everyone at the barn would think he'd just taken off. What else was new with stable lads? No missing person's report would go out. Roch would be pissed at having to get a new boy, but it had happened before. Everyone else would say good riddance. Only the real murderer would be going nuts wondering... But then the real murderer thought he was safe until Monday when the government workers showed up. He might not try to move him until Sunday night, or maybe not at all, figuring the time lapse would make a precise alibi unimportant...

Gilles did not worry about whether they would connect the body with Mr. Jacobson. If they somehow did–and he really didn't see how–Gilles himself at least would not be an obvious suspect. He couldn't get further than this in his mind. He had to get back. He hoped he hadn't made any mistakes.

He looked around. Nobody. Scooping up some damp earth, he smeared his licence plate, just enough so it looked like it could have been sprayed by a passing car in a puddle, enough to foil an alert would–be witness, haphazard enough not to look deliberate.

It was seven a.m. It might take less than forty–five minutes back, because there was no traffic at all in that direction, and he could now drive at the speed limit, while coming in he had prudently stayed under. He was due at the barn at eight a.m. to receive the day's instructions. He was still shaking, his hands were clamped painfully to the wheel and he felt light–headed, but the nausea was gone, just a tightness in the chest and gut. He was starting to be hungry even. He might stop for a McMuffin at MacDonald's and certainly he must fill the tank to yesterday's level, but not here. Maybe in Granby, a big enough town, and close to Saint Armand where his presence, even recognized, would be completely unremarkable.

Fleur licked Gilles' face, very happy with her excursion, very happy to be with the most companiable human at *Le Centre Equestre de L'Estrie*.

Ruthie walked into the warm and spacious country kitchen and poured a cup from the automatic coffee butler, which Manon had thoughtfully programmed for her sister–in–law the night before. The air outside was a bit cool, but she was still glowing from her run, and she thought that even with freshly washed hair she would enjoy sitting out on the sweeping deck. Ruthie loved this solitary time in the early mornings. Funny how evenings alone were inevitably melancholy, but mornings alone were invariably happy, at least whenever she had just come in from running. Sunrise always gave her hope and a feeling that life was beautiful and worthwhile in spite of everything.

Especially today, with the sun climbing slowly up the horizon, the promise of a real spring day in the sweet country air, and this amazing view to feast her eyes on. Hy often boasted that on a clear day you could see virtually to Montreal, and he was right. This mountain was the first to break the flat landscape between here and Saint St. Hilaire, not far from the St. Lawrence River. The Centre was tucked about a third of the way up the mountain, and the views of the property, the stadium arenas backed by a craggy rock face, and the cross–country course, finally verdant and lush after a long winter, were postcard perfect.

How Daddy would have swelled with pride to see this place, and Hy so happy here. She imagined him standing on this deck after one of Manon's gourmet dinners, as straight and tall as his elfin frame would take him, hands stuffed deep in his pockets, contentedly smoking his evening *Romeo y Julieta*, nodding approvingly at the site, and asserting for the hundredth time, "Now *this* is what I call a piece of real estate! You did good, Hymie…"

This morning was the first time she had run here. She could see that she could find any combination of terrains and routes to please her. Well, she would have lots of time to discover them all. She had decided to accept Manon's invitation for an extended stay. It was only an hour back to the city if the girls wanted her. Meanwhile they were happy with their grandmother and their friends, making their summer plans.

Or they could come out here. They liked it here. Both were developing an interest in horses. Funny how the family passion had completely bypassed her. She liked to look at them, but that was it. Jenny and Aviva had been out to Polo's place a few times, and Jenny said he'd offered to teach them to *really* ride, not the baby stuff they did at camp, now that they were back in Montreal to stay.

She smiled thinking about what a nice relationship they'd developed on their own with Polo. She'd never imposed them on him and Nathalie. Childless couples usually found their friends' children boring. But he was genuinely fond of them. He'd seen them several times since Marvin died. Odd that he hadn't called her, though. And hurtful a bit. He'd said at the shiva, *You'll be surrounded by people for a while. I'll be there when they think you should be getting over it.* And maybe things were 'off' again with Nathalie. He always retreated when that happened. Oh well, she was here now. And she'd probably see him later this morning when he came to check on the arena.

She relaxed into the languor of her post–run euphoria. She wasn't a marathoner. About an hour's medium jog suited her. Wonderful in this fresh air, no traffic of course, and lots of interesting little farms and gorgeous weekend homes to look at. On the return circuit she thought she'd seen someone she recognized. No, not someone, something. A car? No. Something, something…oh yes, that dog, sitting up in the truck and looking so pleased with itself. Wearing that cowboy bandanna. She'd seen it somewhere before. Oh well, not important now. Nothing important now, only this perfect day and nothing to do but relax and not think about anything, anything at all….

CHAPTER FIVE

ROCH LAURIN ARRIVED AT THE STABLE EVERY MORNING AT 7:45 a.m. almost to the minute, six days a week. Mondays, the staff's day off and a rest day for the performance horses, he arrived at 8:30 a.m. and spent the day on administrative backlogs and telephone calls.

Today, Friday, he arrived at the usual time, and as always, entered by the stable door in the back. He then performed the invariable routine of which he was by now quite unconscious. Pausing in the passageway linking the round barn to the main corridor, he stood motionless for a few seconds and appraised his domain.

During this time his senses were alert to the environment. His ears heard automatic water dispensers at work and the gentle whoosh of the fan. His nose told him the air was clean and smoke-free. He saw that the barn looked as it always did, with nothing out of place, no stall doors open. From where he stood he could see into the little round barn office; all was tidy and clean there. The bulletin board announced the day's lesson assignments, blacksmith roster, instructors' schedules, and the 'order of go' for schooling of the performance horses. It was all as he had arranged it yesterday.

He also took in the quiet, rhythmic munching of hundreds of blunt teeth on moistened hay, the first course of the morning feed. The hay was tossed in—one 'flake' each—over the chest-high door of each stall. For the second part, fifteen minutes later, when digestive systems were well prepped for the grain, the server would open each stall door to dump the oats into the triangular corner feed bin, at which point any untoward signs of change in the horse's demeanour or behaviour would be noticed.

Morning feed was handled rotationally. Sometimes it was done by one of the working students, sometimes by Benoit, whose regular job it was to muck out twice a day. Occasionally Jocelyne did it, since she never allowed anyone else to feed her charges their special vitamin supplements, and so was there early in any case. Liam worked into the evening hours; so his day usually started around 8 a.m., the same time Gilles was supposed to show up. Today, it was one of Jocelyne's shifts. As Roch began the usual circuit of his own and Michel's horses, he passed her starting on the grain. They nodded cursorily to each other.

In the barn, unless he was chatting up clients, Roch wore the flinty, focused, vigilant expression of a general reviewing his troops. His word was law here, issued casually but obeyed without murmur. Once he had passed through the door leading to the administration quarters, though, his expression softened to that of a decisive but benign diplomat, a more collaborative personality, happy to delegate to others those realms of authority beyond his interest and skills. Away from the horses, in the restaurant and at home, he relaxed and assumed the host-like warmth and spontaneity for which he was generally known and appreciated.

The door from outside into the stable was never locked. This was in order to facilitate evacuation of the horses in the event of a fire, every horseman's nightmare. It had happened once in the Centre some years before. Rats had gnawed through an electrical wire. Fortunately there had still been people in the restaurant and the horses had been saved. But from then on, someone always slept in the barn.

As Roch walked down the main aisle he automatically removed the keys for the admin corridor passdoor and his office from his pocket. He didn't check these main barn horses individually, the clients' and Bridget's, although his peripheral vision was always tuned in for the unusual. He had no premonition today that any of the horses was in trouble.

But he knew something was wrong when he slipped the key into the passdoor and felt that it was already unlocked. His heart jumped fractionally. He hurried down the corridor and realized before reaching his office that its door was already wide open. He ran the last three steps to the threshold and, pausing there, took in the incomprehensible scene.

She–or he–Rock could not make out in the first instant of perception–stood, short, heavy, corduroy–clad legs spread slightly apart in a posture of stolid occupation, a large, mannish hand clutching a spray paint canister. She–he had unconsciously decoded her–had been looking into the inner office, but turned to face him, revealing a square freckled face curtained to shoe–button bright eyes with stick–straight brown bangs, framed by a chin–length Buster Brown bob, and dominated by the biggest, roundest glasses he had ever seen.

"Well, don't look at *me* like that, mister," she asserted trucu-lently, "*I* had nothing to do with all this. Shit, I don't even speak French!"

By "this" she meant the chaotic scene around her, both in Ma-rie–France's anteroom and in his own office beyond. Roch could not attach his shocked initial impressions to any coherent understand-ing of what had happened. The most arresting feature was the walls, every one covered with roller–coasting graffiti: *VENDUS...T'ES QUEBECOIS OU T'ES RIEN...LE CENTRE AUX QUEBECOIS...*

Papers were strewn everywhere and office furniture–chairs, end tables, desk lamps, and bookcases–were overturned. The word processor was upended on a desk. The telephone was off its hook, receiver dangling off the edge of the bureau.

A large, gilt-framed photograph of a proudly smiling Roch standing with the Queen of England, taken at the closing ceremo-nies of the 1976 Olympics, hung askew on the wall, its glass crazed with spray paint blacking out his and her face. Just as pointedly, across the room, another picture of Roch and the original 1969

Hunt Club, a group of laughing men on horseback surrounded by a pack of Jack Russell terriers, was serenely untouched inside a symbolic oasis of clean wall.

Coffee cups, paper clips, pens, notepads, brochures, everything was everywhere in a welter of orchestrated malice and confusion.

In a daze, heart pumping, flooded with adrenaline, Roch whipped back to the strange–looking creature who was peering at him with cautious sympathy. Hoarsely he barked, "Who the hell are *you*? How did you get in here?"

"Sue Parker. That door," indicating with a jerk of her head the main entrance around the corner, "and it was unlocked, in case you're wondering," she added hastily. Then, registering his absolute lack of recognition, she went on, "*Sue Parker.* Journalist. Here to do a backgrounder for the show documentary? Young Riders?"

Roch nodded absently. Some dim recollection had filtered through his amazement, which was rapidly turning to wrath. "Open? Not forced?" he demanded. *Keys. Me, Hy, Marie–France, Michel, Guy, Caroline. That's all. Who–*

He turned to go and check the front door, then they both froze at the sound of a prolonged, high–pitched scream coming from the main barn. They stared at each other in stupefaction. Then Roch was racing down the hall as Jocelyne's wailing voice cried out, "*O non, non, non…*" and Sue Parker, flinging down the canister, was right behind him.

Jocelyne had not yet moved since her first scream. One hand clapped over her mouth to stifle the sounds she wanted to make, but knew would frighten the horse, she used the other to steady herself against the end wall. Roch found her thus transfixed by what she was staring at, hidden from him by the still partially closed stall door. Swiftly but quietly he edged her aside, looked in, and drew a sharp breath of horror and disgust.

Calisse!

The stallion stood, swaying slightly as if in shock or drugged, his head hanging drunkenly close to the shavings. Thick gouty blood dripped from his open mouth. His long white socks were sluiced with brilliant streaks of crimson. The cedar shavings under his front hooves were wet, clumped and blackened. Oats had spilled on the floor in front of him where Jocelyne had dropped the scoop. Roch's glance fastened immediately amongst the grains, nausea rising in him, on a rubbery triangular wad of pulpy flesh–a good half of the horse's tongue–and a bloody length of very thin wire…

Fighting back the urge to vomit, he sank to one knee, swearing and fighting for strength. He heard sobbing behind him–Jocelyne, and the stranger's loudly barked "Holy shit!" as she peered over his shoulder. The horse flinched at the sound. That lent him the surge of energy he needed.

Whirling and rising in a single fluid motion, he had the woman by the wrist in a vise of angry fingers, pressing hard, as he whispered, "Out of here, you. *Now*. Wait in the office."

She winced and tried to free her hand, but his grip tightened. She seemed about to protest, but took a good look at the rising fury in his icy blue eyes, muttered "sorry", shrank away rubbing her wrist and disappeared along the corridor toward the office.

"Easy, boy, easy," Roch crooned softly before laying a tender hand on the horse's shoulder. The ears twitched slightly at the familiar voice, the eyes rolled in puzzlement and a slight tremor passed along his flanks. In a few seconds Roch had ascertained that the animal was not in real shock. He was sweating just a bit, but his heartbeat was close to normal. Gently Roch passed sensitive fingers all over the horse's body, under the belly, up and down the legs, searching for other wounds, but there was nothing. Now he turned to Jocelyne who was calm and awaiting instructions.

"*Ça va?* I need you to do things."

"*Oui.* I'm okay. What first?" She was pale but marginally more collected.

"Get a cotton scrim and a light cooler. And a halter. Not his. The big one from the warmbloods. Get me a thermometer. Then call Guy. Tell him to bring everything, tell him he'll need an I–V unit. If Bridget answers, don't tell her. Make sure you speak to Guy only in French, and tell him not to say anything yet. She'll get here anyway later on, and by then he won't look like this. You got all that?"

She nodded and did what he asked. With infinite patience and a good deal of soothing encouragement, Roch fitted the netted sweatsheet and light wool cover over the length of the horse's back.

He shifted restlessly but accepted the handling without overt tension. Jocelyne returned from the little office.

"Guy's on his way," she said. "Bridget doesn't know yet".

"Okay, I'll stay here with him until he comes. Meanwhile, finish giving the grain to the others"–he had been conscious for moments of the throaty half–whinnies and stamps of frustration emanating from the stalls further along Jocelyne's interrupted route–"and get a bucket of clean water and a new sponge. And–yeah–get Liam."

Roch carefully inserted the thermometer in the rectum, clipping the attached string to the tail, then came back to examine the wound as well as he could. It was coagulating, that was a good sign, and the horse, although clearly tired and woozy, was in no danger of going down. It didn't look like a panic situation, merely a horrible one.

An act of vengeance like this was a complete anomaly even in Roch's lifetime of experience in horse sport. He had seen and dealt with severely injured horses, colicky horses, tied–up horses: all of these were upsetting, heartbreaking even, but were accepted as part of the risks of competition. He had seen many horses destroyed for one reason or another. None of it had prepared him for the dark thrill of disgust in seeing an injury so cold–bloodedly inflicted on a beautiful creature like this stallion. His mind whirled with possibilities and even, reluctantly, some probabilities.

Who hated him so much they would vandalize his office and attack him and Michel personally? Here a dark clot of suspicion was already forming. *I shouldn't have exploded like that last week in the restaurant. Better to avoid open conflict in these things, never does any good to shove reality in people's faces.*

And if they hated him, why choose Bridget's horse to hit on? Everyone knew he kept his horses separately. And if it was Bridget they hated, what use was it attacking his office? How had they got a key to the outside door? How had they opened the pass door? He could handle the sourpusses and the *politicailleurs*, but this was something else. Someone as ruthless as ... *steady, big fella, don't move, good boy, it's going to be okay, poor guy, look at him, doesn't know what's happening, c'mon Guy, get a move on, let's fix up the poor bugger...*

The stable door opened and Guy Gilbert rushed in with his gear. He was by Roch's side in a few seconds, his hands flipping open the bag even as he took his first look.

"J–Jesus," he said softly.

Jocelyne came hurrying back at this moment. "Roch, I have to tell you something."

Roch looked up impatiently. "What?"

Jocelyne shook her head and motioned him away from Guy. Roch frowned, but slipped aside and followed Jocelyne a few paces down the aisle. "What is it?" he asked brusquely.

"Liam isn't there," she said in a low, tense voice. "He's gone–and so are all his things. He's buggered off…"

They looked at each other and at the stall where Guy was quickly and efficiently laying needles, bottles and instruments out on a towel.

Jocelyne said flatly, "Bridget will kill him if she finds him."

Roch shook his head at once. "Liam wouldn't do this."

"Then who?"

It was eight a.m. Gilles entered the barn with the dog. He was tense and he knew it must show. So he said immediately, "Why is Guy here so early? I saw–I saw his truck outside. Is–is something wrong?" His glance slid past them to Guy kneeling outside Rockin' Robin's stall.

Coldly Jocelyne replied, "Somebody cut off Rockin' Robin's tongue. He's bleeding all over the place. And Liam's buggered off. He's gone."

Tongue! Cut off! What was going on? Nobody said anything about–

"How–how can you just cut off–I mean a horse–you can't just take a scissors and–"

Roch was looking intently at Gilles' waxy face. Slowly he said, "With a thin wire, kid." Roch stuck out his tongue, yanked two imaginary ends of wire quickly outwards at the sides of his mouth. "Easier than you might think if you know your way around horses and if they trust you." He turned to include Jocelyne as he added– it seemed almost inconsequential now–"and the office was broken into. It's a mess. I have to go and deal with it now–"

The familiar roar of Benoit's Harley Davidson invaded the barn. Roch's face darkened as he caught the sound of Guy cursing. The horse must have jerked his head at the sudden noise. Roch had asked Benoit a hundred times either to park the machine further away or cut the engine sooner.

A moment later Benoit swaggered in. He approached the little group and, glancing contemptuously at Gilles' pallid face and terrified eyes, asked with routine insolence, "*Qu'est-ce qui se passe, boss?* What's wrong, *hein*? Hey Gilles, you seen a ghost or something?" His tone was clearly intended to be light, but there was no mistaking the underlying menace.

Benoit hissed in angry surprise as Gilles fell back against a stall with jellying knees and slid slowly to the ground. His face was dead white. Roch bent to him and gripped his shoulder.

"*Qu'as-tu?* What is it?"

"No, no, I'll be okay. It's just what you did, what you said–the tongue–the wire–blood–I can't stand–"

"*Maudit*, Gilles, pull yourself together. I got a million things to do. Look, you better go lie down for an hour. Come back when you're feeling better." He added, with rough compassion, "It's normal, son. I got pretty sick when I saw it myself. But he'll be okay, I think."

Gilles nodded mutely, struggled to his feet, glanced with dumb fear at Benoit, and slunk out the stable door. Roch frowned. He had noted the boy's reaction to Benoit's presence. *What the hell was going on?*

"*Écoute*, Benoit. There's trouble here. Someone got to the stallion"–he jerked his head toward the end where Guy was working –"and did a job on him. It's bad, what happened. Cut his tongue off. You know something?" He watched Benoit with laser intensity for his reaction.

Either the youth was a world-class actor or he was genuinely shocked and puzzled at the news. He took a step backwards, shook his head, and lifted both shoulders and hands in disavowal. "Me, I don't know nothing about that. That's really bad news, boss."

Roch's eyes bored into the boy's for a full half-minute, but Benoit held his gaze and didn't flinch. "Okay, Benoit. I believe you. Now maybe you can tell me what you know about my office." He took a step forward as he spoke. His face was very close to Benoit's, and suddenly the boy was no longer meeting his gaze.

"Your office?" Now it was clear the boy was working up a tone of surprise. It was a weak effort.

"Yeah, my office. It's a mess. Looks like some fucking coward-ly *séparatisses* got in there and had a party. But like I said, they're fucking cowards and they didn't leave their names. What do you think of that, *hein?*"

"I don't know what you're talking about," Benoit muttered, squaring his shoulders and affecting a manly spread–legged pose of confidence. But his hooded eyes were darting randomly round the barn and a greasy film of sweat was forming on his forehead.

Jocelyne blurted out, "What do you know about Liam? He's gone. You must know something. You were mixed up in his dirty work, don't deny it–"

"Hey you, you watch what you say there, you bitch," Benoit snarled. His fists balled up and Roch instinctively laid a restraining hand on his arm.

"Where is he?" Roch snapped. Benoit turned sullenly back to meet his fierce gaze, licked his plump lips as if about to speak, then immediately dropped his eyes again. Shrugging, he said, "How should I know? Weren't you the one who told him to clear off or there'd be trouble for him?"

"*What are you talking about?*"

Benoit seemed to sense that he was on firmer ground and, clearly relieved to see the object of Roch's attention shifting from the office to Liam, he assumed his customary impertinence. "Look, all I know is yesterday afternoon he said he had to leave. Said he'd got the push and he had to clear out or there'd be trouble. He didn't say who told him to go, but I just figured it was you. I mean, who else would–?" He seemed bewildered for a moment as Roch and Jocelyne exchanged a spontaneous look of apprehension and un-easiness. Then he licked his lips, assessing the ambiguity of mood to be in favour of a personal initiative.

"Uh, hey listen, boss," Benoit shuffled self–consciously and crossed his arms, "maybe this isn't such a good time to mention it, but you know, I could maybe fill in for a while as head boy, eh? I mean, I'm good with the horses, and I know all the people here, and at least I belong, I can speak English *and* French, you know it was a pain in the ass with Liam only speaking–"

"Are you out of your mind?" Roch had been staring at him throughout this little speech in pure astonishment, as if the boy were speaking some foreign language, but Benoit had been avoiding Roch's eye. His head snapped back in shock at these words. Sensitive to the heat of Jocelyne's scornful gaze upon him, his fleshy cheeks mottled and he drew breath to answer. What he had to say seemed to give him the spurt of extra confidence he needed.

"I don't think you should talk to me like that, boss," he declared loudly, settling his feet wider apart and unconsciously expanding his chest in a gorilla–like gesture of challenge.

"And just why is that, *hein*?" Roch's eyes narrowed and his body shifted to face the boy head–on. Jocelyne backed away, thrilled in some atavistic recess to find herself, however marginally, the catalyst for this masculine face–off.

"Because a lot of people here think I should have my chance." He jerked his thumb at his chest. "My family belongs here. A lot of people say you're forgetting about that. They think you're forgetting about your old friends, who fits in here and who doesn't. They say maybe you think you own this place, and–" his words were choked off by his shirt suddenly tightening against his throat in the grip of Roch's iron fist. Roch's move had been so swift that Benoit was caught off balance. He was slammed against a stall door and found himself staring into the face of a madman.

"*Asshole!*" Jocelyne whispered loudly. She wore an expression of undisguised pleasure at seeing Benoit humiliated. The boy gurgled inarticulately and lunged futilely in her direction. Roch slammed him up against the door again, harder this time, and the boy groaned, pulling desperately at Roch's arms.

"Get out, *pissou*'!" Roch snapped. "And tell the "people" who think you should tell me who works here and who doesn't that as long as I'm in charge of this barn, I decide everything in here. *Everything*! You got that? And tell them I'll be in charge as long as it suits me. You got that too, Benoit?"

Benoit rubbed his throat and muttered something that may have been acquiescence. He made for the barn door and at the threshold, sure of escape, he turned and spit. "It's not over, boss. You should be more careful." He twitched his head toward Guy working on the stallion down the aisle and added softly, teasingly, "Looks like you're not so in charge of everything around here, that's what it looks like to me." And then he was out the door, and seconds later the Harley bucked and roared to noisy life, spraying a hailstorm of gravel against the barn. Guy cursed audibly and made soothing sounds to his patient.

Roch swore quietly, ran a hand over his face, rubbing at his eyes and trying to work out a plan of action.

"Okay, listen," he said wearily to Jocelyne, "go get some of your stuff at lunchtime and move into Liam's room. I want the barn covered at night. We're going to be locking it from now on. I hope you're a light sleeper," he finished grimly.

Jocelyne nodded, eager to please him for a change. And even if he hadn't asked, she had decided to install herself near Michel's horses until things got sorted out. There was no question of leaving them alone after this.

Roch looked around and planned the next moves of the day. *Get one of the working students to cover for Benoit. If I'm lucky, he won't come back. Police, oh fuck, that journalist, insurance…better call Polo and Hy, maybe better not Hy just yet, change the pass door and office and front door locks…a new lock for the stable entrance….*

"Jocelyne, stay with Guy and help him. Get me for anything. When the boarders start coming, when *anyone* comes, just say he cut himself by accident and he's getting stitches. *Compris?*"

"Michel will be here in twenty minutes. I'm supposed to have his first horse ready."

"Send him to me."

"Hey, what does a guy have to do to get a kiss around here?"

Ruthie's eyes flew open, she laughed into the smiling face leaning over the deck chair, and flung both arms up to him in a spontaneous hug of welcome. "Polo!" He slid onto the edge of a flower–

filled barrel beside her. She sat up and hugged her knees.

"It killed me to wake you, but Roch just called here with a message for me, and I can't stay. I thought I'd have time for a quick coffee with you, but–"

"Yeah, I know, it's the story of our lives–love to chat, but there's a horse I gotta see–oh, c'mon, just two minutes to catch up…"

"No, really, Roch sounded pretty worried. And don't say anything to Hy yet. Anyway, I'm coming for dinner. It'll be like old times, just family…"

"Gee, Polo, you look terrific. Is there a picture of you in an attic somewhere getting all old and wrinkled?"

"That's from a book, right?"

"Yeah, how'd you know?"

"You have your book voice on."

"Book voice?"

"Yeah, sort of half a tone higher than normal. Like when you speak French…"

"I speak French in a different *voice*?" Ruthie considered this information with astonishment and the thin edge of pique.

"I didn't say it was a bad thing–just different. Hey, don't shoot the messenger."

"*Touché!* Anyway, to return to my original point, it doesn't mean you don't look fabulous. Weatherbeaten becomes you."

"Well, you don't look fabulous, Ruthie. You look awful. You're too thin and you've got raccoon eyes, so that means you're not sleeping right, or eating–"

"Gee, don't be shy, Polo, tell me what you really think–"

"Hey, don't blame me. I never used to think insulting people was chic before I met the Jacobsons"–

Ruthie pulled at an imaginary knife in her ribs and grimaced. "A palpable hit. We created a monster."

"I gotta go, but–" he laid a finger across her wrist and his voice dropped to an embarrassed murmur–"Are you okay, *ziess*–?"

She wiggled her open hand in the air." *Comme ci, comme ça …* but I seem to be coping. Come early tonight. And set your mood meter to 'nostalgia'. Hy and I had dinner in town with 'The Duchess' yesterday. It was her birthday. She's been clearing out the rec room for when she moves. Wait'll you see…"

Sue Parker mopped up the last of the egg yolk with her toast, speared the remaining morsel of bacon, and regretfully acknowledged her excellent breakfast to be finished. Sipping slowly at her mug of coffee–really, the grub was just super, who'd have thought in a stable, of all places–she pondered whether to order another go-round, but decided that this might seem insensitive considering the atmosphere of worry and confusion swirling around her.

For the moment she was the only customer, although a carefully organized, seemingly casual chat with the owner had already informed her of the comings and goings in the restaurant in the course of a busy day, as Fridays in spring generally were. It was not only the riders who used the restaurant, it seemed. Mountain bikers, joggers, local residents all dropped in for a meal or a beer. And now that the weather was fine, you could sit out under the large awning and enjoy the view of the Jacobson's grounds and the entire vista of the parklands below.

Caroline Laurin, Roch's oldest brother's wife, had been naturally agitated at the news and the sight of the vandalism. Guiltily she had rejoiced that her place had been spared any damage. She had worked very hard to decorate the room so cozily and build up her growing clientele after the indifferent and unimaginative policies of the previous tenancy. In the old days only the Hunt Club members used the place, and then mostly to drink. It was furnished any old way out of people's basements. It had looked *kétaine,* tacky, and the 'menu' was positively *folklorique*: *tourtière,* pea soup and sugar pie were the staples.

From behind the counter Caroline eyed the sole diner with a curious and bemused eye. She was an odd one, all right. But intelligent. Caroline was aware that she had been 'pumped' about the stable's routines, but everyone in small towns was curious, and in stable life the restaurant was the hub for the latest gossip, after all. The girl had been particularly curious about Roch. Everyone was. It certainly hadn't taken long for Roch to make a big impression on this one, though. Five minutes was a record, even for him.

Noticing the wall telephone beside the coatrack, Sue made her way over to it. She'd promised to call her parents in Toronto the minute she arrived. They hated her driving alone on the highways, and were annoyed that she had decided to travel to Saint Armand overnight. She extracted her Bell card from her wallet as she walked.

"I hope that's a local call you're making," Caroline said politely as Sue picked up the receiver. For answer Sue waved the card at her.

"No, I mean you can't call long–distance even with a card on that line. It's fixed so you can only use it for local. But there's a pay phone in the hall and there's a phone in the stable office. Or Roch might let you use his direct Montreal line if that's what you need."

With a sigh Sue pushed open the door to look for the pay phone, and almost collided with a slim blond man, who skirted her in a quick, neat reflex, threw her a sharp, curious glance, and slipped into the office, closing the door firmly behind him.

Nothing had been touched in the office. Roch was on the telephone inside at his desk, passing a hand over his sparse hair in a repeated nervous gesture. Marie–France kept looking from wall to wall, as if she could erase the words by the intensity of her gaze. She held a fist clamped round a balled–up tissue to her pursed mouth. Her pale eyes were red–rimmed and frightened, and her entire plump little body seemed to vibrate with indignation.

Polo tried to take it all in. After several circuits of the room with his eyes, he walked around, looking closely at the objects on the floor, peering at the damaged photographs–one of Michel and D'Artagnan flying over an Olympic jump had been thrown on the floor and stamped on–and lightly examining the overturned machines. It struck him that, the photographs apart, no real damage had been done.

He thought about what he might have seen and didn't: no broken windows, no damaged machines. Whatever was on the floor of any value–a kettle, a Xerox machine, the printer–had been placed there, not thrown down. The graffiti were easily removed, the spray paint was the washable kind, the canister said. The mess was just that–a mess to be cleaned up, sorted through. No files had been broken into, he noted. The three freestanding filing cabinets, which might easily have been overturned, stood untouched. He tried a drawer. It wasn't even locked and slid out accommodatingly to his touch.

There was a message here, to be sure, but a guarded one–a personal act of malice directed at Roch and/or Michel, a warning of worse to come, perhaps. So that didn't jibe at all with the other, the really horrible attack on the horse.

Roch hung up and came around to greet Polo. "You didn't tell Hy?"

"No, but he has to know sooner or later. He was getting ready to go out hacking with Manon, so I thought why spoil his *whole* day–"

"Good, good. Listen, I"–he glanced at Marie–France, and said, "M–F, why don't you go get us some coffee. And relax in the resto a bit." She nodded and scurried gratefully out of the office.

Roch slammed the wall hard with the side of his fist. "Those *fuckers!*"

"You know who did this?"

"I think so. They're just a few, but they're pissed off all the time about *le Centre*–too many of *eux autres,* not enough of *nous autres.* I can't throw them out. We go back too far. And they have too much influence in the town. They got political friends all over the place. And I think, no, I'm pretty goddam sure that little shit Benoit is part of it. He's a cousin or nephew of Jean–Claude, but he's always been jealous of Michel. They're almost the same age, and he used to ride, but there's no talent there. He's a loser, used to have some prestige when *le Centre* was in his family, now he's nobody."

"Why now?"

"I think maybe they heard about Michel going to New York and talking to this guy there. This American guy wants to buy him horses, but Michel's going to have to train in the States. I knew they didn't like that, Michel's like–like public property or something around here–but I never thought"–he gestured helplessly around him.

"Well, they can relax, *papa*."

Roch and Polo looked toward the door that Marie–France had left slightly ajar. Michel was standing there and now took a step inside. His face registered profound revulsion as his eyes roved round the scene.

Normally you couldn't look Michel in the face or he would cast his eyes down and away. He had been stared at all his life and it had long been a reflex response, especially with strangers. Friends knew better than to stare. Now his mind was occupied elsewhere, and Polo allowed himself to glance up and simply steal a rare moment's pleasure.

It was an irresistible impulse. Michel was the most beautiful person he had ever known, male or female, and you wanted to look, as you wanted to look at any wonder of nature–a stallion, a dolphin, an eagle. There were things the boy could do nothing about, even if he tried. He could not help his glossy black curls, or his almond–shaped eyes, a true emerald green, nor his eyelashes, black and thick as mink. He could not hide his short, straight nose, classically sculpted bones, strong, square jaw, the sensuous, curving lips, brilliant teeth, or smooth, olive–toned skin. Then too, he was an athlete, and every move he made confirmed it; he was lithe, strong and graceful as a cat.

Polo felt sorry for the boy. What might have been a woman's dream come true had made life something of a torment for him. Shy and introverted in any case, his evasions usually struck people as arrogance and self–absorption. He couldn't win. When he forced himself to be friendly, people were star–struck and obsequious.

His brilliant success in riding compounded his detachment from the mainstream of social life. He had made a protective circle around himself with the few other riders he was comfortable with. Polo had known him since he was born, and could count himself amongst the trusted inner circle.

Roch said, his eyes narrowing in angry anticipation, "What do you mean, they can relax–"

"I mean, *papa*, that I'm not going to New York. I'm staying here. *Ce n'est pas la peine.*"

"You mean you're going to let this bunch of losers tell you what to do with your life–" he gestured toward the picture of the Hunt Club.

"*Papa,* think a minute. Some of those guys were part of the D'Artagnan consortium. They're thinking about starting a new one. You can't burn your bridges with them over politics, we have to go along with things a bit…and besides, I don't want to go…"

"Oh, *marde,* Michel, *you* think! Think what you're giving up. Think about your life–"

"I do, *papa,* I do." Michel's voice reverberated with repressed passion. "It's all I *do* think about these days, believe me, I–"

Roch opened his mouth to interrupt, and the telephone rang beside Polo. He picked it up, listened a moment, and hung up.

"That was Gilles," he said. "He's at the bus station. The truck is there. He said to tell you the keys are in the ashtray as usual. He's going home. To think, he said. And to talk to his priest."

Roch exchanged a swift and inscrutable glance with Michel. He turned away and bit his lip. Roch thought three things: *Gilles was already scared when he walked into the barn. Michel knows more than he is going to tell me. I don't think I want to know what Michel knows.* Except that only the first two thoughts appeared in his conscious mind.

Marie–France walked in with a cardboard container holding several cups of coffee, which she set carefully down on a square of clean space near the corner of the desk where Polo was half–sitting.

Roch turned back to the inner office, calling over his shoulder, "M–F, get me a locksmith. I want him here *today.*"

CHAPTER SIX

W AITING FOR THE WATER TO BOIL, GUY ARRANGED A TRAY, piled biscuits on a plate, rinsed the teapot with hot water, and reached up to the tin box on the shelf over the stove for two bags of Earl Grey tea. Leaning back to peek around the corner into the living room, he noted that Bridget had not moved. She still lay quietly on the sagging chesterfield, holding a cold compress to her forehead.

"Coming in a minute, Bridget," he called out with somewhat theatrical cheerfulness. There was no response at all. He bustled about the kitchen with exaggerated domestic energy to suggest normalcy, a strategy he thought best under the circumstances.

She had taken the attack on Rockin' Robin very hard. Now she needed TLC and the most generously lavished sympathy. Still, there was no question of his going to her and consoling her in any *physical* way…

The very thought of holding Bridget, or anybody for that matter, made Guy feel quite queasy. In fact, knowing that he would never be called upon to touch Bridget was in Guy's eyes one of the most satisfying aspects of their excellent alliance. That was not Bridget's style in any case, even if they had been engaged in a physical relationship. She would want to *endure* the pain in the most solitary, stoical way.

"Here we are, dear." He set the tray down beside her on the coffee table, deftly manoeuvred several days' accumulated newspapers and a chocolate–coloured Labrador retriever off the neighbouring wing chair, and settled himself to pour out.

"Tell me again," she said in a dull, muffled voice.

"Do you really think it's a good idea to dwell on it, Bridget? I mean, he *is* going to get well."

"Tell me again," she said, as if she had not heard.

Guy sighed. "Well, the tongue was cut about halfway up with the wire. Probably someone had him licking on something sweet or maybe even massaging his back–you know how the horses let down their tongues when they relax–although frankly that would make more sense if there were two people–and, well, I guess there could have been…

"He lost about a pint of blood. That's not a lot for a horse, it just seemed like a lot because it was so visible everywhere. A horse's blood volume is only about eight per cent of its body weight. They can lose ten percent of that without having any serious physiological effects at all. So he didn't go into shock because there wasn't enough blood loss, also because it probably didn't even hurt that much after the initial surprise.

"He's able to drink, although I told Roch I wanted bottled water and a bucket given by hand obviously.

"As to eating I talked to Dr. Forget at St. Hyacinth and he agrees that, as long as he's on a fair amount of 'bute'–I'll inject him myself, and I have him on the maximum dose, along with antibiotics, of course–he can try a little bran mash several times a day. He should be able to take it in, and then the next day grass, hand–fed until he figures out a new way to graze. Well, it'll be a lot of work, and with Liam gone, unless you want the students…"

"I'll do it," she muttered.

"Did I tell you that I read about a similar case in Sweden? A Dressage competitor in second place before the finals, she did it to her rival's horse. Can you imagine? And yet the vets said they couldn't tell the rival *not* to compete in the finals, after stitching him up, because he was still *technically* 'sound'. I guess in a way it's the perfect way to do damage to a horse without actually doing any *real* damage, if you see what I mean."

"There's a journal article for you somewhere in this, isn't there, Guy? I mean, I can tell from your voice that part of you is getting your veterinary kicks out of this."

"Bridget, how can you say such a thing!"

"Admit it. You're feeling pretty bloody chuffed!"

"Well, yes, I was pleased how it all went–I mean, I take some justifiable pride in the stitching job, it's not an easy thing–" he looked at her with mild reproof–"and, well, naturally there's an element of satisfaction in dealing with an unusual situation, and with such a valuable animal. He'll be off stud service for a while, of course..."

Bridget groaned. "Oh Christ, did you call Manon? Did you cancel for today?"

"Oh no, I'm sorry, I forgot all about it in the excitement. I'll call her now. What time is it? Eleven. We said the early afternoon, didn't we?" Guy turned to the telephone beside him and dialed.

Bridget's mind wandered off as Guy chattered on in French with Manon. After ten years in Saint Armand she had barely managed to achieve even a minimal ability to function at the local *dépanneur*. Substantive conversations were quite beyond her. She had given up a long time ago. When she was with unilingual francophones, she resorted to the time–honoured British tradition of simply speaking louder English. This tactic usually intimidated them into pretending they understood her. Fortunately there were very few horse people in Quebec who didn't speak English with some degree of fluency. They wouldn't last long in the sport otherwise.

Guy had been a godsend to her in that respect. He was one of those lucky ones with a perfectly bicultural background, father francophone, mother anglophone, schooled in both languages, and finally so seamlessly at home in both cultures he was often unaware which language he was speaking. Fittingly, he responded with equanimity to both the English and French pronunciations of *both* his names.

When Bridget was with him, he became her unofficial translator and interpreter. He liked that, she knew, because he could then be secondary to the conversation while remaining an integral part of it, and therefore didn't stutter in these situations. It was only when spoken to directly, face to face…

She knew of course that she was also a godsend to *him*, proof of which was that he never stuttered in her presence, even when looking straight at her. Bridget was not, in fact, exactly sure what it was about her that evoked his confidence, but she wasn't looking a gift horse in the mouth.

Bridget heard the conversation picking up animation on Guy's side. Manon must be thinking her stallion was a bloody jinx by now. This was the third rendez-vous with her mare that had been aborted. The first time Guy had been called away on an emergency, and Bridget never liked her stud to cover a mare without a vet handy, the second time the mare had mysteriously failed to come into *estrus*.

And now this.

Bridget could tell from the rhythm of Guy's speech that he was now fairly launched on a blow-by-blow description of the wound. *Christ!* She thought back to the moment of realization in the barn. At first she could not take in what had happened. Then, when she saw poor Robin–and at that point they had cleaned up all the blood, but still…–she had just gone sort of numb. Her mind had shut down.

But she had still insisted that she felt okay physically. Roch had said *you're a funny colour for an okay person,* which was the right thing, she even laughed a bit, and he had insisted she go directly into his office with him and sit down until Guy had finished. Then he pulled a bottle of brandy out of his drawer and made her drink a glass. The fiery draught had jolted her out of her stupor and she was able to absorb the fresh shock of the vandalized office. She was also able to think about what she should say and how she should say it.

Roch was there with her and so was his friend Polo. Polo had been in and around the grounds for two weeks by this time, but their paths had rarely crossed, and then only superficially. He was always at the jumper arena or the Jacobsons' property, while she was always out on the cross–country course or dealing with students. She hadn't thought much about him before, but she began to try and take his measure now, because it was obvious after a minute or so that–whether Roch was aware of it or not–this man and not Roch was in charge of the occasion. He had nodded to her when she came in and looked directly at her with unsentimental curiosity.

Sipping her brandy and saying nothing at first, she watched and listened as the two men continued their discussion, which her arrival had interrupted, about the various possibilities surrounding the morning's disasters. At first they continued to speak in French. It was obvious that Polo spoke a more refined version than Roch. It fell nicely on the ear, not exactly like the kind she had failed to learn in school–what she thought of as *real* French–but rather like that of the news announcers on the telly here. Roch's natural speech patterns just skirted a plangent *joual,* but she had heard him with clients, the press and public figures, and knew he could rise to the occasion if he had to. After a moment Roch remembered her unilingualism and apologized, and they switched.

Bridget made no attempt still to join the conversation, because she was becoming more than a little uneasy about dealing with Polo on such an important matter as this attack on her horse. Who the hell *was* he, anyway? She was listening and looking with total concentration, but she found she could not *place* him, a failure extremely rare in her experience, and given her talent for mimicry based on stereotypical cultural and linguistic norms. His English was accented, but excellent, made more so by contrast with Roch's. Then too, his body language and gestures set him apart from the common background he was alleged to share with Roch.

From what she had gathered via the usual sources, he had been a professional horseman in his youth, a jumper rider, famous, it seemed, for a number of years. Then he had gone on to an eclectic variety of businesses, all horse–related and apparently successful. He was said to own a large, valuable property in St. Lazare, a nice house, an excellent barn and arena. She had heard he was married, but so far there had been no sign of a wife in Saint Armand. On the other hand, she had never seen him with a woman, and he had disappeared for whole days at a time, so probably went home then. At the restaurant he sat alone, reading, or with Michel or Roch or occasionally with the owner.

Nobody had said anything about him being educated–by educated she meant beyond high school, where most horsemen's formal schooling stopped, certainly where Roch's had–but if she met him anywhere else, she would have sworn he was a university graduate. There was about him what in North America was called 'preppiness', an air physically evoked by his urbane carriage, shaggy blond hair and elegant square–framed glasses. She could picture him in khakis and moccasins, a button–down denim shirt, loosened school tie and blazer, a book bag…

These images made her uneasy. He looked far too clever for her liking. She didn't mind intelligence in the service of science, what Guy had, or in the service of her other needs, such as Thea's very useful computer skills, but this Polo looked at her with his cool, hazel eyes as if he knew what she was thinking, and *that* kind of intelligence she normally stayed very far away from. Now she went back over their conversation in her mind.

"I suppose you know that Liam's left with no explanation?" he said to her.

"Do you think he did it? Robin, I mean. It would make sense. He hated my guts," Bridget answered as calmly as she could, remembering Liam's ugly, close–set eyes, his oily, pocked skin, sneering smile and that irritating, insinuating, lisping Irish lilt.

"Why did he hate you?" Polo asked politely. He leaned against the edge of Roch's desk with a foot propped on a chair.

"He didn't appreciate some of my views on Irish inbreeding," she answered with a touch of asperity. "I'm an outspoken person, you see. Some people don't appreciate home truths."

"What particular home truth do you think might have caused him to take offence?"

"I passed a remark one day about the schizophrenia rates in Catholic Ireland being six times higher than in the rest of Europe as a result of inbreeding. He wasn't over the moon about it."

"Is that true?" Polo was clearly taken aback, whether at the information or her audacity in suggesting it, she couldn't say.

"Probably. I think I read it somewhere. Anyway, it bloody well could be. Look, the point is he hated me for a reason. I said those things to him because he–well, he got across me. He hated English people. It's a common enough thing. Losers, insecure people, they think the English are all snobs and take it personally. They either suck up or badmouth us. It's a two–way street. He used to say the Brits were a race of faggots. We were oil and water."

She tossed off the last of the brandy, and gestured at the mess in the office. "What do *you* think? You don't suppose Liam did this little job, though, do you? I mean, he doesn't speak a word of French–he makes *me* look bilingual. Which, as anyone here will tell you, I am bloody well not and never will be."

Roch said, "Me, I don't think Liam, he did the horse. I don't like that guy, for me he's *bizarre,* but one thing it's sure is he knows horses, and it's for sure he cares for them. I got to say he was the best one ever with the horses. It's piss me off I got to get somebody else and train them when it's the busy season."

"Who else hates you, Bridget?" Polo turned back to her after considering Roch's statement a moment.

"There're a few guys around who don't appreciate the fact that I'm an outsider. Things have been getting more political lately–" she broke off to acknowledge an inarticulate growl of frustration from Roch–"well, I'm sorry, Roch, but it's getting worse. Even you couldn't control yourself the other day–" and then she hesitated, suddenly wary, thinking she had already said enough for the time being. The radical separatists made her uneasy. Why should she name them? They might not be so restrained next time.

But she knew them, people like Benoit's cousin, Jean–Claude Desrochers, who still rode at the barn and looked sulphurously out at the Jacobsons' grounds from the restaurant where he always ended the day with a drink. He hadn't made any secret of his feelings. He wouldn't even talk to her anymore, pretended not to understand, even though his English was perfectly fine. Maybe she'd been a little too obvious about *her* feelings, maybe those little 'takes' she did on the '*séparatisses*' at local parties had got talked about–had set somebody off.

God, they were so *fucking* sensitive, these people. Last week when a tableful of Roch's young rider students from Ontario were eating lunch and talking and laughing kind of loudly, one of *their* lot had muttered something about the anglo clients 'taking up too much space', as he had crudely put it…. at least according to Guy, who'd translated for her when Roch overheard too and turned and said *listen, you know how much money those four kids bring in in a season, not just to me, but to Saint Armand,* and then he listed all the revenues from the board, their training, transport in the big van, coaching at shows, the money they spent living in town, eating in restaurants, shopping at the outlets, he'd figured it all out, the whole bit, and it was an impressive amount, Guy had said, you could see they didn't like that, and Roch had ended with *hey, you want to pay the bills here? You want to pay my damn mortgage?* and looked like he was going to hit someone, but walked away instead.

Guy put down the receiver and picked up his cup. "Manon was very understanding, of course. She's only upset for you, and wants to know if there's anything she can do, just let her know." He stirred his tea. "Such a *nice* woman, don't you think? They seem so happy. They go out riding together, and they always speak so *respectfully* to each other. They walk around holding hands, I think that's sweet, don't you? And I think it creates a really pleasant environment when the owners–"

"Oh, do sod off, Guy," Bridget moaned. "I'm going to puke if you keep on with these 'happy families' fantasies of yours. Leave me alone for a bit, go feed your fish, or count anemones or whatever, there's a good chap." Bridget turned her face to the back of the sofa and curled up to ride out the pain.

Before drifting off into a light doze, Bridget's thoughts returned to the office and Polo's questions and answers.

"This may not even be an attack on you personally, Bridget," he had said. "Your stallion is stabled at the end under the window. It was a bright, moonlit night. Whoever it was wouldn't have wanted to put on the lights. It may have been a kind of generic attack on the stable itself. Or on Roch. He rides the stallion, doesn't he? Anyone seeing him–or Michel, for that matter–would think the horse belonged to them. Only an insider would know…"

That was bloody smart of him. She felt better thinking that what he said might well be true, and that she had perhaps not been a target of revenge. But she felt uneasy that *he* had thought of that, and not her. There were certain other things she would not be quite so happy for him to figure out.

Hy returned from the Centre, still in the hacking clothes he had been wearing when he got Roch's call. Manon had showered and changed in the time he was away and looked at him anxiously for more news.

"Well, it's not as bad as it looked at first. I mean the office part. There was another awful thing, though, Bridget's stallion"–

"Yes, I know. Guy called a little while ago. Ugh, it's disgusting. And they were supposed to come today for the mare–it's why I made you hack out so early. So it must have been the same people–"

"Well, I automatically assumed so, I mean, it's too much of a coincidence–but Polo isn't sure, thinks there's something out of balance there–anyway, we decided not to call the police, and there's nothing important enough for the insurance to replace. Cleaning the walls is all, and some photographs ruined. Roch's upset the most about that." He paused, gnawed his lip a moment, frowning.

"Actually I wasn't that comfortable about *not* calling the police. It makes it seem as if we were trying to hide something. But Roch was pretty insistent about the bad publicity, scaring people off if it got known. And then he was right, I guess, when he said they wouldn't have any more idea than us how to go about finding who did it, so…"

"Is there something else? I mean, I get the feeling you're not telling me everything." Manon perched on the arm of the chair Hy had settled into and plucked at the wiry gray fleece that hugged his head.

"Well, it's just–well, doesn't it strike you as another kind of coincidence that nothing happened *here*, at our house? I mean, here we were getting these ominous anti–semitic calls–that's bad stuff, even if it's a prank, there's an influence there…" Hy stood up abruptly and began pacing the room.

Manon answered, humorously, but with an edge, "Hy, I have to tell you that it's actually a lot more fun watching Woody Allen at the movies than living with him."

"You mean I'm doing the Jewish morbid thing? Is that what you're saying?" Hy could feel an edge in his reply, and wasn't happy about that, but couldn't help it.

"I'm only saying"–both of them were aware of the sudden care with which she was choosing her words–"that it's conceivable that bad things can happen which don't involve Jews. Right now, for example, I would say that Roch and Michel and–well, me, for that matter–we're the ones under attack. We're the victims this time. And since it's quite possibly one of my own relatives who's involved here, I would say that it's more than a little insensitive of you to be worrying about why *you* didn't, say, have a swastika spray–painted on the house instead of worrying about how what *did* get painted may affect me," she finished wryly.

Hy felt an unpleasant mixture of shame and anger at what he perceived rationally to be a fair response to his remark. In his heart of hearts he knew, and yearned to say, that a million spray–painted '*vendu*'s didn't yield a millionth of the malignancy or the menace conveyed in one tiny swastika. Ruthie, or Marilyn, his ex–wife, his kids and most of his friends would have understood this without any explanation.

But of course he said no such thing. Hy was an intelligent man, and the lessons of a failed marriage had not been wasted on him. There was a price, however small, to pay in the choice he had made to marry 'out'. He loved his wife profoundly and, he hoped, forever. In a microsecond he had reviewed his priorities in life, and he acted on this assessment.

"Manon," Hy said in a chastened voice, "I've been incredibly thoughtless and egotistical. I'm sorry. Please forgive me."

Manon flew into his arms immediately with a murmur of relief and joy at a crisis, however tiny, averted. They held each other tightly, and Ruthie, who had accidentally witnessed the little tableau, retreated back down the hall. Quietly she walked into the guest bedroom, noiselessly closed the door, curled up in the reading chair, plucked three Kleenexes from the box on the dresser, and had a discreet cry. How sweet it would be once again to have someone to quarrel with, someone to forgive, someone you wished you hadn't offended, someone to hold you, someone to make the frozen sap rise again…*oh no, you don't, my girl, think about something else…*

The pictures, for example, that the Duchess had found and boxed for them in the rec room last night at home on Redfern Ave. in Montreal. There, she was smiling already, thinking of how wonderful they would look when Hy hung them this afternoon as he had promised. There were some Polo had probably never seen. What a cute kid he had been, especially after he got his teeth fixed.

Polo! She had completely forgotten to tell him that Nathalie had called. Nathalie had been as cool with her on the phone as she always was. Ruthie had so often wondered what she had ever done to offend, but couldn't put her finger on a damn thing. Of course she had never mentioned this to Polo. They weren't together often enough for it to matter. Ruthie fidgeted restlessly in her chair. Should she–but thinking back, she remembered that Nathalie had said she would call the condo offices. They would leave a message. So that was okay.

But now Polo and Nathalie were in her head at the same time as the family pictures she'd just seen after so many years: Morrie and Clarice in vibrant middle age, herself in the May of her graduating year from McGill, wearing the same sleeveless sun-dress she'd worn to that horse show, Polo, smiling and handsome in his black wool show jacket and gleaming white stock, stroking the neck of his winning horse, the huge rosette on the bridle…

And of course the capper to this convergence of motifs, Ruthie knew she was in a low and dangerously vulnerable frame of mind. Predictably, the videotape of her life whirred into 'play' mode, opening to that strange and unforgettable day in St. Lazare, and she wasn't making the slightest effort to resist watching.

Why had Ruthie gone to that horse show? Because Morrie and Clarice had to go to an early Sunday wedding and Hy too because he was an usher. Because it was the most important show of the season, a qualifier for Canadian Team membership. Because if Polo won the Grand Prix, there had to be a representative for the owner, as it would be terrible if he won and there was no Jacobson there… Because it was time she saw him doing what he loved.

And how did she explain to herself what had then happened? To begin with it was the only time she had ever been to a horse show. It was a relatively long drive out there, the day was horribly hot, she hadn't brought a hat, and she'd stood watching, sweaty and grimy from the billowing dust, for hours. It wasn't at all the fun and excitement she had expected.

She had been caught off guard when she first glimpsed him too. 'Her' Polo wasn't a boy anymore, suddenly he was a man she hardly recognized, elegantly but–for her–anachronistically costumed in his black coat, white stock, creamy britches and high boots, inhabiting a world in which she had no place, and felt no welcome.

It wasn't her unfamiliarity with show jumping that dampened her mood, though. What irritated and eventually hurt was Polo's complete disregard for her presence. She had imagined the pleasures of reflected importance in her obvious connection to a rising competitive star in this unknown world. He knew she was there, he'd acknowledged her with a wave and a quick smile before he mounted to warm up. But after that he was totally into himself, what he was doing. Amazed at her own growing resentment, she was aware that she had never seen such purity of concentration.

Afterward, when she'd expected finally to share his moment of triumph–Polo had won several classes, including the Grand Prix, she was tremendously proud–there was some kind of delay. Ruthie saw him hand off his horse to his groom, and step aside to speak to some officials. By then she was physically uncomfortable, her face and arms tight and sore from sunburn. Her head throbbed. The heat, the pungent animal smells, the flies, the thick humid air: it was all so oppressive she felt slightly ill, and she couldn't wait to leave. She wandered into the shade of a horse transport, impatiently waiting to congratulate him.

And suddenly there he was, walking slowly toward the stalls, not triumphant, not full of his victory, but curiously dazed. Ruthie had been shocked. It was his hour of glory, and yet he looked as stricken and vulnerable as a lost boy.

She really did not want to remember what had happened next, but the videotape was rolling and she was too fascinated to stop it. She called his name in alarm, his eyes turned slowly in her direction, he stared at her with the puzzled incomprehension of an amnesiac, and suddenly they were wrapped in each other's arms, they were whispering each other's names, she could feel the buttons of his jacket through the thin stuff of her dress, the rim of his glasses pressed into her cheek, she was tasting the damp salt on his skin, the dust of the show ring on his lips…

Wait! Rewind the tape! She was making it seem as though it were a mutual surrender. The truth was, the truth *was* that *she* had run into *his* arms, whispered *his* name, kissed *him*. For a second? For minutes? Did he kiss her back? She would never know, because the next thing she remembered was half–lying on a hay bale, water running down her face, with Polo, pale and frightened, holding her up, pressing an ice–filled horse bandage to her forehead, murmuring incoherent expressions of concern and encouragement.

She recovered, had a coke and some aspirin, insisted she was fine to drive home. And she was. Physically she was fine. But she was covered in shame, on fire with it. Why did she feel so ashamed?

Ruthie knew herself to be compulsively self–analytical. Her mind, like a tongue endlessly gliding across and around the familiar ridges, grooves, spaces and joins of newly–polished teeth, was in constant, sensitive surveillance of her inner world. She could not remember a time when she had not been involved in this restless process of psychological and ethical evaluation, exploring and assessing her motivations, needs, desires, actions, and reactions.

So if she was feeling shame rather than embarrassment, there had to be a reason. And the more she thought about it, the more she fastened on the strange and anomalous relationship of Polo with the Jacobson family, and the more she considered her personal history with him, the more rooted became her suspicions about what Polo was to her.

She had to know, so she waited up for her parents to come home from the wedding, and asked to speak privately to her father. First she told him how well Polo had done in the show. Morrie had been thrilled. It meant Polo had qualified for the Canadian Team. It meant Morrie's horse would be showing in the biggest shows: the Royal Winter Fair, Madison Square Garden. It was what he and Polo had worked for.

–*I have to know something, daddy.*
–*What is it, princess?*
–*Is Polo my brother? Did you ever have an aff –*

–He had smacked her face. Hit her. No one in her entire life had ever–the shock –

–Ruthie. What happened between you? Why are you asking me that?

–I–I–I have feelings for him –

–Did Polo make a move on you?

–She had been very frightened. This voice was not her father's.

–No. No. It's me, I–I kissed him. I didn't mean to. But he looked so–and I suddenly–and then I felt ashamed, so I have to know –

–He's not your brother. Whatever you feel, get over it. It's over. It never happened. Do you understand?

–Daddy, it wasn't Polo's fault –

–I believe you. But it's over.

There were gaps in the videotape after that. Polo had called. Morrie had seemed both distracted and agitated, but he had said nothing about Ruthie. She had been sent to her room. But she heard Morrie making phone calls for an hour. Then she heard his car pull out of the driveway, and when she woke the next morning he wasn't there. He had come home in the late afternoon of the next day. Still in his tuxedo!

The videotape of that segment of her life was winding down, but something nibbled at her consciousness for the first time about that day. *Stop. Rewind. There–freeze frame.* Oh yes. Well, one mystery solved anyway. There she was, coming to from that fainting spell. There was Polo's anxious face. And right there across the aisle was Nathalie, still just a girl, staring straight at Ruthie, and her eyes were glittering with pain.

Fran Briquemont, the Belgian Dressage trainer at *Le Centre*, had finished his morning assignments, and he was eager to go home to the hot, substantial lunch in the European mode that he and his wife Eva continued to favour even after all these years in Canada. However, it would have been unthinkable to leave without recording in his daily log the progress and/or setbacks he had experienced in the morning's routine.

There were four young horses he was bringing along, all

thoroughbreds off the track, all bought dirt cheap by Roch on spec. Race track rejects were–relatively speaking–a dime a dozen here, a continuing marvel to Fran, who found their quick, intelligent response to training a delightful contrast to the dense, plodding mind and physical heaviness of the European warmbloods he had always worked with in Germany. Some thoroughbreds you could have for the price of the dog meat they would otherwise become. (Fran also marvelled at the North American aversion to horsemeat as a cheaper, healthier alternative to beef for their own consumption).

Roch gave these youngsters to Fran to work with because it was understood that he was the only one with the patience and commitment to put in the thousands of hours necessary to set a proper base on them. If you wanted a well–made horse, one that was supple, balanced, obedient, happy in its work, with a mouth like silk and a readiness for the demands of high performance work, like Jumping or upper echelon Dressage, you had to put in the time. There was no other way.

Or rather there was one other way, much more expensive. You could go to Germany or Holland or Belgium where breeders, steeped in their trade's proud history, 'made' their own young horses, separated the wheat from the chaff, and sold 'the wheat' at the astonishingly high prices North Americans were prepared to pay for this convenience.

And this was why the Jumper circuit in North America was overwhelmingly dominated by warmbloods. Of course the warmbloods were more naturally powerful than the thoroughbreds, they had bigger and better natural movement. For purely Dressage purposes they were without peer. But in Fran's opinion, there was no reason why homebred thoroughbreds of high breeding, and trained properly in the old–fashioned ways, couldn't use their superior speed, agility, endurance and intelligence to best the Jumper field more often.

He had seen thoroughbreds here that could stand up to any of the famous warmbloods for talent, scope and heart. He remembered one in particular from many years ago, recalled to mind when he met Mr. Jacobson's friend, Polo. The Grand Panjandrum. And Fran remembered Polo, because he had admired the partnership of horse and rider at the time. A tactful, thinking rider, this Polo.

Fran had admired Polo's skill afresh while watching him ride at *Le Centre* as well over the last two weeks. Polo had schooled Michel's horses a few times when the younger man was busy, and he had also tried out some casual prospects Roch was musing over. A few times he had asked Fran for ground supervision and suggestions, which buoyed Fran's morale. Jumper riders rarely asked a Dressage expert for advice. Polo was one of the few here who realized that extensive Dressage training was the basis for great jumping.

But try explaining that to most North Americans. Riders here, *arrivistes* so to speak, with no deep history in the sport, were impatient. They would grab any shortcut so they could be out competing faster. They ended up ruining their horses' mouths with overuse of strong bits, or making them fearful, over–facing them with too-high jumps, or a hundred other offences against the First Principles of horsemanship laid down by Xenophon centuries ago and never really improved upon.

Fran sighed, thinking of the vast knowledge he had to impart, and the vast indifference with which most of it was greeted. He knew he was not an endearing or charismatic teacher. He was abrasive and uncompromising in his demands. The students here, soft, modern youngsters, resented this. But Fran himself found his methods normal.

Fran had been apprenticed in the military tradition of riding by the great *Reitmeisters,* Ernst Mueller, Karl Schickedanz and Bruno Weill. These riding masters were held in absolute awe, respected and feared by the apprenticing riders of Fran's youth. No student would dare question or criticize them. Indeed no student would even speak at all during a lesson in those days. (Those who forgot were made to wear tape over their mouth during the next lesson). How very, *very* different from the students here.

But it was time to go home. He put away his journal with dispatch as he consulted the time. Punctual, disciplined and considerate of the trouble his wife Eva took to please him, he was rarely late. Today he had a gift, a piece of news, which would please Eva, and he drove through the quiet streets of Saint Armand with a heart less burdened than it had felt in months.

His lightened mood was dampened, of course, by what had happened to the stallion. That piece of news could wait for a more propitious moment. It would only unnerve her, and to no purpose.

He considered the crime. Ugly, ugly. But what could you expect in a barn left so temptingly open to intruders? Fran actually shook his head in wonder whenever he thought about the general naivete and trustingness of horse people over here. Unlocked barns, no entrance gates whatsoever, let alone guards, even the tack room with thousands of dollars worth of saddles, bridles and equipment, all completely on offer to the most minimal of talents for deception or foul play.

And at horse shows it was truly unbelievable. People left their horse vans open and unsupervised for long hours at a time. They left their valuable *horses* in vans, unsupervised. In Europe such negligence would never arise. Your groom stayed in the van. You kept an Alsatian guard dog beside your gear. And for good reason. Really, these people here were like children…

Home for Fran and Eva was a modest bungalow on the outskirts of the village with a tiny garden from which the two aging, but vigorous pensioners managed to coax a surprising number of staple vegetables. The first lettuce of the season was now on the table as their salad, but it was still too early for the peas, carrots, beans, zucchini, and the rest. The main course was a hearty pot roast with potatoes and brussel sprouts, served with coarse, grainy bread, all to be washed down with foamy dark ale.

Fran kissed Eva and went to wash up without a word. He would wait until they were at table. He was tremulous with joy at the anticipation of the peace he would give her with his news. He joined her, taking his usual place at right angles to her.

Together they raised their hands to their lips and murmured a blessing over their daily provenance, thanking God for his material bounty in providing the good food on this table, and not forgetting to thank Him also for their great good fortune, to be living in peace and security in a democratic country, to be living without fear in their own home, to have honest work in a profession that they both loved, and to enjoy the respect of the people they lived amongst. Then they each spent a silent moment in meditation, thinking of those they had left behind, those who had died, so many, so horribly, trying to do right, help others, remain Christians in a world that had forgotten religion of all kind.

For a moment they both ate and drank in silence. Then Fran set down his glass with careful deliberation and said, "Eva, I have something to tell you."

From his tone Eva knew there was something important to hear. She set down her knife and fork and looked anxiously at her husband.

"He is gone, *liebchen*."

"For good?" Her voice trembled slightly.

"*Ja. Ja,* he will not come back. They seem sure of that."

Eva looked down at her plate and automatically picked up her utensils. But she did not use them. Tears trickled down her face, she nodded gently in a mechanical way, and she replied softly, "I am very happy to hear this news, Fran. I think maybe I will sleep tonight."

Fran closed his gnarled and deeply veined hand around his wife's dear wrist. Her knife dropped onto the table. He turned her forearm to reveal her open palm. Then with immense dignity and love, he bent to kiss the warm place on her inside forearm where the ugly row of ink–blue numbers stained her creamy skin.

CHAPTER SEVEN

IT WAS NO USE BEING A JOURNALIST, SUE PARKER THOUGHT IN frustration, if you couldn't get at the news when it was happening.

Since arriving at the Centre early that morning, she had literally stumbled on two potentially fabulous stories, only to be shunted aside before she could start to make sense of things. Plunging innocently into the vandalized office had electrified her. You didn't have to read French to smell the politics in that room. And the horse! Wow! That was obviously something you didn't see every day in a stable, as Roch's response had unequivocally communicated.

Nobody would talk to her about the morning's events. She might as well settle herself in the condo they had arranged for her and get in some of the sleep she had missed driving last night. But she was too wired. She had to find out *something* or she would burst. But where to start?

She had been hovering around the office from which people had been entering and leaving all morning, waiting to see Roch and apologize. She hoped she hadn't wrecked her chances for a decent relationship with him. He was the director; everyone else would take their cue from how he treated her.

111

First the blond guy with the totally sharp designer glasses had gone in. He'd stayed. Then Michel–*what a hunk*!–had arrived, not stayed long, slipped past her, eyes down and averted, just as well, maybe, he might have recognized her from her trip to Palm Beach. Then Bridget, the stallion's owner had arrived, it seemed, word was sent to the office, Roch had slipped out to the barn to meet her and brought her back there. The way *she* looked, there was no point in talking to her or Roch, they would have ordered her off the premises in a shot. But Sue knew she'd get to her sooner or later. She'd had her sights set on Bridget Pendunnin long before this incident.

Finally some time after that the ginger–haired, freckled vet came in from the barn and headed for the office. He was a 'type', Sue could see at once from his uptight body language. And a nerd. He had a plastic pen shield in his shirt pocket. *Quod erat demonstrandum.*

Sue was a world expert on nerds, as they were the only men who were ever attracted to her. This one, she figured, might be one of two types: either he was the anal–compulsive hoarder kind who ranged his pocket change in tidy little denominational piles on the bureau at night, or he had a car littered in year–old chocolate bar wrappers and every pair of sunglasses he had ever owned in his life on the dashboard. He had attempted to answer a few questions for her before going in, but he was stuttering so badly she gave it up and let him escape after a minute or two.

A few minutes later the vet left with Bridget. She looked awful. Sue stayed out of their way. And then the owner arrived. Sue introduced herself. He–Mr. Jacobson–seemed distracted, but was polite and welcomed her to the Centre, adding that he trusted her accommodations were satisfactory, hoping she'd understand why he couldn't give her any time at the moment, etc. Nice manners. And well–spoken, articulate, to the point. He'd make a good interview later.

The owner left at the same time as the cool–looking blond guy. That one stopped to answer a question or two when she pounced, and she could see right away he was too savvy to let on anything important. But he had promised to talk to her when things settled down, tell her about the show, the course he was designing, blah, blah, what a yawn all that seemed like now. Really cute sense of humour, though, also good in an interviewee. *Napoléon Poisson? Whew! Impressive name. Yeah, my dad had a thing for emperors. I think I got off better than my brothers Charlemagne and Vespasian...*

Ah! Finally here was Roch emerging from his lair, wearing a jaunty straw fedora. She noticed that he was nicely dressed in comparison with most of the horse trainers she had so far met. He wore well-cut, modish jeans and a quality denim shirt. His paddock boots were clean, and he smelled pleasantly of some kind of manly aftershave. A pair of chaps were thrown over one shoulder. Without his graying hair and balding dome to call attention from his face, he was astonishingly youthful-looking. "*Encore toué.* You still here, slick?" he asked, smiling as though they were old, casual friends.

"Yeah. Uh, I'm sorry if I was out of line–" she jerked her head towards the barn, causing her helmet of thin, straight hair to jump and sway jerkily–"it was kind of unexpected..."

"No problem." He had already set off briskly down the hall to the barn. She was just another piece of jetsam in his wake of daily problems, it was over, *that was then, this is now*, and she could see she no longer registered in his mind as being of the slightest importance.

"Hey! Hey, wait–" she trotted after him–"hey, give me a break here! I'm supposed to be doing this backgrounder, like interviewing people and finding out how things work around here. Aren't you going to, like, give me any cooperation? I mean, where do I start? Can't I talk to you for a minute?"

"No time, Suzy. Gotta lesson to give."

"Uh, I don't mean to be rude, but I'd prefer 'Sue'. I hate being called Suzy, actually."

"Is your name Sue? I call *all* the girls Suzy. I'm not too good on names...gotta run...speak to you later..." and he was out the stable door like the rabbit in *Alice in Wonderland*.

I call all the girls Suzy. That is so...sexist!

Curiosity and indignation struggled for pride of place in her mind. Yielding to curiosity, she ran out the door and caught a glimpse of him rounding the corner, heading to a warm-up ring, one of several carved level into the slopes of the hill bordering the barn on the storage and utility side. She followed. He wouldn't object to her watching him give his lesson, surely, and she could learn something about his training methods at least.

A rider was warming up in the ring, a tall, slim girl on what looked like a skittish brown thoroughbred. When Sue had started out a year ago on her "E–Quest," as she dubbed it, she knew next to nothing about horses or horse sport. She had learned a lot in a short space of time, and by now she at least knew the difference between a thoroughbred–a hotblood–and a warmblood, between high–strung and what the riders called 'bombproof'.

The girl turned as Roch called out an instruction. Luckily she was English–speaking. "Roch, I can't get her to do *anything* today. She's being such a *brat.*"

"Take her over the X at a trot."

The girl trotted the mare dutifully over a small arrangement of crossed poles. He had her do this several times, then added a 'vertical', a pole laid straight across the standards as a next element. This was the classic warm–up for jumping lessons, and something Sue was familiar with.

Next she would do these two jumps at a canter, and then he would create a small winding course of variegated obstacles, distances and minor challenges–a 'wall' of fake gray stones, an 'oxer', two poles spaced a foot or wider apart in the same element to encourage width of scope, and sundry other combinations. Coming around turns without the shoulder of the horse 'falling in' was a constant feature of the course in order to exercise the rider's ability to balance and set the horse up for the new distance. She was supposed to know exactly how many strides would bring her to her 'spot.'

Finding your 'spot' was the bottom line for all jumper riders. Sue had had this drummed into her by several of the riders she hung out with. You could achieve some proficiency in this through practice, but you needed a natural feel for it too, and some riders never really captured this quintessential technical rubric. The optimum spot determined the horse's trajectory from take–off. Relatively unimportant with low jumps, it became more and more critical to a successful completion the bigger they got. Bringing a horse to a bad spot was, even Sue knew, the cardinal sin of jumper riding, and this girl seemed to be unusually hopeless, as her horse began stopping regularly as soon as the height of the jumps increased.

Finally Roch told her to get off. Sue had noticed that he had strapped his chaps on at the beginning of the lesson, so his interventions must happen regularly with this student. Flushed and annoyed, the girl turned the mare over to Roch. He mounted, took her into a rhythmic canter, just establishing a nice pace for several laps, then popped around, nice and smooth, doing the whole little course in a fluid, classic demonstration of sound horsemanship.

He was relaxed and natural on a horse, very agreeable to watch. On the second circuit of the jumps the horse suddenly stopped at the wall. Roch whipped her smartly, twice, cracking the air and making Sue wince a bit. Then he took her back and jumped the same wall three times in succession. By the third time she gave no sign of hesitation.

Now the girl was back on and did one circuit, without Roch's seamlessly accurate striding, but without mishap. On her second tour the horse stopped at the wall. Immediately she laid into her with her whip. Roch bellowed, "*What are you doing! Why are you hitting the horse?*"

"What do you mean, why am I hitting her? *You* did when she stopped!"

"I hit her because she could jump it if she want, and she doesn't want. *You took her to a bad spot.* She has no confidence to jump it. It's *your* fault. You never hit the horse when it's *your* fault. You understand? *Do you understand?*"

"*Yes, I understand.*" The girl was very red in the face, conscious of an audience. "I'm obviously a totally awful rider, and there's no point in going on today. I'm sorry, but I simply can't *respond* to that kind of bullying."

She rode stiffly out of the ring and back to the barn.

Sue walked over to Roch, who was dismantling the jumps. "I'm sorry if that happened because I was watching."

"No problem. It happens sometimes." He smiled lazily at her, hands on his hips. He bent towards her in speaking, looking directly into her eyes, and she found him to be infringing her 'comfort zone.' This was perhaps a *québécois* thing, she found francophones needed less space between themselves and their interlocutor than English–Canadians. She backed away a fraction.

"Maybe she has her period, what you think?" His eyes were dancing, daring her to take the bait.

Boy, did he ever get my number fast. Bastard.

Determining to take the high road, Sue ignored the barb and even wheedled at him as she pleaded for some time to talk. "Listen, just give me a half hour. Let me buy you lunch. You have to eat anyway."

"Too busy today. But I'll find you someone. Come with me."

They walked down the main aisle. The girl was untacking her horse, whose bridle was tethered by two cross–ties attached either side of the corridor. She looked sulky, and coloured up as Roch approached.

While slipping past her, Roch pinched a fold of flesh at her waist. She shrieked theatrically. He retorted mockingly, "Hey, you better watch out, you, you're taking some weight. What man he's gonna want you then, *hein?*"

Sue stopped dead in her tracks. *He has just managed to offend all of womankind in at least three distinct ways, probably more if I had time to deconstruct all the semiotics at work here. Boy, he must run through an awful lot of female students.*

"*Ro*–och, you are just *so-o bad*! No really, you're *terrible!*" the girl exclaimed. But she had brightened up considerably, and was now going about her grooming with renewed vigour. Her eyes followed him down the corridor.

Roch stopped at the passdoor and glanced back to find Sue still standing with her mouth open.

"That," she said, "was the most politically incorrect dialogue I've ever heard in my life!"

"Ah, c'mon, Suzy. Fuck all that political shit. You think the stable, it's all about politics. I know what you see when you look at us, what you saw this morning. You come with me. I'm gonna show you what's going on here, why it's special. Forget the fucking politics. C'mon."

She started to walk slowly. He clapped his hands briskly. "C'mon, you. Don't keep a man waiting-men don't like it, don't you know that?" And he laughed, very pleased with himself and life in general. She approached him on automatic pilot, her face a study in disbelief.

Roch was enjoying himself hugely with this funny, and funny–looking, little woman. He knew he should be in a rotten mood over the morning's events, but his optimism was a helium balloon, pressing for a chance to soar free. The morning's trauma was a low ceiling, but there had been so many in his twenty–five years here, and things always came right in the end. His mood was improving by the minute. Things would sort themselves out. As she drew level with him, he squeezed her neck in a friendly way and tugged on her hair. She wasn't pretty, but she was female. He couldn't help himself.

Polo found a message from the condo office tucked inside the doorframe. *Please call your wife.* He wondered if he should be alarmed. So far he had always called Nathalie, and he had seen her just a few days ago. Everything had seemed fine–or at least she had been healthy, and intending to spend a few days with her parents in Outremont for the weekend.

"Nath–*ça va?*"

"*Que oui.*" Her words were slurred.

"Are you drinking?" Polo was shocked. Nathalie had never drunk anything stronger than wine or beer, and then only socially, evenings, in all the years he'd known her.

"Yes. Yes I am."

"You were supposed to be spending a few days with your parents."

"And yet, as you obviously have deduced, I'm not."

"What's going on? What's wrong? Your parents, are they–?"

"My parents are fine. Bernard and Pauline are carrying on, setting a proper example for *le Tout–Montréal* in matters social, cultural, fashionable, and financial as usual. Nobody's sick. No, that's not true, I tell a lie. *I*, your wife, am sick. Sick at heart." She was enunciating every word carefully. She was quite drunk.

"You're not planning on driving anywhere today, are you? Nath?"

"No, I'm not. And may I say that I am touched by the sense of responsibility and maturity that makes you ask. And may I say too"–Polo heard a smothered burp–"how typical that you should be so solicitous–as usual–from a distance…no, I am not driving anywhere."

Polo tried to check his rising anger. "Don't fuck with me, Nath. What's going on?"

Nathalie began to cry. "Today is the thirteenth day of my menstrual cycle. I could get pregnant in a minute if–if I had someone–who wanted to make me pregnant…"

"Nath, we have a deal. *Christi*, I could have made sure you never got pregnant–not by me, anyway–just by spending twenty minutes with a urologist. For me a deal's a deal, *hein*?"

She was crying in harsh, jagged sobs now. "Polo, I'm thirty-five years old. You can't *do* this to me any more. I gave you time." She wailed, "I gave you my best, *best* time. Why can't you want this to happen? Why can't I leave you? Why are you always running off to buy horses and build arenas? Why won't you ever talk to me about…stuff?"

She paused hopefully, but receiving no answer, cried, "*Why can't we ever discuss what happened back then?*"

"Nath, Nath–"

"*Why is your whole life such a fucking mystery to me?*" She was sobbing unrestrainedly, like an overtired child.

Polo was by now in the grip of a painful stomach spasm and could hardly talk. He couldn't bear women crying.

He really couldn't bear it.

It was horrible. The knuckles of his free hand were white as he gripped his knee with all his strength. He wanted to smack her, hard, to make her stop. He had never smacked her, or any woman. But he was just as glad she wasn't in the same room at that moment, because the impulse was as bad as he had ever known it to be.

His eyes were irritated. He passed his hand under his glasses to rub them. His fingers came away wet, and he almost groaned aloud in disgust. Of course smacking wives was not what *good* husbands did, smacking kids wasn't what *good* fathers did, but how could he trust himself to remember that forever, especially now when he seriously felt like hitting her–someone,–anyone… Better not to be in situations where women cried, where children cried…

"Listen," he managed huskily, "listen to me. I can't talk to you about this now. Not on the phone. Not when you're drunk. Not when–"

"Not when it's inconvenient, not when it's raining, not when Ruthie's kids want a riding lesson–oh, Polo, you *fool*, do you think this can go on forever?" She sniffed, and blew her nose.

Then she said, her voice low, thick with drink and yearning, "Polo, come home for a day. Not to sell horses, not to buy them, not to wheel and deal. Just to talk. Please. *Please*. One whole day. It's not much to ask." She sighed and added in a tearful, little girl's voice, "There's something–something I want to tell you–finally–tell you– it would mean so much to finally–finally…" she was mumbling, her voice uncertain.

Polo cut her off. He was furious. She was rambling. "Listen, Nath–and this isn't an excuse, this is really happening–there's a kind of crisis here. A horse got cut up badly, deliberately, the office was vandalized. Roch's short–handed, his head boy ran off, I–"

"No, no, *no! You* listen, Polo"–her voice was hard and bitter now–"in horses there is *always* going to be a crisis–when are you going to realize that–a sick horse, a lame horse, a dead horse, a red horse, a blue horse–"

"Nath, come on. This is pointless."

"You're right. But there's a mystery about *you* that needs solving, and I'm going to try to do that while you're away solving horse crises."

Prongs, fishhooks of anxiety lodged inside his gut and tugged gently upwards. "What do you mean, Nath?" he said quietly.

Now she was suddenly listless, mournful and flat. "It's what I said. I am going to solve some puzzles. You won't come home to talk? Fine. You won't come home to listen to me talk? I told you I have something to tell you, but you didn't ask what. 'Cuz you don't want to know, do you, *chou*? You don't want to know…"

Snuffling and movement at the other end. She must be on the portable and walking around, Polo thought. Tearily she said, "You won't see a therapist? Fine. Then I'll have to analyze you myself.

Not the easiest thing when the patient is so good at denial and repression and won't even show up for an appointment. But I will do
my best."

The fishhook dug deeper, tugged harder. A thin, sharp wire of
pain snaked through him. "What kind of shit is this, Nath? You
take a few psychology courses and now you're an expert. What do
you mean by this denial and repression crap?"

"A few courses? Hey, I'm *graduating* next year, remember? By
the way, you didn't even ask how my final exam in Early Childhood
Development was yesterday." She sounded drowsily petulant, like a
toddler resisting naptime. He heard the bedsprings squeak.

"Sorry. Completely forgot. How was it?"

"I'd say B plus or A minus."

"Way to go. Look Nath, I have to get a move on. Can you maybe–could we meet in Montreal maybe? Tomorrow for dinner?"

"Love to, but I already have a date in Montreal tomorrow. Dinner with an old friend of *yours,* in fact." She hiccuped loudly and
he heard a loud knocking noise. "Oops. Dropped the phone. Sorry
about that. Yeah, gonna be on the information highway by Sunday,
I'm betting."

"Don't, Nath–"

"No, I'm serious. I really do have a date."

"Who?"

"Ooh, that would be telling, wouldn't it?"

"Don't play the bitch, Nath. You just come off like a spoiled
brat."

"Oh yeah? Hey, how come I'm not allowed to say when you
act like an ignoramus throwback from *balconville* who thinks psy-
chiatrists put people in straitjackets to cure bedwetting, but you're
allowed to tell me I'm just a spoiled rich bitch from Outremont?
How come?"

There was no answer to this. She was right. They should never
have married. They would be cutting each other up like this every
time they had a fight, forever. Once you started drawing this kind
of blood, you never stopped. *People should stick to their own kind.*
Morrie had warned him. He should have listened.

But who is my own kind? Where would I have found my own kind?

Polo was frustrated and a little frightened. Usually when they fought things never went this far. Usually fighting made them hungry for each other, and they ended in bed what couldn't be solved with words. He was hungry for her right now. But this was very bad. He felt they must be nearing the end of their road together. He couldn't imagine life without her. He wanted to howl like a dog.

"Ruthie's there, eh *chéri?* I mean, I called the Jacobsons to see if you were there. You didn't mention Ruthie was visiting…" Her voice had gotten steadier before this pronouncement, but now it went all weak and trembly again, and he heard tears crowding her words.

"*Et alors?* So what? Are you sugges–you're not seriously–" *How long has she been chewing on this–but that's crazy–*

Silence.

"Aw c'mon, this isn't you, Nath. No really, I don't believe this–"

"Yeah, you're right, Polo. This isn't the me you fell for. This isn't sweet, know–nothing Nath who doesn't want anything else in life but to follow you around and worship you. I guess it's Nath all grown up. Not nearly so appealing, is she–?"

"Just don't ever make those kind of insinuations about Ruthie again, okay?"

Silence. A speaking silence that he felt as a chill, as a witch's curse in a fairy tale. Or as a prophecy. He shivered.

"Okay, Nath?" He kept his voice low so she wouldn't hear the fear. He hated himself, he hated her, he was desperate to get away from her voice and her silence.

Nose–blowing.

"I figure I have five more years at the outside, Polo. I'd like it to be you, because I still love you. I know I'm probably a lifer where you're concerned." She drew a wavy breath and regrouped her forces.

"But blood is thicker than water, you know? And husbands aren't blood. I am *not* going to spend my twilight years knitting ankle boots for horses. You've got a lot of unfinished business to clear up, Polo. Not just with me. With *them.* Ruthie for sure, whether you want to hear it or not, but Morrie too."

"Aw, for Chrissake"–

"And let's not forget your *real* family–you know, *maman, papa,* all those ragtag brothers and sisters–though God knows you've done a brilliant job of forgetting them so far. I'll tell you something for free, since I haven't graduated yet, Polo. I used to think you were the bravest guy in the world. There never was a horse you were afraid to ride. I think it's why I fell in love with you.

"But, see"–she choked up, then hiccupped loudly–"*merde*–I'm realizing that you're not brave enough to be a father. And, see, I have a real problem with that, 'cuz courage in a man–it's–it's–oh *merde*, I'm so tired of feeling sorry for myself! *Salut,* Polo, and lemme know when you're ready to–'scuse the psychobabble–*share* with me..."(this last in English). *Click.*

Nathalie Chouinard claimed to have fallen in love with Polo when she was nine years old, a beginner in Pony Club. He was at that time the rising Jumper star of Quebec. As a youngster and teenager, she followed him around at the shows and pestered him. Polo would let her hang out at his stalls, hot–walk his horses, braid manes for Hunter classes, and help his grooms to organize their comings and goings. When he stopped riding professionally and built a barn on his St. Lazare property, he let her board her horse there, and he coached her at the backyard shows she was satisfied to compete at.

Nathalie had been a gawky ugly duckling. In late adolescence her awkward limbs and slightly goofy–looking features achieved a pleasing harmony and regularity. Like many late bloomers, she was unaware of her transformation. Her youthful efforts had all been directed at self–effacement

Her love for Polo was pure and hopeless. She offered him a dog's devotion and loyalty, and was for many years satisfied with a dog's portion: a friendly pat on the shoulder, the odd compliment on a task well done, the occasional outing for pizza or as transport assistance for the horses.

Nathalie watched Polo's girlfriends come and go without ran-cour–that would have been presumptuous–but with definite opin-ions as to their relative merits and worthiness. She was always pleased by the transience of his liaisons. But she was at the St. Laza-re Classic, the only horse show Ruthie ever attended, and when she witnessed the two of them together and saw how it was between them, she almost swooned with jealousy.

When Nathalie was seventeen, Polo suddenly noticed her one day while she was sitting on an overturned bucket cold–hosing her horse's swollen leg. Or rather took *notice* of her. She was arching her back in a stretch, reaching up with her free hand to smooth a loose strand of hair back from her forehead. It was that one grace-ful gesture and the sweet, buoyant lift of her breast under her thin t–shirt. He was quite close to her and almost reached out to ca-ress her, the impact was so sudden. She stood up in her tight jeans, twisting to turn off the faucet, and he marvelled at the fluid swell of her hips and buttocks.

He realized with a shock that Nathalie was becoming a woman, and a desirable one. She was right on the cusp. Boys–men–would be coming around at any moment. He didn't like that thought. Polo knew how things stood with her where he was concerned, and he weighed the potential for damage if he took advantage of her feel-ings to satisfy what he assumed was a passing physical interest on his part. And he was aware that she was embarrassingly young for him. But he knew that same day that he had to choose. He wanted her, and badly. He had either to send her away or have her.

He compromised by warning her before making his move. It wasn't love, he said. It wouldn't last long. It didn't matter, she declared with her lips. *We'll just see, she murmured in her leaping heart.*

So he made a duvet of clean straw in the four–horse rig, covered it with blankets, and brought her there the next night. Polo had never been with a virgin before. He wasn't prepared, when his mo-ment came, for the flood of joy that followed. When she smothered a whimper of pain, denying it with kisses, he was moved, caught up in the grip of tender possessiveness. What in his life had ever, *ever* belonged uniquely to him?

It was very odd. Holding her afterwards, smoothing her long hair with gentle strokes to comfort and to thank her, he felt at once the pride of exclusive dominion and the humility of a tamed animal. It was the most peaceful, balanced emotional moment he'd ever known.

They were a couple from then on.

As business grew more demanding for Polo, Nathalie became a fixture at the barn, doing his paperwork, overseeing operations, riding and exercising the sale horses. When it came to a choice, she broke off her university education to work for him fulltime.

Bernard Chouinard, scion of an old family, *de vieille souche,* a fundraiser of importance in the federal Liberal party, with generations of learned and distinguished public figures behind him, was furious that his daughter's excellent private school education and her very good mind were going to waste in the coarse and culturally sterile environment of horse sport. The Chouinards had chosen horses as a distraction to boost Nathalie's low self-esteem. Their older daughter was a beauty and a social tyro. They had meant riding to be a hobby and a means of improving her English, not a career.

The Chouinards blamed Polo. He was older, he had seduced her, they assumed. They refused to believe that Polo had also told her she was a fool to give up her education. They saw only that she was in thrall to him, and they assumed he was a fortune hunter as well as an *arrivist.* They were wrong about him on both counts. There were many young women much wealthier than Nathalie on the circuit, and Polo had his pick of them. And he had no social ambitions whatsoever.

The truth was that if there was enthrallment, it was now mutual. Polo wasn't sure that it was love on his part. But he was sexually obsessed by Nathalie. His ardour didn't level out or decrease with the years. He wanted her there with him all the time. When he travelled he wanted to think of her there, in the neat pre-fab house that he had built next to the barn. For the first time in his life he was jealous at even the thought of other men around his woman.

Nathalie adored him. She loved being in his house, working in his barn, waiting for his return. It was a perfect set-up. Except for Nathalie wanting to marry him. And, obscurely, Polo knew that marriage would be the end of something wonderful. But he couldn't arrive at a convincing explanation of why this should be so.

Nathalie became pregnant. By accident, she said. Polo felt betrayed and frightened, and it showed. Nathalie felt betrayed and humiliated, and *it* showed. So when she told him she had miscarried and he needn't marry her after all, he was relieved and so grateful that he rushed to her bedside in Outremont as she lay recuperating, and proposed on the spot. She accepted, of course, but it was not as it should have been. He made her agree that they would wait before having children, that perhaps they wouldn't even want children. Because they would be all in all to each other. It had seemed a romantic notion at the time…

And they were still waiting.

Some years after their marriage Nathalie began to understand that she might never have the family she yearned for, and that in any case no single other person could be a reason for living. Polo travelled a lot and she resented being alone, the caretaker of horses, not children. So she went back to school part time, studying psychology and thinking about a career away from horses. They hired a fulltime barn manager.

Nathalie wondered sometimes if Polo was faithful to her. If he was, he would be truly unique amongst horsemen, or at least the ones she knew. But she never inquired, because what would she do if he admitted that he had other women? She knew she would never leave him. Or if she did, it wouldn't be for that.

Polo *was* unfaithful, but not according to his own standards. He never slept with other women in North America, only in Europe. They were women he had known for years, in the horse industry. He was scrupulously careful and hygienically prudent. He never mentioned these episodes, let alone boasted of them, to other men, as other men did to him. He brought nothing of himself to these women, he took nothing away when he left.

He wasn't proud of himself, and he wasn't ashamed either. It was part of being a man. He was correctly discreet. He would never do anything to embarrass or humiliate Nathalie. He saw nothing wrong in it. And yet if he had thought for a single instant that Nathalie was being unfaithful to him (she never was), it would have ripped him apart. Polo was old–fashioned in this, and other respects.

✤ ✤ ✤

The lunch rush was in full swing at '*De Trot*.' Roch pushed open the door and, as always at the sight of a full house, smiled broadly, as though they were all personal guests attending a party he'd arranged. His eyes searched the room with practiced swiftness, performing a networking triage ritual. Today there were several objects worthy of his attention. But first he had a lesson to teach.

"Okay, Suzy," he murmured as he guided her into the entrance, "take a good look around."

Obediently Sue surveyed the room. There were tables for two, four and six. All were filled but one, a small table at the back. That, as she later learned, was always reserved for Roch and whatever last-minute guest he might show up with. When he arrived, he either appropriated it or sat down with another chosen 'target', nodding to Caroline to give it away to the next comer.

"You see those two men over there? The old guy and the one with the beard?" Roch asked her. She nodded. "The old guy is Luc Boivin, the Minister for the Environment in Quebec. He loves it here, nobody bugs him, he goes out for a ride, clears his head, he forgets all his troubles, goes back to work a new man. Who's he with? Henry Dunton, the best blacksmith in Canada. A Loyalist family, goes back forever. Luc thinks he's a genius because before Henry his horse could never keep a shoe on, and now he has four healthy hooves. Loves the guy."

"Okay, across the room. That youngish guy, curly hair? With the skinny girl? The guy, that's Pierre Tremblay, he runs all the triathlons in Quebec, has one here every July and October. That girl, he's coaching her, she's for sure going to be world champion this year. Sandra Petty, from Westmount. When she wins, they gonna say she's a great *québécoise*, right? But I think maybe she doesn't even speak French, and Pierre, he doesn't give a shit, because he's gonna be a world-famous coach from her. And me, I don't give a shit as long as they come here to train."

"Those four guys in the middle, two from here, the others from Korea. They're big shots looking to set up a plant here, the two local guys are one from the town, one's a *fonctionnaire* from the federal government. Look at them, they're having a ball, they love it here. And over there, that's my kids from Ontario. Do they look sad from the politics? Fuck, no. They love it here, too. You getting the picture, Suzy?"

He pointed out mountain bikers from the city, a Granby real estate agent impressing a would–be purchaser, Claude Lafrenière, the local hay and grain merchant lunching with Marie–France, and even two retired priests who ran a marriage counselling retreat in their family estate near the stable.

"You see how it is here, Suzy?" Again he was peering disconcertingly deeply into her eyes, too close for her usual sense of self-possession. "You got a roomful of happy people here. Why? Because they all got their mind on something they like to do. They're all different. Some of them are rich, and some of them are poor, some of them are French and some of them are English, but who cares? They all got lives, they all got something to think about except politics. Why don't you write about that for a change, *hein?*"

Sue was about to reply when a low, musical voice behind them said, "Hello, Roch."

Roch grinned with spontaneous pleasure as he greeted Thea Ankstrom. He saluted her warmly and she blushed slightly. "I'll never get used to both cheeks," she said demurely. "It makes me feel quite wicked and Continental."

Roch introduced Thea to Sue. Sue made an immediate bid for time with her to discuss Thea's role in the show and her views on the sport in general. Thea responded graciously and cooperatively, ending with the suggestion that they get started immediately by eating lunch together. Roch smiled a little smugly at having so smoothly facilitated this tiny networking accomplishment. Trivial as it was in the scheme of things, it seemed to him a nice cap to the thematic thrust of his preceding speech to Sue on the magical social properties of his kingdom.

"Don't run away so fast, Roch," Thea said warningly as she read his body language. "You've *got* to help me with Bridget. Eventing is the only discipline I can't get up to date on, and the only reason for that is Bridget's lack of organization. She hasn't given me any of the lists I need: volunteers, jump judges, final choices for *chefs d'équipe*. She hasn't even given me a map of the course, and I can't possibly have a program ready without it–" She scanned the room. "I was actually hoping to find her here, but no luck."

Roch sighed and filled her in on the morning's upsets. Sue, watching Thea's reactions very closely, felt that she took the news with remarkable sangfroid. When Roch shook his head and confessed that nobody had any convincing argument for the target of the attack on the stallion, Thea mused ironically, "I suppose it could be me!"

In response to the baffled look on Roch's face, she went on, "Well, think about it. The two horses look quite similar over the top of the barn door. So it may be that the attacker was after *my* horse opposite and got mixed up."

Roch's frowned in grudging concession—one more frustrating possibility—and, almost sadistically, or so it seemed to Sue, Thea continued in a wry, detached tone, as if she were speaking of a complete stranger, "Had you also considered the fact that it could even have *been* me that did it? I mean, it's no secret that Bridget and I have an unsettled score between us—"—here Roch looked puzzled—"I mean, it's well known that I hold Bridget responsible to some extent for what happened to Stephanie."

Thea looked calmly and without flinching at Roch throughout this little speech. He found himself troubled and even unnnerved by the strength of her poise and obvious resolve. But resolve to what? Not for the first time he found himself wondering what on earth could have persuaded her to look for therapy in an undertaking of this kind. He was grateful, selfishly, for the sake of the show. She was doing the work of three people. But such coolness, and to say these things in front of this nosy journalist....

He shook off the cloud of gloom that was threatening to re–descend, and with determined good cheer, responded, "I got to admit, Thea, you *anglais*, you got an interesting sense of *l'humour*. Me, I don't believe a nice lady like you is going to do that. And lunch, it's no time to think about those sad things."

Briskly, and without leaving them an option, he concluded, "You girls are lucky. There's no tables, but I insist you gonna have my space. I know you got a lot to talk about. Ladies always got lots to say, *n'est–ce pas?*" He winked cheerfully at Sue, who glared back at him in completely futile irritation.

Shepherding them cavalierly to the table, he tweaked Sue's hair, touched Thea lightly on the shoulder and was about to slip away to 'work the room' when Thea added, "Roch, you really *must* help me out with her, in spite of everything. I hope you haven't forgotten that Sunday is the last plenary meeting before the show. I *won't* have it said that I was the disorganized one. I'm going over to Bridget's tomorrow to make her walk the course with me and do those lists, and I expect you to back me up!"

"No problem, Thea, no problem," Roch replied heartily over his shoulder, already halfway across the room. Thea sighed in resignation and gave her attention over to Sue.

CHAPTER EIGHT

SUE WAS EAGER TO GET TO WORK ON THEA ANKSTROM, AND IF she had been a more seasoned journalist, she would have been more patient in her attack. She quickly realized that she was no match for Thea's sophisticated defence system. Even before ordering their lunch—all–dressed burger, fries and coke for Sue, *Salade Niçoise* and Perrier for Thea—several of Sue's opening gambits had been neatly deflected, and before Sue realized it, she found herself being interviewed by Thea. How had Sue gotten started in equestrian journalism? What did she know about the eventing world in particular? What did she hope to get out of all this?

Well, Sue explained, it was JoJo Katz, a Communications Studies friend who had gotten Sue started on her project by sharing with her the ongoing saga of her family's troubles in the horse industry. It was a perfect story for a novice investigative reporter because JoJo had all the facts beautifully archived. JoJo and her family became the first of the celebrated lawsuits Sue had written up for her series in the Financial Gazette. So actually she knew quite a bit about eventing, for an outsider, and what she hoped to gain was a story that would grab readers' attention, further her career, and maybe, just maybe, shake things up in an industry that obviously needed it.

"I'll be frank, Mrs. Ankstrom, I wanted to talk to you in particular because I'm seeing a pattern emerge. It's a small world, eventing, and you could help me a lot if you could answer some questions for me about your horse, Robin's Song."

Thea was not to be drawn in so quickly. "Tell me the details of your friend's case," she said. Sue must have looked a little impatient because Thea added, "My dear girl, I've just met you, and you're a reporter. I know nothing about you apart from your writing, which, by the way, is extremely good. I'm simply doing some due diligence to see if I can trust you to do justice to what I choose to reveal." She sipped at her Perrier. "Due diligence is a concept not often associated with horse people. I have been as guilty as others in that respect in the past, and the only difference between me and most other horse people is that I tend to learn from my mistakes."

Sue sighed. "It's a long story, but fair's fair. Here goes." And it was a long story, but Thea listened with quiet attentiveness to every word. Sue stopped every five minutes for a gigantic bite of hamburger, and Thea, nibbling methodically at her salad, waited politely at each of these intervals without comment.

The Katzes had not been sanguine about JoJo's passion for horses, particularly not about her interest in the riskiest discipline, eventing. But when all their attempts to deflect her from her goals had failed, they reluctantly rallied round and came to the decision that, if she were going to 'go for the gold', she might as well do it right, and get a horse worthy of her dreams.

They went to England. They met with Philip Fairclough who assessed JoJo's abilities (excellent, he said) and riding style, and assured them he would find a horse compatible with her needs and ambitions. The horse would be vetted in England and sent off via his 'partner' in Canada, Bridget Pendunnin, who, happily, lived not an hour's distance from Montreal. Lucky JoJo. And what a coincidence. She had already attended some eventing clinics with Bridget, indeed it was Bridget who had sent them to Fairclough, and JoJo felt confident that under her guidance it would be a perfect set-up.

The horse arrived in due course. The Katzes paid an "obscene" (Mr. Katz's word to his lawyer) amount of money for it. Within six months, the horse had been through five expert trainers, all of whom had pronounced it a variant of 'unsuitable for any girl', 'a horse for a strong man', 'a pig,' 'half-broke', and 'dangerous, not worth breaking your neck over.'

Mr. Katz conferred with Larry Klepper, a very expensive and successful litigation lawyer who happened to be representing him at the time in a business lawsuit. Normally the horse case would have been beneath a senior partner's notice, but under the circumstances, and mindful of the "obscene" amount of money he was likely to make on the business suit (*not* the word he used with his client), he agreed to review the details. Having done so, he said he wouldn't touch the case.

'You have no case for misrepresentation–legally, that is–although it's clear that in *fact* you've been royally screwed,' Klepper had said flatly. 'The agent here will say your daughter is a bad rider, that she somehow ruined the horse, or that you should have exercised more caution in buying it. And your daughter will become a pariah in the sport. You have nothing in writing. You will lose. Is that what you want?'

Mr. Katz was a stubborn man, and was not used to being made a fool of. Also, in his business–he raised millions of dollars of venture capital annually in the field of biotechnology–a person's word was his bond. A handshake meant something. He concluded deals worth hundreds of thousands of dollars over the telephone on a routine basis. If he were to dupe a potential investor he could be held accountable to the Securities Commission, face huge fines or worse, lose his standing amongst his peers, risk censure in his own, the Jewish, as well as the general Montreal communities.

The consequences of acting in bad faith in his business were therefore unequivocal and far-reaching. Even if he were not an intrinsically ethical person–which in fact he was–he would have had to be a fool to transgress the rubrics of good faith that were the cornerstone of his prosperity and sense of self-worth. This horse business was a new and ugly experience for him.

Because what it came down to was that the Katz family had absolutely no recourse for their complaint. The Federation–C–FES–

didn't want to know about it and stonewalled every attempt Mr. Katz made to have the problem adjudicated within the "profession". In the end it became clear that he would have had more support from the Consumers' Protection Act in buying a five thousand dollar used car than any horse buyer had in purchasing even a million dollar animal. It was shocking.

Equally enraging was the reaction of other owners to whom he told his story. Most of them shrugged and offered unresolved and unrequited horror stories of their own. It appeared that this kind of duplicity was so pandemic in the sport–like black flies in the Laurentians in summer, an irritation that spoiled your fun, but about which you could do nothing–that his decision to pursue justice was the exception that proved the rule of passivity amongst the other victims.

Mr. Katz went to England. He spoke–not to Philip Fairclough, whom he by now suspected of being a charlatan and a world–class creep–but to grooms, other riders and even a private investigator in London.

He was astonished to learn that a 'pre–purchase vetting' in England was a rather casual affair. If the horse was sound on the day he was vetted, then he passed. If not, he failed. His former history of injuries, operations or whatever were never mentioned in the vetting report. The private investigator made discreet inquiries about JoJo's horse and found that the animal was not only considered a maverick by his previous riders, but that he had suffered a bowed tendon several years before. It had healed, but it was a weak spot most eventers would be chary of, and should at the very least have been reflected in a lowered purchase price.

Armed with this knowledge and, more important–and rare–written proof of it, Mr. Katz returned to his expensive lawyer who informed him that he now had a case for civil fraud. It was presently still before the courts. Rumours flew around the circuit, but the sport insiders instinctively sided with the professionals or refused to comment. C–FES had deflected Sue's numerous attempts for information and interviews with practiced insouciance and thinly veiled contempt.

JoJo meanwhile had quit the sport in disgust. She was presently training enthusiastically for her first season of mountain biking competition. And, she had added mischievously, the sport of bik-ing had a great advantage over riding: your coach wasn't trying to sell you bicycles.

Here is where Sue's narrative ended. She would wait for later to add that what had intrigued Sue about the Katz case was the ease with which the horse had been palmed off on these really quite intelligent people. She had begun to ask around about horses ac-quired for eventing through the Fairclough/Pendunnin connec-tion. What she had discovered had surprised and intrigued her.

And so now, munching on her fries, waiting with willed pa-tience to take back control of her agenda as Thea continued to sit in pensive silence, Sue clucked over the tragedy of the stallion and the office mess. No response worth noting, only the implacable banality of clichés. They then discussed some of Thea's plans and responsibilities for the June show. It was all rather benign, predict-able and, to Sue's aroused professional sensibilities, soporific. She wanted to return to the topic of the stallion as a springboard to her major theme, curious to elicit some real feelings from the woman. Sue's professional instincts told her that Thea's cool reception of the story was definitely bogus.

She began with a global and innocuous comment on Thea's personal involvement in the sport. "You've had a long volunteer history in horse sport, Mrs. Ankstrom. The chairman of this com-mittee, Mrs. Smy, tells me you're one of the most dependable and helpful people around. And I believe your husband was even chair-man of C–FES for some time?"

You're one of us, my dear...

"Oh yes, yes he was. Many years ago. I was actually quite a bit younger than my husband, so I came into the sport pretty wet be-hind the ears. But very eager to be of service, oh yes indeed. But what is it the young people say? That was then, this is now."

Sue started. "Oh, that's so weird. That is exactly the expression that came to mind when Roch was putting me off earlier today, as if the whole strange business with the stallion were a thing of the past, yesterday's news. And yet it was such a scary thing. If you had seen it..."

Thea waved her hand dismissively. "Roch is like that. He's the most charming man in the world, and I don't suppose he would ever do anything to hurt the sport, but he simply doesn't want to know about bad news." She paused, sipped at her Perrier, and added bitterly, more to herself, it seemed to Sue, than to anyone else, "They all want to think everything is just going swimmingly all the time."

Sue could see that the mood had shifted dramatically, she couldn't think why. Thea was distracted, dealing with some internal conflict as her gaze fastened on empty air and her lips compressed grimly. Sue waited it out. Her gut told her a story was hovering in the air, but it was a fragile thing. She waited as the seconds dragged themselves through empty space, almost biting her tongue in impatience.

Finally, dreamily, Thea went on, her voice low and vibrant with some intense but indecipherable emotion, "And I believe you. The stallion, I mean. Terrible, an ugly thing to do." Slowly her eyes came back into focus and she gazed solemnly into Sue's sharp little monkey's eyes. "Imagine the sense of grievance behind such an act. Just imagine." She spoke these words calmly and thoughtfully, but Sue's heart bumped hard in her chest and she shivered involuntarily.

But the moment was propitious and she had to grab it. "Mrs. Ankstrom, I am sure it must be very painful for you to talk about your daughter's horse, Robin's Song, and I have no wish to intrude on your privacy, but the question I now want to ask has directly to do with some of the statements you just made–I mean, about bad news and people in the sport not wanting to know."

Bull's eye! Thea had gone pale and her face was tense with apprehension as her hands gripped the table edges "Go on," she said quietly.

Sue plowed forward doggedly. "Okay, here it is. Mrs. Ankstrom, during the time your daughter trained and rode the horse, did you ever notice at any time whether there was something physically–or even mentally–let's say not quite right about him?"

"Why do you ask that?" Thea's voice was so low Sue had to strain to hear.

"Because," Sue replied, "I have made inquiries about practically every horse Bridget Pendunnin has ever brought over from England, and I would say that in virtually half the cases, an old injury or serious character defect has revealed itself within two years of purchase. That is an extraordinarily high number. And her clients are spread all over North America. No one has ever looked at it globally before. Every client thinks they are the only hard luck case. None of them think it's deliberate. But I'm beginning to wonder."

Thea had recovered her composure. She looked purposefully at Sue and seemed to think hard for a few moments. She nodded twice, as if she had been asked to sign yes or no to some privately heard question. She reached for the check. And then she posed a very unexpected question to Sue. Nodding towards the telephone on the wall near the coatrack, she asked, "Did you know that you can't make long distance calls from that telephone, not by reversing the charges or even with a phone card?"

Sue just knew there was a super–excellent reason for her question and excitedly replied, "Yes, I did! I tried to make a call when I got here this morning, and Caroline explained there's a block on it. Why?"

"Yes, the same thing happened to me. Come to my condo for dinner," Thea said, pressing her lips to her napkin and placing it neatly across her plate. "I will tell you what I have been told about telephones and horses. And then I will tell you what I believe."

She rose gracefully from the table, smoothed down her skirt, and said, "It would seem that we have a great deal in common, my dear," Thea said.

"_?"

"We both appear to be here to praise equestrian sport, when in fact," she smiled mirthlessly, " we may be here to bury it…" Sue shuddered as Thea's glittering gray eyes bored intensely into hers. *She could be ruthless. She is capable of anything.*

Sue's adrenalin was pumping. She had come to do a promotion for the bank, and she would do it. But the bank directors knew what she was really after, and they had not discouraged her. It was in their interest to know the truth for any future sponsorship plans they might wish to review.

When Sue had returned from Palm Beach in March, she had hinted to them that a big story, a really dirty story, was about to blow up, a story that was presently confined to events in the United

States, but that might have ramifications in Canada. The Bank had millions of dollars sunk into equestrian sport. They were nervous, and it had been clear to them that Sue was not bluffing.

And now there was this new information. Sue's only problem was to know which story to run after first. There were at least four at the moment, all of them very promising.

Her eyes fell on Thea's salad plate. Goody, she'd left the olives. With a little sigh of pleasure, Sue reached for the unexpected treats.

CHAPTER NINE

POLO'S CONDO, A SEMI−DETACHED ONE−BEDROOM UNIT, WAS the mirror image of Thea Ankstrom's. His living room adjoined her bedroom and vice versa. Long after he'd finished working on his own computer, he often fell asleep to the pleasant, rhythmic click of her typing and the less pleasant rasp of the printer or the growl of the photocopier.

Other times he heard her pacing the floor, very late at night, after the computer work was finished. She must be lonely and troubled, he assumed. She was divorced. Her daughter had died tragically. He could not even imagine how terrible that must be.

Sometimes he thought it would be the neighbourly thing to invite her in for a drink or a coffee, but her manner with him was so diffident, even when they met for sharing information on the show: lists, course designs, exchanging disks, stabling logistics and the like, that he felt even the most casual of social overtures might be considered an intrusion. So he had let the instinct pass.

Looking out the kitchenette window he noticed Sue Parker moving about the condo unit across the driveway. What an odd−

looking girl she was. She was dying to get her teeth into the mysterious events at the Centre. What journalist wouldn't? He liked her. She was bright and amusing, full of mission and energy. And, he reflected ironically, she was the only person at the Centre who could safely be said not to be involved in either the vandalism or the mutilation, assuming she had an alibi in Toronto for last night.

Thinking back over the day's events as he showered and dressed for dinner at the Jacobsons, Polo found himself tense and restless in a way he hadn't been for years. It was how he used to feel at horse shows when he was 'on deck' after the warm–up, before going into the ring for the big classes, when the distilled essence of solitary, personal responsibility flooded his being and made his heart pound with excitement and dread. For those few minutes, every time, he never knew if he would come out of the ring ecstatic or humiliated. He felt himself somehow responsible now for finding out who had done these things, and he was nervous about what such an investigation might yield.

Quietly pacing the living room, Polo reviewed the things he had seen, and what he had gleaned from Roch's and Bridget's opinions and behaviour. There were so many unanswerable questions it was hard to know how to approach the affair.

Chief amongst these questions to Polo was the seeming lack of connection between the bold and ruthless attack on the horse, which had all the earmarks of a highly personal revenge–whether it was the Laurins or Bridget as the target–and the restrained messing–about of the office.

Aside from the difference in style of the two events, there was the question of motive. The motive for the office vandalism was crystal–clear: *le Centre* wasn't *chez nous* enough for some people. Possibly Michel's rumoured departure for the States had been the trigger. The obvious suspects were the Desrochers clan or somebody sympathetic to their bitterness.

It might have been Benoit. Roch was insistent about the boy's evasiveness–or he might have helped to set it up. Benoit didn't have a key to the front door, but there were at least five floating around. And most people around barns were pretty trusting. You had to be. There were too many people in and out of the place to be on your guard all the time. And whoever had access to Roch's home would have opportunities, too. A friend, a trusted relative…. someone who was, say, invited to dinner occasionally…a piece of wax, a moment's swift work…

And that could mean Gilles. His abrupt flight home was incriminating. But here Polo shook his head intuitively. Gilles was clumsy and inept at times, but he wasn't a political animal. He seemed to think of his work as permanent and it was clear that he was trying hard to impress his uncle.

And the way he looked at Michel–well, you could see the pride in the family connection struggling with his wish to be 'cool' and hide his hero worship. He had been eager to learn the things Polo was willing to teach him. Why would he jeopardize his future here over politics that had no personal meaning for him? As to the horse, it was out of the question. Gilles was still a little timid working with horses, and stallions scared him, as well they should any inexperienced handler.

Polo thought back to the time he had spent with Jocelyne in March. He remembered very clearly her anxieties and fears for Michel and her deep suspicion of Liam. What had she said about Liam and Gilles and Benoit? That they were like *some weird club or something, as if they were spies.* It may have been that Liam's influence over them had somehow coerced their cooperation. But then again, why would Liam be involved in this particular political scenario? If he were, he'd be more likely to be on the opposite side. So that didn't make sense.

But the horse? And Liam? Both target and motive were otherwise unclear. If someone were going to take the chance of being discovered in what was obviously a criminal action, wouldn't he or she want the impact to be felt, and felt instantly, by the object of the attacker's hatred? There was simply no way that it was a random act by a stranger or even a boarder. If something were going on in the barn generating that kind of friction, one of Bridget, Joc or Roch would have noted it.

Okay then, how *about* Liam and the horse? Roch said no, in spite of his dislike of the boy. Also in his favour was the vet's, Guy's, admiration for his nursing skills. Liam's respect and affection for the horses themselves seemed to be the one decent thing everyone agreed on. And even Bridget agreed it was unlikely to have been Liam. But was Roch any judge of character? As long as the boy behaved in his presence, Roch wouldn't have taken too much notice of him. As for his nursing skills, it also meant he knew more than the average groom about physical problems, and wasn't afraid of animal distress. And why should he take Bridget's assessment at face value? Polo didn't know her, but she seemed pretty tough, and there was obviously very bad blood between her and Liam.

Okay, what about Liam and Bridget? What if the tongue were a kind of code between them, a warning of some kind as well, just as the office mess looked more like a warning than a final act of destruction? Today the tongue, tomorrow something else, something more permanent. Far–fetched, though, he had to admit. On the other hand, who was it that had sent the kid packing? Was it Bridget? Anyway, what was to stop him coming back in the middle of the night?

He sat down on the living room sofa and propped his feet on the coffee table. Tongue was another word for language. In French the two words were one, *langue*. Language–or at least accents– was apparently a sore point between Liam and Bridget. The Irish and the English were worse than the anglos and the francos, even though English was their common language.

Or was that the connection with the office? Was this whole business some sick, but sophisticated attack on the anglophone influence there? Not done by Liam, but in fact with him as a target or one of several targets of hatred? This proposition was one that at least joined the two acts symbolically. The cutting off of an 'anglo' tongue–the horse a substitute for the owner–a kind of Mafia godfather warning, only less terrible than the horse head in the bed… *allez chier, les anglais…*

Words, symbols. Unconsciously Polo's hand, draped over the sofa arm, grazed the cover of a thick book he always brought with him for solitary stays away from home: *Dictionnaire des*/Dictionary of *FAUX AMIS*. Anglophones studying the French language seriously–and vice versa–eventually had recourse to it. *Faux Amis* meant 'false friends' and was, Polo felt, an apt description for the words the fat text covered.

The dictionary had been a gift from Ruthie at some point in his study of English. It had been a fantastic help to Polo when he was struggling to break through into fluency. There were thousands of words in English that came from French, but their meanings in English had altered with time. *Avertissement* meant 'warning' in French, nothing like 'advertisement' in English, but the root was the same. *Prétendre* in French looked like 'pretend' in English, but it meant to 'claim' or 'intend'. It was easy to make mistakes, and sometimes the mistakes could be significant, could materially alter your communication with people. Every time he dipped into the dictionary he found something new.

So far, so bad. The more he thought about who was, or might be involved, the more baffled he became. And sooner or later he was going to have to consider if Michel had some role in all this. Had it been Michel who told Liam to clear out? Or Bridget? Or even Fran? They all, according to Jocelyne, had reason to hate him. And they all had credibility and authority in their various areas. If Liam had felt their reason was strong enough to make an appeal to a higher authority–Roch–useless, he might have conceded defeat and slipped away. Or if any of them had threatened him with some kind of exposure or punishment and he had estimated it to be serious enough, Liam might have decided to bolt while the going was good.

What if–he really hated to moot this proposition, but it had to be considered–what if Jocelyne had got it all wrong about Michel and Liam? Could there conceivably have been some relationship between them that went sour? It was a repulsive thought for Polo, but it had to be faced, if Michel in fact was gay.

Was Michel gay? Polo had told Jocelyne it didn't matter, but that was just to make her feel better. It mattered to Polo. He knew about the new school of thought on gays–his wife hewed to the cutting theoretical edge in these matters–how it was supposed to be as normal as being straight, and sometimes just another lifestyle choice, but where Polo came from, theories like that were so much bullshit, and he had never struggled very hard to overcome this particular bias. He felt sorry for gays, because they weren't normal. Maybe they couldn't help it, and he didn't think they should be ashamed of what they were. But he didn't think it was something to be proud of either.

Polo had always been disturbed by that aspect of the circuit, that so many of the male riders were gay, and he had no explanation for it. He himself had been verbally baited often, but only actually physically touched, once, in a tack room when he was sixteen, by an older American rider/trainer, one of the stars in the sport. The approach had been sophisticated and subtle, but unmistakable.

Without reflecting on the crudeness and disproportion of such a gesture, Polo had turned and punched the man hard, squarely in the side of the head. He might have damaged his ear, because he saw it bleed. The man had staggered away, stunned, humiliated, and frightened. Polo had been a little frightened, too, at his own kneejerk reversion to methods of confrontation he believed he'd left behind in St. Henri.

If Michel were gay, it would matter a lot to Roch as well, and Polo knew it for a certainty. Polo and Roch had chummed together when Roch was still competing. There weren't many francophone riders taking the sport seriously in those days, and Polo was grateful for Roch's sunny, upbeat nature and his unfailing ability to find a good time in whatever small town they were billeted in.

Polo had been shy and something of a loner. Without Roch he was unlikely to have had any social life to speak of. Wherever Roch was, a party was sure to emerge. The girls adored Roch and flocked to him, an added bonus for Polo, since casual romance was the only sort he wanted, and he couldn't be bothered looking very far for it.

There had never been any tension over which of them was successful more often in the ring. Roch liked to show and compete, but he wasn't hung up on the necessity of getting a ribbon in every class. Polo was preoccupied with putting in 'personal best' performances. It was a little different from, say, Michel's fixation on winning, because Polo knew he himself took the horse's limitations more into consideration, but not much. So he and Roch were able to be comfortable and easy with each other and they had their common cultural background to unite them.

When Roch had told him he was quitting the circuit to get married, Polo was shocked. They were almost the same age–Polo was nineteen, Roch twenty–and Polo still thought of himself as a boy. It was almost inconceivable to him that a peer of his could be settling down so cheerfully to the enormous responsibilities of marriage and a family. For of course the only reason Roch was marrying was that Michel was on the way, and because Ghislaine's family–and Roch's too–held rigidly traditional views in these matters.

Nothing had ever fazed Roch for long or dimmed his optimistic view of the world. He had jokingly told Polo that he didn't expect to stay married for long, but when Michel was born, the fact of fatherhood transformed him instantly into the picture of bourgeois contentment. He adored Michel, he was delighted to have a pretty wife fussing over him, and he was proud of their first tiny *ménage*, a mobile home behind *Le Centre*, where he began as a trainer before assuming control of its management a few years later. He gave up competing without a backward glance, and turned his energies to the development of *Le Centre* with an enthusiasm that had never abated.

Michel was the centre of his universe. Polo had often envied Roch the settled life and fixed certainties, the well–lit emotional runways that the boy's existence had given him. Michel's talent was the icing on the cake. Roch had poured himself into his training. The father and son had been inseparable throughout Michel's youth. Roch was a man's man. Having a son meant certain obvious things to him. As flexible as he was in other ways, Polo could not imagine Roch tolerating any deviation from his dreams for Michel with understanding or acceptance.

Why, Polo asked himself, was he taking these disasters so personally? It wasn't his barn, it wasn't his horse. Part of the answer, he knew, lay in his lack of confidence that Roch would deal with them effectively. True, Roch had been furious at such arrogant invasions of his realm, but his follow–up reactions were, more typically, to equivocate and downplay the significance of events.

Roch hated problems, hated conflict, and wanted above all else that *Le Centre* should be a happy, routinized place. As soon as the stallion looked more normal, as soon as the office was set to rights, he was half way to denying that anything had happened at all. Much more worrying to him, Polo assumed, was Michel's enigmatic decision to throw over the chance of permanent security and a dream sponsorship deal. But Roch no doubt believed that a lifetime of paternal domination would reassert its normal sway and, in time, put that situation right as well.

Far more evocative had been Hy's face when he arrived at the office. Polo had seen his shock, of course, but also fear. Suddenly, in Polo's eyes, he was once again the anxious, insecure child of a demanding, success–obsessed father. Polo had known him since Hy was fifteen and he himself was eleven. Hy had been an obedient only son, totally dominated by a need to vindicate his father's immigrant struggles from grim poverty to ever–expanding achievement. So Hy had spent most of his adult life fulfilling mandates set first by his father, then by his wife and community. And now, just when he'd claimed his reward for a lifetime of uncomplaining responsiveness to the needs of others, he saw his long–deferred paradise under siege, most likely from within.

Polo was dressed. That is, he wore a clean, crisp, newer version of the denim shirt, and khakis instead of the jeans he wore during the day, and Timberland moccasins instead of paddock boots. But it was still too early. And he was suddenly uneasy, remembering the weird and depressing phone call with Nathalie.

What had she meant by *unfinished business?* And what was that crazy innuendo about Ruthie? Because it *was* crazy. Never once in their whole married life had Nath ever had cause to think that Ruthie was anything but the–well, okay, not his sister exactly–but damn close–of his youth. He'd never even been alone with Ruthie since she got married. *That was over twenty years ago.* It was a complete mystery to him. Nath wasn't the jealous type. Why now? And was this a good or a bad sign for their marriage? That she was jealous, that is. That she was jealous of *Ruthie* was simply intolerable. *Intolerable.*

He felt his jaw clenching with anger again as he reviewed the accusations she had levelled at him. *Denial. Repression.* God, he hated those buzz words. He hated jargon of any kind: political, psychological, professional. It was the clubbiness, the members–only implications of such words. Pretentious. Nathalie had never been that way before she started taking university courses. And Ruthie too, always quoting from books and poems.

He fought against these prejudices. He knew it had to be envy and a lack of confidence in himself that made him sensitive to what after all was perfectly normal usage for *them*.

If you can't stand the heat, get out of the kitchen. Who said that? Good advice, though. Except the kitchen is the warmest room in the house, and the people I care most about in the world are perfectly at home there.

He would leave in a few minutes. First he would record a few notes. He took a small notebook from his pocket. It was something he always carried with him. In it was noted information: bits he heard or read, but mostly new vocabulary, expressions he saw in magazines or gleaned in conversation. It was a habit he had acquired in his teens when he had started reading and learning English properly, from the ground up. Every once in a while he would review his notes and transfer the most useful of the material to a file he kept in his computer. Tonight he jotted down the bit about the schizophrenia rates in Ireland. He wanted to check that out.

He flipped to the beginning and scanned entries that went back about a year. He had noted the distinction between 'gambit/gamut', for example, because anglophones themselves often confused the two, and he hated making mistakes–really, it had started as a game, and then he'd got addicted. He smiled as he looked at the very last entry–'nosy parker'–

–Hey, Sue, you ask an awful lot of questions.
–Yeah, that's why they call me 'nosy.'
–Mm.
–Don't you get it?
–Get what?
–'Nosy Parker'?
–?

–It's an expression, it means someone who's always sticking their nose into other people's business, I'm sure there must be something like it in French…

He'd got addicted, also, to the good feelings that came from speaking a language in the way educated people did. He liked what it had done for his self–esteem when he was young and needed it badly. And he liked the automatic respect it engendered in other people. It was important to appear to be on a social level with sponsors, and later, clients. Even the appearance of ignorance or cultural inferiority in someone in his position could set up illusions of power in the people he dealt with. Language properly spoken, he had discovered, was a potent commodity, as good, in its own way, as money in certain situations, and better than money in others.

His now excellent English and even his better–than–average French–not to mention a fair sprinkling of Yiddish words and expressions–he owed to the Jacobsons, along with his perfect teeth and properly occluding jaw, his opthalmologist–prescribed–as opposed to drugstore–bought glasses, his table manners, clothes sense, taste for sarcasm, and his brilliant career in horse sport.

Only his marriage had been entirely his own doing… And even then Morrie had warned him.

You're marrying 'up', Polo. It's not easy. Trust me, I know. What's a little Yid like me doing in Westmount with all these Wasps? I should be in Cote St. Luc with the rest of the tribe. But no, Cote. St. Luc is a ghetto, she says. I'm a 'greener', what do I care, but Clarice's family–the Levys–goes back like a hundred generations here. One of her ancestors from Germany was peddling steamies and frites to the frenchies or whatever the hell they ate then on the Plains of Abraham. Can you imagine? If there were more Jews jobbing supplies back then, maybe you guys would've won, who knows? Seriously, be careful. You'll always wonder if you're good enough. It takes confidence. You got enough, kid?

CHAPTER TEN

ST. HENRI IS ONE OF THE POOREST NEIGHBOURHOODS IN Canada. Nobody would choose to be born there, one of eight children in a family dominated by a volatile, hard–drinking father, and badly managed by a credulous, browbeaten mother. One of St. Henri's positive features, and the one that saved Napoléon Poisson from a life of illiteracy, ignominy and possibly even crime was its proximity to Westmount, one of the country's wealthiest, and at the time almost exclusively anglophone, communities.

The Poissons lived on the corner of Ste. Marguerite and St. Antoine Streets in a run–down, too–small duplex. His father worked for his brother in a butcher shop. His mother struggled to keep her swarm of children fed, clothed and out of trouble. She hoped they went to school when they left the house in the morning, but if they didn't, she would be the last to know. The schools of St. Henri had enough to do in those days without calling the parents of absentee children.

Polo was somewhere in the middle of the family pack. He hated school. He couldn't see the blackboard properly and he had terrible headaches. His stomach hurt too, almost all the time. Nobody knew about food allergies then, and nobody he knew went to doctors unless it was an emergency. He grew up before the advent of Medicare. The school nurse accused him of complaining to get out of doing homework. He couldn't concentrate on anything the teachers said, and he never learned to read or write.

In Grade Five the teacher called his mother in to tell her that Polo had *'difficultés d'apprentissage'*, that he was not backward exactly, but eligible for special instruction. Ignorant in these matters and a slave to authority, his mother accepted this diagnosis and presented him to the assigned classroom. Polo took one look at the drooling children playing clumsily with blocks, and informed his mother that he was finished with schooling. He was eleven. His mother sighed and said as long as he looked after his own expenses, got a job, well... And nobody from the old or the new class ever followed up on his case. He was free.

He roamed the streets and thought about how he would look after himself. His teachers, parents and siblings had all by now labeled him stupid or worse. Strangely he himself felt no doubt but that he was very smart, smarter than everyone else in his family. He felt himself to be different in many other ways from his siblings, and somehow slated for a destiny apart from the life he had so far known.

By the age of ten he had already discovered Westmount. You just walked up De Courcelles until it turned into The Glen and kept walking under a bridge and up a hill and suddenly you were in a world of elegant Victorian homes and quiet streets overhung with feathery canopies of gracious old trees, and parks with green playing fields, wading pools and children's playgrounds, all neatly tended, safe, clean, and serenely monitored by well-dressed mothers and uniformed nannies. Now, in his newly liberated state, he found himself drawn there.

The parks even had an area consecrated to dogs, 'dog runs', the equivalent of the children's playground, where dogs could get exercise and socialize. Squinting to assimilate their expressions, he watched the owners with their dogs. He had never seen such affection, concern and animated discussion so focused on animals in

A Three Day Event

his life. This phenomenon fascinated Polo and his thoughts took an entrepreneurial turning

Polo evolved a scam that soon brought in snack money–he was always hungry in spite of the stomachaches–but wasn't criminal enough to warrant police intervention if it failed. He would 'lose' dogs tied in the front yard, walk them around for an hour and then 'find' them. *Les anglais* were mad for their dogs, and the rewards–money, food, sometimes both–were considerable by his standards.

On the day he stole the Jacobsons' white poodle, his timing was off. Normally he would work the scam around midday and return the dog no later than three, to be sure of being clear of the house before the children or the father got home. On this particular day he had been careless, and didn't actually take the dog until mid–afternoon. When he brought it back, it was close on four–thirty, uncomfortably late.

The scam worked like a charm at first. The mother, a large-boned lady with a patrician face and upswept hair, had noticed it missing from the front porch about fifteen minutes earlier and was just working up a nice lather of panic. When she saw him with the dog, she laughed with relief and insisted he come in for a treat. Seating him at the kitchen table and fussing over the dog a bit, she peered at him closely and took in the clues to his provenance.

'*D'où viens–tu, petit?*'

He squirmed and pointed vaguely to the south. She just nodded and got busy at the stove. In a few minutes he was working his way through the best bowl of soup he had ever eaten, a golden broth full of noodles and a fluffy dumpling, along with some sweet, soft cakey bread. He ate so fast he almost choked on it, and amazingly there was another bowl, this time with noodles and chunks of chicken, and more bread, as much as he wanted. And a coke! He couldn't believe his luck.

Noisily scraping the last of the soup into his mouth and stuffing a huge wad of bread in after, he glanced up to see a girl, wearing an expression of fastidious distaste, staring at him from the doorway. She was petite, poised, scrubbed–looking. Her dark, curly hair was drawn up in a high pony tail, decorated with a bow that exactly matched her pretty ruffled blouse, which matched her pedal pusher pants and capezio ballet slippers. Her big gray eyes studied him under pixie bangs and her rosebud mouth was pursed assessingly.

'What's your name?'

The mother said something to her, and she began to speak to him in French. But it was not a French that he felt comfortable with. It was fancy. Nobody he knew spoke like that, not his teachers or even people on the radio. And his mouth was still crammed with bread. So he didn't answer her.

'You may see my room, if you wish,' she said haughtily. He felt like smacking her, she was a spoiled little bitch and no mistake, but he had eaten their food, so he got up and followed her upstairs.

Her room was bigger than the living room and kitchen combined of his duplex. It was like a picture in a magazine. The windows were swathed in some gauzy pink stuff. Plush toys spilled from shelves. There were dolls and a huge dollhouse in one corner. Whole shelves were stuffed full of books of every size and colour. Comic books were piled high on a little night table. Her canopied bed was covered in a thick quilted fabric, and decoratively frilled pillows of different sizes and shapes were scattered at the head. A cozy, plump chair, slipcovered in a pattern of giant roses, sat near her bed, with a pretty white ceramic floor lamp beside it. He was aware that his feet were cushioned–a new sensation–by a thick, shaggy carpet, pink to match the curtains.

She watched him taking in her possessions with frosty pleasure. 'Would you care to cast an eye on my schoolroom?' she asked in her impossibly precise and rolling French.

Schoolroom! He had thought she was a spoiled brat, but now he began to think she was not quite right in the head. He started to back out of the room, but she motioned imperiously to him to follow her through a door at the end of the room. Curiosity drove him forward and he peeked around the door to find another room, a winterized porch, where someone had created an exact replica of a schoolroom for her: a fullsize blackboard covering one wall, in front of which was placed a real teacher's desk and chair. Facing this desk were three one–piece school desks, the kind where the desktop opened up. There were more bookshelves, chalk, erasers, a map of the world…*it was the real thing!*

He stared at her with incredulity and a little fear. She was *insane.*

She took a book down from the shelf. 'I can read Hebrew', she said airily. 'Look!' She opened the book the wrong way, from back to front, held out a page with funny black dots and squiggles on it. Then she started to make weird gutteral noises, pretending to read. Now he was angry and flushed up. He was tired of being polite. He felt his fists balling up and suppressed an impulse to strike her.

'You're making fun of me. That's not writing. Those aren't words. You're a real bitch. And you're crazy, too.'

He backed out of the room before she could say anything. Her mouth was open in a big round O of surprise. He tried to look for the stairs, but his eyes were inexplicably glazed with tears, and he blundered instead into another bedroom. He swiped at his eyes and oriented himself. He couldn't help stopping to look around. This room was also like a picture in a magazine, but it appealed to him. It was simple, done all in brown and gold. The materials were nice and ordinary, not fluffy and mysterious. There were bookshelves here too, and they were full of books, but a lot of them he could see had pictures of airplanes and warships on them. There were models of ships and airplanes too.

Then his glance fell on a photograph on the bureau, and his heart started knocking painfully in his chest. It was a picture of a boy, maybe the owner of this room. The boy was riding a horse over a jump. Polo reached for the frame with both hands and held it up close to his eyes. He put a hand over the boy's face. Then he imagined himself in the photograph.

He felt himself on the horse. He knew what it must feel like. The muscles in his legs tensed. He remembered this moment all his life, and always wondered if he had superimposed a later knowledge, because though it seemed impossible, incredible, he knew that the boy was not in perfect balance, he felt the extra weight in the boy's hands pulling the horse out of alignment in his trajectory and the tension in the horse's back. He felt a pure desire for something, for this experience, the first time ever, he felt light–headed and frightened, he…

'*T'aimes les chevaux?* You like horses, kid?'

Startled by the man's gravelly voice, and dazed by the clarity of his vision, Polo dropped the picture in its heavy metal frame onto

153

the bureau. The glass cracked loudly. Horrified, Polo threw a hand up to protect his head from the blow.

'For Christ's sake, kid, I'm not gonna hit you!' the man barked. Warily Polo brought his hand down and tried to look at him without panic. The man was a dapper little guy with an elfin, heart-shaped face, a shock of thick, graying hair and, under a set of steepled devilish eyebrows, fervid black eyes, which were drilling into Polo's at the moment with a disturbing intensity.

He knows. I'm fucked, thought Polo.

'I asked you if you like horses,' the man said calmly, but in a tone that demanded an answer and pronto. *What was the right answer?* 'Ch' suppose,' Polo shrugged.

The man just kept staring at him, and Polo started to be afraid. He looked around. The man was blocking the only exit. 'Don't be scared, kid,' he finally said. 'I'm gonna take you home now.' At least *his* French was normal, not even as good as Polo's, it was actually full of mistakes, so that was a little more comforting.

Polo said he didn't have to bother, but he could see there was no hope, the guy wasn't letting him off. He marched stoically downstairs and, passing the kitchen, thanked *madame* for the good food. She smiled and murmured something conciliatory to *monsieur*.

The man settled him into the front seat of a late model Cadillac with all the gimmicks. Momentarily Polo forgot to be afraid as his eyes darted around the dashboard, and his body registered the plushness of the seat.

'St. Henri?' the man asked. Polo nodded. They set off.

'My name is Morrie Jacobson. My next door neighbour's kid asked me why I don't pay *her* to walk my dog if my own kids don't want to, why should I get a kid who's not even from around here.'

There was nothing to say. It had to happen sooner or later. Fatalistically he gave himself up to the pleasure of the cushioned ride. In a few minutes they were sitting across the street from the duplex. Polo had never looked at it objectively before. Now he knew it was a dump and he wanted to get away from the man who had made him see it for what it was. Mr. Jacobson was looking at it too and Polo could see he was thinking hard, he was that kind of guy, so intense you could practically hear the wheels turning in his brain. Polo reached cautiously for the door handle.

'You strike me as a smart kid,' the man said brusquely. Nobody had ever said that to him before. Polo turned to look at him to see if he was joking. Mr. Jacobson looked gravely back at him.

'I take my son Hymie riding on the weekends. That was Hymie in the picture. We have a horse. You want to come this Saturday?'

Again that painful thumping in his chest and the lightheadedness. He was scared, but he knew that this was his chance, and maybe the only one. Even if the guy was a pervert–it wouldn't be the first time some old guy had approached him–he reckoned he could handle it. No guy could hold on to you if you were prepared to fight really dirty, and he certainly was, so…

The next thing he knew, Mr. Jacobson was talking to his mother, showing her his business card from *Tissus Clar–Mor*, asking her if she liked to sew. She nodded yes, but explained that her machine was not the very best and often broke down, so she couldn't sew as much as she would like, and threw an embarrassed glance at Polo's torn clothes, seeing them through the eyes of this rich man in his impeccable gray suit. Overwhelmed by the Cadillac and his courteous solicitation of her permission to take Polo out with his family–he showed her a photo of himself with his wife and two children–she nodded dumbly that it would be alright…

The next day a Singer sewing machine from the distributor arrived at the duplex, the top of the line model with all the fancy options, and later on a *Clar–Mor* truck screeched to a stop outside, and the driver dumped a package of materials in the hall, there must have been forty yards of chintzes, boucle, batiste cottons, liner material, denim, corduroy, everything… His parents stared at each other with ambiguous excitement and then at Polo. 'If he lays a hand on you, tell him I'll kill him,' his father growled.

Saturday morning at nine–thirty sharp, as he had promised, Mr. Jacobson's Cadillac slid smoothly to a stop outside the duplex, and Polo's real life began.

It didn't take long for Ruthie to find out he couldn't read. By the time he was thirteen (she was then eleven), Polo was spending more time at the Jacobsons' home than at his own and he spoke a fluent functional English. She begged him to let her teach him how to read and write. He would never have asked her, but it was what he had been longing to hear. He still considered her to be a spoiled brat–her father called her 'princess' in affection, though it was no joke to Polo–but he knew he had to get started soon (and nothing would induce him to go back to school).

Ruthie had been 'pretend' teaching with her friends for so long she thought she knew what she was doing. She was enthusiastic, but he didn't make any progress. One day she cried out that it was no use trying to teach someone if they didn't want to learn. He retorted in frustration that she must be a bad teacher because he *did so* want to learn. She said maybe he was just *stupid,* that was all. He overturned the desk, smashed his fist into the blackboard (it cracked, and he broke a finger), and stormed out of the house, vowing never to set foot there again.

One week later Morrie showed up at the duplex in the latest Cadillac. Polo said there was no point in going on if they thought he was stupid. Morrie made him come out for a rib steak at Moishe's, and begged him to come back. Ruthie was miserable, all she did was cry. She wouldn't eat. What was a father to do?

Listen, Polo, you know you're smart and so does Ruthie. She's just mad at herself. Don't be a putz and lose an opportunity. We're gonna find the right way, and you're gonna learn to read, and then you're gonna feel like a million bucks. Come home–I mean, come on back with me, kid.

So he came back. Ruthie, flustered, blushing and red–eyed, apologized, looking at the floor, and muttered that she would never call him stupid again. They started the lessons. This time she was different. She was patient and reasonable. She was thinking about him learning, not about her teaching. Ruthie was different altogether. Something had changed in her. She was a nicer person now.

So he learned to read and write. Ruthie had asked which language he wanted. Having studied for so many years at College Marie-de-France, she felt equipped to teach him both, but by now Polo was only too aware that the riding circuit was so heavily dominated by anglophones, even in Quebec, that he would be foolish to concentrate on anything but English. Then too, once he started to succeed, he would be in the other provinces and the States a lot. Nobody he ever came into contact with spoke a very good quality of French. His would do for now. Besides, what was the point of him learning to speak and write and roll his r's like a Frenchman? He'd just be laughed at by everyone he knew.

And those were the most important things in his life for the next seven years: riding, and the hours he spent with Ruthie. He had his own room in the basement, and a side entrance through which to come and go at will. It never occurred to him at the time how peculiar it was that a man in Morrie Jacobson's position should take him on, feed him, clothe him, get his eyes tested and buy him glasses (he would never forget the ineffable joy of seeing distances for the first time), fix his teeth, buy him horses to ride, drive him back and forth to the stables, and ask for nothing in return but the pleasure of seeing him fulfill his talent for competitive jumping. It also never occurred to him to ask how peculiar it was that he should be allowed to spend so much time, unsupervised, with a pretty daughter whose safety, purity and general comportment were otherwise as strictly monitored as a nun's.

Ruthie did more than teach him language skills. She introduced him to books. She read to him, which he loved. She told him one day that she was going to read him a story about a horse so famous that he would be recognized and talked about as long as literature existed by millions and millions of people all over the world. Could he guess? Of course he couldn't. It was Boxer from George Orwell's *Animal Farm*. He loved that story, which she read in half–hour installments over weeks, and always got a little weepy when he thought about Boxer going off to the knacker's. He was also touched by her efforts to match his interests to an appreciation of the finer things, although it would have been sappy to tell her so.

Then she would sometimes read to him in French and make him read aloud to her, to improve his pronunciation, and he remembered above all Gabrielle Roy's *Bonheur d'occasion*, which, she said, was popular in English as *The Tin Flute*, and which she had chosen, of course, because it was about life in St. Henri. He rarely alluded to his family, and she didn't ask, but he was glad she had read that book, because he knew she understood a lot about him without his having to talk about it.

Other times she set him compositions to write. This was difficult, tedious and unpleasant work. He sat at one of the child–size desks in the little schoolroom, chewing on a pencil, labouring over the simple themes she set him: 'The Horse, Man's Special Friend', or 'My Favourite Christmas.' Later she would correct them, tactfully explaining how important it was to stick to your theme and try to make your reader visualize what you were thinking of. It was dispiriting to see all the red marks, but there was no question of giving up.

Through the open doorway, as he gnawed on the pencil top and toiled to find the words to please her, he would see Ruthie sprawled on her stomach on the pink bed, lost in a book. There were books all over the room, some of them in English and others in French. He could not believe how much she read. She read with a concentration and intensity that piqued his curiosity and aroused in him an inchoate fusion of yearning and envy. He would feel lonely watching her, and something worse that he could not properly identify. A kind of shame, as though he were spying on her.

Sometimes he would call her name softly just to catch her elfin face in mid–flight between two worlds. The rapt languor in her smoky eyes and parted lips as she swam back to awareness was sweetly shocking to him. Where had she been? Was it like where he went in his head when he rode? At these moments he came closest to admitting to himself what she was to him.

He still went home to the duplex, but it became more and more difficult to fit in there. His siblings and father were wary around him. At first they made crude jokes about his braces or the new glasses, and that was all right, but it was different when they noticed his speech patterns were changing. Then they became self–conscious and sullen in his presence. He felt himself to be more and more an outsider.

For his part he began to notice that nobody had much to say to anyone in his family. Or at least nothing of any particular interest to him. It was either sports–never riding, of course–or who lost their job and was on welfare or who got picked up by the cops for whatever, or what neighbourhood girl was knocked up, and was the guy going to marry her or not (or sniggers if the paternity was in obvious doubt). It wasn't conversation, it wasn't an exchange of opinions. It wasn't *ever* about something anyone had read. Conversation was something he'd learned about at the Jacobsons.

The Jacobsons, on the other hand, never seemed to shut up. They had *too* much to say. They never stopped talking, laughing, describing, judging, explaining, criticizing, complaining. They carried on debates, sometimes pitched verbal battles, even shouting, at the table. It often made Polo very nervous, and he rarely, almost never, joined in when things heated up

When he first started joining the family on a regular basis, listening to Hy and Ruthie and their frequent guests argue about whatever subject was on the agenda from school or the news, Polo had looked at Morrie, waiting for him to tell them to shut up and let him enjoy his food in peace, or to smack one of them. Instead he was usually laughing, awarding points to one or the other, goading them to further excesses. It was *bizarre*.

In fact, if the conversation was just going along normally at the table (that was a whole other thing, dinners–and what dinners!–at a set time and everyone sitting together), Morrie usually got restless and said something inflammatory to get them started. You could bet on it at Friday night dinners, which were long, elaborate affairs. The Jacobsons weren't religious or anything, but Friday night was always a bit of a deal and nobody was supposed to have other plans. More often than not conversation then was about Jews, the Montreal community or Israel, or the war. Morrie never got tired of that stuff. It was pretty interesting, though. Or if it was about other things–Canadian or Quebec politics–then it was about that and how it affected the Jews.

His visits home became infrequent. By the time he was eighteen, they had stopped altogether, although he kept in touch with his mother by telephone. He loved his mother, but couldn't think of a way to include her in his life. He didn't miss his father at all, and was not much moved when he died–Polo was twenty–of a stroke at the tavern, although he attended the funeral, of course. For some reason, he was embarrassed to tell the Jacobsons, and shocked them when it came out months later.

Mme Poisson for her part became shy with her son, and they never talked about what had been, and was, happening. She was embarrassed by the continuing gifts of fabric, but they had made a substantial difference in the household. She made money sewing for other people, and her own children were finally dressed nicely.

Her social status improved, but deep in her heart she knew she had sold her son. And to *les juifs*. It was disconcerting. And it wasn't something she could share with anyone. He lived in another world, and when she saw him in person, so obviously happy, her feelings were conflicted. It was easier when she didn't see him, only thought about him. Eventually it was easier not to think of him.

Polo wasn't aware of being in love with Ruthie. He only thought of her as an indispensable part of his life, like horses. It was a hopeless kind of love, hopeless in that nothing material could ever come of it. Polo didn't articulate these thoughts to himself. Ruthie as a female was *taboo,* he knew unconsciously there was a line he must never cross with her, even in his thoughts, and that was it.

And so the love of his mother was lost to him and what might have replaced it was forbidden, but he was not an introspective or a self–pitying boy, and he didn't think along these abstract lines. He was conscious of his blessings and happy in the intensely physical, demanding work he had chosen. When he wasn't riding Morrie's horses, he earned money working around the stables. Feeding, hot–walking, mucking–out, hauling hay. Nothing was beneath him, it was all part of his plan, his determination to become a complete professional.

He never thought he knew enough. He followed the vets around, pestering them as they worked and afterward with questions and further questions until they begged him to leave them alone. The same with the blacksmiths. He took in what they said with the whole and lasting memory of the longtime illiterate.

He also trained and competed for other people as a 'catch' rider. He was a quick study with difficult horses, and earned a reputation as a last–resort rider for desperate owners. When he showed them to advantage in the ring and 'sold' them, the owner usually gave him ten percent of the profits. In time it was a modest living, along with his winnings, and he had self–respect in addition to his other advantages.

Polo loved Ruthie, but he wasn't faithful to her. What would have been the point? He had started sleeping with the wife of the stable owner where Mr. J. boarded his horse when he was fourteen. He had learned quite a lot about what women were like–and liked–

from her, and he had gone on to girl riders and later groupies when opportunities presented. He never had a romantic girlfriend. None of his sexual partners thought for a minute that any possibility of a deeper relationship existed.

Ruthie never came to his horse shows. She had her own life, and he never expected her to cheer him on. The riding was always a thing apart from whatever it was that they shared. Except once. She drove up to St. Lazare, to the "Classic", representing Morrie, who had to go to a wedding. It had been a hot day, though, and it was too bad her one and only horse show had ended with her getting sunstroke.

But other important things had happened that day too. As soon as he got his ribbon and sent his horse off with the groom, Mr. Ankstrom had taken him aside. Mr. Ankstrom had told him that in spite of his win having qualified him for the Canadian team, they felt the team's "cultural homogeneity" would be compromised by his presence–those were his actual words–and he had even suggested Polo, or rather his sponsor, lend Panjandrum to another, more recognized rider of their choosing–to which Polo, stunned more than angry, had curtly said no. He had called Mr. J. to tell him the bad news. And then the next day Ankstrom had called to say they–the board of C–FES–had reconsidered and he was mysteriously back on the team.

And that was pretty well it, as far as the Jacobsons were concerned. Morrie told him, as soon as Polo's place on the Team was confirmed, that he was getting out of horse sport. After the Royal Winter Fair. When Polo cleaned up at the Fair, won pretty well all there was to win, Morrie took him to breakfast at the Royal York Hotel and told him he was selling Panjandrum. He'd had an offer five minutes after the show closed the night before. It was for a crazy amount, crazy. From an American, of course. Now Polo had a choice to make.

Polo, you know I never jerked you around in all the time we been together. I'm telling you straight, I'm not leaving you anything when I go. The business, the money, it's all for Hy and Ruthie. But I want you to have a good life. I want that you shouldn't be dependent on these schmucks in the horse business. So I'm giving you half the money from the horse. It's a lot of money. You can do what you want. You can buy three more horses and blow your brains out on the circuit trying for the jackpot again, and end up kissing some rich jerks' asses and eating shit for the next thirty years just so they'll pay your way—you know as well as I do, this kind of luck is one in a million—or you can take the money and make an investment: buy a piece of land, build a house, put it all into T–bills, I don't care, but an investment, Polo, you see what I'm saying here? Something to build a real life on. A man's life.

Morrie gave him a week to think it over. Polo would have liked to discuss it with Ruthie. But she had decided rather impulsively before the Royal even began to spend a year in Europe (topping up her already exquisite French, he supposed). There was nobody in the horse world he could count on for objectivity. Hy, surprisingly, told him that doing what you loved was just as important as security. But then Hy was speaking from a position of absolute, life–long security.

So Polo took a hard look at the professional riders who stayed in. Morrie was right. They were still boys in many ways, ego projections and tools of their parents' or sponsors' escalating social ambitions.

Polo bought land with the money, a hundred acres in St. Lazare, and put the rest to work in a safe portfolio that Hy recommended. But he was still young. It was too hard to quit cold turkey. So he stayed on the circuit for a few more years to test Morrie's thesis about Panjandrum being one in a million.

He had no trouble finding sponsors. But it was a rude education to find out some of the things they expected from him. The sponsors–or sometimes their wives or girlfriends. Polo rode some very fine horses, none ever quite as wonderful as Panjandrum. He enjoyed success. Once he won the *Puissance* at 6'9" on a 15.1 hand palomino. That caused a stir. He had a little fan club for a while. He was 'Leading Rider of the Year' at Madison Square Garden two years later. But he had already proven himself, he was lonely, the peaks flattened out, and the successes weren't enough to offset the growing resentment that came with dependence on his sponsors. Or to offset some of the depressing training strategies he was forced to witness in some of his more unscrupulous peers.

He wanted to be in charge of his own life. He became a general entrepreneur in the world of horse sport. Polo had a knack for choosing horses, spotting raw talent in the field. He 'made' young horses and competed, but only to sell them. He travelled widely in North America and Europe for a growing and increasingly prestigious client list in Canada and the States. Being an honest horse trader who was free from conflicts of interest, he was something of an anomaly in the sport.

By the time Ruthie came back from Europe, Polo was no longer spending time at the Jacobsons' Westmount house. But he came over to welcome her home. She wasn't alone. There was a handsome medical intern there, Marvin Cooper, who shook his hand politely and said he had heard what a great rider Polo was. That was all. Polo looked at Ruthie. Her eyes slid away. He realized then that this Marvin was her future and that he was already her past.

On the day of their wedding Polo found himself in Holland assessing young Jumper prospects for one of his sponsors. He imagined that Ruthie was secretly relieved at his absence. Before leaving he had looked for a suitable wedding gift. He went to Eaton's and chose an old–fashioned pitcher, decorated in a sentimental tea rose motif, which he thought very English, and therefore appropriate.

Polo had not realized that Jewish brides of Ruthie's status were 'registered' for pre–chosen patterns in their china, crystal and flatware. Polo's gift stood out as the odd piece amongst the starkly modern designs and crisp colours of the kitchenware Marvin had pressed for.

The couple had left for Winnipeg, where Marvin built a solid career as a neurologist and Ruthie taught high school French, and where they raised a family. Ruthie and Polo continued to think of themselves as friends, saw each other on family occasions. But Polo wasn't a letter writer, and Ruthie was busy. Mainly they stayed in touch through Hy, with whom Polo remained close.

Some years later–he was thirty–three–Polo married Nathalie Chouinard in a hastily arranged, families–only ceremony at the Chouinards' gracious Ste. Adele country house. It was the only occasion on which Hy and Ruthie ever met Polo's mother and siblings.

(Morrie and Clarice were on a long–deferred trip to Israel, Marvin had to give a medical paper in Toronto, and Marilyn had committed months before to chair a Combined Jewish Appeal's Women's Division fund–raising event.)

The wedding party was a curious assortment of negative vibrations. The Chouinards had succeeded in masking their hostility to a union they had long fought to sabotage, but the charade left them with little energy to simulate much pleasure in the event. As the Poisson clan, overdressed and overcoiffed for a country wedding arranged themselves in the circle of wooden chairs on the lawn, Bernard Chouinard asked himself what he had done to merit his daughter's leaving all this to join the real–life version of the TV Plouffe family.

For their part the Poisson family were intimidated by the magazine–ad perfection of their surroundings, and only too acutely aware of the yawning social chasm between the two groups. They huddled together in a stiffly self–conscious agony of discomfort that Polo and Nathalie, keyed to distraction by the tension of the day and all that had preceded it, did absolutely nothing to relieve.

So it was left to Hy and Ruthie, fascinated and intensely bemused by the cultural and psychological crosscurrents of the affair, to summon a lifetime's formidable arsenal of social skills and perform the successful role of buffer between the two parties. When they said their good–byes, the Chouinards expressed fervid gratitude for their presence.

Ruthie had wanted to steal a private moment with Polo to offer him a special personal wish for his happiness, but the opportunity never presented itself. Nathalie never left his side, and in spite of the bride's demure and proper behaviour, Ruthie felt an unmistakable chill coming her way every time their eyes met. At the time she couldn't imagine why.

It was time–past time–to have children. Polo knew it. But he couldn't. Whenever he pictured Nathalie pregnant, desire died in him, and he felt the urge to run away. She begged him to see a professional, a therapist. He couldn't do that either. She pressed for joint counseling at least. He wouldn't go.

Finally one day, bitter over his stubborn–in her eyes peasant–like–resistance to some kind of systematic analysis of his problem, and aiming with a lover's unerring instinct for the armour's fatal chink, she said she guessed you could take the boy out of St. Henri but you couldn't take St. Henri out of the boy.

Inarticulate with rage, Polo had come so close to hitting her, his heart racing so fast, it frightened him. He stormed out of the house and stayed away for a week. When he came back, a subdued and chastened Nathalie promised him more time.

She thought she'd lost him, and thinking that, believed she would die of grief. That had been a year ago. Now he'd had his time. And now Nathalie knew she wouldn't die of grief if he left her again. Or if she left him. But she thought she might die of grief if she didn't have a child.

And that was it. And that was it…

It was time to go to the Jacobsons'.

CHAPTER ELEVEN

THE MOOD WAS SUBDUED IN SPITE OF THE CHAMPAGNE MANON insisted on serving to celebrate their reunion. They gathered outside on the deck in the soft evening air to appreciate the view, and as if by consensus avoided discussion about the unpleasantness at *Le Centre* that morning. Polo commented on the afternoon's progress in the arena. Ruthie praised the scenic pleasures of her morning run.

Manon commended the new gardener's skill and efficiency in bringing along the landscaping plans in the gardens–they peered over the railing to admire M. Boulerice's work on the vibrantly coloured, densely planted borders–and down at the stadium too.

"He's wonderful," Manon said, "he seems to know exactly what shrub or bush should go where, and his flower sense is excellent. I really enjoyed working out the designs this afternoon. But you know, Hy," she turned to him with a frown, "I was surprised to see that all the material for the show was just sitting out on a table in the V.I.P. section. I mean, it's protected from the rain, but I would have thought they'd deliver it wrapped in bags or heavy paper or something to keep it clean."

Hy looked puzzled. "But it *was* wrapped. I was there yester-day when it arrived. In fact, I remember thinking that there was so much material we should have it locked up somewhere until they get to work on it." He shrugged. "I guess somebody needed the wrapping for something else. I should have locked it all into the press room."

No one commented for a few seconds. Then, mustering a host's requisite animation, Hy said, "Ruthie, why don't you show Polo the pictures we brought back from Montreal. And I'll help Manon get dinner together."

Polo followed Ruthie into the house. She *was* thinner, her face more angular than he remembered, not as attractive in his eyes, and she still looked a bit peaky, but it was clear that she was making every effort to avoid the usual pitfalls of depression. Her clothes were new and expensive–looking. Her feathery dark curls bobbed gently in a chic, cloudy swirl around her heart–shaped face, and she wore enough make–up, subtly and expertly applied, to cover the dark rings around her eyes and bring a soft touch of pink to her lightly–tanned skin.

She hadn't seemed at ease up to now, and Polo wondered why. He asked himself if he was sending subliminal messages of his own leftover discomfort from Nathalie's call. They stopped in the hall-way where Hy had arranged a balanced, attractive grouping of pho-tographs, many of them featuring Polo at various stages of phys-ical development and equestrian achievement. Ruthie seemed to relax and enjoy herself as soon as the distant past became the focus of their conversation. For a few moments they each let their eyes roam amongst the pictures.

"Do you remember that pony? Look how proud you are here…"

"That's Nikki. I remember every pony and horse I ever sat on…"

"And this is cute, you must have just won something important, you're grinning like the Cheshire cat, you forgot all about having a full set of braces…"

"Oh God, don't remind me. It was torture." He bent down to peer more closely at a smallish photo. "This is nice, the one of Mor-rie and Clarice dancing…"

"And rare. He was so self-conscious about being shorter than her. He loved dancing, but he didn't usually like to see pictures…"

Hy joined them with the champagne bottle. "Dinner will be ready in a few minutes. I can hear the nostalgia is flowing nicely." He gestured to one of the larger pictures, occupying a place of honour at the centre. "Do you have a copy of this one?"

Polo shook his head. "Not the original, but I have the newspaper clipping of it." The photograph featured Polo on a handsome bay horse sporting a huge rosette on his bridle. Standing to each side of the horse's head were Morrie and a tall, Nordic–looking man staring directly into the camera with gelid eyes and a tepid smile.

Ruthie asked, "Who's the uptight guy? When was this?"

Polo smiled ironically. "That was when I was twenty–one, the year I won five out of seven classes at the Royal Winter Fair and became their first French–Canadian Grand Champion ever. Which is why Harold Ankstrom, chairman of the Federation, is looking like he's come straight from a proctology appointment. Not to mention that he's not exactly ecstatic to be sharing the moment with Morrie."

Hy added drily, "You'd have seen a real smile if it were Rob Taylor on the horse and George Montagu Black as the owner. You can almost see his teeth grinding."

Polo now remembered how curiously aggressive Morrie had been in that moment of triumph. "The photographer took the picture and said, 'That's a really beautiful horse you have there, Mr. Jacobson', and Morrie looked right at Ankstrom and answered, 'Yeah, I wanted to own him the minute I saw him. Reminded me of the horse this Polish general used to ride through Lodz on his way to the whorehouse.'"

Ruthie shrieked, "*No*! Oh, you're not *serious*! That's tacky, even for daddy. I mean, really…"

Hy and Polo were enjoying her retroactive embarrassment hugely. Hy chuckled, "That's nothing, Ruthie, you never worked with him in the stores. He could be pretty crude. But it was all part of his charm, eh Polo?" Polo laughed in agreement.

Ruthie went to take a closer look at Harold Ankstrom. "Ankstrom. So is this the man who's married to the lady I met this afternoon? Thea?" She looked at Polo who said, "*Was*. They divorced a long time ago."

"Oh. Because he isn't the type I would have thought…because when I was introduced to her today, I remembered I'd met her years ago–at that horse show I went to in St. Lazare." She resisted the urge to glance up at him.

"Too bad about that show for you," Polo said, and then Ruthie did look up quickly. "You got heat stroke. Bummer, eh?"

"I'll never forget it," Ruthie agreed ironically, but Polo just kept running his eyes over the pictures. He's forgotten, Ruthie thought. And that's a *good* thing, she reminded herself.

"How do you remember Thea from so many years ago?" Hy asked Ruthie, refilling their glasses as they settled into chairs in the living room.

"Oh, by her voice, of course–'her voice was ever gentle, soft and low, an excellent thing in woman…'–and don't give me that look, Polo, I'm allowed to quote something once in a while if it's really appropriate–and in this case it truly is."

"I agree," said Hy. "I found the same thing when I first met her at the C–FES meeting. It has a hypnotic quality."

"Anyway, I kind of recognized her face, she's quite lovely still."

"How did you meet her?"

"Oh, I was standing around looking terribly out of place, which I was, and she asked if I was looking for someone, and I said I'd come to see Polo ride, and she immediately kind of took me under her wing. It was lucky meeting her, though. She explained about all the different classes, and who was technically good, and who was a natural, and who looked good but really wasn't–it was quite an education actually."

"What did she say about me?" Polo asked.

Ruthie coloured up again and laughed a bit self-consciously. "Well, if you must know, I thought she had a bit of a crush on you. She waxed quite poetic, said you were one of the true artists in the sport, the Nijinsky of the jumper world–I *mean*, okay, graceful, yeah, even I could see you were special, but *Nijinsky*, jeez–and all kinds of other stuff. I remember I was sort of taken aback, and even a little annoyed."

"But why were you annoyed? I certainly don't mind being compared to Nijinsky–whoever *she* is–"

Ruthie automatically started to explain, caught the gleam in his eye, and laughed. "Got me again. Still the same old *mazzik,* I see. I never can figure what you know and what you don't, Polo. Your referential stock is so uneven it's hard to know when you're bluffing."

"*Je vous en prie,*" Manon announced with a flourish toward the dining room...

Dinner was gazpacho in glass bowls, poached salmon with dill–yogurt sauce, steamed asparagus, new potatoes, and watercress salad. Manon preened a bit in the glow of the usual accolades. Hy expatiated on the wine he had chosen for the occasion. It was sipped and also duly praised.

"What did I hear you calling Polo before?" Manon asked Ruthie.

"*Mazzik?* Oh, that was the nickname The Duchess gave him. It's a Hebrew word but a Yiddish pronunciation. It means–I guess 'a lovable rascal' would be closest."

"And your nickname was *ziess,* right? That means 'sweet', doesn't it?" Ruthie nodded.

"Obviously wishful thinking on the family's part," Polo added flippantly. Ruthie lightly stuck her fork into the back of his hand. "Okay, okay. I take it back. Gosh, we seem to be reverting to childhood at quite a furious pace here. It's the downside of nostalgia."

"So what was yours, Hy? What was your nickname?" Manon asked.

"You don't want to know," Hy chuckled and Ruthie nodded vigorously in agreement.

"No, really."

"*Kaddish.*"

"*Kaddish?*" She frowned. "Isn't that the prayer you say over the wine?"

"'Fraid not. The wine prayer is *kiddish. Kaddish* is the prayer you say over the dead." At the look on her face he protested, "Well, you insisted. Honest, that's what he called me when he got sentimental. Because I was the son and I would be the one to go to *shul* and say *kaddish* every day after he died."

"*Mon Dieu,* but to use it as a nickname..." she murmured.

"Yeah, and it's really so out of character," Hy retorted with a sly grin, "I mean, Polish Jews–especially from his generation–are

171

normally such lighthearted, fun loving, larky people, you wouldn't think he'd be capable of that kind of morbidity, would you?" Ruthie giggled guiltily, but appreciatively.

Manon sighed and Polo patted her hand sympathetically. "Death by sarcasm. It's slower than arsenic, but just as toxic."

She smiled good–naturedly, and Polo went on, ignoring the miscreants across the table, "Have you noticed he only gets really bad when Ruthie's around? What do they call it–co–dependency? You know, you should make him talk to you more often in French, he only has the knack for sadism in English." He winked at Hy and Ruthie who tried without success to look penitent.

"Old habits die hard," Manon sighed ruefully. "Remember, he was my boss before he was my husband." She turned back to Hy and said, "I was going to ask how your mother got to be called The Duchess, but now I'm afraid to."

Hy chuckled and set down his cutlery. "Now that actually is a funny story, *les enfants,* and I happen to remember it vividly be-cause as an eight–year old what did I know from metaphors, and what dad said seemed pretty amazing to me." He laughed again, shaking his head at the memory.

"C'mon, Hy, let's have it," Ruthie prodded impatiently. "I always thought it was because she just looks so aristocratic. But is it go-ing to bruise my shell–like ears? I mean, is this going to be daddy speaking English or Chabanese?"

"Oh, definitely Chabanese." And in response to Manon's puz-zled expression, "We used to say he was speaking Chabanese–you know all the *shmatta* factories are on Chabanel St.–when he was particularly crude."

He sipped his wine. "Okay. Dad was in the kitchen with Izzie Bienhacker, who got into curtains and blinds after peddling some of dad's lines when he first came over from the old country. Izzie was thinking about renting space in this little strip shopping centre in St. Laurent, the first one dad bought with *Clar–Mor* as the an-chor.

"And Izzie was *kvetching* that the unit rent was too high, he could probably do better 'by Shapiro in Laval', and dad was such a hustler, I don't have to tell you, and so anxious to make the sale, so he says to Izzie, he says, 'listen Izzie, you won't do better with that *goniff* Shapiro. You won't do better anywhere than the price I'm giving you. I'm not bullshitting you, I mean, *I'm puttin' my schlong on the table here...*'"–

Hy started to choke with laughter, Ruthie moaned '*oh no*' and sank her face into her hands (but giggling) and Manon looked in puzzlement at Polo who whispered something to her at which her eyes widened and her mouth fell slightly ajar.

"And my *mother*," Hy went on between fits of laughter, "and my *mother* overhears this and says in this really to–the–manor–born kind of way, '*you know, Morrie, a simple 'I'm being very sincere' would convey the same message in a more civilized way*.'" Hy and Ruthie were roaring uncontrollably now. It was infectious.

"You had to see–" Hy broke up again, and mopped at his eyes with his napkin–"you had to see the look on Izzie's face." Ruthie was by now doubled over in giddy abandonment. "So does that–oh God, it was funny–does that answer your question, pumpkin?"

Manon opened her mouth to reply and the telephone rang. "I'll get it," she said and slipped into the hall. Hy was still shaking his head, repeating, 'a simple I'm being very sincere would convey the same message...' and started to laugh again.

"It's for you, Hy," Manon said, "Albert Legendre from the Taschereau store. He says Howard's left for Stowe and it's important."

Hy excused himself, still chuckling.

The three relaxed into a companionable silence for a moment, the glowy intimacy of shared laughter circulating in the air amongst them.

"I don't mean to sound pathetic or anything," Ruthie finally said, her voice still weak from laughter, "but that is honestly the first really good laugh I've had in"–her eyes looked into the distance and her fingers counted against her thumb–"thirteen months. Because," she continued almost dreamily, "it was a year ago April that we knew it was cancer," she sipped at her wine, "and not the right kind...." Her eyes stayed focused in the distance for a moment, then suddenly she startled.

"I can't believe I said that," she apologized in obvious embarrassment. "I'm so sorry, Manon. And–and Polo. And it's such a beautiful dinner." Her eyes filled and she shook her head in self–reproach.

Polo was stunned by the emotional punch he felt at Ruthie's un-expected and intimate offering after the lightness of the last hour. He wanted to jump up, pull her to him, hold her and comfort her.

And before his conversation with Nathalie he would have felt at the very least perfectly comfortable to do what any friend would–give her a hug. He had hugged her this morning. She was his oldest friend. But now he felt suddenly guilty about his instinct, and even recoiled from it. He felt a surge of terrible anger at Nathalie. She had spoiled something important in his life, perhaps forever. And she was wrong. It was a lie. He should ignore it.

And yet he made no move toward Ruthie. He couldn't feel right about it any more. It was terrible

Finally he leaned over to squeeze her hand in a brotherly way. "What are friends for, Ruthie. Don't be silly." *Gee, fella, that's really profound and original. That ought to cheer her up right away.* He cursed himself in a variety of swear words covering every object, article of clothing and ritual ever associated with the Catholic church.

Manon murmured something comforting to her in French, and the two women continued to speak softly of the things Manon was well–equipped to sympathize with: the difficulties of living alone for a woman who has spent a lifetime under the protection of men, explaining the injustices of life to frightened and bewildered children, the struggle to rediscover a sense of normalcy...

Listening, making no attempt to pretend that he had anything to contribute, at first so sunk in his own frustration that he didn't realize they had switched languages, Polo gradually became aware of the charmingly flawless Parisian accent which never failed to take him back to his earliest memories of Ruthie, her pink bedroom and the absurd little schoolroom.

It was paradoxical. She had seemed so sure of herself back then, sure of what she owned and what she had to offer, confident of her value and importance to the world, that arrogant little slip of a child, and now, a woman in late, but still full bloom, she was vulnerable, sure of nothing, humbled. His heart went out to her. Which, he knew, was what it mustn't do. *Think about something else. Think about why you like her better when she speaks English.*

It was interesting that he had never liked to talk to her in French. He supposed it was because it only emphasized the yawning educational and cultural chasm between them. It was humiliating to be outclassed in your mother tongue. There was less shame when it was your second language. And in English, they were pretty much of a sameness now.

As the conversation gradually shifted back to normal ground, Polo felt free to remark that Hy had been on the phone for quite a while. It was true. And it was unlike him to take his guests for granted, even family, Manon knew. She half-rose to see if anything was really the matter, when Hy strode back into the room.

Manon could not stifle a cry of shock at the sight of him. His colour was very bad and he was breathing so raggedly it sent a chill of fear through her limbs.

"Hy, what is it? Howard? Elaine? Your mother? *What is it?*"

Hy grasped Manon's outstretched hand and tried to muster a soothing tone. "It's not the family. It's nobody we know. Or rather–listen, just give me a few minutes with Polo." Polo had already risen and was waiting tensely. His mind was roving–irrationally, he remembered it was store business–amongst the horses at the barn, wondering if the door had been locked, if Roch had checked before leaving…

"No, Hy," she cried, "You can't expect me to look at you, and see how upset you are and not tell me." Ruthie murmured a reinforcing bid for enlightenment.

Hy nodded grimly and took a deep breath. "Okay, you're right. It's–oh, God–it's that stable boy, Liam. They found him out back of the Taschereau store. Dead. Strangled. No identifying marks." The two women gasped.

"How did they know it was Liam?" Polo asked, feeling instinctively this was the wrong question.

"*They* didn't know it was Liam. They–the police, the store people–they still don't know who it is. It's *me* who knows it's Liam. Because–" he was still gripping Manon's hand and shook it a little as he looked fiercely into her frightened eyes–"they described what he looked like, and at first because they didn't mention a ponytail, I just thought it could be anyone, but then they told me he was wrapped in *Clar-Mor* paper! And from the size, I knew it was the paper that's missing from the stadium!"

Polo now grasped the real source of Hy's extreme anxiety. "So you didn't tell them."

Hy's face sagged with the comfort of confession. "Polo, I couldn't. I know it was wrong, but I suddenly saw what it would mean, and I thought of Roch, the police swarming all over the place, the publicity–I had a vision of that funny little reporter dashing to the phone–it was wrong, but I froze. And I didn't even lie. I didn't have to. Albert wanted to know if I thought he might have worked for *Clar-Mor* somewhere else, at some other store, and I said truthfully I couldn't think of any store employee that fitted that description. So technically–" he slumped wearily into a chair and rubbed a hand across his face and eyes.

Polo's mind was racing back through all the postulations he had made about the stallion and the office. All bets were off. Whoever had sent him packing had hated him enough to kill him. Or again, maybe not. A hundred new possibilities leaped to mind…but first things first…

"When do they think he died?"

"Late afternoon or early evening, no precise time yet." Hy's voice shook slightly. Manon slipped her arm across his shoulder.

"And they think he was killed in town?" Polo probed.

Hy shrugged. "They have no reason to think otherwise. But it's obvious he was killed here."

Manon nodded, but Polo frowned and was about to speak, when Ruthie said thoughtfully, "Why is it obvious? The killer may have brought the paper into town for that reason. Or anywhere along the way. They might have had a rendez-vous planned. He–or she–might have given the boy a lift to town, planning all the time to kill him. So we can't even be sure it was someone on the grounds here."

Polo nodded and looked at her in admiration for her swift grasp of the alternatives. They all fell silent for a moment. Finally Polo said, "What do you want to do, Hy?"

Hy groaned. "I was hoping you'd tell me. I'm out of my depth here, I admit it." He sank his face into his hands. "This is a nightmare. I'm the kind of guy who declares every pair of socks I buy in Plattsburgh when I cross the border. How did I get mixed up in a murder?"

"We have to let Roch know," Polo said. "He should be part of the decision. I'll call him." Hy nodded dumbly.

Manon rose stiffly. She grasped Hy's hand, squeezed hard, and began mechanically to remove the dishes from the table

Ruthie walked briskly into the kitchen. "I should make some coffee," she offered.

"Make a lot," Polo said quietly, and their eyes met as he reached for the telephone.

CHAPTER TWELVE

T HEY HUDDLED AROUND THE ANTIQUE PINE COFFEE TABLE IN varying postures of frustration and tension. Ruthie was curled tightly into a wing chair, hugging a pillow. Roch sat on the edge of a hard chair, elbows to knees, and rocked back and forth on his heels. Manon and Hy sat very close to each other on a loveseat, fingers tightly interlaced. Polo paced the width of the room, sat for a few minutes on a Turkish ottoman, got up to pace again.

It was very late. The air in the living room was acrid and blue from Roch's Old Ports. Smoking was normally an offence in the Jacobson household, but under the circumstances, and in the light of Roch's intense agitation, Hy and Manon hadn't the heart to enforce a ban. Periodically Ruthie picked up his ashtray with careful, shrinking fingertips to rinse and empty into the garbage compactor. Roch was oblivious to her expression of fastidious distaste as she did this, but Polo flashed back in his mind to his eleven–year old self and that first awareness of her cool, assessing presence in the Jacobsons' kitchen.

There were a few areas of agreement. Of this little group Polo and Ruthie were taken to be disinterested parties in the affair, unless some stunning new piece of information came to light. A police investigation would be unlikely to involve them in anything more than a cursory investigation of their whereabouts at specific times. Even without alibis for time and place, neither of them had any but the most tangential relationship to the Centre and its business. But Roch and Hy and even Manon, on the other hand, because of the circumstances of Liam's job and the link to *Clar–Mor* in his death, would be fair game for deeper probes of both motives and opportunities for the murder.

Roch had argued passionately against disclosure of Liam's identity to the police. He spoke eloquently and stirringly of the years of commitment and unremitting work he had devoted to the Centre. A scandal of this kind would be devastating. If even ten percent of the boarders left–and they were sure to if the murder and the stallion attack were publicized–the cash flow of his business would be in jeopardy within two months. Six months of sharply reduced business would finish him.

The parents of his young Ontario students would whip their kids out of Saint Armand as soon as they heard about it. You didn't get students that easily in the horse business. One way or another a public enquiry would be the end of his career, he was convinced, no matter who was–or more likely who was not–found to have done it.

"*Écoute,* Hy," he pleaded instinctively to the one he knew was most inclined to empathize, "it's not only *Le Centre* I'm thinking of. Let's face it, this *affaire,* it looks bad for my nephew. When Gilles left like that, I thought well, he's scared about the stallion, and I've been tough on him lately, maybe he thought he'd be blamed. But now I don't know…and let's say he had nothing to do with the murder, the police, they're going to make him the first suspect, that's for sure."

He turned to include Manon and Ruthie. "You have families, children…you understand what that means. My sister, Gilles' mother–she's got a lot on her plate right now. This would–"

Hy groaned and held up a weary hand. "Don't, Roch. No more. I give up. I understand where you're coming from. It wouldn't be any picnic for me either as owner to see the Centre exposed to that kind of publicity. And anyway it's not just *your* family's reputation that's at stake." Manon buried her face in her hands and sighed as Hy sympathetically caressed her shoulder.

He said, "Look, you all know what I'm most inclined to do, and that's go to the authorities. But I want to do the right thing for everyone. I think we all realize that the best thing in terms of our own interests would be to try and solve it ourselves. If we can prove who did it and hand him over to the police, it'll blow over fast." Roch nodded eagerly.

"But," he continued firmly, "we have to agree on a time limit. It's Friday night. The C–FES people are coming down on Sunday for the final meeting before the show. The government grant workers are coming Monday. We can't keep it quiet after that. Rumours will spread. And if we wait too long, we may be liable to all kinds of charges–criminal charges, maybe, obstruction of justice or whatever. If we haven't found the murderer by Sunday night–"

Ruthie stood up abruptly. She had not spoken much since Roch arrived, and not at all during the general discussions about the barn, where she had little to contribute, but now she exclaimed, "But this is crazy, Hy. I know I don't stand to lose anything, so it's easy for me to take the high road, but we're none of us equipped to deal with this. I mean, look at us. We're ordinary people, not private eyes. The only detective work you've ever done is to dig up new donors for Combined Jewish Appeal. How do you propose we go about finding a *murderer*, for God's sake?"

Roch was nettled and flustered by her intervention. He cast about in his mind for an appropriate form of rebuttal. She was not someone he could either flirt with or openly dominate. She wasn't a client or a sponsor or a committee member to be charmed, flattered or manipulated. Her confident, but neutral manner with him this evening told him she was used to dealing comfortably, directly, and on even terms with all men. Then too, her fluty European French was disconcerting. He was self-conscious and unsure of his footing with her, and so smothered the patronizing or dismissive reply he might have offered most other women he knew. He looked to Hy for support.

Hy said wearily, "I don't propose to find out who it is by myself. And I wouldn't ask any single person here to do it either. I'm looking at it as a group job, a business project, and I'm looking around the room and seeing a team of very smart people with different talents. If we put our brains and our abilities together, we might be able to do it, don't you think?"

Everyone looked at everyone else. There was a short silence. Ruthie said, "Even if you did agree to work together, you'd still need a *responsable*. And it's too much for you, Hy, you shouldn't have that responsibility." Manon nodded.

Hy smiled. "I'm way ahead of you, *ziess*. Remember, I've put together a lot of business teams in my time. Polo. How about it?"

"You want to trust me with this, Hy? Are you sure?" Polo felt rather than saw the swiveling gazes and the sudden heat of everyone's hopes trained on him like searchlights. He waited for someone to say "don't be absurd" or "no way". But they didn't. They were silent and big-eyed and respectful of Hy's choice. Except Ruthie, who pointedly looked away from Polo, got up and made herself busy taking cups to the kitchen.

"Yeah, I guess I am," Hy answered levelly. "We'll all cooperate, of course. But somebody has to lead, and I think it should be you."

"Why?"

"Because you're smart as hell, because you know everything there is to know about horses, because nobody I know has an axe to grind with you, because you already know most of the principals, and because you're above suspicion and nobody else is." He sighed, and added, "But mostly, I guess, because apart from Manon, my kids and Ruthie–and none of them has applied for the job–I trust you more than anyone I know."

"But seriously," Manon said, frowning, "this is no joking matter, Polo. If you agree to take this responsibility, you may be putting yourself in danger. Think about it a minute. We aren't dealing with some cranky political extremist anymore. Somebody has *killed* someone. And we're all agreed it's most likely someone at *Le Centre*, aren't we?" Everyone nodded glumly. She shivered and Hy pulled her to him protectively.

Polo considered her words thoughtfully. She was right, of course. How much did he owe Hy? His life? It would have been easy to counter Roch's pleas for containment. He knew he could have swayed Hy to do the right thing, call the police, continue to play the good citizen. But then, didn't he owe Roch something. too?

Who else did he owe?

I used to think you were the bravest guy in the world.

And finally, most important, there was his own inner voice, asking him when he had last felt so keyed up, so mentally charged, so–so *sharp*? There was no use denying the excitement he felt, a ferment of youthful drive he hadn't realized was missing from his life since he'd stopped competing. He'd tried to recreate that unique 'rush' in a hundred different ways–never with drugs or alcohol, he'd seen too much human misery in his life in St. Henri and on the circuit conferred by those false friends–but he'd never achieved those peaks again, no matter how much travelling, building, buying and selling, wheeling and dealing he packed into the days and weeks and years.

Now, suddenly, Polo scented a tantalizing fragrance from the past. A past where no one ever questioned his courage, his manliness, his choices in life. His heart was beating to a sweet, familiar rhythm. Short–circuiting any complex theories of the whys and wherefores, he knew that he yearned to test some atrophying aptitude, some creeping intellectual sclerosis. He had been wasting psychic energy in futile and insoluble struggles at home. He welcomed Hy's summons. He even looked forward to the potential danger.

'Cuz courage in a man, it's–it's–

Gravely he reviewed the expectant faces of his friends. His mind was already teeming with strategies and shortcuts. *Time to walk the course. Big fences. Tricky footing. Off–stride distances. Hard to find your spot. A seat–of–the–pants ride.*

"Okay, then. I will. First important decision. Do we tell the main people at *Le Centre* what's going on? I say yes. It's a good bet the killer will know that we're after him–or I suppose we should get used to thinking 'her' as well–but he isn't going to expose himself if he thinks he has a good alibi, which he probably does. On the other hand, he may panic and run or even confess if we're lucky. In any case, I think we have to take the risk.

"The other reason is that reporter, Sue Parker. She's very sharp, very persistent, and I'd rather have her on our side, working with us, than nosing around on her own. I don't want *her* getting hurt. If we promise her an exclusive story if and when the truth comes out, well–"

Ruthie had come in and taken her seat again. She looked at Hy as she spoke. "I can't stop you from doing this, but I want it clear that I am very much opposed to this plan. But if I don't cooperate, my only choice is to go back to Montreal. And I can't do that, Hy, I'd feel like a coward." Turning to the others, she went on, "So I'm in, against my better judgment, and possibly without being able to help at all, since I know nothing about horses, and I hardly know anybody here.

"As to that reporter, I think she had better be onside. Once we're not going to the police, we may as well have someone with an investigative background. I spoke to her a bit today and she was almost twitching with curiosity about everyone." She still hadn't looked at Polo, and he interpreted this to mean that she hadn't put her stamp of '*kashrut*' on his leadership. He felt unreasonably piqued at this, unreasonable because her concerns were perfectly valid. Still, a vote of non–confidence from Ruthie, if that's what it was, stung deeper than he liked to admit.

Polo sat down and pulled out his notebook. "We have to know where everyone was yesterday afternoon and early evening. Since we don't know if he was killed here, there or somewhere in be-tween, just about everyone without an ironclad alibi for the whole time is going to be suspect unless and until we establish the exact place of the murder. How we're going to question Benoit and Gilles is another problem. But we'll worry about that tomorrow."

Roch said gloomily, "I called my sister. Gilles won't talk to me, and I didn't want to upset her, so I let it go." He sighed. "And Beno-it–he was pretty pissed off when he left. I don't know if he's coming back."

Polo nodded and made a note. Then he looked soberly at each person in turn. "We may as well decide right now that we have to be as ruthless as the police would be. We can't exclude anyone, even ourselves." He checked his watch. "That's the only thing we can do tonight. We all need some sleep. Anyway, starting with myself, I spent the afternoon at the arena with the workers–they left at five–and the evening alone. I ate in town at one of the bistros–that's verifiable, but doesn't account for much time–came back to the condo, worked on some data for the show, read a bit and went to sleep. No alibi whatsoever."

Manon sighed. "Oh dear, I'm in the same boat. Hy went to Montreal. I messed around in the garden, did some shopping in the late afternoon and made the gazpacho. Then I ate dinner in front of the TV and watched and dozed until Hy got back at–what was it, about midnight?"

"Yep. I went into town around four p.m.–unless we establish that Liam died here, I suppose I could have given him a lift to Montreal, and I suppose I could have packed the *Clar–Mor* paper in the trunk, and I suppose I could have killed him somewhere on the way, dumped him at the Taschereau store, dropped in at the office to chat with Howard, and showed up with Ruthie at my mother's place at six–thirty, no problem at all," Hy offered drily.

"Don't be ridiculous, Hy," Ruthie snapped. "Do you think I wouldn't have known something was wrong? And the Duchess? You're as transparent as glass. You never *could* lie about anything."

"Ruthie, this isn't about what you and I think about each other. It's about what could have happened in time and space. That's what concerns police," Hy answered testily

Polo said, "Look, obviously none of us wants to believe anyone we know could do anything wrong. The police act on the principle that any*one* at all is capable of doing any*thing* at all if the circumstances are right. Which I tend to agree with–with the possible exception of Hy," he added lightly to defuse the gathering tension.

"Then you're wrong, Polo," Ruthie said crossly. "I hate that theory. So did daddy. He always said it was the kind of defense the Nazis used after the war. Anybody would have done the same, they all sang the same tune…"

"Oh *marde,* Roch said, "excuse me, Suz–Rut'ie–but please let's not get into politics. Polo, you're right that we have to try to get past the personal stuff. Me, I was in the office or giving lessons all day. I ate at the resto, sat around with the usual gang and left at ten. So I guess I have an alibi."

"Didn't you go home to shower and change before dinner?" Polo asked. He knew Roch was particular about his grooming and appearance, and never used his profession as an excuse to look like a slob, as so many other horse people did.

"Yeah, I did…*c'est vrai*… I did," Roch nodded reflectively. "And I was alone then, it's true. Ghislaine is away looking after her mother–she's very bad, cancer, a terrible thing–" Ruthie flinched slightly, but Roch's eyes were fixed and unseeing, reconstructing his evening. "So that's maybe forty–five minutes…"

"Well, at least you're off the hook if it happened in Montreal," Polo said dispassionately. He snapped the notebook shut and stood up abruptly. "Let's call it a day. Roch, I think you better telephone everyone–that is, Bridget, Guy, Michel, Thea, Fran, and Jocelyne, and Benoit if he'll come. Call them early in the morning and get them to a breakfast meeting, 9 a.m., say, that's the most efficient way. After that it's a question of talking to everyone and comparing notes. It'll be a long day."

Ruthie saw Polo out and walked down the steps toward the driveway with him. She took a deep breath of pine–scented air and gazed appreciatively at the thickly starred canopy of night sky above the mountain. She sighed. "Not quite the reunion I had envisaged."

Polo nodded. He stopped and turned to her. "Ruthie, before I go, there's something I wanted to ask you… I mean, I did ask you, but you didn't really answer. That day at St. Lazare, why were you annoyed at Thea Ankstrom for being such a big fan of my riding?"

He sensed her embarrassment. "I don't know," she shrugged. "Maybe it was the way she talked about you as if–as if you *belonged* to her–to them–the horse people–as if you had no other life…oh, I don't know, it's irrational. Of *course* I should have been proud and happy for you. I was. I *was*, really. And–and I apologize retroactively, if that's any use…"

"Don't be silly," Polo said quickly. "I was just curious."

They were at his truck. He reached for the handle. "Can I ask *you* a question?" Ruthie said quietly.

"Of course," Polo said promptly, but he knew, and his gut tightened in anticipation.

"What's with you and Nathalie?" She glanced at his expression and shook her head. "I shouldn't have asked, I guess."

"No, no, why shouldn't you–you're always honest with me." He shrugged awkwardly. "Not too famous at the moment."

"Is it something in particular, Polo? I always thought you were such a good match." She smiled mischievously. "In spite of your having robbed the cradle to get her."

She'd meant it as a joke, of course, to lighten the mood, and was expecting a flippant comeback. But Polo flinched as if she'd shied a stone at him, and Ruthie bit her lip in self–censure. It must be serious, then, this 'not too famous' thing.

He cleared his throat. "Yeah, it's something in particular. It's me. Nathalie deserves someone better than me."

"Give me a break, Polo. I mean this is *me* you're talking to, you can't use self-pity with *me*," Ruthie retorted crisply. She would have liked to show some sympathy–he looked tormented–but was afraid to.

"Nathalie wants to have kids. One at least anyway."

"And she can't? I always wondered. Well, that's a shame, but you know these fertility clinics nowadays are fantastic, they–"

"Whoa, Ruthie. She can and she would. It's me. I'm not letting her. It's not self–pity. She really does deserve better. And don't waste your time coming up with some diplomatic answer. I know what you're thinking."

"Okay, no diplomacy. You're right, she *doesn't* deserve you. How can you be such a shit? More to the point, how can *you* not want to have children?"

Polo shrugged. "I guess it's something you never even thought twice about." He leaned against the truck.

Easy for you, *ziess*. Easy for Hy. Easy for Roch. When you're part of a real family, you know how to make one of your own. You're not scared stiff. You know automatically how to make it work.

"No, I never did. Life without children–it's unthinkable for me." Ruthie glanced affectionately at Polo. She realized she had never seen this expression of naked sadness in his face in all the time she'd known him. Her heart reached out to him. She yearned to comfort him, but how–safely? So she chose instruction, which was what she knew how to give.

She said, "You know, Hy once said to me—well, he's spent so much time with community leaders, and a lot of them are, you know, quite wealthy, and they have these big businesses, or they're partners in law firms or whatever.

"Anyway, some of them are getting on in age, and Hy says that when he has lunch with them or they're *schmoozing* at meetings, these guys, they never want to talk about their businesses or their deals or whatever, they just want to talk about their children, and their grandchildren, what they're doing, who they're marrying, all that stuff. It's the only thing that's still fresh for them, you see, still exciting and interesting."

Polo nodded curtly and looked away. End of topic. Ruthie noted the rigid set of his jaw, sighed, moved discretely away a step or two, and was about to say good night, when Polo suddenly took her wrist in a firm clasp and said, "There's something else, Ruthie. I shouldn't probably mention…but I don't understand it. Nathalie said my life is a *mystery* to her. She knows everything about me—and she's known me since I was a teenager. I never had any secrets from her. What does she mean, do you think?"

Ruthie's eyes widened in genuine surprise. "But Polo, it's obviously that she—Polo, don't *you* think your life is something of a mystery?"

"What do you mean? I expected you to"—Polo passed his hand nervously through his hair. Why was she looking at him like that, as if he'd said something absurd or inappropriate. Everything seemed suddenly unreal, this whole crazy, unending day, the stallion, the office, the call to Nathalie, the surreal discussion about a murder that didn't yet seem actual, the pictures, the memories, and now Ruthie, calmly telling him that his life was a mystery. How could she, when she was there with him all the time? Why was *his* life a mystery and not hers?

"Are you all right? Polo?" Her eyes were big with concern and contrition. "Polo, forgive me—gee, that's all I ever seem to say tonight—I didn't mean to scare you, you suddenly looked so weird… Listen, I only meant that Hy and I, we never really understood how you suddenly came to be such an important part of our lives. You were just suddenly …there with us…another child in the family…

and yet not as we were…not in school, no rules, no responsibilities–or at least none that made any sense to us–*and it was never
talked about*. D'you see what I mean? How it was for us? Wasn't it
strange for you?"

"Truthfully? No, it wasn't strange at all. I always knew something would happen to me, something that would take me away
from my home. And–and, you see, it happened. I never questioned
it. I was doing what I wanted to do. I was where I wanted to be. I
never thought about your feelings, yours or Hy's–or anyone's, for
that matter. Of course I knew I wasn't growing up in the usual, con-
ventional way. But I felt normal. Obviously I was completely self–
centred, self–absorbed. But my life never seemed mysterious…not
to me…"

They both looked down at his hand, still clutching her wrist,
and he hastily dropped it. In a low and urgent voice, he asked,
"Were you jealous? Were you angry? Didn't you ever talk to your
father about it?"

Suddenly he wanted to know everything she had thought and
felt for all these years–not out of concern for her, but because he realized she was both right and wrong at the same time. And Nathalie
too. A claw of apprehension nipped at him. How had he never seen
it? Yes, yes, there *was* something terribly strange about his sojourn
with the Jacobsons–and Ruthie's memories might give him a clue,
might fill in the gaps in his knowledge.

The mystery wasn't about him, though. It was about Morrie.

"I'll only answer one and a half of your questions. It's too late
tonight for the rest. There's too much else going on. Yes, I tried to
ask my father about you–not once, but a hundred times. And it was
no use. He wouldn't talk about you. At one point–God, it was a horrible moment–I even asked him if you were his illegitimate child
from some romantic adventure. Talk about naïve. He smacked me,
the first time ever. The only time."

Polo visibly startled at this, and she smiled ruefully. "Yes,
I know. It was so out of character. I'll never forget it. Anyway, it
seems you are *not* my brother." Polo knew he was supposed to smile
encouragingly at this feeble joke, but he was transfixed. He had
wondered the same thing. Once maybe, and buried the thought

forever. Because it was just so ridiculous. But apparently not so ridiculous that Ruthie hadn't wondered too.

Now she was saying, "He just made it clear that you were there, under his protection, and we could like it or lump it. I don't know how much my mother knew, but she wouldn't discuss it either. As for our feelings, I think—well I know—Hy was quite jealous for a while—another boy, you see, and with your looks, the riding and all…but he grew out of it."

She turned away as if she had nothing more to say, struggled with some conflicted impulse, stopped, and finally, in low, muffled tones, vibrant with emotion, added, "Years later, you know, when all these awful stories about child abuse started to surface in the news—I mean, when I was young, I was so sheltered, I never dreamed such terrible things existed…but as an adult, and hearing about men, the most respectable even, I sometimes thought… but how could I possibly have asked you—how could I think such horrible thoughts about my own …and now hearing you say you don't want children, I wondered if back then…" her voice wavered, she bit her lip and hugged herself, suddenly, shivering.

"*Morrie?!* Oh God, Ruthie, no, he—oh God, *never, never, never.*" He stepped forward instinctively to grab her, as if to shield her from some gory sight, then checked himself. "Whatever it was, whatever his reasons for wanting me around, it wasn't—oh shit, I'm so sorry you let yourself suffer, even thinking for a second…"

He could see her trembling and ached to hold her, but jammed his hands into his pants pockets instead. *Damn you, Nathalie.* "It was just the riding between us. He loved the horses. I don't know why he wanted me around the house. But he was very good to me. Always honest. I'll never forget that. And after the riding stopped, we hardly even saw each other. I swear, *ziess.*"

"Thank you, *mazzik,*" she whispered softly. "You don't know how"—she shook her head and wiped surreptitiously at the corner of her eye, and Polo's heart contracted with pain.

Taking a deep breath, she mustered an attempt at a cheerful, no-nonsense tone. "Well, I–I think I've had about as much nostalgia as I can bear for one day. This really is goodnight."

She turned to leave, hesitated, then reached up for a hug. His arms were already embracing her before his mind gave them permission. He held her more tightly and a second longer than he should have, but she didn't seem to notice. "Goodnight, *mazzik*", she murmured, and smiled shyly with the old affection as she slipped away.

There was another note tucked into the condo door. *Oh fuck no. I can't take any more shit tonight.* But it wasn't from Nathalie this time.

It read: *'I would very much like to discuss an issue of some importance to me regarding my horse, Robin's Song. I would also appreciate it if you would agree to ride him once or twice over the next few days. I hope this will not be taken by Michel or Roch as an insult, but I am anxious to have a disinterested opinion. I will call on you early tomorrow for your answer. Thank you. Sincerely, Thea Ankstrom.'*

Polo sighed. He was exhausted. Another mystery. He went inside and scribbled a short note in return: *I will be happy to discuss your horse with you tomorrow. There is going to be a breakfast meeting for several of us at the restaurant in any case, so we can talk on the way over. Until then, P. Poisson.* He slipped it under her door.

He thought he would have trouble falling asleep, with all that had happened, but he was towed under as if drugged within seconds of his head touching the pillow.

He dreamed he was struggling to cross the parking lot behind the Taschereau *Clar–Mor* where he had sometimes worked as a stock boy in the Christmas season. In slow motion, as if running through water, he strained to reach the other side where he could make out a shapeless bundle wrapped in *Clar–Mor* paper, and from within whose folds he heard the forlorn wail of an abandoned baby. But *it's dead,* his dream voice was saying. *How can it be crying?*

And then he saw both Ruthie and Nathalie were there too, and neither of them could (or would) pick the bundle up. Ruthie stood looking at him reproachfully, sadly shaking her head. But

Nathalie was weeping and wringing her hands, calling to him to hurry, or it would be too late, too late, too late. He pushed on, but it was no use. He was plowing through mud. And the baby's cries grew louder and more anguished...

His own voice crying out and the pain in his hands woke him up. His heart was pounding, his t–shirt was damp with sweat and his palms showed angry red crescents where his clenched fists had driven in his nails. He got up, showered and changed, then dozed in fits and starts until, towards dawn, he fell into a deep, dreamless sleep.

CHAPTER THIRTEEN

"That was Roch," Bridget said pensively, her hand lingering on the receiver. "There's to be an emergency breakfast meeting at nine. For both of us. And most of the others."

There was no reply to this statement, though Guy was within easy hearing distance. His attention was focused elsewhere.

"It's serious, Guy," Bridget continued sternly. "Roch says it's something the police might have to deal with eventually, and he wants us all there to discuss it. And it's not about Rockin' Robin." She frowned and stared at him, willing a response. Silence. "He mentioned Liam," she prodded teasingly. "Roch says he didn't just run off. He says something happened to the little bastard."

Guy burst out petulantly, "He's dead! And it's entirely my fault. As fascinating as he is, I had no business bringing that vicious little predator home in the first place."

Totally nonplussed by this startling confession, Bridget gazed at her housemate, making no effort to conceal her irritation. In measured tones, laced with the excruciating irony of the British upper class at its most theatrically frosty, she replied, "Guy, do you think I might possibly intrude on your grief over your dead anemone–"

"It's not an anemone! It's my shrimp! And there were only two like that, all red and white striped! And this damned hawkfish is so clever–look, look, do you see him? He's stalking the other one already, he–"

"*Guy!*"

Guy swivelled obediently round to face her, although his pale eyes twitched, magnetically pulled to the massive, 500–gallon reef tank, explosively colourful and dense with tropical marine life, where so much real eco–drama was in progress. "Sorry, Bridget, but this really is a bit of a crisis. I may have to take the whole tank apart to get at that hawkfish. A net isn't the slightest use with a character like–"

"*Guy!*"

"Sorry, Bridget," Guy said meekly, frowning in concentration and not daring to look away from Bridget's menacing topaz eyes. "Did you say something about Liam? Everyone thinks he ran away..."

"Yes, I am saying that there is something very much wrong about Liam. I am saying that Roch is saying that he's dead. Let's see, how did Roch put it? Oh yes, *H'its priddy damn serious, dat's all what I'm saying, là, and we don' want la police mixing demselves in h'our affair, là...*" she went on in an exaggerated, but devilishly accurate parody of Roch's confused syllabic stresses and synthetic verbal structures.

"Oh Bridget, you really are very cruel sometimes. Roch is always so nice to you." He did not dare add that it seemed doubly insulting to make fun of Roch who had at least gone to the trouble of actually *learning* a second language, however *approximativement* it came out at times.

"Oh, it's just for fun, Guy. Lighten up, for God's sake," she snapped. "I can't help it. It's how I deal with stress. Everyone has their way, and that's mine." She glanced at her watch. "Look, I'm going to the barn first to check on Robin and see if he can take a little grass. There's still plenty of time. You'll look in on him before we go to this meeting, won't you?"

"Of course, Bridget," Guy said crossly, already turned back to the tank. "When did I ever *not* start the day checking your horses?

I just want to–"

"If you forget, I'm not kidding, you can kiss all your little mates good–bye: Mr. Purple Fins, Mr. Polka Dot and the rest, not just Mr. Shrimp," Bridget added sardonically, nodding at the tank as she shrugged into her nylon windshell.

"That really isn't very funny," Guy retorted uneasily. *She would, too.*

Polo knocked on Thea's door and her timbred contralto called out immediately, "Come in, please."

As he entered she emerged from the bedroom, impeccably groomed and attractively dressed in a khaki cotton pantsuit. Tilting her head to adjust a pearl earring, she smiled so warmly that Polo was taken aback. The cobweb of diffidence that she had spun between them was gone. Her eyes sparkled and her voice was vibrant with purpose as she greeted him. Her colour was fresh and healthy. A different person entirely. What had happened?

His eyes swept around the tiny space. They came to rest on the drainboard at the sink, where two plates, two wine glasses and two cups and saucers were plainly visible in the drying rack. A dinner guest. An overnight guest? But he would have heard a car pull away in the morning. Dinner, then. Who?

"Roch just called. I gather we have something far more important to talk about than my horse at the moment," she said briskly.

"Maybe we can do both. It's still early. If you like, we can walk over to the barn first to look at your horse and I'll tell you what's up on the way."

Thea was almost as tall as Polo and an energetic walker. She matched his stride without effort as they made their way to the stables under a lowering sky. Listening intently as he recounted the events of the previous evening, she received the news of Liam's death with characteristic detachment and aplomb.

"Dead? Strangled?" she murmured. There was a pause. "With what, do they say?"

"Whatever it was had been removed. Wire, probably, or very thin rope. But there weren't any rope burns, as far as I know, and the skin was broken, according to what the police said, so I would assume wire."

"Wire would be faster, I should think. Harder to get your fingers under once it was tight." She paused to reflect. "Even a woman, if she used wire, might have an added advantage. He wasn't tall, or big..." Polo did not reply, waiting to see where this speculation would lead her.

She thought a moment and added, "I suppose you have already considered the coincidence–the stallion, I mean, and the wire used on his tongue"–

"Yes, we did, of course."

"And you say there were no distinguishing signs? What was he wearing?" Thea demanded.

"T–shirt, jeans. Sneakers."

"Not the sweatshirt?"

"What sweatshirt? The blue and brown vet school thing?"

"Yes," she replied curtly. "He wore it all the time. It used to make me sick to see it."

"–?"

"You didn't know? That Stephanie–she–that's my daughter, she"–her voice faltered for a second, "she was a student there. She was going to be a veterinarian. She was so proud of that, she loved wearing that sweatshirt."

"And Liam was wearing your daughter's sweatshirt?" Polo struggled to find a connection between a girl dead a year and a groom hired only months ago.

"No, no," she shook her head impatiently as they continued on up the rough path through long grass that painted their pants with dew as they passed. "Not Stephanie's. I mean the Tufts sweatshirt in general. Guy was a visiting lecturer there, you see. At Tufts. He was one of Stephanie's advisors in the Large Animal program for a semester. He was helping her with a study she was doing on cattle–on growth promotion."

"Cows?" said Polo. "I would have thought horses would be her line, and Guy's too."

"Guy isn't really a practicing horse vet, except here in this barn, although I can see where you got that impression. He's a research freak. Cows are his actual academic expertise, although all large animals are his general domain. Taking care of Bridget's horses is their quid pro quo arrangement. He shares her house, you know." Polo hadn't known this, thought it quite interesting, and mentally filed it for future reference.

Thea continued, "Of course it's wonderful for Roch to have a kind of resident vet around for emergencies, and I think he gives him small perks, office space, clerical time from Marie–France, that kind of thing. As for Stephanie, of course horses would have been her preference but, you see, it's always a question of funding, and what topics are available. A veterinary pharmaceuticals company wanted work done on this cow business, the money for it was there, so there really wasn't much choice. Anyway, Guy and Stephanie became friends over that research–very good friends, actually." Her voice drifted off a bit here, as if other thoughts had diverted her attention.

Then she was back. "So it was Guy who gave the sweatshirt to Liam. For helping him when one of the horses colicked. It was touch and go, apparently. Liam stayed up all night with him. It was cold. And Guy lent him the sweatshirt. And then gave it to him." She shrugged. "Stupid of me, but when I first saw that sweatshirt, I almost screamed. He must have thought I was crazy."

"I'm glad you told me that. It means that if he was wearing it when he was killed, then the killer knew it would be a clue and might lead somehow to an investigation of stables in the area. I'd already noticed that they didn't mention a belt. The buckle he had was distinctive, too. Which makes it all the more probable"–

"–that it's very likely one of a very small group of people, one of–well, *us*, not to put too fine a point on it. And that's the reason for the meeting."

"Yes."

"And that's why the police haven't been told. Because it's–in-house, so to speak."

"That's right."

"And you're assuming that it wasn't Liam who cut up the horse, then."

"No."

Thunder rolled faintly in the distance and the sky darkened.

"So the obvious question now is–why are *you* up to your ears in this? You're a transient here, like me."

"Friendship. Roch and I go back a long way. Hy and I even longer. Manon–she's become a friend since they married. *Le Centre*, too. If anything happens to *Le Centre*, Michel won't have a base. His career would be in trouble."

She smiled bitterly. "Personal loyalty, in a word."

Polo searched her face to read the emotion behind her words. He felt judged and defensive. "Loyalty isn't a bad reason for doing something. It counts a lot for me." He shrugged. "I guess I assumed most of us would feel loyal to Roch at least. If not for him, most of the people here wouldn't have jobs, or at least not such a good place to work. You know how few stables in Canada have the kind of resources *Le Centre* has to offer."

"You haven't mentioned C–FES and the Young Riders show. Don't you feel loyal"–she swished a mocking hand to her heart–"to us too?"

Stupidly, Polo did not pick up on her irony immediately. "I'm sorry, I don't really have much of a group mentality and, to be honest, I've never had more to do with C–FES than was necessary when I was competing–"

He said this, tensely conscious of who she was in the sport and whose wife she had been, and broke off. She gave no outward sign of discomfort, but she was suddenly looking down at her sensible leather walking shoes, not at him. He added a little lamely, "I didn't mean to minimize your particular loyalties–"

"Polo, really, you're a hoot," Thea laughed, flinging her head up, "or is that something people ever say anymore? Probably not. Don't you know sarcasm when you hear it?"

"As a matter of fact," Polo retorted coolly, "I was surrounded for a good part of my youth by geniuses in the field and I consider myself something of an expert at recognizing it. I just never expected it from you. I never thought you had"–

"–a sense of humour?"

"I wasn't going to say that. But let's just say I've only ever seen one side of your personality. Why should I imagine you'd be sarcastic about an institution you're so obviously devoted to?"

Tears glittered suddenly in her eyes and she turned quickly away from him. "Look down there," and she pointed at the cross–country course below them. They had been climbing steadily towards the stable, and the view from their rutted path, strangely luminous in the pre-storm light, encompassed a slew of cross–country obstacles, tiered embankments, water crossings and the entire steeplechase oval. He looked. To the left he could also make out the stadium and the mound of sand waiting to be spread in the arenas.

"Isn't it pretty? Isn't it green and bright? Doesn't the water look pure? Don't you just long to gallop over it? Don't the jumps seem like they'd be fun to just–you know–pop over?" Emotion thickened her beautiful voice.

Polo's gut tightened in anticipation. *Jesus, what is it about me that makes women want to start bawling all the time?* "Thea, listen, maybe this is all too much for you right now. I shouldn't have just thrown this murder story at you. Think a minute before you tell me something you may be sorry for later."

"Loyalties. Loyalties." She stared hypnotically down at the course below. "A lot of things turn on them, don't they?"

She poked with the tip of her umbrella at a crouched toad hiding in the long grass, and it leaped away. "Are you politically inclined, Polo? I mean, who would have a better right than you, after what my husband and the others tried to do to you? And you must have known it wasn't just him. They all felt the same in those days." She laughed harshly. "Even I never saw how ludicrous and wrong it was. I didn't like it, but I never said anything. I was so *loyal,* you see."

"You mean trying to keep me off the team because I was French–Canadian?" Polo shrugged. "That was a long time ago. Not worth joining a political party over. I told you, groups aren't my thing. And anyway, it was no big deal. He changed his mind within a day. So I don't see–"

"*Changed his mind?*" Thea whipped back fiercely. "You know very well he would *never* have changed his mind if your sponsor hadn't done what he did!"

"My sponsor? You mean Morrie?" Polo stared at her uncomprehendingly. "You've got it wrong, Thea. Morrie wasn't even at that show. They had a wedding to go to. He only found out when

I called after the show, later that night when he got home. Morrie didn't do anything. He didn't even say very much about it."

Polo frowned as memory washed back the disappointment he had felt at Morrie's almost detached reaction on the phone, his too-easy acceptance of the bad news. *'Cultural homogeneity', eh? That's rich. That's a good one. Ankstrom, eh? What's his first name? These guys, they're real handy with the words when they wanna fuck you over without any bruises showing. Hey, don't sweat it, kid. What goes around comes around...I gotta go, some stuff I gotta do, speak to you tomorrow, eh kid?'*

Polo added slowly, "It seemed a little strange, in fact. He was so excited about his horse going all the way. He was frustrated about missing the show."

Thea nodded with satisfaction. "A wedding! Ah, well, that at least explains the tuxedo. I always wondered..."

Polo felt as though the ground had shifted slightly. The thunder rolled again, closer now, and the dampening wind plucked at their clothes. "I don't understand, Thea."

She peered closely at the candid bewilderment in his expression. "You really don't know, do you? He never told you. How truly *extraordinary* ... how very–*gentlemanly* that was. I misjudged him. I thought he'd be the kind to strut and crow, tell the world..." She shook her head slowly, clearly bemused by private memories. "More than loyalty. To take the risk of looking a fool for someone who doesn't even know..."

Polo was by now churning with impatience and foreboding. He wanted to grab her and shake her. He was still strung out from last night, and he knew the day ahead would be hell. He was fed up with being polite and deferential to her. "I think you'd better tell me what you're talking about," he said coldly, with barely suppressed aggression, and she smiled apologetically.

"I'm sorry, Polo," she said quickly. "I'm not trying to create mysteries for you. I'll tell you what happened that day–and the next. But it's not a good time now." She looked up at the ominous sky and shivered. "I want you to know the whole story. You've a right to it. And to other information that's come my way. Can we meet later? Perhaps a drink later on–around five?"

He wanted to insist on knowing now, but hesitated, then nodded. Better to wait. He felt intuitively that what she was going to tell him would be something he would prefer being alone to digest. Today would be crowded with people. The first fat drops began to fall. They pressed on quickly.

"Good. Now let me tell you about my horse, and why I would appreciate your riding him. Today, if possible."

"It's probably not on for today, Thea. This crisis will take up most of the time."

"Oh, but I think you should ride him for that very reason, Polo. I think there is a connection with my horse and what's going on here, and when, or if, you find out what's wrong with him, we may know more about someone's motive for getting rid of Liam."

"Are you saying that Liam knew something was wrong with the horse? And if he did, how come Michel didn't? Wasn't Michel riding him regularly? Michel would know if it was something physical, at the very least."

Thea shook her head impatiently. "Of course Michel is a top rider, but you see he always rides the horse in the arena. He does a basic warm–up, jumps him a bit, keeps him supple and all that, but"–

"Thea, what do you want me to do with him that Michel doesn't?"

"Put him through a real workout, Polo. Take him outside, work him on asphalt, *push* him…"

"Hallo, Michel! You're on the early side this morning, aren't you?" Bridget ducked under the crossties tethering one of the large warmbloods in the aisle of the round barn.

"Morning, Bridget," Michel replied politely, bent over with his attention directed to the thick tendon along the back of Amadeus' left foreleg, which Jocelyne was palpating in firm, practiced movements of her fingers. Beside her waited two gigantic rubber boots, attached by hoses to a small generator. A bag of ice lay on the floor. Jocelyne did not look up or greet Bridget.

"Not bowed, has he?" Bridget persisted solicitously, noting the whirlpool boots, ready to act sympathetic if it was bad news and hide her secret sense of triumph–*your horse, not mine*–in the traditional way of horse people.

"A little heat and tenderness, that's all. The footing was soft yesterday. He'll be all right with some treatment and a few days off." Michel spoke civilly, but didn't look up.

"Well, that's all right, then. You can take Robbie out first today. I mean, after this breakfast meeting, I shouldn't expect it will take too long."

"Polo's schooling him today," Michel stated laconically. He kept his eyes averted, but his body tensed slightly for her reaction.

"What do you mean? I haven't asked Polo to ride him." Her voice was sharp and bordering on hostile.

Michel shrugged. "It's already fixed up. The owner wants Polo to ride him. She called me this morning." His face and his tone were equally impassive.

"*Thea* asked him? Without consulting *me*?" Patches of colour rose quickly up her neck and jaw, and her voice tightened with the effort to sound normal. Jocelyne peeked up at her, a tiny smile playing at the corners of her mouth.

Michel straightened up and looked directly at her for a brief moment. "Seems that way." He then kneeled on the other side of the horse and began a close inspection of the right foreleg.

"Don't come over all professional with *me*, Michel," Bridget snapped. "What the hell is going on?"

But Michel was nothing if *not* a complete professional, and he hadn't the slightest difficulty in displaying both ignorance and indifference in the matter, neither being feigned. In horse sport there were motives it was prudent–and even safer at times–to know nothing about. Michel knew better than to take it personally when an owner suddenly fancied another rider for her horse. It happened all the time. He didn't consider it an indictment of his skill. And he never resented the next rider. Sometimes another guy's style was better with a given horse than yours. No big deal. Once you let feelings and sensitivities interfere with your riding, you were a dead duck.

"Ask the owner, Bridget," he said with terse finality, and began talking to Jocelyne in French. Bridget glared at him, but knew it was useless. His face, drawn and abstracted, was closed against her.

She knew he would never back her up in an argument with Thea over it. He felt no loyalty to her. None at all. He should have felt some gratitude for the exposure he got riding her horses, not to mention the pleasure he must have in schooling such exceptional, talented creatures. But he didn't. He didn't appreciate what she had given him. Nobody at the stable appreciated what she had done, was doing for Three–Day Eventing, for horse sport here in Saint Armand, here in Quebec, in Canada. Nobody was loyal to her. Except Guy, of course…

"Amazing, isn't it?" Guy cried with delight. "Not twenty–four hours later, and he's managing with the grass. A lot's falling out, but he's working on it, you can see he realizes he'll have to learn a new way. Amazing!" Guy was preparing a needle to inject the antibiotic.

Bridget glowered at the stallion. "Amazing," she echoed half–heartedly.

Approaching footsteps roused her from her contemplation of Rockin' Robin's slowly masticating jaws.

"Good morning, Bridget," Thea said quietly, shaking out and folding her umbrella. The old veil of inscrutability had fallen over her features as soon as she entered the barn, Polo noted. He nodded to Bridget, who only glared at him and turned back to Thea.

"I won't mince words, Thea. It's considered very bad form to go over your trainer's head with a horse's training program, " Bridget said brusquely. "If you weren't happy with my methods or my decisions, you should have come directly to me. Although frankly I think I'm the best judge of who should be riding Robbie."

Bridget was studiously ignoring Polo's presence, but he could feel the waves of animosity coming his way. He pointed to the clock, exchanged a brief glance with Thea, who nodded understandingly, then immediately withdrew to rendez–vous with Roch and Hy in the office. The meeting would begin in ten minutes.

Thea's eyebrows arched in a nice imitation of surprise at Bridget's words. "Oh dear, Bridget," she said trenchantly, "I'm afraid you've got the wrong end of the stick if that's what you thought. I mean, if you thought you were my horse's *trainer.*"

Bridget's creamy skin went crimson. She opened her mouth to speak, but Thea put up a hand and continued, "I consider you to have *been* my daughter's coach, Bridget. After that role ended, I simply left the horse here to board. If anyone was in charge of him, it was Roch. I didn't care what he did with him. From what I gather, you simply took responsibility for him. As if, in fact, he were *your* horse."

"I did what was best for him. To keep him fit and saleable. I assumed you would want to sell him. I'm the one with the contacts in the Three–Day scene." The tone was belligerent, but Bridget had regained her composure.

Thea shrugged. "I may or may not sell him. I have questions I want answered first."

Bridget's eyes narrowed. "What kind of questions? And why can't Michel answer them?"

Thea regarded her coolly. "When I have some answers, I'll tell you what the questions were. And I wanted someone who was, let's say, *disinterested* to ride him. I have nothing against Michel, but his career depends on pleasing owners, telling them what they want to hear. I need someone who is"–, she hesitated, seeking the right word–"free." She nodded, satisfied. "Yes, free."

"Thea, I want you to consider something," Bridget said quickly and in a more conciliatory tone. "I want you to consider donating Robbie to the team. Listen a minute before you say anything. You can donate him to the team and C–FES will give you a tax receipt for the full value of the horse. That way you know you'll have a top rider on him, and you'll get the tax advantage. It's easy, and I can arrange it for you fast."

Thea laughed. "Bridget, you must be joking. I'd end up with only fifty percent of what I paid for the horse in a tax deal like that."

Bridget gestured impatiently. "Don't be naïve, Thea. Naturally we'd value the horse at double what you paid."

"We?"

"I mean whoever we get to evaluate him. Nobody from the barn he's coming from, obviously. But that's no problem. I've done it for others, I can get someone to do it for me." She crossed her arms confidently and waited for a response. She seemed very pleased with herself.

To Bridget the proposal was a piece of sharp thinking, something she was proud to have come up with. Thea wondered at her carelessness in speaking about it so openly. Bridget clearly thought she might go for this scam. Why not? It was only cheating the government. A lot of otherwise honest people had no qualms about that.

Thea knew it was done fairly frequently. It was a great deal–not for the unwittingly subsidizing taxpayer–but for the donor. The donor got the tax write–off for the so–called 'value' of the horse, as well as for all incurred expenses, *and* he got all the prize money. A sweet deal.

And if he actually liked the horse and wanted to have it back one day, he could buy it back for a dollar. At this moment Thea knew of two 'team' horses who hadn't competed in over two years. One was lame and basically retired in his 'owner's' back pasture. But that donor was still enjoying tax benefits and probably would until the horse died (and maybe beyond if no one investigated), and Sport Canada didn't seem to care.

Thea said, "Not a hope, Bridget. I've heard that this is done by some people, and I'm sure you'll consider me quite old–fashioned, but I actually don't think cheating the government is something to boast about at dinner parties or even something to have on my private conscience."

"Do make *some* kind of decision, then, Thea. The horse should be competing," Bridget retorted acidly.

"Wouldn't it be wonderful if the decision was taken out of all our hands, and no more questions had to be answered?" Thea said. She walked over to her horse's stall and looked at him intently. He stretched his lovely, chiseled head towards her, looking for treats or a caress. She raised the tip of her umbrella and poked him, not altogether gently, in the chest with it. He backed off at once with his ears flattened and kicked hard at the back of his stall.

Thea turned back to face Bridget and did not attempt to conceal her pain and anger. "Wouldn't it be convenient if he just dropped dead? That would certainly put an end to all the tension between us, wouldn't it, Bridget?"

For a long moment no one said anything. A gust of rain pattered suddenly, smartly against the window. Outside, quite near now, angry thunder rumbled. Then the silence inside was broken.

"It's amazing, really," Guy said softly." He looked up, seeking Bridget's attention. "You know, I think you were right, Bridget. I think there could be a journal article in this incident, after all…"

CHAPTER FOURTEEN

R UTHIE WAS RUNNING, RUNNING AT A FASTER PACE THAN SHE could hope to sustain for more than a few minutes, but unable to slow down. She was wired, frightened and alarmingly indecisive about what she should do. She hadn't been able to sleep past 5 a.m., so had written a few thank you notes for some belated sympathy cards she had received the past week She had gone to Hy's study to look for stamps. She was going to mail them during her run. She had found the stamps. Applying them her glance fell on the fax machine. What she saw had made her knees go weak and her heart start to pound.

She'd seen it before, this vile anti–semitic cartoon from *Der Sturmer*, reproduced in history books. The spider–Jew, the globe, the drops of blood–it was a product of the most loathsomely evil minds of the twentieth century. That it should be sitting here before her in her brother's house sent a wave of fear and disgust coursing through her whole body.

Her first thought, irrational of course, was *oh I'm so glad daddy isn't here to see this*. Then she reminded herself that he had probably not only seen this particular psychological bombshell, but hundreds of others like it when he was young in pre–war Poland. The originals! The inspiration behind this one. Wasn't that why he had set out, alone, barely out of boyhood, over the opposition of his family, to come to a country where such despicable propaganda wasn't part and parcel of the fabric of daily life?

What should she do? She didn't want even to touch it but she had to know…yes, it had come from *Le Centre*. Hy's instincts had been completely accurate. He had figured there would be graffiti on the house, a swastika. This was simply a more subtle touch, but with the same animus behind it. And safer, because they wouldn't want to approach the house and risk being seen just to paint something on the wall.

Who was behind it, though? The same people who had vandalized the office? The separatists? Somehow it didn't jibe. This was a different order of magnitude on the malevolence scale. But those phone calls starting months ago. Manon had been pretty sure they were from Benoit, so it probably was the same group. Only where would a bunch of disaffected francos pissed off at anglos in general and Jews in particular for buying the Centre come up with this–hate literature? These diabolically vicious reprints were not common currency in rural bookshops and libraries. You didn't just happen on these things. You sought them out. Or you belonged to a group that had access to them, that encouraged you to use them.

It was a paradoxical thing. Ruthie knew that this kind of hate literature, while it appealed to the crudest, most marginalized mentality, was rarely to be found outside of an organized and fairly sophisticated network of hate–mongers. In her heart Ruthie didn't believe that Saint Armand was that sort of place. But she did know exactly how she could find out where in Quebec such places, such cells of activity, existed.

She was breathing hard but couldn't slow down. Should she wait a few more hours and do a bit of detecting on her own? Right now Polo and Roch and Hy's priorities were focused on finding Liam's murderer. This flyer might have some relevance to that. Or it might not. She glanced at her watch and a drop of rain spattered on her wrist. She looked up in surprise. It had been quite sunny when she left the house. Now it looked like more than a shower on the way. As if in corroboration, thunder rumbled and the sky began to darken.

She picked up her pace. She had time to shower and change for the breakfast meeting, and twenty extra minutes, enough for a quick phone call to Jacques Lallouz, her ex–sister–in–law's Significant Other.

A phone call to their Old Montreal condo this early on a Saturday morning might not make her very popular with Marilyn, who loved to sleep in. But Jacques was a pretty cheerful morning type, and, as chairman of the Communities Liaison Committee of Canadian Jewish Congress /Eastern Region, knew more than anybody in Canada about racist activities in Quebec.

It was good to run in this freshening, damp wind, good to do something physically demanding after last night's sedentary hours of tension and alarm. What a weird, unsettling day and evening it had been altogether. She hadn't slept well. She had been annoyed at Polo for accepting Hy's challenge to coordinate this investigation. He shouldn't have. He should have insisted on calling the police in. He should have sided with *me* is what it comes down to, eh Ruthie? And then that little scene outside. Polo's going through some personal crisis, this isn't such a great time for him to be dealing with this, she thought. And what about me? I'm not exactly in top emotional form myself. Oh dear, oh dear. Daddy isn't here, I may end up having to smack my own face…

Fran and Eva Briquemont left the house together. Eva watched while Fran locked the door and tested it. Silently they walked to the polished old Saab and installed themselves, seatbelts carefully fastened, for the short ride to the stable. Thunder growled threateningly in the distance.

As they entered the parking lot and nosed into their usual spot under the generous protection of a spreading red maple tree, Fran cleared his throat and said, "Well, Eva, it is good to have you with me again at the stable. I have missed you."

Eva smiled lovingly at her old partner. "I also." She clasped her hands tightly and made no immediate move to get out of the car. "I am a little nervous, Fran."

"That is quite natural. You wished he was gone away forever." Fran covered her two little twined hands with his own large one. "And so it seems he is. But it was not you who killed him." She nodded obediently, but the apprehensive look on her face did not fade. "He killed *himself*, Eva," Fran said authoritatively, squeezing her tightly balled fists and gazing gravely into her worried eyes.

"You mean he–"

"No, I do not mean he is a suicide. What I am saying is that he was playing a dangerous game. He played with the secrets, the deepest secrets of other people. Some he guessed at and was wrong. Yours, for example. About others perhaps he was right. Either way this is fire he was playing with, Eva." He opened his car door. "And so you see he became consumed in this fire." He stepped out. "What eventually must happen to all those who serve the forces of evil."

He walked around to the other side of the car and gallantly opened the door for his wife. She stepped out and drew her scarf over her hair to protect it from the lightly gusting rain. "So," he said encouragingly, "you will remember to say that I arrived home at 3:30 in the afternoon on Thursday."

"It is difficult for me to lie, Fran. I have to say this to you one final time."

"And I must say to you once again that if we do not look out for each other, we may not expect strangers to do so on our behalf." He tucked her hand firmly under his arm. "If it were of any consequence where I was after leaving the stable, do you think I would ask you? One is not obliged in life to invite suspicion where it is not necessary. In telling them this, you remain still an entirely innocent person."

"Oh," she said tremulously, "I am not sure they will think I am innocent when they see how afraid I am. I'm not good with many people, Fran. With horses I am a different person."

He chuckled and tucked his arm under hers. "My little bird, there is nothing to fear. Be silent and observe the others. Perhaps you will see something of interest. And afterward it will be as it used to be, a normal day, with students, schooling the young horses, all what you love to do"–

"Yes, of course, my dear. I shall think only of that."

✤ ✤ ✤

Sue Parker sat in front of her laptop computer and literally pulled at her lanky hair in frustration. There was just *so much shit* here. She didn't know where to start. She'd thought she had her hands full with the stories she'd dug up on her own. Now here she was with her own stories–the lawsuits–demanding regular follow-ups, then the unexpected and really big story in Florida that she needed time to develop and verify–*I have got to get some time alone with Michel. He knows a ton of stuff about what went down in Palm Beach*–and then out of left field the shit that was going on here at the barn. *Mutilation, vandalism and now a goddam murder.*

She walked over to the dining room table where all her various folders were spread out in a neat grid for cross–referencing. She picked up one marked 'Correspondence.' Correspondence was actually a euphemism for what this folder contained. Most of it was hate mail that the newspaper had passed on to her after her little series of articles appeared, the material on the lawsuits and the op-ed piece panning the industry as a whole.

You ignorant slut. You don't know what you are talking about. There is nothing wrong with horse sport except a few rotten apples just like in any sport or business. You are giving a great sport a bad name. Go fuck yourself.

This advice was not welcome, but at least involved no harm to her person apart from whatever she chose to inflict herself.

How dare you take it on yourself to criticize a whole sport. You must hate trainers. What harm did they ever do to you? My friends and I are going to find out where you keep your horse. You better watch out.

This was simply puzzling. Did they imagine that only a rider was capable of finding out what was going on inside the sport?

You are a first class bitch.

She shivered. What had she gotten herself into? At the last show she'd attended, the organizer had tried to throw her out, had even jostled her about a bit. She'd stood her ground, but she'd been scared.

And if this was the reaction from people indignant about a few lawsuits, what would happen when the Palm Beach wire fraud story broke? If it was just Americans involved, maybe she wouldn't be pilloried, but she knew in her bones that there had to be Canadians in it somewhere down the line. Because not all of the mail was against her. There were hints of some pretty hairy stuff going on in Canada that might somehow be linked to the Florida story.

If you think the crooks who cheat riders in horse sport are bad, wait til you start digging deeper. I can't give you my name, but why don't you look into the fire that burned down Clay Hardacres' barn in Perth with three horses inside? You may find out it wasn't an accident. One of those horses was insured for a lot of money.

She sighed. She felt lonely and afraid, but she knew she mustn't let feelings like that get in the way of her job. She loved journalism. She knew she'd found her life's work, and if she let herself be scared away on her first major assignment, what kind of future would she have?

Intuitively, seeking a morale booster, she fished out a letter from one of her favourite people, Carla Nemic, the first of the plaintiffs she had met to have finished their case. It had arrived just before she left Toronto.

Dear Sue,

*Thought you might be wanting a little cheer about now. You sounded so down on the phone after getting those disgusting anonymous letters. They **would** be anonymous, wouldn't they? Cowards! Just remember that you have a lot of people rooting for you. Just because they don't write letters, they are the silent majority in the sport and they are really happy someone is finally going public with all the stuff that's been swept under the carpet all these years.*

Winning our lawsuit taught me a lot about how important it is never to back down when you're right. And it has taught Joe a lot about life. He went through hell at the shows for two years, as you know. It's tough for a teenager to be isolated like that and still concentrate on competing. The other riders treated him like dirt.

But now that we've won, it's a different story. A lot of them have asked him (in private, of course) how we got started getting evidence. They admit they're too scared to do anything, and they still don't want to be seen being friendly to him, but he's getting a lot more respect. Of course C–FES still hasn't done a darn thing about suspending that

awful BeeBee Rogers as a Technical Delegate or making her resign as
Chairman of the Ontario Jumper Association, but we will never give
up our campaign to put teeth into the so-called Ethics Guidelines.
What a joke they are now!

So what I'm saying is, don't give up. You are not alone! And you
have done a lot of good already. I have sent your articles to Sport
Canada and to my MP, and Leo and I have an appointment to see
one of the bureaucrats next week. See you soon, we hope,

Love from Leo and Joe,

Carla

P.S. I am thinking of starting a new organization as a lobby group
to pressure C-FES to take a stand when their own professionals break
the rules. I am calling it O.U.R. V.O.I.C.E.S. That stands for Organization of Unseated Riders / Voicing Opposition to Insider Corruption
in Equestrian Sport. What do you think?

Sue found herself feeling better already. The Nemics were terrific people. They had become friends. It was one of the perks of her
trade. Leo Nemic's father had faced down Russian tanks in Hun-
gary in 1956. So Leo didn't feel threatened or intimidated by the
tinpot dictators of a mere sport. And this was something Leo and
Carla had discussed with Sue at length.

Why, Sue had asked them one night over dinner in their home
town of Kitchener, Ontario, did they think there were so many
people suddenly making trouble for the sport, pursuing grievances
that would have been swallowed in silence even ten years ago? Leo
had smiled and spread his hands wide, saying, 'It's so obvious, Sue.
Look at the plaintiffs. We're all newcomers to the sport. We have no
awe of these people. And also, we are all educated. Isn't it so?'

It was true. The plaintiffs in every case—she was covering four—
were professionals or business people with MBA degrees or, in
Leo's case, a pharmacist now heading up a chain of drugstores he'd
founded only ten years after immigrating to Canada.

He was one of a new breed of horse owners. People who were
not afraid of lawyers and courtrooms, people who knew their rights,
people lacking the colonial mentality of the past, people who didn't
think getting ripped off, even by the stars of horse sport, should be
accepted as a privilege or even a necessary fact of equestrian life.

She picked up the file marked simply 'Pendunnin.' Now *that* had been a stroke of luck, Thea Ankstrom being in a snit over her horse and nobody so far to talk to about it. Mentioning the horse to Thea had been like poking open a *pinata*. It certainly looked promising. Thea had said she would ask Polo to ride him, to get a disinterested opinion. What a *coup* if there was something wrong with him.

On top of everything, who would have thought that as one of the insiders from C–FES, Thea would not only be willing to talk about her own horse and its problems, but would suddenly start blowing the whistle on all her cronies at the top?

Who knew that even this Young Riders show was a hotbed of corruption? That the whole Ontario jumper team had been hand-picked by the *Chef d'équipe* who just happened to be the committee chair for the whole damn show. Conflict of interest? Just a *tad*. It was trivial compared to some of the other stuff, but if the sponsors of the show found out, it could tip the scales in terms of their global policies in horse sport. But how the hell was she going to approach the redoubtable Marion Smy on this one?

Say, Mrs. Smy, could you give me a comment on how it is that three of the four riders on your Ontario team didn't actually qualify for this show on the horses they're riding in it? I mean, isn't that like against the C–FES rules? And, uh, is it a coincidence that they all train with this famous Rob Taylor, in whose syndicate you happen to be a founding member, and that his son who didn't actually qualify is somehow on the team too? Wanna comment on that, Mrs.Smy?'

Jesus, where do I start?

She looked at her watch and groaned in frustration. She couldn't miss this meeting. Thunder rolled in the distance. Sue jumped up and rummaged in her duffel bag for her poncho. But Roch had made it very clear that he was only including her in order to keep her mouth shut for the time being. Well, that was fair, if she got an exclusive when the story came out. Her heart leaped in anticipation of the professional triumph within her grasp. And anyway, she had already proven she had the makings of a good detective. What true journalist didn't? Maybe she would be the one to find the killer. Oh God, imagine that.

✤ ✤ ✤

Gilles Lefebvre sat on the edge of his bed at home in Brossard and strained, over the howling wind and lashing rain at the window, to hear the conversation his mother was having on the hall telephone with Uncle Roch. The agitation and bewilderment in her voice cut him to the quick. He felt miserable at the thought of what his predicament was doing to his family. But he didn't know what to do. Not yet.

It was obvious, at least, that he couldn't possibly tell his mother the truth. So far he had fed her scraps of partial truths: that he didn't feel he was very good at his job and that it was just a matter of time before Roch fired him, that he wasn't sure he was cut out for a life in the country, that he didn't get along very well with some of the other staff…

How much had Roch told her? Obviously Liam's body must have been found. Had he told her that? Obviously by running away and by refusing to talk to Roch he had made himself a prime suspect. His heart drummed painfully in his chest and he clutched at the bedspread as he imagined the police already on their way to the house to question, or even arrest him. He knew he had to tell somebody about his secret or he would burst. He didn't want it to be the police. There was no way he could make them understand why he had done something so crazy.

He hardly understood it himself. Somehow he had thought at the time that by moving the body he was distancing himself and his relatives from the murder. And if he'd only stayed at the barn and gone about his business as usual, maybe that's what would have happened. But when Roch had pulled the imaginary wire across his tongue, just as the killer must have pulled the wire around Liam's neck, he'd come pretty close to fainting.

And then the humiliation of Benoit and Roch and Jocelyne seeing him fold up like that. The mortification of being sent away to recover, made worse somehow by Uncle Roch's unexpected sympathy. Then crawling off like a little girl to lie down and rest. But instead of resting he'd started to have that panic attack, the sweating, his heart pounding so fast and hard he thought he was going to die, and all he could think of was getting home and being safe within these homely, familiar walls.

Being home and talking to Father Pascal. Which he hadn't been able to do yet. But this morning he had an appointment and if he could only get through the morning, and if only the police didn't come to arrest him, and if only Roch hadn't told his mother the whole story, and if he didn't die of terror and confusion in the meantime, then Father Pascal would tell him what to do.

In Ottawa Marion Smy, Barbara Lumb, Bill Sutherland, and Stuart Jessop ranged themselves around the small arborite conference table in Stuart's office for an informal breakfast meeting. They were conferring this early in the day in order to accommodate Bill Sutherland. Bill had to catch a plane to Calgary whence he would be whisked by limo to Cedar Meadows Equestrian Centre, there to officiate along with several equally high–powered European technical delegates at the enormously important and richly sponsored Intercontinental Royal Dominion Jumper show, which was to begin there in three days' time.

Coffee and bran muffins had been distributed. In spite of the pressures of time, they had begun with the obligatory five minutes of insider gossip. The topic today was, understandably, Jumper gossip. Canadian Jumper talent was to be quite thin on the ground at Cedar Meadows, and C–FES took this fact as an affront. They would look like poor cousins beside the Americans and the Europeans, and on their own playing field. It was embarrassing, to say the least.

"So it's a complete mystery, you say, Bill?" Barbara Lumb trumpeted, leaning forward with her ear cocked and her raddled face screwed up in eager anticipation of his answer.

"That's correct, Barbara," Bill Sutherland blared back, thinking, not for the first time, that in this posture of pained suspense, Barbara bore a striking resemblance to Mr. Magoo. "Michel Laurin withdrew his entries a week ago, and refuses to give any explanation why. He won't leave Saint Armand. Very unlike Michel to miss a chance of going up against Europe's finest."

He looked round the table and directed his next remark generally. "Naturally this weakens the Canadian component of the show considerably. Rob Taylor being out with his injury and now Michel–well, the Cedar Meadows people and their sponsors are *not* very happy campers, as you can imagine."

Marion said, "I call it *most* inconsiderate of Michel to let down the side like that. I am sure that his syndicate members can't be very pleased. Stuart, have you asked Roch what the problem is?"

"Indeed I did, Marion, but Roch was rather evasive on the subject." He cleared his throat. "If I may say so, I don't think Roch would tell us anything of a personal nature about Michel's motives. Not unnatural in a father, of course. And I *do* rather get the impression that something quite–er–*personal* is at the bottom of his decision not to go."

Marion bridled and was clearly prepared to expatiate on the subject of Michel Laurin's disappointing behaviour, but Bill cut her off with a pointed glance at his watch and a restless recrossing of legs.

Marion shuffled her papers and announced, "Well, everything seems to be more or less in order for *our* show, although Roch is *not* very cooperative in returning calls. I don't believe his secretary actually gives him all my messages."

Bill Sutherland was studying his copies of the reports and data pertaining to the Young Riders show. "I notice we have the Jumper technical delegates confirmed, and we have a preliminary drawing of all the Jumper courses with distances, heights and materials properly marked, and they all meet FEI standards and regulations.

"I am quite satisfied with the dressage tests and the judges, all of whom, I see, have signed their contracts. But–" he frowned, riffling through the papers and failing to find what he sought–"as to the Three–Day Event, there is no cross–country map, no details on Roads and Tracks–either Phase A or Phase C–no information on ambulance back–up, no list of jump judges or indeed a whole host of other FEI concerns that we should have in hand by now. Madame Chairman?" He folded his hands and looked at Marion with mild but implacable inquiry.

Marion squirmed and pinkened under his accusing gaze. "I have every confidence that Bridget has the Three–Day under *complete* control, Bill. She always comes through in the end, and she has given me her *personal assurance* that everything will be ready on time. I realize that she can be a bit disorganized on occasion–"

"Disorganized is putting it mildly, Marion," Bill interrupted, now uncharacteristically vexed and impatient. "I spoke to Thea the other night. She's quite distressed at the lack of cooperation she's received at that end. There's no use having all these wonderful computerized schemes if she can't get the data to enter. I've told her–I trust you won't be offended at the liberty, Marion–that she absolutely *must* do a course walk with Bridget today at the latest and inspect the jumps. There can be no question of their failing to meet standards, or I–that is to say the FEI–wash my hands of the show. Fortunately we have a fallback position. I have it from Ron March that Cedar Meadows is well equipped to offer their site in an emergency and have indicated their willingness to step in, should the need arise–which I very much fear"–

Stuart moved hastily to dispel the gathering tension. "How right you are, Bill. There can indeed be no question of any irregularities. I am sure that Thea will manage to get the information she needs today. And if not, well, that's exactly why we're all going down to Saint Armand tomorrow for the final meeting."

Bill Sutherland did not look reassured. He said, "I have given my Cedar Meadows telephone number and central fax number to Thea. I have told her to let me know if she finds even the slightest irregularity at the Three–Day end of things. I am not at all sanguine with regard to Bridget's methods of putting on a competition, and I believe I said as much at the outset." He bent to retrieve his briefcase, stood up, nodded curtly to the table at large, and left.

Stuart sighed glumly. "Marion, I cannot impress upon you too urgently the importance of our maintaining FEI approval for this show. On top of everything else, we would be the absolute laughingstock of the industry if we fail to come through on this one." He ran a finger round his shirt collar. "Moreover, if Quebec loses the show to Alberta, it will be seen in a larger context–it will be a political hot potato, an absolute gift to the separatists, the very last thing we need in our sport at this critical moment."

Marion responded coldly, "You can be quite sure that Thea will not be in correspondence with Bill Sutherland regarding the

Three-Day Event." She gathered her papers and stood them in front of her. "Thea knows where her loyalties lie. And as of tomorrow," she added grimly, chopping the pages smartly into alignment, "I will be there to remind her."

"What's that you say, Marion?" Barbara quavered plaintively, her hand cupped round her ear.

"I SAID I AM GOING TO MAKE SURE THEA DOESN'T FORGET WHO HER FRIENDS ARE!"

"No need to shout, dear, I'm not deaf, you know…"

Manon set the glass of just-squeezed orange juice down on the counter beside the row of pills and capsules: one huge multi-vite, supplementary doses of the anti-free radicals A, C and E, half an aspirin, three Spirulina tablets, plus three capsules of shark's cartilage (why not? who really knows?).

Hy came into the kitchen, freshly shaved and handsomely turned out in Ralph Lauren's latest interpretation of rural chic, but pale and glum. Absent-mindedly he kissed Manon lightly on the cheek. Robotically he drank the juice and downed the supplements.

He cocked his head toward the ceiling and frowned. "Was that thunder?"

"Yes. It's supposed to rain most of the morning, then clear."

"Mm." He studied his orange juice. Then he stared abstractedly at the kitchen table. "Papers?" he asked. Manon looked mildly taken aback at this near-rudeness, but took sympathetic note of his mood.

"I forgot. I'll get them." She was back in a minute, laden with the extra-thick Saturday editions of *The Globe and Mail*, *The Gazette*, and *La Presse*. "Hy, we're an environmental menace." She plopped the stack on the kitchen table.

Hy smiled faintly, but didn't pounce on them as he usually did. "Is Ruthie up? Is she coming to the meeting?"

"Up, ran, showered, blow-dried, dressed, and has been in furious consultation on the phone and writing madly for the last fifteen minutes in your study."

"Mm."

As if on cue, Ruthie appeared in the kitchen with a slim briefcase. "Ready when you guys are," she said with forced brightness. Manon could read the brittleness of mood in her face. You two would be the world's worst poker players, she thought.

The telephone rang. Hy was closest and looked dully in its direction, but made no move to answer it. It rang twice more before Manon sighed, rolled her eyes in mock–exasperation, and snatched the receiver up.

"I'm sorry, he's not available right now," she said in response to Hy's slight shake of the head. "Who? What? A comment? About what? Who did you say wants a comment? What story?…What headlines?… Just a minute…" Manon covered the mouthpiece and whispered urgently to Hy, "It's *The Gazette*. They want a comment from you. It's the lead story, he says. He can't believe you haven't heard about it."

Hy and Ruthie both lunged for the stack of newspapers. Hy yanked *The Gazette* from the bottom of the pile and drank in the front page. First blankness, then puzzlement and finally relieved comprehension chased each other across his features. He waggled his fingers towards the phone and Manon handed the receiver to him, utterly baffled. As he began talking, Manon picked up *La Presse*. Ruthie grabbed *The Gazette* from Hy's now–relaxed hand.

The headline read: MONTREAL MEGA–BUCKS MIRED IN MIAMI SCAM. She skimmed the lead paragraph, which in bold strokes outlined the collapse of a grocery warehousing pyramid scheme in Florida, promoted and manipulated by former Montrealers, involving upwards of four hundred million dollars from Montreal investors.

Hy was saying to the reporter, "…and all I can tell you is that I turned it down and advised my friends against it because after I looked into it I could see that it was too good to be true…"

Ruthie's heart began to race a bit as she read on. The names of the victims leaped at her from the page: Caplan, Lifshitz, Greenblatt, Stein, Cohen, Zimmerman… Almost every name familiar, if not because she knew them personally, at least because they were Jewish. At the same time she was reproaching herself. Her first, irrepressible reaction had been, *Almost all Jews. What will the goyim say?*

"...look, a company doing those huge volumes can't make re-turns of thirty per cent–not legitimately, anyway. I mean, you take a normal sales arbitrage company–there's one in New Jersey I can put you on to–they're pretty nimble and the profit margins are small, so they can cherry pick their buys. And yes, they can give an investor, say, 10–12 per cent on his money..."

How could she think so–well, politically incorrectly was what it was for someone of her lofty, global overview of life. That was *other* Jews' voices, Cote St. Luc, ghettoized Jews, certainly not *hers*. She disowned her response. She was educated. She prided herself on her lack of parochialism, on her many inter–cultural friendships. What did it matter if they were Jews who'd been stung? It wasn't as if they had been found running a heroin ring, after all. It must be because of that horrible cartoon. She wasn't herself...

"...a thirty percent return! So then why did these Florida peo-ple have to come to Montreal for money? But sure, I was curious, and it seemed like so many people were raking it in, so I asked the general partner in Montreal for the financial statements. I wanted to actually see how they were doing it. He showed me *his* statement. Well, hell, I said, that's no use to me. Let me see the statements of the sales company's that's doing the arbitrage. But then he got eva-sive and I knew right away something wasn't kosher."

Four hundred million dollars, they would say. *Do you see how rich they are? And how greedy?* Or maybe, *Aren't Jews supposed to be so smart? How did they all get taken like that? There's more to this than meets the eye...*

"...classic. Absolutely classic Ponzi scheme...every pyramid scheme is really the same old story..."

Ruthie read on. It was appalling. Houses mortgaged, RSSPs raided, money borrowed, capital decimated, golf and tennis club memberships dropped, private school educations forfeited, retire-ments deferred, ignorant wives dumbfounded...There would be divorces, suicides maybe. Combined Jewish Appeal would have its work cut out for it this year.

Her heart beat faster. *There but for the grace of–well, not God, but fate...* and she thought with fervent gratitude on her children's behalf of Hy's conservative administration of her own secure and steadily growing portfolio and, of course, her half interest in *Tissus Clar–Mor…You'll be quite a catch*, Marvin used to say when the medication made him high and everything seemed hazy and funny to him. *Oh don't don't don't…But it's true, ziess…*

"…all the due diligence in the world is useless if you don't check out the principals… I'd be very surprised if their personal record is clean… On the record? a quote? Well, I guess it's what I just said. You want to check out the principals if you're investing in something. Because it's their characters that will determine what kind of deal you're getting yourself into."

CHAPTER FIFTEEN

THEY SAT AMONGST THE DEBRIS OF GLASSES, COFFEE CUPS AND plates of buttery toast ends in the empty restaurant, Polo poring with quiet absorption over the scabrous cartoon, Ruthie restively scanning his face for the nuances of feeling underneath.

Ruthie had waited until after the meeting. Now they were alone. Ruthie had decided to show it first to Polo to see whether he thought there was any point in burdening Hy without a specific target for his anger. And since she was eager to have Polo's opinion, she could not account for the profound resentment she was suddenly experiencing in witnessing his fascinated contemplation.

"Have you ever seen this kind of stuff before, Polo?"

"Nope."

He didn't look up. Ruthie waited impatiently for him to say something else. But he just kept looking, frowning, lips compressed in a meditative line. Why wasn't he waxing indignant on her and Hy's behalf? Why wasn't he saying out loud that he was repelled, morally outraged? For this was what it seemed necessary for her to hear from him. Yet it appeared to be, for him, just another vexing tangent to the general mystery, an odd–shaped fragment in a 1000–piece jigsaw puzzle.

Ruthie felt vulnerable, anxious and disoriented. Part of her longed to flee this too–open rural spill of undefended dwellings. Her thoughts turned westward, with renewed appreciation for the protective anonymity of the city, the tall, solid, jammed–together fortresses of brick and stone in lower Westmount, her once and future home.

Ruthie's thoughts still resonated with the story in the morning paper and her own defensive reaction to it. The public story of that business scam–*Jews Jews Jews*–and this terrible private intrusion–it was a bad psychological cocktail. She had not wanted to face the turbulence of her own feelings in realizing that she was either a hated and possibly hunted creature or an envied and resented one. The cold wavelets of fear lapping at her gut during her run that morning were now great rolling breakers beating hard against the porous wall of reason she had erected against them.

Overnight her cosmos had divided itself into 'them' and 'us'. This had nothing to do with the environment she lived in, of course. Ruthie knew her history. She was engaged in the collective cultural life of her people. She knew she lived in a Golden Age of tolerance and freedom unprecedented in Jewish history. Naturally she followed the escalating progress of global anti–Zionism and anti–semitism (almost invariably one and the same, of course) with concern and apprehension. But that was a mental process. It had nothing to do with what was churning inside her now.

To be confronting racial hatred in a personal way for the first time at such an advanced stage of life–it was an odd and very unsettling feeling. But why didn't Polo speak? Why wasn't he *connecting* with her fears and emotions? Why wasn't he offering some kind of *comfort*?

Ruthie felt herself suddenly alienated, detached from Polo. Mysteriously she took against him. There he sat, a cool, blond stranger (a professional horseman, of all absurd things), and a *stranger,* and some deep tribal impulse counseled retreat from intimacy with him.

"What do you think, Polo?" She heard frostiness in her voice.

Did *he*? "Or rather what would you think if you got that over *your* fax machine?"

"Assuming I was Jewish? I'd be scared…angry…frustrated… mostly scared, I think. All the feelings we want to spare Hy."

"Yes, well let's assume you're not." now she heard the edge, the uninvited sarcasm in her voice.

If he noticed, he didn't betray it. Impassively he considered her suggestion. "Not? I guess…I guess my first thought would be, well, somebody really hates Jews…and then maybe—why are they sending this to me? Do they think I'm Jewish?"

"And you'd feel—what? angry? scared? …maybe you'd feel *insulted*? That you should be thought to be Jewish, I mean…?" There could be no mistaking the accusation in her voice. *What is happening here? Why am I saying this?*

Startled, his eyes flew up from the page and, meeting the misgiving in hers, the spark of disbelief exploded into a flame of anger. "I'm feeling pretty fucking insulted right now, *ziess*," he said in a low but feeling tone.

"You mustn't use that language with me!" she snapped.

"Yeah, well I'm sorry if my *stablese* has 'bruised your shell–like ears', but if you were a guy, I'd have done more than *bruise* them for accusing me of that kind of shit."

"It was natural for me to wonder," Ruthie protested. "I watched you. You didn't seem to think there was anything so terrible about that piece of filth. You're not Jewish. How can you possibly understand what it *feels* like–"

–*You're not trying to learn. You're a bad student.*

–*I am so trying. Maybe you're just a bad teacher.*

–*And maybe you're just plain stupid…*

He leaned forward, gripping the table edges. For a frightening second, Ruthie thought he might overturn it. He spoke quietly in a voice she'd never heard before–raw, male, implacable, "*Fais plus de ta maîtresse d'école.* It's finished, the pretty little schoolroom. I'm all grown up now. Nobody tells me what to say or think."

He sat back in his chair, but his face was hard and closed. She shrank from his antagonism. It was disproportionate. Wasn't it? She started to let him know this, but he held up his hand.

"I'm grown up now, Ruthie," he repeated. "I live in the real world. It's full of hypocrites and creeps. You just don't have a clue. Your whole life you've been surrounded by people who made you think the world turns around you, and that it's so goddam important to share every little feeling, every little thought, every little worry. And everything that came out of your mouth was special. *Ruthie's so smart. Ruthie's so sensitive. Ruthie's so good.* And suddenly somebody's calling your brother dirty names, so you think the world's coming to an end and everyone has to drop what they're doing to hold your hand. You know, I hate to tell you, but where I come from, people would say you've got High Class Worries, lady."

He saw he had got to her. She looked furious, but embarrassed and miserable too. And yet she had been the one to strike the first match. He couldn't stop yet. He still felt like cracking a blackboard. One final shot. "Part of you will always be *daddy's little princess*, eh *ziess*?"

"*Ohh!*"

Oh fuck, why did I say that, she's going to cry...

"And maybe part of *you* will always be just a...just a...." her voice shook and her face flamed, because she couldn't manage to say it, and couldn't think of anything to replace it with.

"...just a..."

Maudit. This has to end.

"–an ignorant *habitant* from St. Henri? It's okay, I've been called worse."

"*Ohh!*"

Polo had meant it as a joke. But Ruthie's eyes were brimming and hot with shame. They stared at each other in an agony of suspense to see what was going to happen next.

"I never meant–" she finally whispered–

"It was a joke–" he murmured.

Thank you, her eyes said. She drew a shaky breath and then, to the command of some invisible baton, they both chose laughter at the same instant. It was precarious and uneasy laughter, but it threw a bridge over the terrible fissure. They were safe. They were quits. Still, they knew now that there would always be a scar in a place they had once assumed was solid rock.

Returned to herself at last, Ruthie took a deep breath and shook her head. "Look, I'm sorry," she muttered. "I–I know it seems like paranoia. This whole business seems to have done something to my judgment. This place–it's so beautiful, but there's something evil going on." She shivered, and pulled her woolly cardigan tighter.

"And today," she went on in a murmur, "knowing one of them was probably lying, but not knowing who–I don't know–it's that nothing in this place is what it seems to be somehow. And you said it yourself last night. Anybody is capable of anything under the right circumstances. I said it wasn't true, but maybe it is. Seeing that–" she gestured brusquely to the paper in front of him–"it was upsetting. Not an excuse, I know that…" she trailed off miserably.

Polo didn't absolve her in words, but a softened glance of understanding had replaced wariness. He rolled up the paper and tucked it into the pocket of his Australian driver's coat, hanging over the back of the chair.

"No problem," he finally said, lightly, with no discernable emotion. "Let's move on. It wasn't Jean–Claude Desrochers who did the office, I don't know if I told you. He was and still is in Quebec City. He really is there and didn't know a thing about the damage. Either that, Roch says, or he suddenly took acting lessons. Not possible. Roch's known him a long time.

"That brings us back to Gilles and Benoit again," Polo went on. He shook his head impatiently. "Benoit, okay, but I still can't put it together with Gilles…What about you? Got any theories yet?"

She cleared her throat and responded tentatively, still embarrassed. "About the horse business, no. Horses are definitely 'not my onions.' But the office attack and the fax–well, actually, I think I do. Or at least an orientation with potential. I spoke to Jacques Lallouz from Canadian Jewish Congress this morning. He thinks it could be serious. An indication of a cell, a racist network, maybe. That didn't help my mood any, by the way. Again–no excuse…. But do we tell Hy?"

Polo drummed the bowl of his coffee spoon rhythmically on the table and stared moodily across the room and out the far window towards Hy's house. In the quiet of the restaurant they could hear from the courtyard the steady glug of water pouring out of the gutters into rain barrels that served as water troughs for the horses on turnout.

Polo considered the pressures burdening Hy already, and he considered his friend's not entirely perfect state of health, and he considered especially Hy's heightened sensibilities on the issue of anti–semitism, not unnatural in the only son of a man whose entire family had been wiped out in the Holocaust.

Finally he said, "I don't see it as being very constructive right now, do you? I mean, you've already stolen his mail," he smiled wryly at her, "now it's just a question of how long before you give it back."

Ruthie smiled back gratefully, relieved to be forgiven and a target for teasing once again. Seeking a neutral subject as a breather, she looked out the near window into the courtyard, and cried, "Oh look. He's so sweet."

'He' was 'she', Popote, the shaggy little blind pony, now marching stiffly but eagerly through rapidly widening puddles in the direction of a beloved voice. Daisy the goat danced nimbly around her. A second later Michel, his riding gear covered by a split–backed waxed riding poncho, came into view, a handful of carrot bits outstretched. The pony's worn teeth found the treats and she nuzzled her dripping face into Michel's stomach while Daisy complained noisily at his interference with her companion. Relaxed and laughing, Michel pulled affectionately at his pet's hairy ears, scratched her flaccid neck and even bent to kiss the top of her soaking wet head.

"It's a side of Michel most people don't see," Polo said with obvious approval. "He's pretty closed up around most humans, and he's all business with his competition horses."

"You've known him his whole life, haven't you?"

"Yeah. We get along pretty well. He's shy like I was, and ambitious–like I was."

"So then he's the opposite of his father, in fact."

"Yeah. People, and making things happen are Roch's bag. You'd never catch him mooning over a horse, even if it was his very first, like this one was for Michel."

"What about you? Do you moon over your horses?"

"Not hor*ses* plural, but I did once. I was crazy about The Grand Panjandrum."

"Oh, *Hamish*. He was beautiful. No wonder."

"Oh, it wasn't his beauty. Looks aren't much to a competition rider."

"What then?"

"Hamish had the most heart I ever knew in a horse. Plus he was a hundred percent honest. *And* he had great natural athleticism. You often get two out of the three in a horse, but all together–very rare."

"Honest…That's a funny word to use about an animal."

"If you rode, you'd understand."

"I thought it was so odd that daddy gave him that name, didn't you?"

Polo laughed softly. "It was typical Morrie, that's for sure."

–He should have a stable name, Morrie. Panjandrum's too long.

–I thought about that. We'll call him Hamish.

–Hamish? Isn't that a Scottish name?

–Yeah, but in Yiddish it means someone who's a good guy, comfortable, easy to live with. A person who likes his home. It'll be our secret. You can tell people your mystery sponsor is Scottish. MacGregor, McDuff, McCoy, McGoy…whatever you want. 'Til you make the team. Then watch their faces when they find out…'

"It went as well as could be expected, didn't you think?" Ruthie asked, meaning the meeting, which had been attended by everyone they wanted except Benoit and Gilles.

The self–condemning absence of the two stable boys had worked out to their advantage. With Benoit and Gilles to focus blame on, nobody else felt particularly threatened, and volunteered information about their movements on Thursday afternoon and evening with no obvious signs of guilt or constraint. This was pretty much what Polo had expected. If the killer lurked amongst this group, he or she had had ample time to think about an alibi or a reasonable cover story.

It had been readily established that Liam had been last seen Thursday afternoon out on the cross–country course patching the soggy footing at jumps 9–A and 9–B (the Chevrons) with wheelbarrow loads of sand borrowed from the jumper arena mound. Bridget admitted talking to him, giving further instructions at about four p.m. when she left in her truck to meet with Roch in his office about stabling needs for the show. Roch confirmed this. When she went back out on the course around five, she said, Liam was gone, and so was the wheelbarrow. When Roch asked her if she had told him to clear out, that he was fired, she had appeared mystified. Nobody admitted to 'giving him the push,' as Benoit had put it to Roch.

Where Liam had been situated was out of sight from the road, indeed at the farthest remove possible, deep into the woods. It was common knowledge that he was spending most afternoons working on the course. Nobody's schedule was so tight that they couldn't slip away for fifteen minutes. Trainers, competitors, students, vets, managers: in a stable timetables are so highly individualized, nobody pays much attention to what anyone else is doing.

Michel, for example, riding down to the warm-up ring to school a horse as he claimed, could just as easily have hacked around the cross-country course and met up with Liam, on purpose or by chance. Hacking out wasn't unusual if the horse was fussy or ring-stale, or had been schooled hard for several days running.

Hy could have ridden out on the cross-country course instead of through the trails above his own barn as he normally did. And he could have left for Montreal later than he said. There'd be no traffic going *into* Montreal in the late afternoon. And he hadn't arrived at his mother's house before seven.

Roch could have gone into town for supplies and whipped onto the course in his truck instead on any pretext whatever. A rough service track, wide enough for a car or truck, necessarily wound through the course, sometimes paralleling the jump course, sometimes wandering off through more hospitable terrain, but always within easy walking distance of the next jump. No one would have noticed a vehicle out on the course because it was such an ordinary sight.

The same held true for Gilles or Benoit, Guy or even Fran. They all drove around the site for one reason or another at various times of the day. In fact, however, Guy said that at four o'clock he was in his car coming back from St. Hyacinthe where he was checking data at the vet school for a monograph he was writing. He went directly to the house and worked on his reef tank from then until dinner. He had been oblivious to all else.

Fran claimed to have finished his last lesson at three and left the barn for home. His wife confirmed his arrival home shortly after, although her voice shook noticeably in the telling. But this seemed natural because she was known to be shy and rather timid. Her English was weak and her French not much better. She and Fran spoke German together.

Thea said she had been working at her computer all afternoon, but when Bridget claimed to have telephoned her from Roch's office (confirmed by Roch), she remembered she had taken a break and gone for a walk. Nobody challenged her. Nobody had seen her. Which meant that she was lying–or that she had gone for a walk and forgotten, that is to say it meant nothing at all.

Jocelyne's time was her own once the horses were looked after, as long as Michel didn't need her to set up jumps for a schooling. As it happened, his last horse of the day was being schooled on the flat, so he didn't need her. She might have been in the stable yard, cleaning out the horse van, as she claimed, or she might not.

It would be impossible to question every person who walked in and out of the barn about their movements at any given minute or hour. In a barn the routines are either completely invariable–feeding, mucking–out–or completely individual. Time is an elastic notion in a stable. And even feeding time, rigorously observed–was just a fifteen minute operation. Before or after…

Really the meeting had only served to give notice that the body had been found, that the police were not being called in yet, and that everyone present could expect to be interviewed at length in the course of the day. Polo emphasized that nobody in particular was under suspicion, that they were only trying to accumulate as much information as possible to keep publicity to a minimum in the long term. This explanation was accepted at face value. Everyone pledged their cooperation with varying degrees of enthusiasm and confidence.

The whole tone of the meeting had been curiously dry and detached. It was, Polo realized, because the victim in the case was so peripheral to the lives of the people here. He was–*déraciné*–

disconnected, not just from his cultural roots as the French word usually implied, but alienated from everyone here who knew him. Nobody had *cared* about him, to put it kindly. They had thought him gone from their lives forever, so the fact that he was dead made little additional impact.

That Liam had been tolerated by all with feelings ranging from neutrality to dislike to hatred made the meeting seem like a year-end inventory at *Tissus Clar-Mor*, as Hy had put it. And even without his encouragement, Polo noticed, everyone was impatient and more than ready to go on with their routines. As though nothing of any importance had occurred. A sad requiem, he thought, even for a loser like Liam.

They had split up their functions. Roch said he would follow up on Benoit and Gilles. Polo said he would talk to Michel, Jocelyne, Guy, and Bridget in the course of the day. He added (without saying why) that he had made a date with Thea later on in any case. Sue Parker had not been assigned any particular role and maybe, Polo now mused, that was a mistake. Left to her own devices, she might stir things up in the wrong places.

Ruthie had insisted on taking part. Polo suggested talking to Fran, and Eva too if she wanted. Hadn't Jocelyne said something about her being afraid of Liam? 'You can show off your fancy French with him or your German. Either way he'll appreciate it instead of thinking you're a snob.' What Polo didn't add was that he thought Fran was 'safe' for Ruthie to talk to. He was a long shot as the killer in Polo's mind. Too old, not strong enough.

Caroline had cleared and cleaned the tables and shoved them back into their normal alignment. Boarders were arriving in singles and groups for pre-or post-ride breakfasts. Polo and Ruthie moved to a table at the back and Ruthie started to walk him through the notes she had made during the phone call with Jacques Lallouz.

"The report isn't going to be published until August," she said, "but the proofs are ready now. It's going to be called "Violence and Racism in Quebec." The committee's made up of a whole group of interested organizations: Congress, of course, and the *Commission des droits de la personne du Québec,* and the *Centre maghrébin de recherche et d'information,* amongst others. It's sponsored by the

Department of Multiculturalism and Citizenship. Jacques says the research is first–rate.

"Let's see," she said, flipping the pages of her steno pad back and forth, "so where should I start…? Well, there's a lot of stuff in the report that's either plain old common sense or stuff most educated people know. Like that poverty and unemployment and political uncertainty and the lack of action by political leaders all contribute to making people feel marginalized, and that's why they blame minorities and immigrants for their problems. No big surprise there.

"Then there's all kinds of stuff about racism in schools and how it can be prevented, blah, blah, initiatives the police can take, which by the way they're doing a lot of, only you'd never know it from the bad press the police here get, and stuff on media responsibility, blah, blah.

"Okay, but here's where it really gets interesting–or at least I think it does for this situation. See, they pose the question of whether Quebec is actually a racist society. Not whether there are racist incidents, 'cause there are all kinds of them. So what else is new? There are racist activities going on all over Canada, but somehow people seem to have this idea that Quebec is more–you know–*inherently* racist than other parts of Canada?"

Polo sighed. "I always wondered if that was really true. I always thought we–French–Canadians, I mean–were just more up front and open about our feelings and prejudices."

"Oh, Polo," Ruthie sighed, her equilibrium restored, "calling yourself French–Canadian is *so–o* old hat."

"Old hat?"

"*Vieux jeu.*"

"What am I then?"

"You're q*uébécois*. You've been *québécois* for ages now."

"Oh yeah? Who says?"

"Oh, come on, Polo, I don't believe you're that out of touch with what's politically correct here. Don't you even read the news?"

"Ruthie, you have no idea how out of touch with *everything* most horse people are. I mean, I spend half my time travelling in the States and the rest of Canada and Europe, and even when I'm not, my contacts are almost all horse–related. Trust me, these people never, but *never,* think about provincial politics. Unless it's a question of whether you can get better grants for shows from the province or from the feds.

"And every competition rider I know who's serious thinks internationally. You think Michel considers himself *québécois*? No way. Maybe when he's buttering up his syndicate or for stories in *La Voix de L'Est*. But you listen to him in English language interviews. It's Mr. Canada then. Because the big show sponsors are all national or global–banks, insurance companies, brokerage firms, car companies…"

"It just has such a quaint, *folklorique* ring these days, 'French–Canadian'…"

"Don't care. That's my story and I'm sticking with it." He gestured to her notes. "Okay, go on. What's the scoop? *Are* we more racist?"

"Well, *that's* what I find so interesting. This report makes a distinction between *racism* and *xenophobia*. And it looks like *les québécois*–are more *xenophobic* than racist."

"Meaning…?"

"Sorry. Well, it means a fear of strangers. And you see, *fear* is the operative word here. *Afraid* of others is not a great thing to be, but it's a more benign form of *true* racism–the neo–nazis and all–which is based on a feeling of *superiority* over other races. For example, the Ku Klux Klan and Heritage Front, the worst of the racist groups, have never really taken hold in Quebec. Probably partly because of the language barrier. But also because racism in Quebec, I mean racism as a *philosophy,* has only been really active amongst the intellectuals–I mean, *Le Devoir* up until the sixties was sometimes viciously anti–semitic–but it never took serious hold in the popular imagination, the really bad stuff, the stuff that leads to violence.

"Now look at these two columns I drew up, and you can see how the one is different from the other."

Polo took her pad and perused the two scribbled lists. Under the column headed 'Racist', she had cryptically jotted: 'imported!' (this was double–underlined), 'feeling of superiority', 'segregation of groups (white supremacy)', 'recruitment of youths *en mal d'identité*', 'promotion of racial conflict'. Examples: Longitude 74

(Mtl section of KKK), Aryan Resistance Movement, *Le Mouvement des Jeunesses Aryennes de Ste Foy.*

Under 'Xenophobic' she had scrawled: 'indigenous!', 'defensive rather than aggressive', 'insecurity', 'focus on *l'Autre* as intruder rather than inferior', 'fear of cultural and economic takeover by strangers (immigrants, *l'Autre*)', 'fear of disappearance'. Examples: *Mouvement Pour La Survie de la Nation, S.O.S. Genocide* (tied to *Carrefour de la Resistance Indépendentiste), Le Mouvement pour une Immigration Restreinte et Francophone.*

"Well?" she asked eagerly.

Polo shook his head. "It's interesting, and it makes sense, but what does it prove for this affair?"

Ruthie was disappointed. "Don't you see? It looks very much like we have two distinct things going on here. We have the radical separatists–they're the xenophobes and did the office stuff–and then we have the racists who sent the hate literature!"

"But if the cartoon was faxed from the office, it would be an impossible coincidence if it were two different groups."

"I'm not saying it was two different *groups*," Ruthie explained as patiently as she could, "I'm saying there were two different *sensibilities* at work."

Polo understood with a slight kick–in of adrenaline. "You mean the hate literature is *imported*–Liam–and the office stuff is local."

"Yes, yes, yes. And Liam sent the fax *before* he was bumped off"–

"Whoa!"

"What?"

For answer he turned and took out the rolled paper from his coat. Smoothing it flat, he pointed to the line of computerese on the top. He was sorry to see disappointment shroud the rosy animation he had been admiring in her face.

"The time," she said dully.

"Yeah, it doesn't work. Not by a long shot. And that's what had me wondering so long before. I mean, Liam had to be dead by early evening latest. So this thing was sent by the vandal. And it was sent at 4:17 a.m. Why did the vandal choose that time? Why so close to dawn and take the chance of some early bird coming in?"

"*Merde.*"

"Hey, don't be discouraged. I mean, I like your theory. Just because Liam didn't send the fax, it doesn't mean it didn't come from him in spirit. He could have had a collaborator." And he thought again of Jocelyne's discomfort around Liam's relationship with Benoit and Gilles. *Like some kind of weird club, she had said...merde, it always came back to Gilles....*

"So we're back to Square One."

"Maybe not." He rolled the fax paper up again and returned it to his pocket. He stood up. "Lots to do, Ruthie. We better get started."

Ruthie nodded, but made no move to leave. Her chin propped in her hand, she watched Polo shrug into his raingear, sighed and looked gloomily into the dreary courtyard. Jocelyne was leading the pony and the goat back into the stable. In a few seconds she returned leading a big horse in a waterproof cooler. She was unhooking the lead shank from his halter when Ruthie suddenly bolted upright, knocking over her chair, and clapped a hand on Polo's sleeve as he was heading for the door.

"The dog!" she cried. "It was the dog!"

Puzzled, Polo followed her hypnotized stare into the courtyard, where Fleur was capering at Jocelyne's feet, wagging her tail in yet another futile bid for her mistress's attention.

"Fleur?" he asked. "What about her?"

"Whose is she?"

Polo nodded out to Jocelyne. "Hers. Why?"

"I saw her. Not Jocelyne. I mean I saw the dog. Yesterday morning. When I was out jogging. It was the bandanna made me remember."

"*Et alors?*"

"In a *truck*, Polo. I saw her in a truck. *Leaving* Saint Armand. Early, early in the morning. *Too early for anyone to be working.*"

They stared at each other in wild conjecture.

"Who was driving?" Polo urged. "What make of truck?"

"Oh, Polo," Ruthie wailed, "I'm such a crummy detective. I didn't *see*. I haven't got a *clue*..."

CHAPTER SIXTEEN

S UE WAITED PATIENTLY FOR HER CHANCE TO SPEAK TO MICHEL alone. She wandered up and down the long aisle where tacking, untacking and grooming procedures were in full progress amongst the diehard boarders willing to ride in the rain. They worked and chatted to the accompaniment of oldies music blaring out of an ancient radio slung from a nail over the bulletin board.

... it's been the ruin of many a poor boy, and Gawd, I know I'm one...

Sue was prepared to wait until after his first or second ride or until he took a bathroom break, whichever came first. But she was determined to speak to him. Right now Jocelyne was finishing tacking up his first mount of the day, one of the warmbloods. Michel had shed his poncho in favour of a white nylon windbreaker that sported a bold red maple leaf and the Canadian Team logo.

Then Sue got a lucky break. Just as Michel was about to swing aboard, Jocelyne handed him the wrong whip, it seemed, a short, thick one. He shook his head at it and, when Joc turned toward the tack room, he stopped her and handed her the reins. Sue followed him.

Another lucky break. The tack room was empty. Sue slipped inside and quietly shut the door, eyes admiringly fixed on Michel's tapered muscular back and taut, defined buttocks as he rummaged through his tack box. She leaned noiselessly against the door and planted both feet solidly in front of her. Would he lay hands on her to force his way out? Sue doubted it, but felt a little faint as he straightened up and turned, a long, thin dressage–type whip in hand.

Surprised by the sight of her, Michel uttered a wordless sound of exasperation, and swished the whip against his tall boots in eloquent, elegant reproach. Sue's heart began to pound.

"Let me pass, please," he said neutrally.

"I have to speak to you, Michel," Sue said quickly, cursing the tremor in her voice.

"I'm busy," he answered curtly. It was a flat rejection with a hint of warning.

Sue was nervous and afraid, but weirdly, a part of her mind was coolly and independently working up a riff for her friends at school.

Okay, so picture it. It's Harlequin Romance time. And trust me, Fabio is road kill next to this guy. Okay, here's me pressed up against the wall. A windowless room. Two feet away is this gorgeous stud, gleaming cat's eyes, dark Byronic curls tumbling over his forehead, full, sensual lips–got the picture?–in these, like, skintight britches, black leather riding boots and–ooh–a long, long whip. Everywhere you look there's leather straps, hooks, chains. He's coming toward me. I'm panting, terrified, trembling with emotion...

Michel's emerald eyes and thick black lashes were stunningly near to her. She could smell his breakfast coffee. She felt sweat trickling down her stomach. *Oh, that's very attractive, Sue. Sweaty bodices are quite the rage this year, I hear.*

"Please, Michel, I have to know what went down in Palm Beach. I know you were there. You can even tell me off the record. I just have to know. *Please!*"

"I don't know what you're talking about." Anger was creeping into his tone. She didn't have much time.

"Yes, you do. Your horses were stabled right next to hers. To the Panaiotti girl the FBI are after. Your friend–your girlfriend–"

"She was never my girlfriend!"

"That's not her story, Michel. The buzz in Palm Beach was that you two were just a step away from being engaged. That her father wanted to sponsor you. People here at the barn are saying you're going to New York."

He was furious, but scared too, Sue could see. He glanced quickly around the small room, as if another exit might magically appear.

"My private life is my own business," he said tightly. "I don't know how that story started."

"It doesn't matter how it started, Michel. The more they investigate, the more your name will be associated with hers," Sue pressed, leaning harder against the door.

Michel said nothing to this, but his face darkened. "Let me pass," he growled softly. He reached out with the handle end of the whip and nudged her arm with it. But it was a half–hearted gesture. He looked unsure of what to do. His eyes shifted away and down. "Move, Sue," he almost pleaded. "Jocelyne will come looking for me in a minute. You'll be embarrassed."

He's the one that's embarrassed, Sue thought. He's tough on his horses, but he won't beat up on a woman. That's nice at least. It was now or never. She shivered and plunged.

"*Mr. Lullabye*! What do you know about Mr. Lullabye, Michel?" *Bingo!*

Fear has a smell, kind of like smoldering wet wool, Sue thought wildly. Michel stood transfixed, his olive skin draining to a sickly khaki. Sue's mouth rounded in an O of fascinated empowerment. *I did this to him*! Wow!

There was a discreet knock at the door. Jocelyne! "Michel?"

"Listen, Michel," Sue burst out in low, but rapid–fire delivery, "you're better off talking to me. I'm sympathetic. I'm Canadian. I have a shred of respect left for human dignity. When the American journalists get hold of you, they'll tear you apart like a pack of dogs."

She saw him waver. His eyes flicked to the door and Jocelyne's repeated, puzzled query. One last pitch and he was hers.

"I know you didn't do anything wrong, Michel. But you know stuff. Believe me, you'll feel better when you've told someone. No priest can help you with this one. But maybe I can. Let me try at least."

He passed his tongue across dry lips. Another knock, more insistent. He swallowed hard and nodded. Immediately Sue moved away from the door and let Jocelyne in. The girl's eyes flew back and forth between them. Michel spoke low and rapidly to her. Sue blasted her decision to drop French in high school.

Through the open door the wail of the radio could be heard.

Let the sun shine, let the sun shine in, the su–un shine in…

Polo passed Michel and Sue in the corridor as they headed for the restaurant. Michel didn't meet his eye. He was clearly tense. And the girl had the look of a jungle cat returning to her lair with fresh kill. She was on to something. *Maudite merde.* There were too many people involved in this thing.

He found Jocelyne removing the ankle boots from a clean horse, with no sweat marks, and a dry, unused mouth.

"Why isn't Michel riding?"

Jocelyne should have been irritated at the breach of Michel's routine, Polo thought, but she was in a surprisingly sunny mood.

"Oh," she shrugged, smiling indulgently, "he said he promised that journalist an interview about his glory days as a Young Rider, and he wanted to get it over with so she wouldn't bug him all day."

From the look he had seen on Sue's face, Polo knew there was no goddam way she was interviewing him for the show. "Look," he said, "I wanted to talk to you for a few minutes. I guess you have some free time right now, eh?"

"Yep. About an hour", she said. "Just let me put this beast away." She was positively *chirping,* Polo noted suspiciously.

She invited him into her new bedroom, Liam's vacated cubicle. She had added a battered stool to the room for use as a night table and she offered this to Polo while she plopped on the bed, one leg tucked up beneath her. She looked at him expectantly, an air of eager candour to the fore. Polo placed the stool opposite her where he could see her face and its reactions plainly.

"Where does Fleur stay at night?" he asked.

Jocelyne blinked in surprise. It was not the question she was expecting. "Fleur? Fleur lives here, at the barn. Why?"

"Is she locked up somewhere? Who lets her out in the morning?"

Jocelyne shrugged dismissively. "I don't lock her up. Fleur is supposed to be the watchdog. At night I think she's in the office on a blanket," she indicated with a slight sideways jerk of her head. "And whoever gets here first lets her out, I guess."

"What would she do if a stranger came in?"

"Not much except bark, really. I mean, she wouldn't attack anyone or anything. And she wouldn't do anything if it was one of the regulars."

"Would she go anywhere with someone? In a car? In a truck?"

Jocelyne became wary and her eyes narrowed. "What are you getting at?"

"She was seen in a truck early yesterday morning. Around 5:30." He watched her closely. She looked tense, and her merry air had fallen away.

"Well, it wasn't with me, that's for sure," she said firmly. She added promptly, "Fleur's pretty friendly. She'd go with anybody she knew." Her eyes held his without wavering. "It wasn't me." Then she seemed to remember something and her earlier sunny mood surfaced again as she added, "And it wasn't Michel either." *Ask me, ask me*, her eyes said.

"Okay, now I have to ask you about where you were and what you did Thursday night, Joc," he said, then adding after a deliberate pause, "and early yesterday morning, too." He watched her face intently.

This had been what she was expecting and hoping for. She was delighted with this line of inquiry, there was no mistaking the glow of triumph he had evoked. "Well, let's see," she said, trying very hard to appear as if the question were unexpected, something she needed to reflect upon.

It was no use. The words came tumbling out, pre-sealed, stamped and addressed. "Thursday. Okay, I left the stable at the usual time, after the horses were fed and rugged for the night. I got home about 5:30. I was going to make some hot dogs and beans.

Then Michel called. He wanted to talk about something, but he didn't say what. So I invited him over."

"Hadn't you just left him at the barn?" Polo asked.

"Yeah, but there were people around. This was something he wanted to talk about in private." Her eyes were dancing. She was thrilled to have this story to tell, Polo could see. Couldn't wait to get on with it.

"Okay, so Michel comes over at–six, say?"

"Yeah, about like that. And we had dinner. And talked a bit, and–" at this point she half lay down on the bed, propped up on one elbow, and cocked her head coquettishly at Polo. She smiled meaningfully and cast her eyes prudishly floorward in an unconscious parody of a happily deflowered virgin.

"And–" for a scarifying second Polo thought her vampy smile and half–closed eyes were for his benefit, an *invitation,* and he felt his face freeze in astonished recoil, then realized that she was only enacting an explanation too delicious for mere words.

"And–you're saying–Michel stayed? Stayed the night with you?" He hoped she hadn't noticed the accent on the 'you'. He really couldn't help it. It was just inconceivable to him.

"Yes!" Jocelyne crowed. "The whole night. We were together the whole night. We had breakfast together and went to the barn separately, in two cars. Me at my usual time, and he came later like always. So no one would know!" A proud smile and an excited flush lit up her insipid features. She was, for this moment, pretty. Polo remembered the sweet, eager girl she had been at fifteen when she started grooming for Michel. She was almost that same girl again. Could it possibly be true, what she said?

As if reading his thought, and humiliated by his skepticism, Jocelyne took up the challenge against him. And like most well–intentioned, but bad liars, she went one step too far. Jutting out her chin, smugly sure of herself, she cried, "Ask Michel! Go ask him! He'll tell you exactly the same thing. Exactly!"

Oh, you poor little fool. Of course he'll confirm it, since he invented it and gave it to you. What a sweet set–up. He gets an alibi for whatever it was he was doing both Thursday night and Friday morning, and you not only get an alibi for the whole night and the

242

time when Ruthie saw the truck, you get to tell the world Michel is sleeping with you. I guess it's the next best thing to actually doing it, but girl, when are you going to get a life?

He stood up to leave. There was nothing else to learn here. She had her story and she would cling to it. Replacing the little stool he turned and felt his paddock boot touch something under the bed. He looked down and saw the edge of a cardboard box peeking out from under the rough gray blanket. He looked inquiringly at Jocelyne, who shrugged to indicate ignorance. "Do you mind?" he asked and reached to drag it out without waiting for an answer.

"It's not mine," she said with surprise but without apprehension. They both looked at the scattering of comic books, stamped 'Le Centre Equestre de L'Estrie'. "Must be Liam's. They're stamped. Looks like they came from the Client's Lounge. Everyone brings in their old magazines and comics."

"Everyone? The boarders and the students too?"

"Yeah. Even the staff. Like for example Bridget brings in these gossip magazines back from her trips to England all the time, 'Hello' and 'Majesty'. They're a scream."

"And you're sure these're Liam's? Not someone else's?"

She shrugged. "Liam's the only one who used this room for all these months."

Polo peered down to find the date of one of the Jughead comics. Two months ago.

"And I don't read comics," Jocelyne said scornfully. "But I'm not surprised he did. He was a retard."

But Polo was puzzled. Then it came to him why. Slowly he asked, "Do you know whether Liam could actually read? I mean, did you ever see him reading anything?"

Jocelyne frowned, concentrating. "Yeah, sure he could read. He used to have to sign for deliveries from the grain merchant. He must have read them before signing them."

"Not necessarily," Polo said thoughtfully, remembering the thousands of subterfuges he had accumulated to fool people into thinking he could read when he was young. "What about newspapers and magazines? Things without pictures."

"Um, let's see." She took a good minute to think. "Oh yes, I'm sure he could, Polo. I remember he was laughing at one of the signs Roch put up on the bulletin board to announce a clinic for the boarders, with a sign–up sheet. Liam said the English translation was full of spelling mistakes, and he even corrected them."

"The translation? Yeah, that's right. Bridget said he didn't speak any French. Is that for sure?"

"Oh, absolutely. Not a *word*."

Jocelyne's eyes followed Polo's as he stared down at the box. She now saw what he meant. That they were almost all French–language comic books. He bent quickly to riffle through them. They were a random mixture of action, kidstuff, *Archie et Veronica*, and love comics. Only two or three were in English. The box was a foot deep, room enough for hundreds of them.

Polo was by now deeply suspicious. No kid he'd ever known read *all* kinds. And this particular kid wouldn't have been able to read *any* of these. And yet if the students and staff and boarders were all bringing stuff to the lounge, then there would have been a good choice of English–language comics as well.

These weren't for reading. They must be for camouflage! With a quickening pulse Polo started to dig, and in a few seconds he had found it. Liam's stash of hate ammunition.

Instinctively he blocked Jocelyne's view. She flopped back down on the bed, incurious. He riffled through it, taking a quick inventory. Cartoons, tracts, newspaper clippings in English and German, neo–nazi medallions and promotional kitsch, photos of parades, all manner of war memorabilia, Holocaust hoax argument summaries, a few books by David Irving and other Holocaust deniers (he'd learned a lot just listening at those Friday night dinners at the Jacobsons, and holocaust denial was high on their list of interests). Accounts of the Zundel trial in Ontario. Pictures, lots of pictures, some Heritage Front role models, skinheads on parade, some of Hitler giving pep talks to the *Volk*. The English stuff was printed in Flesherton, Ontario, the German material came from Passau, Bavaria.

"Joc," he said, keeping his voice level and reassuring, "I'd like to take a closer look at this stuff. Could I have a few minutes alone here?"

"Yeah, sure, Polo," she said, swung off the bed and left. Polo realized that she didn't have any idea what she'd seen.

"*Hostie toastée!*" he whispered softly as he began to spread the stuff out on the bed. "It's one up for you, Ruthie. And I take back what I said. These are *not* just High Class Worries, lady."

Sue and Michel had ordered coffee to justify their use of a table, but neither had any intention of drinking it when it came. It was warm in the restaurant. As soon as Caroline had put the cups down and walked away, Michel took off his jacket, hanging it neatly over the chair back, then turned back to see Sue drawing out her steno pad and pen. Michel immediately stiffened and leaned back in his chair with both hands gripping its arms.

"Relax, Michel," Sue said kindly. "I'm not the police. You're not making a statement. But I have to get things straight. I can't rely on remembering everything."

"I don't want my name on this," Michel muttered.

He looked ill, Sue thought worriedly. She hoped he didn't barf or anything before she found out what she wanted.

"Listen, Michel," she said firmly and reassuringly. "It's like this. You tell me stuff and I take it down. You're what's called my source. If I use this stuff, it's going to say 'from a reliable source.' I promise you I will not reveal who told me. And nobody is allowed to make me tell. Unless of course someday you want me to."

He shook his head rapidly in a full range of motion like a child refusing medicine.

"Okay, Michel," Sue said, her pen poised. "Let's get started. I'm going to ask you questions and you just tell me what you know. What you *know*. If it's what you *think*, you gotta tell me that. Okay?"

He nodded and leaned forward, elbows on the table and hands clasped in the air. *Portrait of the penitent rider at prayer,* Sue thought irreverently.

"Let's start with Mr. Lullabye, Michel. His real name is Tim Brill, is that right?"

Michel nodded. "I *think* so, anyway. It's what he said it was."

Sue beamed at him. "You're a quick study, Michel. It could very well be an alias." She made a note to check for a.k.a's. "And they call him Mr. Lullabye because he puts horses to sleep, right?" Michel nodded again, but he was looking at the table and muscles were jumping up and down his arms.

"For the insurance money, am I right?" Michel nodded. His knuckles were turning an alarming white, Sue noted. She jotted down a few lines.

"He did the Panaiotti girl's horse, didn't he? What was its name, Urban Cowboy or something–"

"City Slicker."

"City Slicker, yeah. Yeah, but he didn't do it in the usual way this time. This time he decided to make it look like the leg got broken in a pothole or something, like the horse escaped and ran into a field. But he screwed up, and there were witnesses who saw him with the crowbar, right?"

"Yes."

"Were you there, Michel? Did you see it happen?"

"I–I–"

Take your time, handsome. I got all the time in the world for this.

"I saw him take the horse out of the stall, but I–I–"

"You didn't want to see where he took him maybe, or what he was going to do?"

"No, because I–I–"

"Knew why he was there?"

"I wasn't sure. It wasn't the usual–he usually didn't–"

"Why wasn't it the usual way, Michel?" *Calm down, Sue. Stop leading him. Let him tell it.* Sue was trying very hard to keep her voice neutral and pleasant, but she was trembling all over with excitement. She had to hide this and act professional, she knew, or he would bolt. She wished she had about twenty years' experience on her. She was too raw for a story this powerful.

"The horse–City Slicker–he had had an operation for colic before she bought him," he said, and sat silent again as if this were sufficient explanation.

"Sorry?" Sue didn't have any idea what he meant by this. She wished she were more familiar with horse terminology and diseases and stuff. She knew colic was a common problem with horses, that they couldn't throw up, so their insides got all knotted up and they therefore sometimes died from it, but that was all.

He looked at her in surprise. "Well, that meant he had an exclusion in his insurance policy. He couldn't be insured for colic attacks. He was too high risk."

"But the horses Brill killed didn't die of colic," Sue said, puzzled.

Michel was frowning suspiciously. "I thought you knew all about this stuff," he said. His eyes flicked to the door.

Oh no you don't, friend. You're in for the count.

Quickly she said, "I know that the guy has been killing horses for insurance money. I know he has some way to do it so the vets never figured out what was going on when they examined the horses. I just don't know the details." She paused and sipped at the cooling coffee to look relaxed. "Come on, Michel," she urged finally, "help me out here."

His hands were playing with the paper place mat, pleating and unpleating the corners. His eyes stayed down, but he began to speak, and without hesitation, as though he'd come to the end of some occluded patch of highway in his mind and the road now stretched clear before him.

"Colic is one of the most common problems with horses, and nobody knows a whole lot about why it happens. I mean, it happens sometimes when a horse changes barn and starts on new feed. Or if he's overworked or drinks a lot when he's too hot or gets stressed in some other way. Some horses get it a lot, some never. Some just get a passing little attack and you walk them out and it's gone, others die from it no matter what you do."

"So you mean there's ways to give a horse colic?" Sue asked. "It sounds chancy, if you don't know how serious it will be from horse to horse."

Michel shook his head. "No, he didn't give them colic. He just made it seem like they died from colic–or a heart attack."

"How, then?"

"He–uh–*comment dit-on*–he electrified them." The place mat was now an accordion. Michel passed a hand across his mouth, and beads of sweat were forming on his brow.

"Electrified?" This was a word Sue associated with great

performances by rock bands. What did he mean? Michel was looking distressed at her lack of comprehension.

Agitated, he pressed, "You know, an electric current–like when you get the death *peine.*" In a remote corner of her mind, Sue noticed that stress was bringing out more of a French accent in him and a slight loss of English vocabulary. Interesting.

"*Electrocuted!*" Sue had a crazy image of a horse sitting up in an electric chair. "Wha–how?"

Michel took a deep breath. His eyes were glued to the table. "It was like a simple thing. He had two–ah–*ces trucs-là*"–he made pinching gestures in the air–"at the end of wires–like jumper cables, split, and together at the top, and he put one on the ear and one on the ass of the horse. Then he–ah–plugged in the other end, in a light bulb *récepteur.*" He swiped at his gleaming forehead and gulped at the coffee. "Then the horse just dropped dead, in a second."

Sue shivered and wrote. She felt a bit sick herself. "Go on, Michel."

"He kept his stuff in a little black bag. Like a doctor's bag. When we saw him at the shows with the bag, we knew a horse would be dead the next day. It was so simple. Two very little burn marks. But the vets never looked at the ears or the ass. What for? They always said it must be a heart attack–or a colic in the night. A bad one that went fast."

'*When we saw him at the shows'...Oh Michel, how many of you knew? Why didn't you do something? There're so many of you, only one of him. You're so strong...*

"So this happened a lot? For a long time?"

"A few years, maybe," he whispered.

"Were there any Canadian riders involved?"

"I don't know." *Too quick, love, much too quick. But we'll let it pass for now.*

"Is this why you didn't go to Cedar Meadows? Because you didn't want to see the Panaiotti girl there? And maybe Brill too?"

"Wha–uh, yeah, I guess so. Yeah, I thought it would be better if I didn't go this time, that's right–"

Nosy Parker, you stupid, stupid woman. That's what comes from leading the subject. You just blew it, babe. He didn't go to Cedar Meadows for some other reason and now you'll never know. Idiot!

"Michel, this Panaiotti girl, I hear she's from the cellular phone fortune, I mean, she's a rich girl, isn't she? Like a kazillionaire, I heard."

He nodded. Colour, too much now, was flooding up his neck and jaw.

"How much was the horse insured for?"

"A hundred thousand…" Sue could barely hear, he spoke so low.

Sue couldn't help herself. She cried, "Oh Michel, for a lousy hundred grand, she had a beautiful horse killed!"

He was very red in the face and his chin crept lower and lower. "She bought him to win. He wasn't winning. She wasn't–such a great rider. It didn't look so good in front of the other riders."

"But she could have sold him for *something*, surely!"

"She maybe was afraid a new rider might start winning. He was quite a good horse, you know."

Polo had almost finished replacing everything in the cardboard box–he had spent about a half an hour looking at everything–when a voice beside him made him jump. Roch's voice, and it was as clear and loud as if he were standing beside him.

"Claude, You're going to have to come get some of that hay you brought last week. There's mould …yeah, about forty bales…yeah, and listen…"

As Roch continued talking to Claude Lafrenière about the hay and grain situation at the barn, Polo looked wonderingly in the direction of his voice. This cubicle abutted the barn office, but surely the walls weren't that thin? He crossed noiselessly to the wall. There was a small fragment of mirror hanging there on a nail, just big enough to see his face. Why over here where you had to kneel on the bed to use it? Unless–

Gently sliding the mirror over a bit, he had his answer. There was a hole under it, a small, but perfectly round man–made hole, and through it he saw Roch's hand on the receiver, so close he could count the hairs on his knuckles. Roch finished speaking and hung up. Polo heard his footsteps receding briskly down the corridor.

Polo sat down to consider the various possibilities this new piece of information offered. Liam must have overheard hundreds of phone calls this way. This telephone was–ostensibly–in the most private and isolated part of the barn. People who wouldn't want to make a personal call from the restaurant or the pay phone in the public corridor, or from Roch's office where Marie–France and visitors could overhear, would come here.

God alone knew what secrets the boy had picked up this way. He looked around himself at the monkish cell. Once, when he was very young, he had gone to church with his mother when she said her confession. He had been fascinated by the sight of her troubled face and the whispered secrets she was confiding to the grille, behind which, he knew, a mysterious judge–like figure sat in ominous silence. With his ear to that hole in the wall, listening to the revelations not meant for him, Liam had been a kind of…anti–priest, offering the opposite of absolution. And in his own way he had ended up acting as a judge, hadn't he, conferring on himself the right to decide the fate of others? Talk about poetic justice, then.

It was probably just luck that Jocelyne had not yet gotten clued in. She had only moved in yesterday. She left the barn at lunchtime, and probably never went to the room until after hours when the barn was empty. He would have to seal the hole right away. And then borrow a bag to put all this crap into.

Just as he was about to leave he heard the receiver picked up again. This near to the wall he could hear the individual sounds of the push tones. Child's play to figure out even the numbers being called if you wanted to. He was about to make his presence known, to forestall embarrassment on both sides, when a low voice said "Claude? Can you talk?"

It was Michel's voice, intimate, conspiratorial and tender. For a crazy second Polo thought, *Michel and Claude Lafrenière, the grain merchant?* Then he realized it must be some other Claude. Not a huge coincidence. Claude was probably the single most common name in all of Quebec. But there was no mistaking, as Michel went on, the lovesick quality of his voice. *So Liam was right. And this is how he knew.*

Then Polo began to feel the full weight of the shame of what he was doing. He hadn't moved or spoken. He was officially eavesdropping. But how to get out of it? And did he really want to? He was supposed to be sleuthing. So he listened, fascinated and increasingly sick at heart by what he heard.

"Claude, I just spoke to the journalist. I told her about Palm Beach…yeah, I'm sure, it had to come out sooner or later…I don't know, I hope so…but listen, never mind that shit…what did the doctor say? I mean, the tests, are they…then when?…I should have been there with you…how can I not blame myself…do your parents suspect anything? …Good. Thursday? Don't worry, Joc is covering for me…Oh Christ, I just want to be with you, I want to tell them, it's making me crazy not being with you…My father? No, he thinks I'm out with a hundred girls every night, I told you, he thinks I'm going to marry this rich bitch in New York. Oh, shit, Claude, I have to tell somebody soon or I'll explode…yeah, me too…yeah, as soon as this crazy stuff blows over here…okay, okay…me too… bye."

As Michel's steps receded, Polo got slowly to his feet. Every muscle in his body ached. He felt a hundred years old. Old but not wise. He hated his own reaction to what he had heard. If it were anyone else but Michel, he wouldn't have questioned himself. Nathalie had told him he was homophobic, and he had laughed at her. Phobic meant afraid. But that wasn't it. Not where Michel was concerned. What was it then? Why take it so personally? And– what tests? *Tests for what*? He could only think of one medical test that would provoke the tension and worry he had heard in Michel's voice. He took off his glasses and rubbed his eyes and forehead.

Polo had never given much thought before as to how he felt about Michel as a person. The boy was a friend's son and a prodigy in the profession. How could he not have a special interest in Michel's well being and a natural curiosity about his life's trajectory? It would be a rotten trick of fate if Michel were the killer–getting Jocelyne to lie for him was incriminating, a foolish and desperate move on the face of things–but it did not account for the misery and frustration Polo felt or his irresistible urge to shield the boy from discovery or further harassment. Protecting, comforting, understanding. That wasn't his job. It was a father's role. Roch's.

Polo thought about Roch learning that his son was gay and/ or a killer. Which would he think was worse? Polo could imagine the uncomprehending pain and anger either of these terrible imagined revelations would arouse in Roch. Whatever happened, it would be crushing for Michel. Roch could be hotheaded and impulsive. He had invested too much in Michel's success. There was no Plan B for Roch. Michel was his one throw of the dice. Michel was only too aware of that. How strong was the boy? How much courage did he have? He was going to need some–more than some. Jocelyne had said he acted like a kid when his father was around. He had looked almost ill this morning following Sue down the corridor.

This is what comes of having children, Polo thought stupidly, knowing it was stupid, but needing a peasant's simple understanding of a stubbornly complex pattern of circumstances. They raise your hopes, they make you needy, you depend on them to make sense of life, you think they want the same things you do. And in fact you haven't got a fucking ounce of control over what they do. They can tear your heart out in the end. His fists curled tight, and for the second time that morning, he longed to crack apart a blackboard.

CHAPTER SEVENTEEN

THEA KNOCKED AT THE DEEPLY SCRATCHED AND PEELING OLD door. It was Guy who ushered her inside.

"B–Bridget's in the kitchen with some of her students, Thea," he said, taking her waxed rain poncho delicately between thumb and forefinger and hanging it on one of a row of hooks beside the door, all similarly laden with riders' foul weather gear.

"She's exp–pecting you," he went on. "But she didn't th–think you'd want to walk the course in the r–rain."

Thea made a moue of exasperation. Guy went on hastily, "Actually, it's wh–what she's doing now with her s–students–going over the c–course, that is. T–talking it through."

"Well, that's no good to me, Guy," Thea answered. "I have to actually see the jumps, measure them and check their construction and so forth. I brought a camera, too, so we can have a permanent record, for the archives." She nodded at her briefcase.

"And," she added tartly, "I'm not made of sugar. It wouldn't be the first time I've had to walk the course in the rain. I must have done that fifty times at least with Stephanie." Thea was relieved to be able to finally say her daughter's name without making a spectacle of herself. She had steeled herself for this trip down Memory Lane, the course walk, and she had managed to keep her professional self at a remove. But her eyes stayed fixed on Guy to measure his reaction to Stephanie's name. She felt sure he had not dealt with his own feelings. She knew how few friendships he had sustained in his life.

Guy flinched a little, but Thea wasn't sure whether it was the reference to Stephanie or the implied confrontation she would be having with Bridget over the promised course walk. She knew Guy couldn't bear 'scenes' and that he was afraid of Bridget's anger. Everyone knew that. What everyone didn't know, she thought with sudden compassion, was why he was that way. She knew why, because Stephanie had told her. Poor Guy. Thea didn't want to involve him in any difficulties her presence might cause. So without waiting for any further invitation, she simply headed for the kitchen.

An animated conversation broke off and four heads turned toward her as she arrived at the threshold. Bridget, charming in an old–fashioned floral Viyella blouse and green cotton vest that made the most of her vivid hair and creamy skin, dominated the tableau. She was sitting on the ancient kitchen counter with a large cross–country course map in her hands. A well–padded calico cat lounged in blissful indolence on the breadboard beside her. Three girls, ranging in age, Thea guessed, from fifteen to nineteen, sat taking notes at the white deal table in the centre of the room.

The girls were clearly not sisters, but they had enough about them in common to suggest kinship of another kind. Thea was singularly well placed to recognize their breed. They were Three–Day Event riders. They all had on the scruffiest of outfits, torn jeans and none–too–clean oversized sweatshirts. They wore no make-up or jewelry. One had her hair cut as short as a boy's, the other two sported no–nonsense ponytails worn low, and scrunched, unadorned, into fat elastics. Their fingernails were clipped, square and lacquerless. And they all looked annoyed at this interruption of their course 'walk.'

Thea could not suppress a tiny smile of bemusement as she took in this typical scene. For a bittersweet instant she was back with Stephanie in the agreeable intimacy of a post–show dinner, dissecting the performances and characteristics of the other riders, reliving the triumphs and/or disasters of the competition.

Amongst the three disciplines, the eventers were universally acknowledged to be the grungiest of the riders, Stephanie had admitted complacently and not without a certain pride. She revelled in her tomboyhood, and boasted of her spartan social life. Boys could wait, she had always said (citing the more promiscuous Jumper riders with disdain). Eventers had to put their hormones on hold. Her horse took too much time and care to admit of rivals for her affection. After all, they were the triathletes of the sport. And the last of the great amateur tradition in riding. They did it all. Event horses gave so much of themselves, Stephanie used to say, that they had a special right to their riders' unconditional love and single–minded devotion.

Bridget's voice, unusually husky today, brought Thea back to the present. "I'm right in the middle of things with this lot, Thea, but you're welcome to muck in, if you want."

"As long as we actually get out on the course itself at some point today. I really must have things in place for tomorrow's meeting, you know."

"Would it be a tremendous *bore* if you went without me, then, Thea, because, you see, the thing is, I also promised you the list of jump judges and outriders and that sort of thing, and if I don't do it this afternoon, *that* won't be done for the meeting either." She coughed emphatically and blew her nose. "And I'm starting this bloody awful *cold*, it seems. I mean, I know it's rotten of me to go on *whinging* like this, but if you *could* manage on your own, I'd be jolly grateful–" and she smiled appealingly at Thea.

Thea was acutely aware of the impatient stares of the students and fought back what she knew to be futile resentment. It was not a good time for an argument. "Well, I don't see that I have much choice," Thea said, thwarted and knowing it. She could not in all (public) conscience ask a person who might be on the verge of a flu to spend two hours tramping up and around fifty acres of rough, sodden terrain in this weather. "I'll look at the map while you talk to the girls."

She accepted Bridget's offer of coffee and sat down to review the grubby, much-handled copy of the course map that was cheerfully pushed at her by a pony-tailed member of the trio. Each of the girls politely murmured her name–Lucie, Chloe and Claire–and promptly forgot Thea was there as they turned their rapt attention back to Bridget's discourse.

Bridget carried on with her coaching session, punctuating a general discussion of the pitfalls and challenges of the twenty-four obstacle Young Riders' course with individual warnings and bits of advice uniquely tailored to the talents and weaknesses of each girl and horse combination.

"Now let's remember our goals here," Bridget was summarizing. "You've done your Dressage. Whatever happened there is best forgotten. Spilt milk. And if you did well, thinking about it's bound to make you overconfident. The cross-country is what you're in the sport for. Here's where you don't want to blow it.

"You have to ask yourself if your horse is fit enough to make the optimum time if it's a really hot day. Don't forget: it's a hilly course. There won't be many without time penalties. And you have to have enough *go* left for Sunday and the Jumping. So Chloe, you're going to have the advantage here, because you've done all that hill work in training, and your 'Sting' is a nice, go-ey kind of beast.

"But Lucie, let's admit that your 'Hilarious' is a bit of a slug. Now you'll have done well in the Dressage, so there's no use getting hot and bothered for nothing, just don't go for time on the course, go for accuracy and no other penalties. Your best bet is to kick on and take the safe options, and especially watch out he doesn't suck back at the water, you know how you tend to take your leg off at the water…"

This is where she's at her best, Thea thought. She's a born teacher. Look at their faces. Absolute trust and confidence. And she loves this. She never gets tired of it. If I only ever saw this side of her, I'd like her, I really would.

"Claire, I don't want you flying out of the start box and using 'Mastermind' up. You want to steady him without riding backwards. Eyes up, leg on and try to get a rhythm. By the time you get to the 'Orrible 'Ole, he should be all settled in."

The familiar admonitions and jargon took Thea back to the early days of Stephanie's training program with Bridget. The enthusiasm! In those days it was nothing but excitement and progress. Those were the days when Stephanie was getting to know her first *real* competition horse. 'Boy George' they had named him because he was such a flashy mover and so full of himself.

And in the first two seasons, between semesters at Tufts, she had moved quickly up the competitive ladder, winning several Open Preliminary Trials–at Timberline, at Ledyard and Fair Hill–then capping the second season as Ontario Reserve Champion at Glen Oro. She and Boy had been a wonderful partnership.

"Now Chloe, you're going to have to be very accurate at The Coffin. You've had your good, strong gallop up to the Ogre's Table and then a direct shot up The Ziggurat, and now you've had a breather coming down hill where you've your choice of this very attractive fourteen foot bounce with good ground lines on both elements, or that quite unattractive right–hand corner. I wouldn't take the corner. It's too easy for the horse to run out at it. Especially Hilarious, not–let's admit–the most *honest* bloke if he sees an opportunity. In any case you'd only save two seconds. Actually, the bounce *looks* gruesome, but it's quite straightforward if you get a nice, collected pace and set up properly."

When had things begun to go wrong? Thea was sure that it was the transition from Prelim to Intermediate that had marked the turning. The amateurs stayed at Prelim or fell away from competition altogether when their horses proved to lack the necessary scope to move up. Only a handful went on because Intermediate was riskier, a lot harder, and required a bold, scopey horse. The jumps were huge. Downright scary, in fact. It was a major transition, much more so than from Training to Prelim.

Suddenly there was too much at stake. At the Prelim level all of them had been happy amateurs, pulling together. There had been stress, certainly, but it came from within. It was the rider challenging herself, setting her own goals.

But at Intermediate, most of the riders were committed to making it big–that is, they wanted to go all the way, compete internationally, be chosen for the Talent Squad, then the long list, then the short list, then Team Alternates, and finally The Team. *Making The Team*. It was political now. It was who your trainer was, if they were 'in' with C–FES, if the C–FES committee liked your horse, liked your odds, thought you would reflect well on them.

So now the stress was external too. The mood changed. Stephanie wasn't happy any more. She thought her chances for making the Team were slim. What did it matter, Thea urged, as long as she was enjoying herself?

You don't understand, Mom. You have to have an internation-al level horse. Bridget says Boy isn't good enough. He's not scopey enough. He'll let me down. Even if he goes okay at Intermediate, he'll never go Advanced. I have to have a better horse. I have to.

And Harold had backed her up. Thea hadn't wanted to quarrel with him. The divorce had been a painful experience. She want-ed to keep their relationship civil and as amicable as possible. She didn't want Stephanie to become an object for wrangling over.

And of course Harold was so taken with Bridget. He admired spunky, pretty women, he was easily seduced by posh British ac-cents, and he liked the thought that his daughter might make the Team, where Bridget seemed to be in a position–perhaps not to guarantee a berth, but certainly to oil the wheels of the political machinery involved.

Eventing was a small pond in Canada in relation to the big lake that was England or Europe. Compared to Jumping, where compet-itors were more numerous and the struggle at the top much fiercer, you could go pretty far pretty fast in Canadian Eventing. Even so, in its parochial way, Harold had found it no small thing to be the parent of a Team member. And on top of his honorary life mem-bership on the Board of C–FES–well, it had an irresistible appeal.

Bridget was deep into her subject. "Now you want to remember that the second water jump will be harder than the first. Your horse will be tired. And you should keep in mind that statistically, more refusals happen jumping *out* of the water than at any other obsta-cle. So for God's sake once you're out of the water, look up, keep your leg on, ride forward, and get over the next jump. That's the vertical–here, you see it? And then, heading for home, your horse is really tired now, so he'll want to flatten out and be on the forehand. It's absolutely critical not to let him *dive* at the Hay Ride…."

Thea found herself engulfed in the blackness of mood that always coincided with this point in her memories, the acquisition of that damned Robin's Song. Why hadn't she spoken out? Why hadn't she said aloud what she had come to realize after following Stephanie around on the Three–Day Event circuit for all that time?

That Stephanie wasn't experienced enough for the big time. She was brave, certainly, and talented. But not ready to leap so high. Oh yes, perhaps with a very special horse, a horse with more experience, that knew the ropes at Advanced. But really, Steph should have stayed at Prelim for at least another year, ridden more horses at that level. Only to have competed with the one horse, Boy–it wasn't enough. She had gone on to Intermediate too fast. And there was no question that Robin's Song wasn't the right horse for her. Not at all.

How had it been that she, Thea, was the only one to think so? Bridget had told Harold that Robin's Song was ideal for Stephanie. He was a Team prospect, no question, she had said. Out of Rockin' Robin, the best stallion she had ever brought over from England. And Harold had believed her. Why was she, Thea, the only one to remark–only in her mind, of course, not out loud–that it was Bridget who stood to gain financially from the sale of the horse? That there was a terrible conflict of interest involved?

But no, the horse was incredibly beautiful, Bridget produced a list of his amazing accomplishments so far, Stephanie fell in love with him at first sight, and it was, emotionally, a *fait accompli*. Harold had put pressure on Thea because, after all, *she* would be the one to pay for the horse. Harold was not embarrassed about this fact. He had gotten quite accustomed to the luxuries that her family fortune had provided during their marriage.

Harold had resisted the divorce. A life of budgetary restraint after so many years was socially humiliating for him, and Thea understood this. In spite of her excellent reasons for divorcing him (most of them blonde and nubile), she felt obscurely guilty about his ouster from the easy life her money had provided. She, after all, had not worked for it. It hadn't been a hardship to share it. And so it was out of her need for expiation and a sense of closure that Thea had, however reluctantly, written the cheque for $70,000, the absolute high end of the spectrum for an Eventing horse of that level.

It wasn't Robin's Song's lack of talent or scope that worried Thea. Even Thea could see that the horse's athleticism was incontestable. His natural balance and the purity of his gaits could rival any Hanoverian or Selle Français or Belgian warmblood. He could jump the moon from the laziest of trots.

She simply knew that the partnership was wrong. She didn't trust him with Stephanie. And she'd never had a satisfactory answer as to why she felt this way.

Michel and Roch had always been very circumspect about what they said about him. They praised his abilities, but were reluctant to say anything negative. Thea assumed that this was because they knew that their criticisms might result in a lower sale price and trouble for Bridget.

They all stick together, Thea thought. Trainers with trainers against owners. Horse people in general against the world. She hoped Polo would at least be honest with her after he rode him today. Perhaps he was riding him right now.

Still, even if his opinion vindicated her suspicions, it was too late to help Stephanie. Too late for a second chance to speak out, to be brave. And for her timidity, for her unwillingness to make waves, she had paid a disproportionate price. A dead daughter seemed a very high price to pay, indeed, for simply not wanting to quarrel with one's ex–husband.

Bridget was wrapping it all up. "…and what is the most important thing you have to remember? All of you? All the time when you're out on that course? You tell me now. I've told you so many times it should be engraved in your brains."

"Don't be afraid," said Lucie.

"Fear is the enemy," said Chloe.

"There are no bad horses, only bad riders," said Claire.

Bridget saw her students out, then gathered up her own things. She was going up to the barn to feed the stallion and hand walk him around the indoor arena.

"Don't rush out on my account, Thea," she said. She peered out the window. "It's letting up a bit. Why don't you have another cuppa' before you go out on the course. Guy will be 'mother', won't you?" she asked teasingly of Guy who had just appeared in the doorway. He smiled politely in affirmation.

"Oh, that's all right, I really ought to be–" Thea began.

"No, stay, Thea," Guy suddenly said quite firmly. "I was just about to fix a c–cup of tea myself. C–company would be nice." He walked quickly to the stove before she could decline.

"'Ta, Guy,'" Bridget said. "I'm off, then." A few seconds later her car growled to life and she was gone. Thea felt an immediate lessening of tension in the house. She wondered if it was her own presence that had produced the tension in the first place, or if Guy always relaxed a bit when Bridget went out. The kettle sang out and Guy fixed up a tray to take into the living room.

Thea followed him in and looked around with curiosity. She'd been so intent on her duties before that she hadn't noticed the rather oddly arranged living quarters. Guy was watching her puzzlement with amused understanding.

"That's Bridget's corner over there," he said, nodding to what should have been the dining room end. It looked to Thea like an office that had been vandalized. There was a desk, barely visible under a heap of papers, folders, horse passports, framed eventing photographs, and other evocative testimony to a life spent in equestrian sport. To Thea it seemed as though a huge garbage pail had been emptied over the desk.

A filing cabinet stood in the corner with its drawers yawning open, and files half–pulled or lying on top of the rest. A year's accumulation of *Eventing Magazine* from England rested precariously on a small table. A box of chocolates sat open on top of the pile. Folders with paper sticking out everywhere were stacked up on the floor beside the desk. A Xerox machine stood on its own little rickety stand, too low for a user's comfort. There were papers and a telephone sitting on top of it. A fax machine squatted on the floor next to a dog bed where a chocolate–coloured labrador slept with his drooling mouth resting on the machine's panel of instructions.

Viscerally insulted and mentally aghast, she turned to Guy and shook her head in speechless wonder. He simply nodded sympathetically. There was nothing one could say.

"And that's my space," he indicated, inclining his head to the other end of the room. The contrast was actually shocking. Here was an oasis of order and routine. A clean desk, except for three folders, an open cheque book and a pen, and an excellent, expensive-looking study lamp. Bookshelves full of medical tomes and journals, all neatly ranged and catalogued. One section featured books and periodicals devoted to fish and aquarium literature. A small computer unit module with printer and paper storage components to the side of the desk. A pretty little jewel-toned Persian rug on the threadbare broadloom beneath.

Between the two camps was the living room, which consisted of a sagging leather couch and two shabby wing chairs facing an *armoire*, a television and VCR set on a trolley, and a drably beige arborite coffee table. Newspapers and horse magazines were tossed about everywhere.

Instinctively Thea moved closer to Guy's workspace, the only corner in the house that looked as if anybody cared about it. Surreptitiously she ran her finger along the desk edge. Clean. How very strange it all was. She looked down at the folders on his desk. One was marked 'Hydro', one 'Telephone', and one 'Misc'.

She looked inquiringly at Guy who had followed her movements with comprehending eyes.

"Those are the bills we share in c-common," he explained. "I l-like to know where they are," he said without a trace of irony. "I keep my research notes and v-vetting records up at the office at *Le Centre*."

"In the filing cabinets? Polo said they weren't locked. That surprised me."

"They usually are. Perhaps Marie-France forgot before leaving."

Thea nodded gravely. "Lucky they weren't tampered with by the vandals."

"Yes. Y-Yes, of course that *was* lucky."

Thea looked again at Bridget's end of the room and shook her head. "How do you tolerate it, Guy?" And then, quite rudely, knowing it was none of her business, "I'm sorry, I shouldn't ask, but this kind of environment–" she gestured at his space–"I mean, the way you are–"

Guy smiled and nodded again, not at all insulted. "I l–like it here, Thea. Bridget is g–good company. We don't–well, we d–don't *interfere* with each other." He looked from one end of the room to the other. "We just ex–p–press our need for privacy in d–different ways."

Thinking about his unhappy past, Thea nodded. She could see the attraction. He didn't have to live alone this way–total solitude would be too much to bear–and yet here he could carry on with invisible walls all around him. The British are so very good at that sort of thing, Thea reflected grudgingly. They understand the necessity of doors between rooms, invisible barriers between people, secrets kept, the obvious unmentioned. They do not intrude.

"But also b–because she gives me enough s–space," Guy added.

"Well, yes, that's what you just said," she replied, puzzled.

"No, no," he said, with a rare laugh, "I mean s–space. Real s–space. For"–he gestured with an outstretched arm across the hall.

Thea then turned and looked across the hall and gasped. Practically the whole wall on the other side of the house was an explosion of tropical colours.

The reef tank! Guy's famous reef tank.

"Ohh!"

Guy's face lit up with pleasure. He motioned an invitation to come closer. She walked over to it and Guy quickly produced a second chair to sit alongside his own.

"It's–it's so *huge*!"

"Five hundred gallons," Guy said proudly. "I had to have the floor reinforced."

"My goodness. It's–it's beautiful! The colours!" Her eyes were darting everywhere, hungrily trying to take it all in at once. "Can you explain it to me, what everything is?"

Could he *explain* it! He looked at her with blissful gratitude and launched himself into his personal paradise. The moment he turned to look at the tank, he stopped stuttering.

"Well, those rocks you see piled up everywhere. They're all covered with that heathery, mossy vegetation now, but when I first got them from Bali–"

"From Bali?"

"Oh yes, it's living rock. It has to come from the tropics. At first when you get it, it's bare, it looks just like pieces of lunar landscape. Then when you get the water temperature and salinity and bacterial levels just right, after a few weeks things start to grow and come out of the rock. Those anemones there–the pink ones–they fasten on and spread themselves out, so now the rocks are kind of fused together by the vegetation and the corals and all–"

"Oh, I thought they were grass, those fronds waving like that–"

"Oh no, they're alive, and so are those yellow wheaty things–if you touch them, they shrink down and close right up"–

"–and the gorgeous little mushrooms there? The blue things? Like Ladyslippers?"

"Yes, they're alive too." Guy's normally sallow face was rosy and his eyes sparkled behind his glasses.

"Ooh, look at that funny praying mantis–but all candy-striped–"

"No, that's a shrimp. I had two, but one of the fish ate him." Guy's face darkened and his tone lost energy.

"Oh, what a shame."

"Yes, it was my fault. I took bad advice from a so–called expert. I should have checked for myself whether a hawkfish would fit in to this particular eco–system. And now I'm stuck with him." Guy was quite gloomy now. "There he is. Can you see him?"

"You mean that pretty purple and yellow fish?"

"No, no, behind that rock. He's sort of brown and spotted, with eyes like antennae, and he kind of jumps from rock to rock. He's a *stalking* fish. I've been trying to get him out, but he's wily, you see. It's as if he knows what the net is for. You wouldn't think a fish could be intelligent, but this one is–"

"So how will you get at him?"

Guy sighed. "I may have to take the whole thing apart."

"Oh, but that would be terrible. Everything else is so perfect. And the time–it would take so much time and energy."

"I know. But I have to protect the others, you see. It isn't fair to them."

"You really love this, don't you Guy? Stephanie used to tell me about your hobby, but I never took it very seriously. I didn't realize what a–what a *world* it is."

264

"You used the right word, Thea. A reef tank *is* a world unto itself. A complete eco–system, self–perpetuating and flourishing once you get things going. You don't even have to feed it. It's all symbiotic." He frowned and pushed his slipping glasses up his nose. "It was inexcusable for me to make an error like that hawkfish."

"That's life, Guy," Thea said lightly, becoming a little uneasy with his fixation on the one problem.

"No, Thea," Guy said intensely, jabbing a finger toward the door. "*That's* life, out there. Or our human life at least. But in here, where I have the power to be in control of what I do, I shouldn't make mistakes. A reef tank is the most complete captive environment you can create, and the most easily manipulated if you prepare things properly…"

Thea suddenly felt strangely empathetic to the change of mood and Guy's extraordinary intensity. She was not convinced they were even talking about reef tanks any more. She felt sure Guy was unconsciously referring to the dark secret in his own life that he had shared with her daughter.

She said, testing, "Wouldn't it be nice if we could keep the life we humans create as safe as the creatures in a reef tank?"

"Some people should not have the right to create life at all," Guy said with a curious lack of affect, still staring moodily at the tank.

"What do you mean, Guy?" Thea asked quietly.

"Look at my creatures, Thea," Guy answered. Obediently Thea turned her eyes back to Guy's enchanted Eden. She saw sparkling, clean blue water and weird–shaped, brilliantly–tinctured fish–purple, yellow, blue, orange–gliding effortlessly in and around the mossy grottoes and limpid shoals of the rocks. She saw anemones dancing and swaying to the pulse of the currents. Snails and shrimps made their slow, delicate progress wherever atavistic impulse demanded. It was extraordinarily beautiful, protected and peaceful.

"I know what happened to you, Guy," Thea finally said. "Stephanie told me."

Guy drew into himself. Like an anemone when it's threatened, Thea thought. "She shouldn't have," he said softly.

"She cared about you, Guy. She felt terrible about what happened to you at that school. The headmaster. And you never telling.

Protecting your family. Protecting *his*. His own sons at the same school. Unthinkable, really. She felt very privileged that you shared this with her. But it was disturbing. She had to share her pain. It was only me–she never told anyone else. And I never did. Or would."

"Don't feel sorry for me, Thea. I have things under control. I'm pretty happy with my life on the whole." Guy spoke gently, but there was a warning underneath. *Don't try to get close.*

"It's not pity I feel. It's sympathy. And indignation. Anger, too." She paused, groping for the right wording. "Did you never want revenge of any kind, Guy? You hear nowadays about lawsuits, successful often"–

Guy shuddered visibly. "I could never, *never*–in public–the publicity–and my parents–no, no, *never*. And then, I was raised to be a Christian, you see. I believed what I was taught. So revenge– well, it's just not the right thing."

Thea smiled grimly. "Oh, I was raised to be a Christian too, Guy. But I've come to find that being a human being keeps getting in the way."

Guy nodded, but said nothing.

Thea straightened up and cleared her throat. "I don't mean to belabour the morbid side of things, Guy, but now that I have the opportunity, I want to thank you–I never really thanked you for all that you did for Stephanie," she said, her voice low and rich with feeling.

"But I failed her, too, Thea. She was the only real friend I had, and I failed her. You shouldn't be thanking me," Guy said, his voice sinking almost to a whisper.

"How can you say that, Guy? You were her good friend. You were always there for her when the pressure got to her. She always told me how much she depended on you."

"But I w–wasn't there at T–T–Timberline, was I? It was the only show of hers I missed all season," Guy said, his voice tight now and trembling with emotion.

"You *couldn't* be there, Guy. You got the flu. And even if you had been there, you're not saying–you don't suppose you could have *prevented* what happened–"

"I don't know... I don't know... I don't know..." he was

whispering–to himself or to her? Thea could no longer tell. He sat in a kind of trance, staring blindly at the reef tank.

He reached out for something on the shelf above the tank. Thea couldn't see for a moment what it was that he was clutching. Then he raised that hand toward the tank. It was a net.

"I thought you said a net was useless with that fish, Guy," Thea said in a voice she hoped sounded normal and neutral. "You said he knew to avoid it."

"I've decided I'm going to leave it in the tank for a while. Eventually he'll get used to it. He'll think it's part of the system. I'm going to put bits of food in it, bits of scallop. Pretty soon he'll start going in to eat. Then he'll hang around for a while. He'll feel safe. And then," his voice sank to a murmur, "I'll have him. I'll have him…"

CHAPTER EIGHTEEN

A FTER HE HAD BUNGED UP THE LITTLE ROUND HOLE IN THE wall with hoof packing, Polo rummaged in the tack room storage cupboards and found an old, empty duffel bag with the logo of *Le Centre* and Roch's initials on it. He stuffed everything from Liam's carton into the bag, except the comic books. These he took to the Clients' Lounge and replaced on a bookshelf with the others he found stacked there.

He was about to leave the almost–empty room–there were two boarders, a man and a woman, chatting together in an alcove beside the window–when he noticed the magazine the young woman had tossed onto the coffee table in front of her. *Majesty,* it was called. The title seemed familiar.

Polo picked up the magazine to flip through it. It seemed to be all about the Royal Family and the aristocracy. Most of the stories featured weddings, society outings and scenes of country life with big hats, dogs and posed happy family portraits much in evidence. Princess Di, chic and morose, and a glum, jug–eared Prince Charles occupied pride of place. Now he recalled that Jocelyne had mentioned the magazine. She had said it was a 'scream.' Bridget, she had said, brought copies back from her trips to England

He shrugged and tossed it back on the table. Then something caught his eye and he frowned. Something not making perfect sense. He picked it up again and his finger traced over the thin white paper rectangle and the curled–up edges where the glue had lost its sticking power. Faintly the computerese script revealed what was puzzling him: Bridget's name and her address, here in Saint Armand.

He turned back to the bookshelves and riffled through the stacks of magazines. There were other 'Majesty's and some 'Hello!'s as well. And they all had subscription labels on them. So they were sent to her here. She didn't buy them in England. Jocelyne was mistaken. Then why hadn't Joc said, 'Bridget *gets* them from England'? Curious. And hadn't Bridget just been to England recently?

How did he know that? Nibbling at the edge of his consciousness was a vague recollection of himself and Roch, sitting together out on the patio over a beer when he had first arrived at *Le Centre*, and catching up on each others' horse news. They had spoken about hunting, he remembered. Gregarious Roch loved hunting, a swarm of excited riders thundering over the countryside together in hot pursuit of a fox that rarely failed to escape, then the back-slapping jollity of the lunch party at '*De Trot*', generously lubricated by drink and embellished recitals of the day's adventures. Polo had never enjoyed social riding of any kind, and (unconsciously) held the hunting crowd in particular in a virtuoso's contempt for the thrill–seeking amateur.

But now he remembered that the conversation had swung round to the various disasters in their past season of the Saint Armand Hunt Club, and Roch had remarked in passing that Bridget's father in England had died in March from injuries sustained in a hunting accident, that she'd missed the planning meeting for the show in Ottawa because of it. This had led to further reminiscences of famous hunting tragedies. And that was all he could recall for now.

Perhaps she received other things from England here at the stable? She was away a lot, and it was obviously more secure for her to have her mail sent here and kept for her return, rather than trusting to a rural mailbox or *poste restante* in the village. On an impulse he walked quickly down the corridor to the office. Marie–France was off for the weekend, but after the locks were changed yesterday Roch had given him a key for the duration of his stay. It was possible that in the confusion of yesterday's events the mail hadn't been sorted and distributed. One day's mail was unlikely to tell him anything, of course, unless he was extraordinarily lucky.

He was lucky. The wire In–basket on M–F's desk was piled with messily heaped mail, and thirty seconds' of shuffling through it brought up a letter addressed to Bridget. Not a letter, though. Clearly a bank draft, a thin long envelope with the English bank's return address, and Bridget's machine–drafted name in the cellophane window. Well, Hello, hello, hello! Polo found this terrifically interesting, though he couldn't have said why. All he could think of for the moment was that Bridget's relationship with England could be a strong factor in this case. If she had lied about something so trivial as the magazines, who knew what else she was making up? More due diligence in order here. He was about to put the envelope back in the pile, hesitated, then slid it into the pocket of his coat.

Polo borrowed Roch's truck to take the duffel bag over to the Jacobsons'. There was no question now of putting off telling Hy about this discovery. He was somewhat worried about Hy's reaction; he wondered whether the shock might cause some physical downturn in him. And he hated to even think of what Ruthie would say or do. He fervently hoped she wouldn't burst out crying. Better to get it over with fast.

He let himself into the house without bothering to knock. From the poncho thrown casually down on the antique settee in the foyer, he saw that Hy already had a visitor. He now heard the murmur of voices in the living room and he recognized Sue Parker's urgent pitch and rapid–fire delivery.

At the same time he was conscious of a telephone conversation taking place in the hallway around the corner from the entrance. It was Ruthie talking to one of her daughters. Polo didn't know how he was so sure it was one of the girls. It couldn't be the words, as he could barely hear what she was saying. It must be her voice, he supposed, some soothingly maternal tonal varnish he had unconsciously picked up on. The usual tension nipped through him and was almost instantly gone.

Polo liked Ruthie's girls equally: Aviva, dark, brainy, serious, and Jenny, the high-spirited clownish extrovert. And he enjoyed having them come around to ride or just hang out and help the groom at his barn. Jenny had a natural talent for riding. She could be good if she took it seriously. He heard Ruthie hanging up the phone.

Without greeting, Ruthie announced to Polo who had just stepped into her line of vision, "Well, *that's* very strange!"

"What is?"

Ruthie was frowning and smiling together. "That was Aviva. She thinks the Duchess may have a *boyfriend*. Can you *imagine!*"

Polo considered Mrs. Jacobson for a moment. Funny that he had never called her anything but that, long after he stopped calling Mr. J. anything but Morrie. There had always been that narrow but formal corridor between himself and Clarice. Not that he'd minded. He'd taken comfort in that neutral zone. He had appreciated her never trying to move in close on him. Lucky, he supposed, for both of them, she hadn't been looking for another kid, and he hadn't been looking for another mother.

Thinking of her now though, from the vantage point of adulthood, Polo realized that she'd probably arranged for that distance between them on purpose, consciously, so he wouldn't feel like a foster kid having to choose between his real home and hers. Some women might have thought they were being selfish, or that they would look bad if they didn't give a kid in his position a lot of love and attention. Mrs. J. had known better. Smart lady.

"I suppose I could," Polo said in answer to Ruthie's question. "She's only-what-seventy-two, three? She's got that look that goes so well with white hair-you know, that high-class, *'on se connaît'* look-and she dresses so well. She's healthy and bright and interesting, not to mention rich-well, sure, why not?"

Ruthie wrinkled her nose in a childish *moue* of distaste. "Because she's my *mother*, of course. Mothers aren't supposed to have *boyfriends*. They're supposed to knit sweaters for their grandchildren and do good works in the community and go to Florida spas. Ick! What a yucky thought, and here's daddy's funeral meats barely cold on the table–"

"Don't be silly, *ziess*," Polo said, cutting off what was clearly some bookish illustration of her theme. "It's been nearly three years. I think it's nice, if it's true. Has Aviva met him?"

"Oh no, it's purely speculative still. I'm just playing detective," Ruthie admitted.

"What are the clues?"

"Only one, really, but it's highly suggestive," Ruthie confided with a raised eyebrow. "She cancelled out on having the girls stay over tonight, and even told them they'd have to make their own dinner arrangements, *as she had other plans*." She nodded conspiratorially. "Plans she refused to be specific about. Very suggestive, I'd say. I mean, the girls always have Saturday dinner with her before going out with their friends. It's a tradition since we moved back."

Polo smiled and shook his head. "You were right this morning."

"About the report?" Ruthie's eyes widened.

"No, about being a crummy detective. Not very convincing if that's your only clue about your mother's love life." Then, more soberly, and reaching back for the duffel bag he'd left in the foyer, "Actually, you may have been right about a lot of things, and I guess I owe you an apology." He glanced around to ensure their privacy and added softly, "I was rough on you, and it turns out you weren't over–reacting after all."

Her eyes fastening on the bag, Ruthie struggled to frame a reply that would cover both vindication and rising apprehension.

Polo added quickly, "I'll explain, but I want you and Hy together." He cocked his head toward the living room. "What's with the reporter?"

Ruthie's eyes grew larger and she exclaimed, "The *reporter*. Oh Polo, what the hell kind of sport are you involved in? From what Sue's been telling us, it sounds like–more than just tough–more like the Mafia's factory outlet–*thugs*, *hit* men, *horse* murders–"

"Okay, now you really *are* over–reacting–" he said this automatically, but in fact he'd been waiting to hear very bad news about the horse business for a long time. And from the expression of bafflement and distaste on Ruthie's face, it looked like the rumours had substance.

"No, no really," Ruthie protested. "She said she's working on a story that just broke in Palm Beach that's going to blow the Show Jumping world wide open. In the States and Canada too. Horses being killed for insurance money. Big money. *Contracts*. She said we'd be *sick* if we knew the details. Except that she's beginning to wonder if Liam's murder had something to do with it–with this story, it's something that could really end a lot of riders' careers, she said. And since Liam was so into finding out secrets about every-one, she thought maybe he knew something connected with it, and got murdered for it."

Polo thought immediately of the lioness in Sue's expression as she led the way for Michel to the *resto*. "Did she say who she sus-pects? Or where she got this information?"

"No, she wouldn't tell us. She said she has to protect her sourc-es. But it began in Palm Beach and she was there on a tip, and now the FBI are into it because it's wire fraud, and she says it won't be long before the RCMP get going on a bunch of cases here."

"But how does Liam come into it?"

"Well, that's why she came over. At breakfast she asked Hy to get some information from the office about Liam to see what could be found out about Liam's background and his whereabouts this winter. She should really have gone to see Roch, but she's pretty sure he'd worry that Michel might be involved and wouldn't coop-erate."

"Why should she think that?" Polo's heart was beginning to thump hard.

"What? Well, because it's kind of obvious, I guess–I mean, who else from here was showjumping in Palm Beach this winter?"

"Go on–"

"Well, that's just it–it was really coincidental, because Hy had the same idea–I mean, not about Palm Beach, but about trying to put together a history of where Liam had been before coming here. But then Manon remembered that Liam and Gilles *both* helped Michel make the trip down to Palm Beach. It sounds like a huge project, by the way, going down to the winter shows."

Gilles again. The kid is involved in every scenario.

"It is," Polo agreed dryly, "it's like moving house every three months." He thought about the exhaustion and aggravations of those days-long trips up and down the continent in cumbrous convoy, one of the features of competition he'd been delighted to see the back of. He looked expectantly at Ruthie for more information.

"Who did what on the trip down?"

"Oh. Well, if I remember right, Michel drove the horse van, and Jocelyne followed in his car, and Liam drove the mobile home, and Gilles had the pickup truck full of hay–apparently they charge an arm and a leg for hay at the show sites–which he and Liam drove back together to Saint Armand. I think Michel went down with four of his own and Roch's horses, and five others, some from students here and two he picked up en route in Georgia–and the whole trip took four days."

"They laid over in Georgia?"

"They stayed one night there. Some small town north of Atlanta where they have all these carpet mills–Dalton, was it?"

"And how long did Gilles and Liam stay in Florida?"

"Not long. Several days, just to help set up the stalls and lay in supplies and rest up a bit."

They heard Hy and Sue's approaching voices. Sue looked startled and a little embarrassed when she met Polo in the hall. Quickly she stuffed her steno pad into her briefcase and swung her shiny white poncho over her head. With her huge round glasses and shoe–button eyes, her brown helmet of raffia–straight hair, and her now tented near-dwarfish trunk and legs, she looked to Polo like a kind of oversized doll.

Seeing her out and shutting the door behind her, Hy turned to Ruthie and murmured slyly, "She's a smart kid and I love her enthusiasm, but doesn't she remind you of 'That's my dog Tide, he lives in a shoe, I'm Buster Brown, look for me in there too!' Not the dog part, I mean the Buster Brown kid on the label."

"Gee, that takes me back a few years. I think TV only had one channel in those days. No, being a postmodern type myself, I see her more as Honey from Doonesbury," Ruthie said.

"Y'know, you guys are *not* nice people," Polo mused.

"Thank you, *mazzik*," Ruthie smiled complacently. "I can't think of anything I'd rather *not* be called than 'nice.'"

Chuckling, Hy excused himself for a minute and Polo and Ruthie went into the living room to wait for him. He set the bag on the coffee table and Ruthie's face, which had softened with the comforting pleasure of sibling banter, now tightened, and worry lines appeared on her brow.

The men settled themselves around the coffee table, and Ruthie jumped up to make fresh coffee. Manon called out from the kitchen that she would be there in just a minute. Polo and Hy filled each other in on the morning's offerings. Polo didn't mention Jocelyne's phony alibi or Michel's telephone call.

In the silence the steady, light patter of the diminishing rain showers on bushes could be heard through the slightly open window in back of them. Fresh loam and flower-scented air drifted round them. There was a brochure on the table that Sue must have left behind, the Prize List from the Palm Beach series of shows. Polo leafed through it idly.

Polo was pretty sure he had an idea of what this Palm Beach story was about. Rumours had been flying around the circuit in Canada for the last few years about suspicious horse deaths. There had been a number of sudden, unexplained—or poorly explained—deaths of otherwise healthy and mostly young horses. Horses that had passed their pre–purchase exams with flying colours and without any serious history of colic. Then there had been that fire in Perth. Clay Hardacre had collected insurance on a lovely thoroughbred–Hanoverian crossbred Polo recalled for her gutsiness and consistency in the ring. She'd been a tick short of the scope for Grand Prix, but what a lot of heart she'd had.

Polo's heart sank as he remembered the look on Michel's face when he'd passed him in the corridor with Sue this morning. In a lightning scrolldown of all the horses Michel had ridden in the last three years, he searched for suspicious deaths. None of Michel's, he was sure he would have remembered. But now that he thought of it, there had been a colic death, a client's or a student's. No big deal. It happened, after all. There hadn't been a breath of scandal about it. The only reason Polo remembered was because Michel had called him in St. Lazare to arrange for the client to see him about a replacement. There was a certain urgency because the client had booked to go south for the winter to train with Michel and he wanted to buy a horse in Canada, not pay American dollars in Florida.

Had there been insurance paid on the horse that died? Maybe. A lot? Who knew? Who had thought even to ask? And what would the client have to do to arrange these things? Pay the go–between half? A flat fee? The go–between would have to be a trainer or rider, someone who knew who to contact and how to set it up.

The morning was wearing on. Polo had thought that by now he would have been able to ride Thea's horse, but this new information took precedence, and he was sorry now that he had promised her he would. Sue Parker had left the house casting a greedy eye on the bulging duffel bag. Now Polo and Ruthie and Hy were studying its contents, and Manon brought in a tray of sandwiches, soft drinks and coffee. Polo looked at his watch and excused himself to tele-phone the barn.

"Joc? Who's on lunch rounds today? Okay, tell them *not* to give any grain to Thea's gelding. Yeah, I'll be on him in about an hour or so, I think, and I may want to work him pretty hard, put him through all the hoops…and listen, if Fran is around, tell him I'd really appreciate some observation time… Would you? Good…see you then."

You couldn't second–guess how people were going to react to provocative information, Polo reflected, even people you thought you knew intimately. Because it had been Manon who cried out in disgust and refused to look any further after she'd seen the first few items, while Ruthie and Hy, after the initial low whistles and gasps of surprise, gathered closer in passionate curiosity, eager to see and devour everything.

Polo was disconcerted. From the care and attentiveness of their touch, and the soft exclamations of wonder that passed between them, you would think they were museum curators who had un-earthed some long–hidden cache of ancient cultural artifacts. For a few moments, as the brother and sister drew close to each other and bent their heads over the materials, Polo even felt a bizarre sense of exclusion, as though he were an outsider at some tribal rite of passage.

As if delegated to answer his unspoken thoughts, Ruthie lifted her eyes to his in apologetic understanding and said, "You must think we're awfully cold–blooded, especially after what I said this morning. But"–she shook her head in partial bewilderment at her own behaviour–" it's like, once you know where it's coming from, once you can put a *name* and a structure to the enemy–well, it gives you a place to stand and fight back."

"It's true, " Hy added. "I felt much worse getting anonymous calls a few months ago than I do right now looking at this *drek*. Maybe that's why I always loved studying history. I guess the mind needs something concrete to work on, to give you a feeling of control. Even if that turns out to be an illusion."

Ruthie had appropriated the pictures and cartoons, Hy was more interested in the texts. He said, "There doesn't seem to be any doubt. It's Heritage Front, and the stuff in English seems to have its publishing centre in a place called Flesherton, Ontario. Anybody know where that is?" Hy asked. But he was already up and heading for his book–lined study in search of his Atlas of Canada.

"It's familiar to me," Polo said, "and probably for some horse reason, but I'm not sure why. It isn't a Show Jumping centre, or I'd have been there."

"And I'm sure I've heard it somewhere too, but I'm betting it must have come up in connection with the Zundel trial or something," Ruthie said.

"Here it is," Hy said, returning with the large book open and a fingertip on a page. "North of Barrie, near Georgian Bay, must be the boonies, the nearest sizable town is Collingwood." He looked up and frowned. "Wait a sec', wait a sec'"–he laid the atlas down on a hassock and went back to his study, returning with a file folder.

"This is one of the files I took from Roch's office on the way out this morning," Hy said. "It's Liam's. Not much in it, but there's a letter of reference–a very good one, by the way–from a Brian Jones who owns a place called Timberline Farms. I remembered it was in Ontario, but I didn't look at the address closely. But look, here it is–RR #2, *Flesherton*, Ontario."

Polo took the letter from Hy and looked at the logo of the farm: a horse and rider splashing down into a water jump. "It's a Three-

Day Event stable," Polo said. "That's why I didn't recognize it." He mused a moment. "So if he was working at a Three–Day stable, he may very well have come into previous contact with Bridget. From what I gather, she's either the organizer or the course designer or the Technical Delegate at every recognized Three–Day in Canada. Maybe he knew something about Bridget she doesn't want to get around."

"Well, this is terrific," Ruthie quipped sarcastically. "Forget Bridget for a minute. Because now, in addition to a whole new set of horse–related leads, we have a murder victim who seems to have been a member in good standing of this country's most active and virulently racist organization. Great. So now there's a whole other possible motive for his murder, and a whole other group of suspects to consider."

"I don't understand," Manon said, frowning. "What other suspects?" Manon, Polo observed ironically, was the most agitated and unhappy of the four of them. She wasn't thinking clearly. But he himself could see where Ruthie was headed, and he saw Hy nodding in anticipation as well.

Ruthie sighed in frustration. "Well, I think it's clear that Liam was here for a reason. I mean, he *chose* this stable, and even brought a reference letter. Either he came alone to start a new cell–that's how these things work, I think–or he came to join an existing one." She looked round the table and everyone nodded to say they were following her logic so far.

"Okay, so let's say he quarreled with his cell buddies–or he got uppity and wanted more power–or he was hitting on the leader's girlfriend–or *anything* really. What I'm saying is," she finished gloomily, "this could be a whole new ball game–the point is, he could easily have been killed by *someone totally outside Le Centre*, but someone *who knew everything about it,* the people and its routines, from Liam." She spread her hands in an 'I–rest–my–case' gesture.

A tense and pregnant silence followed Ruthie's proposition. Hy's eyes met Polo's, and Polo took in his friend's profound and growing uneasiness.

"Look, Hy," Polo said, feeling his way with extreme care, "we can change our plan if you want. If you want to end it here and call the police, we can. We can get Roch and show him"–he broke off, aware that he hadn't seen Roch all morning–"by the way, where *is* Roch? I haven't seen him since breakfast."

Manon said, "I'm pretty sure I saw him driving towards town about an hour ago. In his car."

"Must have been his car," Polo said. "I drove his truck over here." He shrugged. "We can talk to him this afternoon then."

Hy sighed. "Well, we can't decide anything without him. Let's plough on in the meantime. Ruthie's right about this new ball game, though. It's possible we're completely off base thinking it's a stable person. And from what Sue Parker told us, it could be a horse person from outside our barn, someone who was involved in this Palm Beach story." Hy shook his head in frustration. "This Liam was like an octopus–he seems to have had a tentacle in every door."

"Except that"–Polo began and stopped, carefully beading his thoughts along a delicate wire of logic.

"Except what?" Hy and Ruthie asked in unison and flicked a quick, wry smile at each other.

"Except that the stallion, cutting his tongue–I'm sorry, it doesn't go with the Heritage Front theory, with Liam being murdered by a fellow racist. No, the killer simply wouldn't be a horse person as well as a racist–and not just a horse person, one used to dealing with stallions–that's too coincidental. And let's say Benoit was in on it with this racist, so the Heritage Front guy gets Benoit to do the French stuff in the office. But can he get Benoit to do the stallion also? No, it doesn't work."

"Unless"–Ruthie broke in excitedly–"unless the fellow racist was *Bridget*! She was probably in Flesherton often for horse shows, didn't you just say she was everywhere where they do three–day events? What a great pretext for a job as the liaison for cells in small towns all over the horse scene. And this whole *feud* thing between her and Liam that everyone seems to have known about. Maybe they were protesting too much. Maybe she was only *pretending* to hate Liam to cover up their common cause. How about that as a possibility?"

Polo shook his head impatiently. "There's no way Bridget would cut up her own horse. Simply out of the question. I saw her yesterday. She was really in shock."

Ruthie chewed at her lower lip and frowned. "Okay. Okay. Gimme a second. There's something–something"–She was thinking furiously. Polo was reminded in her expression, in her little heart–shaped face, of Morrie staring at him in the car when he'd driven him home that first day. He remembered how he had thought you could almost see the wheels turning in Morrie's mind. And Polo's whole life had changed because of whatever it was that passed through Morrie's mind in those two minutes. A premonitory chill coursed through him now as he saw in her face that Ruthie had pounced on an idea. He knew it was something, ever since Ruthie had mentioned the Palm Beach story, that he himself had seen and deliberately turned his eyes away from. Something he couldn't bear the thought of. Her eyes glowed and her colour was up.

"Okay," she said breathily, "the Bridget thing is weak on some points, but the Palm Beach bit–a fellow rider–that *does* work–because it might have been a warning to other people," Ruthie said with rising excitement. "Sure, look. Here's a Palm Beach rider–an American, say, or a Canadian from somewhere else, not Saint Armand, obviously, not Quebec probably–and Liam has a hold on him. So he comes up here and kills Liam but also does the job on the stallion as a warning to somebody else, maybe to Gilles, who he figures Liam may have told, or maybe Michel, who might have known stuff–or even–" she caught the look of sudden anguish in Polo's eyes and faltered. "Who might have known stuff…" she trailed off.

She's almost there, but not quite. Maybe she won't–

"Okay, but then what?" Hy demanded impatiently. "Are you saying that this outside rider/horse killer who strangles Liam and cuts up the horse as a warning then tops off his excursion to Saint Armand with a little office vandalism and, working with a French dictionary, decides to stir up some political trouble for the hell of it, not to mention sending the fax off to me? And how did he know about the *Clar–Mor* paper?"

Ruthie wouldn't give up. "No, look Hy, in this scenario–the fellow rider scenario–the office is done by Benoit. It's a coincidence, maybe, but it could happen. And the fellow rider does the stallion and murders Liam." She looked puzzled for a moment. "And the fax is done by–Benoit too, then–and the *Clar–Mor* paper…" she trailed off and sighed. "No, that's no good at all."

Polo took over. "No, it doesn't work. An outside killer–the fellow rider–would have had a different plan all worked out where he wouldn't be seen by anybody at this stable. Certainly he wouldn't have taken the chance of bumping into Michel or Gilles or even me or Roch, any or all of whom might recognize him. It's a pretty small world, Show Jumping. I'd say all of us know ninety percent of the professionals on the circuit, or at least would recognize them. And this guy wouldn't have been snooping around the Jumper arena looking for something to wrap the body in, it's wide open down there."

"But Polo," Ruthie suddenly blurted out, "there's one possibility that covers *all* your objections, and I know you don't want to hear it, but you were the one that said we have to look at everybody objectively–"

Oh why do you have to be so clever, Ruthie. Give me some time to prove it couldn't be–

As if she were reading his mind, Ruthie continued, "I'm sorry, Polo, I know how fond you are of him, and I'm sorry the thought occurred to me, but listen, if it *were* Michel, he had the strength, the skills, the knowledge, and the opportunity to have done everything: killed Liam, cut up the horse, vandalized the office, sprayed the French words, sent the fax as a false lead, and–*and,* let's not forget–a perfect right to be anywhere on the grounds, so he could have taken the paper whenever he liked. Oh, and the truck–with the dog in it. Would a stranger have taken the dog with him? If it was in fact the killer in the truck I saw yesterday morning? No, it would have to be someone the dog knew.

"And let's face it, there are plenty of possible motives. He could be protecting a fellow rider in this wire fraud business, he could be protecting *himself.* And Liam may have known. And he was looking to get at Michel. Remember Jocelyne told you that Liam hated Michel because he was rough on the Irish horses. There's a very tough and determined streak in Michel. Everyone says he's obsessed with winning. So the psychological profile fits. And you just told me this morning that Michel is a complete professional with his competition horses, that he's not sentimental about them. Competing is expensive. He may have been desperate for money. There could be any number of–" her heart suddenly twisted in remorse at the misery in Polo's expression–"I'm sorry, *mazzik*, but it has to be said…" she ended softly.

Polo felt whipped. Ruthie's words had been landing like blows. He was aware that all three of them were looking at him. With contempt and disillusion, he imagined, for their mistaken confidence in his judgment. He had made quite a show of the need for impartiality. But now that a crude, but plausible hypothesis was emerging, one that he didn't like, he couldn't cope with it.

Hy began to speak, and with such obvious compassion that Polo felt the urge to get up and rush out of the house. He had to force himself to sit quietly in his chair. "Polo, it's just one possibility. We don't have all the information in yet. And we haven't even asked ourselves all the pertinent questions. For example–" he drew Roch's duffel bag over to look at it more closely–"this isn't Liam's, is it?"

Polo breathed deeply, glad of the diversion. "No, it's Roch's. I borrowed it from the tack room. And I wondered the same thing. How did Liam get the stuff here in the first place? Where is the bag he used to carry it here?"

"Because all his clothes were gone from his room, right?" Hy asked.

"Yeah," Polo said. "So it made me think that if he knew he was leaving the place for good, if he was leaving because someone threatened him, 'gave him the push', he would have packed this stuff up. I mean, he would need it, and he certainly wouldn't have wanted it to be found after he left. He'd want to just disappear with everything he owned, without leaving a trace."

Ruthie abruptly set down her coke, swallowed hard, and added excitedly, "But then we can definitely eliminate one of the possibilities. See, it *couldn't* have been a Heritage Front mate who murdered him, because he would know to look for that stuff before taking off. And he would know where Liam's room was and the set–up at the barn. So he would have found it, it would have been important to him to find it and get rid of it, right?"

She beamed guilelessly at everyone in turn, as though she'd just got the highest mark on a school exam, and Polo suddenly wanted to hug her, not for this twist of cleverness, which only turned the spotlight brighter onto Michel, but because she looked in this moment of minor triumph like her twelve–year old sucky schoolgirl self, and because she was the living wick to the bright and eager flame of his youthful dreams, to all that was pure and uncompromised in him.

CHAPTER NINETEEN

POLO JOGGED OVER TO THE BARN, MENTALLY RUNNING THROUGH the schooling tests he would use for Thea's gelding. He decided to come in through the office end to see if Roch had come back. He hadn't. It was odd that Roch had just taken off like that without mentioning where he was going. Polo had put himself down to speak with Michel, Bridget and Thea. Thea was slotted in for that drink later on, but realistically he wondered if he'd have time to speak to all three in one afternoon. The 'team' had agreed to meet for dinner at the *resto* to compare notes.

Roch was supposed to pursue the Benoit and Gilles line, but he hadn't spoken to Polo about the best way to do it. Benoit had disappeared, and Gilles was still holed up at home in Montreal. Was Roch playing a lone hand with some theory of his own? Had he gone to Montreal to confront Gilles? Maybe he had told Michel. Polo would ask him. But now it occurred to Polo that Michel might be the last person Roch would confide his theories to. In fact, though normally in the day's routine Polo was used to seeing Roch and Michel connect a dozen times a day, sometimes just for a few seconds in the corridor, sometimes for a coffee or meal, he hadn't seen the two of them together for maybe a week, since well before the stallion got cut.

There had been tension between them already when Michel stepped into the vandalized office yesterday morning to announce he wasn't going to New York. Then there had been his unexpected withdrawal from the Cedar Meadows show in Calgary, forfeiting his place on the Nation's Cup Team. That was pretty huge. Everyone was talking about it. He'd been keen to ask Michel about it himself, but Michel seemed to shrink from all but superficial contact every time they met.

Now, knowing what he did about Michel and this–*Claude*–and putting it together with the news about Palm Beach, he wondered how much Roch already knew or suspected on both fronts, even while he was still pressuring Michel about marrying the New York girl. And if he did suspect–either about Claude or the Panaiotti girl's involvement in the insurance killings–then could even Roch, driven as he was to see Michel stay at the top of the sport, ignore this sure recipe for his son's unhappiness? Was Roch that single-minded underneath the bonhomie and unfailing optimism? What kind of father was he, anyway? Well, whatever Roch knew or didn't know, he was clearly freezing Michel out lately–maybe because he knew his sometimes volatile temper might make him say or do something he would regret later.

Polo glanced at his watch as he walked down the corridor. Too bad he didn't have his own groom here. He'd have to prep the horse himself, a waste of valuable time. Ordinarily when riding a new horse he liked to do the first grooming, to check out sore spots and conformation quirks from the ground. These were not ordinary times, though. He stopped at his locker, hung up his coat, buckled on his spurs, and threw his chaps over his shoulder.

Walking down the long barn corridor, ducking under a cross–tie where a horse stood having his hoofs picked out by its owner, he noted that not more than eight horses were out of their stalls. Roch had cancelled lessons for the weekend. Only the boarders were around, hacking out singly or in pairs–the weather was sunny and fine now after the storm–or hanging out in the *resto*, completely oblivious to the life of the barn beyond their own horses and their needs.

286

Polo had almost reached the tack room when Michel, changed from britches and tall boots into jeans and paddock boots, suddenly appeared in its doorway. "Can I speak to you, Polo? I've been waiting here for you," he said gravely. He seemed tense, but he was looking him full in the eye, Polo noted.

"I was going to ride the Irish gelding, but I wanted to speak to you too, and if this is when you're free"–

"The horse is one of the things I'd like to talk to you about–before you ride him. But–not only that"–

"Well then, yeah, sure." Polo came to a quick decision. Before he let Michel ask or tell him anything, he had to let the kid know he'd been overheard on the telephone that morning. Polo didn't want to hear more lies and have to refute them later. Besides, the secret had been weighing on him. Revealing what he knew was going to be one of the most unpleasant things he'd ever done. Best get it over.

"Do you want to go to the *resto*?" Michel asked.

"No," Polo said. "I want to show you something." Motioning Michel to follow him, Polo walked around the circle to Liam's bedroom. The door was closed. He knocked. Jocelyn opened it, yawning.

"Sorry, I must have dozed off. Hi Polo. Michel, did you want to school Amadeus already? I'll start on him."

Michel shook his head. "Just turn him out. I'm finished riding for today."

Polo said, "Actually, we need this room to chat in private for a little while. If you wouldn't mind…"

Jocelyn looked swiftly from one to the other. Their bland expressions told her nothing, and nobody seemed angry at her. So her alibi for Michel was holding up, and that was good. Polo deserved a reward for validating her story. She smiled sweetly. "Polo, do you want me to prep Robin's Song for you? Oh, and Fran said to just call him when you want him at home. It'll just take him five minutes to get here."

"I'd really appreciate it, Joc. I can use the extra time."

"All–purpose or jumper saddle?"

"All–purpose. It's the"–

"The Steuben? Third rack up on the right?"

"You know every saddle in the barn?" Polo was impressed. As a groom she really was peerless. Joc pinkened at the praise. Michel rarely expressed admiration or overt gratitude. Not that he didn't feel it, she knew. Still, it was nice when someone actually said something…

"Bell boots?" she continued enthusiastically.

"Couldn't hurt."

"Leg wraps?"

"No, just ankle boots."

"Martingale?"

"No."

"What kind of bit? D–ring, twisted wire, pelham?"

"I like a snaffle first time out."

"Sure? He can be a bugger."

"Yeah, I'm sure."

"A snaffle it is, then." Jocelyne slipped past them and took herself off to the tack room.

"Michel, what bit did the owner's daughter use?"

"Pelham, I'm pretty sure."

An amateur using a *pelham*. A pelham could be extremely punishing in a thoroughbred's sensitive mouth. Polo looked inquiringly at Michel who shrugged and said, "I know, but Bridget was her coach, not me. I told her, you need perfect balance and a velvet hand for a pelham, you don't even get that with professionals sometimes, but you can't talk to her. She likes her riders to have a crazy amount of speed control. Me, I use a D–ring on him, sometimes a twisted wire. He can get a little… nappy, and it's better than fighting with him."

"Nappy?" Polo was instantly alert to the professional rider's tendency to understatement. "Nappy as in doesn't like to go forward heading away from the barn, or nappy as in rears, flings himself backward and deliberately rolls on you to crush you to death?"

Michel just smiled. "He's never actually reared on me. But you can see he's thinking about it sometimes. He's smarter than you want a horse to be. Don't worry. You can handle him."

"Yeah, but could that girl?"

Michel's mouth pursed Gallicly, while his shoulders and eyebrows rose in unison.

"Is that what you wanted to tell me about the horse?"

"Just to watch him. He's very athletic, but he isn't..."

"Honest?"

"Yeah."

"Thanks. I'll be careful."

Polo then moved to the mirror, took it off and laid it on the night table, and beckoned to Michel. With his Swiss army knife blade he worked the hoof packing out of the hole. "I plugged this up yesterday, but Liam had the use of it the whole time he was here. Look through here, Michel."

Michel brought his eye close to the hole, and a second later Polo heard him suck in his breath. Seeing the telephone two inches away, he had understood instantly. He sat down on the bed and stared hard at the floor. Polo dragged the stool out to face him and sat down and waited a moment for it to sink in.

"Michel," he finally said, "this is going to be a little tough for me to say, so hear me out before you say anything back. First of all, as you've probably figured out, this hole is how Liam knew so much about everyone in the barn. And it's what makes it so hard to pin the murder on anyone. It seems a lot of people might have had a motive for shutting him up. Joc told me in March what Liam was threatening to tell about you, for example."

Michel was listening quietly, but he didn't seem particularly tense or upset, just attentive, which was unexpected, disconcerting even. Polo took a deep breath. "Now I have to tell you that I found something out when I was here this morning after the meeting, and after you met with Sue, when you were on the phone. I didn't come here to spy on you, but I also didn't do anything to warn you once you started talking. I heard every word of your conversation with–ah–Claude, you know?"

"You did?" Michel asked, his mink–lashed eyes focused wonderingly at Polo. Polo's whole body was tensed for action in case Michel blew up at him or threw a wild punch, or stormed out of the room. So the last thing in the world he had expected was the sweet smile and hopeful eyes that now illuminated Michel's face. Polo felt broadsided somehow, and less sure than ever that he could pull this off.

"Ah, yeah, I did," Polo confessed nervously, nodding stupidly over and over and rubbing both sweaty palms on his knees. He had tried to prepare himself for this moment by asking himself what Nathalie would have said to the kid. She would have been in her element, that's for sure. He imagined her marshalling all those re-assuring bromides about equality, dignity, diversity, lifestyle choice, rights, finding your voice, empowerment–they were like a new dia-lect of a language he sort of understood but couldn't speak–and he wished with all his heart that he could have handed this off to her.

Meanwhile Michel was grinning happily at him, and in the pause before Polo delivered his little speech, the words just tum-bled out of him. "But Polo, Claude is what I wanted to talk to you about. I'm glad you found out. You've always been a good friend. It's been hell keeping this secret, you have no idea…"

"Well, Michel,"–and Polo could hear the unnatural stiffness in his voice–"I'm glad you're not pissed off about my eavesdropping. That's a good start. So to go on, ah, I feel actually quite…*honoured* that you feel *comfortable* about…*sharing* this so openly, and–*merde*, it's hot in here, isn't it–and…if you want to tell me more about this–*Claude*"–

"What did you just say, Polo?"

"About what?"

" Did you just say '*ce Claude*'?"

"Ah, yeah…why?"

"Why? *Why?* But you told me you heard everything I said!"

"But I did…"

"And you thought… Polo, are you *nuts*? Would I be talking like that to a freaking *guy*! *Merde*, Polo, it's '*cette Claude*', *cette cette cette*, not *ce*. Claude is *ma blonde*, my girlfriend. We're in love. And you thought…"

Tabarnouche.

It was as though he had slipped his hand into his pocket and felt his fingers close around the unfamiliar bulk and shape of some-one else's wallet. Claude! *Claude!* Well of course it was both…but almost always a man… with girls it was normally Marie–Claude or something, not usually by itself… but of course it *could* be, why hadn't he…because Roch had just finished speaking to Claude, the grain merchant…and from Joc he had gathered that Liam had been so sure…and because you never saw Michel with a girl, and because he was so beautiful, and so meticulous…and because, because…

Polo passed a hand through his hair, bit his lip and shook his head in wonder at this spectacular failure in the detection business. "*Jésu*, Michel, I feel like such a *putz*," he said.

"A what?"

"*Un vrai poisson…*"

Michel punched Polo affectionately on the knee. "Don't take it so hard. I see what happened with Liam. He doesn't speak French, he thinks Claude is only a man's name, he hears my lovesick voice every night, and he's completely convinced he's got me by the balls. He tells Joc, Joc tells you…seriously, I'm not as insulted as you think. It's kind of funny." He clapped him on the arm. "Hey, cheer up, Polo. I can see why you believed it."

"You can?" Polo felt ridiculously grateful for the way Michel was taking this.

"Polo, look at me." Polo looked at him. "I know what I look like," Michel said with candour and not a trace of his usual shyness. "I get hit on every other day by guys in this business. You kind of… get used to it, and shrug it off."

"I never did."

"I bet you used to slug them."

"I hurt someone. Then I made sure it never got as far as the 'hitting on' stage."

"It's different now, Polo. You can't…act like that anymore, no matter what you're thinking. It's like being a racist or something. The sponsors–they watch how you are in public more, you can't get away with things, even kidding around. Gays in sport are starting to become trendy."

He took note of Polo's expression. "I know. It sort of amazes me too. But I have to say," Michel shook his head a little in bemusement, "some of the guys who are right out of the closet, the ones who have relationships–they're pretty happy, it gets to seem normal, it's easy to be with them…"

Polo found himself nodding and smiling sympathetically. At this moment he fervently hoped homosexuals all over the world would be happy. He was definitely okay with that concept, which he would have resisted five minutes ago. But five minutes ago he had thought Michel was gay, and now he knew Michel wasn't, and the lightening of his mood and the new benevolence in his attitude to gays was nothing short of remarkable.

"Michel, what a trip, *Seigneur*, there are so many things I want to ask you, I don't know where to start"–

"And there's lots I want to tell you. You saw me with that journalist. Before I started talking to her, I was sitting on a mountain of secrets. It seems like it's been forever. I was like a volcano about to blow. I thought I didn't want to talk about Palm Beach, but–oh sorry, I'm getting ahead of things, do you even know anything about what went down there this winter?"

"I heard rumours for a long time. Sue told the Jacobsons and they told me. I wouldn't mind hearing the details."

"Did she say she got it from me?" Suddenly Michel's voice went from confiding to high alert.

"No way. Don't worry, Michel, she's an honest journalist."

"I suppose it doesn't even matter now if people did know I blabbed…anyway, but when I finally told her, I felt… I felt like I'd been dragging these big lead balls around and I finally cut the chain to one of them"–

"Michel, did you kill Liam?" It had just jumped out, he hadn't known he was going to ask. But he realized instinctively that this was the one moment he could count on getting the truth from him–or knowing if it was a lie.

Michel smiled broadly, didn't clutch or hesitate. His eyes held unbroken contact. "No, Polo. I hated the little creep, but I didn't have any reason to kill him. He could push my buttons, and I had to smack him around a bit to put him in his place sometimes–and sure I resented him making up that shit about me being gay. But it was the nerve of the guy thinking he could muscle in on my private life that got me mad, not what he was saying about me."

There wasn't the slightest doubt in Polo's mind that Michel was telling the truth. His spirits soared. Sweet, narcotic relief rinsed through him in a sudden rush. He felt like jumping up and hugging Michel, but of course did no such thing. He allowed himself only a broad idiot's smile of infinite happiness, and a full half minute to savour the information while Michel smiled gently back at him in amused indulgence.

Finally it came to him to ask the obvious question that any real detective would have pounced on at once. Merrily, as though it were nothing but a tedious corroborative formality, he asked, "Then why did you ask Joc to cover for you Thursday night and Friday morning? She told her story very convincingly, by the way, but you didn't really think I would believe you were sleeping with her, did you?"

Michel squirmed a bit. "Yeah, it was a lame alibi, but I couldn't think of anything else at the moment. I couldn't tell anyone I went into Montreal to see Claude."

"Why is it so hush–hush about Claude? Is she–married or something?"

Michel laughed. "No, of course not. Although she soon will be–to me," he said with boyish self–congratulation. "I know it's old–fashioned to want to get married, but we're going to. My grandparents will appreciate it. No, it's because of *papa*. If even one person in the horse world found out about it, it'd be sure to get back to him. He's going to have a shit fit when he finds out."

"I take it Claude is not in horses, and not rich…"

Michel leaned forward eagerly. "She's not in horses, she's not rich, she isn't into cocaine, she isn't anorexic. Her parents are nice, ordinary people who treat me like a real person, not some fucking movie star. She's smart and ambitious, she's studying hotel management, and she's the most wonderful thing that ever happened to me." He sat back with an air of satisfied achievement.

This conversation is so much fun, Polo thought. *Nothing but good news. What could he say? I am so proud of your values I could burst? Way too sappy. A joke instead, then.* "She sounds much too normal to be attracted to a professional horseman. What does she see in you?"

Michel grinned, smacked his knees, stood up and stretched. "Can we get out of this dungeon? It's kind of creepy."

Polo bunged up the hole and replaced the mirror. He grabbed his chaps from the bed and threw them back over his shoulder. They started to walk around the circle. *But wait, what about–*

As if reading his mind, Michel stopped, touched Polo's arm, and murmured shyly, "There's one more thing you should know about Claude..."

"The tests you mentioned on the phone," Polo said apprehensively.

Michel blushed, but his eyes danced with excitement. "She's pregnant."

Polo took a hit to his gut. *What are you talking about? You can't have a kid. You're a kid yourself.* Except that Michel was 24 years old. Why did he keep thinking of him as 'the boy' and 'the kid'? *Say something, stop staring at him as if he just announced he has AIDS.*

"And you're...okay with that..."

"*Okay*? I can hardly sleep at night, thinking about how great it's going to be. Except," Michel added soberly, "we're a little nervous. She's been bleeding a bit, so she went for an ultrasound...I feel like such a shit not to have been there with her." He chewed at his lower lip. "That's why I have to tell *papa*. I can't let her go through this alone anymore."

Polo nodded approvingly. He hadn't yet absorbed Michel's news fully, but one thing he knew without having to think about it was that it didn't matter whether you were happy or scared shitless. If your girl was in the club, whether you were going to try and talk her into an abortion or see the thing through, you didn't let her deal with it by herself.

He said, "You're doing the right thing. So...is that the last lead ball...or is there something else?" Because Michel looked a little relieved, but there was still a cloud, still tension in his face and body.

Michel seemed to struggle with his thoughts a moment. He looked down the corridor, Polo too. They saw Jocelyne working vigorously on Robin's Song with currycomb and brush. She was giving him the de luxe grooming package, and the saddle was still propped against the stall door. They had time. Michel touched Polo's arm and signaled the outer door. Polo dropped his chaps on a hay bale, they left the barn, and started walking around the parking lot.

And as they walked, Michel talked. And talked. Soon their footfalls joined cadence, taking on the rhythm of his words, and as they strode up and down the lot, absorbed in their subject and oblivious to the outside world, they might have appeared to an imaginative observer, the two smoothly muscled athletic bodies, the same height, the dark head and the light, in their similarly graceful, loose–limbed gait, like brother acolytes in the cloisters of some equine–worshipping religious order.

"…and Polo, what's really weird is that, as horrible as it is, these killings for the insurance, it wasn't what finished it for me. I hated myself, yeah, for not saying anything, but until the last one, breaking the horse's leg, which was just off the charts for…" he broke off as his voice faltered, and Polo forced himself to say nothing, just keep walking until Michel found his composure. "Anyway, up to then, it was like an external kind of thing. I never saw the dead horses, and this…hit man…he wasn't one of us. So it was like, yeah it's criminal, and disgusting, but at least the horses didn't suffer, and it didn't have anything to do with me…or it's what I told myself… and it worked…"

"And then it got personal?" Polo asked quietly.

"Yeah," Michel said jerkily. His breathing was more ragged now, and Polo hoped he would get it out before he choked up completely. "The horse whose leg got broken, it belonged to Gail Panaiotti. It–it was a good horse, Polo. Grand Prix, I know he had it in him. It was just–he's difficult, he needs–he needed–a really good rider. And she's not great. She mainly just pays whatever it takes to get made horses. So she couldn't ride him, but she hated to admit it. I offered to school him or at least coach her, but she was so stubborn." He sighed deeply, and went on.

"He started to stop at the higher fences. She wasn't finding her spots, he had no confidence in her, that was the whole problem. She was okay at Preliminary, but…anyway, after she got eliminated for stopping in one of the classes, at a vertical coming off the water jump, I saw her going to her trailer and coming out again, and taking the horse away from the groom.

"I followed her. She took him to the warm up ring, and she had her groom put the vertical up high. Then she rode him like a maniac back and forth over that jump maybe twenty times. And he didn't just jump, Polo–he flew over them. And yet he was dying, he was so tired. So I knew there had to be something…and finally I made her stop and I looked at her spurs and…"

Michel suddenly clapped the heels of his hands over his eyes, and barked a short convulsive sob. "Sorry, sorry," he muttered, dragging an arm across his eyes and sniffing. Polo's arm was half-way around Michel's back before he realized it. Just before he made contact he managed to yank it back. Then he jammed his hands into his pockets so he wouldn't touch the boy. One kind word, one pat on the head, and Michel would dissolve. He had to be left alone, or it wouldn't happen.

"Electric," Polo murmured bleakly.

*Been there, seen that–the shock spurs, the rapping, the raking over the nailed practice bars, the BB guns blasting on their rumps when they wouldn't jump over water–*cristi, *how I hated those fuckers. No wonder Morrie lost his taste for the sport when I started riding elite. That was when all this shit started to go down.*

"Yeah." Michel took a deep breath, and another. Polo waited. "Polo, I've seen a lot of bad stuff on the circuit. It's been hard to accept, because, you know, growing up here, you know my father can be tough, I can too, but no horse in this barn ever got treated anything but fair, you know that"–

"*Cela va sans dire*, Michel. I could never have been friends with anyone who abused horses."

Michel nodded gratefully, then went on, "And that's why Gail decided to have him whacked. Because I told her if she ever competed on him again, I'd turn her in to the Association, and she'd be off the circuit. At least for that year. So that's when she must have decided to…but there was a colic exclusion, so"–

"So now you figure this horse's death is your fault."

"Well, it is," Michel said with sad finality. "And it's the end for me."

The day was still humid, and the sun was intense. Polo was suddenly conscious of sweat trickling down his spine. He was also aware of a rolling inner turbulence, as memories he'd thought shoveled under forever crowded and jostled for his mind's attention. The combination of heat and dampness–like today–and Michel's guilt. That was why.

The really, really bad memory took the lead, was mounting in him, hot and fast as lava. It wanted out, and he knew its telling was long overdue. Telling would do himself no credit, would never bring absolution, but it might help Michel to know he was not alone in his torment. So this was the time, and he couldn't think of anyone better placed to understand than Michel, even if empathy was out of the question.

"Michel, let's sit in the shade a minute." A grassy bank dotted with wild flowers and flat rocks bounded the parking lot at the far end, and they sat down on adjoining rocks under a maple tree.

"I've never told anyone about this before." Polo felt very calm and detached as he began, and at first the narrative flowed smoothly and coherently.

"Michel, when I was about your age I went out with a rider from Virginia for a while. Andrea was mega–rich, just like yours. I wasn't serious about her, but she was hung up on me. I was her flavour of the month, I guess, because I was at the top those years. Her family was into horses in a big way. She invited me to spend some time at her place after the Washington show. I'd heard about it–the guys called it 'the Other White House'–I was curious, and it was close by, so what the hell. Nice rest for my horses before the long drive home, if nothing else.

"The house, the barn, the setting, it was–like Hollywood–it was something else." Polo shook his head at the memory of the manicured lawns, the undulating pastures, the English gardens, the sprawling neo–classical mansion. "I was–I dunno, kind of dazzled." Polo grabbed a fistful of long grass, opened his hand between his knees and watched the blades scatter to the ground. Michel watched his own fingers pluck petals off a daisy, listening carefully.

"There were servants who did everything for you. They made the bed, they tidied up your clothes, they brought fresh flowers to your room, cold drinks, whatever you wanted." He smiled, remembering. "It was wild. I felt like the guy in that story, where the two kids are switched at birth, and it was like I only thought I came from St. Henri, and then I found out I was this prince.

"Anyway, after a day or two, I'm feeling no pain, the food is great, she's sneaking into my bedroom every night, her parents are treating me like I'm visiting royalty because, after all, I was such a fucking *winner* in those days, right…?"

He paused, squinting out and across the paddocks toward the Jacobson house. He plucked another handful of grass, let it scatter. "So I'm riding every day, hacking out my show horses just to keep them loose, and she's letting me try out all these beauties"–Polo sensed impatience in Michel–"I'm getting there. Hold on.

"And then on the third day I'm handing off my horse to the groom to put away, and from behind the barn I hear hooves going like crazy and horse noises I don't like–I had bad vibes right away. So I go out back, and there she is, Andrea, and she's got her tacked-up horse on the *longe* and she's driving him at a full gallop, but you can see the horse is crazy tired, I don't know how long she's been at it, he's black and foamy with sweat all over his body, his eyes are rolling, he's labouring, can hardly breathe, and she's whipping him on…"

Michel lifted his eyes to meet Polo's. They were dark with anger and suspense, and his nostrils flared. "Did you grab the whip and break it over her head?"

Polo swallowed hard. He had been wrong about the Claude business. This was certainly going to be by far the toughest thing.

"Actually Michel, I didn't do a goddam thing. I was kind of–frozen in place. I wanted to do something, but I waited a second too long, which gave me time to think. Bad mistake. Because what I thought was, first of all, it was her house, her barn, her horse"–

Michel hissed and turned away. His inarticulate disgust was brutal in its purity. Shame, like the roused dragon in the fairy tales, rose up and smote Polo with its scorching breath. His mouth dried to flannel, and the words wouldn't flow, they had to be dredged.

"Michel, listen, I–I say this not as a real excuse, but as a kind of explanatory factor–there was something else stopping me. See…I wasn't the only one there watching her…and this other guy was also not doing a goddam thing about it."

Michel whipped around to face him, his eyes glittering with curiosity. "Who?"

"Dr. Dennis Stryker."

"*The FEI vet?*"

"One and the same."

"But…"

"Yeah, that was my reaction. But…But…But if the most prominent vet on the circuit, the guy who actually makes the rules on where the line is between discipline and abuse, is standing here watching this horror show, then either it's really not happening, and it's my imagination, or there must be some plausible explanation for it."

He paused, breathed deep, pulled at grass. "So, as I say, I waited that split second too long. By then, the horse had collapsed, and was on the ground, just heaving and groaning. And while my eyes were seeing…what happened next…it was like my body was completely paralyzed."

"What happened?" Michel whispered.

"She kept on…whipping him…but he couldn't get up," Polo whispered back. He would have spoken aloud, after all, they were completely alone, but his throat was suddenly closing up, and twenty years after the fact, he could feel himself shivering slightly all over his body, just as he had then.

"It was…like a dream. My hand was…" he had unconsciously lifted his hand, his fingers fanned open in a 'stop' sign. "I kept… looking at Stryker and trying to talk…but the words weren't coming out…and there he was…just–just *watching* this with no expression on his …" Now the lump in his throat was cutting off even the whisper, and he sketched a vague air gesture to Michel as he got up, took off his glasses, and walked off a few paces.

My turn now. This weekend's theme, eh? Okay, I'm okay now. Oh Nathalie, you'd love it. Let it all out. I'll hold you. Not good. Michel knows better. Good guy, just pretending not to notice. Best thing, all this modern stuff is bullshit. Grief counseling. Closure. Gimme a break. There, no more tears. All gone. Blow nose. That's better. Clean glasses. Back on. Finish story.

He sat back down, and made micro–adjustments to his spurs. Michel was looking very intently at his fingers, which were separating individual blades of grass into perfectly symmetrical strips. Polo cleared his throat, and continued in a tight, but steadier voice.

"Then Andrea just got tired herself, I guess, and she threw the whip down, and flounced off. And then–finally–I could move again, and I ran to the horse, and so did the vet, and–this is the weird part"–the scene was whole and vivid before his eyes–"the two of us just worked on that poor sucker together without saying a word or even looking at each other.

"I somehow got the bridle and saddle off, and he was taking his temperature and his pulse and checking for shock, and then we were washing him down, giving him water and electrolytes by syringe so he wouldn't tie up, and eventually we kind of hauled him up and he staggered back to the stall.

"He was half dead, though. Stryker set up an I–V, and the two of us took turns sitting with that horse for the next four hours to make sure he was okay, never saying one thing to each other, and then I hand walked him a couple of times, and eventually he settled down and ate a bran mash and dozed off, and we left him with the grooms."

Michel exhaled noisily. He had been holding his breath without realizing it. "And then you went and found her and gave her shit?"

Polo sighed. "No Michel, I went back to the house and packed my things after telling my groom to get the horses ready for shipping. But this part is going to disappoint you"–

"You didn't"–

"Michel, you know better than anyone that it takes hours to get ready to ship out. It was late afternoon. Her parents had given me and my horses three days of hospitality."

"So you actually"–

"Yes, Michel. Yes. I showered, I dressed, I went down, I drank a glass of fucking sherry, I sat across from that cunt and the vet at dinner, I made pleasant conversation with her parents, and I listened politely as they yapped away about the new, the amazing, the magnificent Volvo horse van that they would be the first on the circuit to own. I didn't look at her or speak to either of them. I then thanked the parents, told them I had urgent business at home, excused myself, and left. And I never saw her again."

Michel looked confused. Polo didn't blame him. "I just don't understand...how could a vet..."

"How? Because he has a living to make, because this family is powerful and influential. If he lost their business, it would be more than their ten horses, it could mean half his other fancy clients in that area, not to mention his status at the major shows.

"When I thought about it later, I felt sorry for him. I was only going to live through that hopefully once in my life. How many times do you suppose that bitch got angry when a horse didn't do what she wanted? I had the distinct impression this was not his first go–around."

They both got up and started slowly back to the barn. Half way there, Michel turned to him and said, "Polo, I didn't mean to judge you. I have no right. Sometimes I wonder about how these things happen. I think about us being like–I don't know–students at school. We study, we follow the rules, and we write tests and exams. Winning in the ring–it's like acing an exam. You're on top of the world. But then you see other people are cheating. So you want to tell the teacher. But when you see they really don't want to know, and they're breaking the rules too, it's hard to be sure–to know–and so we end up doing nothing–and that's wrong, too…"

"It's why I got out, Michel," Polo said, spent.

"It's why I'm getting out," Michel replied morosely.

"What do you want to do?"

"I'm not sure. One thing I know is, I'm sick of being a nomad, living out of trailers and trucks. I want to come home, Polo. Here–not just *le Centre*"–he gestured expansively to include some greater landscape of the heart–the townships, Quebec–"it's the only place I ever felt I really belonged. But I can't come home to stay if things aren't right between my father and me."

"It's too bad you couldn't tell him about the Panaiotti girl and her horse."

Michel looked pained. "It's hard for me to say this, but I was afraid that even if he knew, he might say, he might want"–

"You think Roch would still want you to marry her, even knowing she was a horse–killer?"

"I don't know, Polo. Isn't that terrible? I don't know how much he wants this success for me. He can't see any other way. The money is the key. He wouldn't hurt a horse himself, he's a good man, but I can almost see him putting it out of his mind, if it meant I would have what he's worked for all these years. You know how he is…"

Polo nodded. Nobody could set aside bad news like Roch in the service of a higher priority.

And then in a tentative tone Michel said, "Polo, would it be very wrong if I asked you to be there with me when I tell *papa*? He trusts you. You go back a long way together. And it's going to be very bad. All his dreams…He's done everything for me…I know what I'm taking away from him…"

"No, of course it's not wrong. Of course I'll be with you." He cuffed Michel lightly on the shoulder. "And–*félicitations*, Michel, I'm sure everything's going to work out for you and *ta belle Claude*." Michel's eyes glowed with relief and gratitude.

And would it be very wrong, Michel, if I gave you a massive bear hug and told you I wish I could be your father for the hour of your independence, so I could bless your new life, so you could embark on it without guilt, and so you wouldn't have to go through this pain that I am so weirdly feeling as my own?

"Thanks, Polo." Michel shifted awkwardly from foot to foot for a moment, then said shyly, "You know, I never went to church or anything, but I think I feel the way you're supposed to after you–you know, confess to the priest." He swallowed hard and took a deep breath. "So–thanks again," he winked, "s*alut, Père Polo*…"

"*De rien, Michel*. Me too… *Salut*."

In a fugue, Polo gazed after Michel as he walked away, his shoulders broad and square, head high. Then very slowly he moved toward the office to call Fran. He felt old and troubled by a nameless sorrow. He had never felt less like riding a horse in his life.

Michel, self–absorbed in the afterglow of relieved stress, ambled down the long corridor on his way to the lockers. As he passed Jocelyne making the final adjustments to the chestnut's bridle, he casually remarked to her with unintended, but profound cruelty, "Joc, you don't have to lie anymore about Thursday night. Polo knew all along it was a completely impossible story. But don't worry, he knows you did it for me. So if he asks you again, just tell him where you really were."

And he sauntered off without remarking that Jocelyne was suddenly fumbling blindly with the straps she couldn't see because her eyes were shot with tears of humiliation and rage.

CHAPTER TWENTY

RUTHIE ARRIVED AT THE ENTRANCE TO THE INDOOR DRESSAGE arena and saw Fran standing with arms crossed mid–way on the short side of the huge rectangle, intent on the progress a horse and rider were making around the arena's perimeter.

She walked over and was about to greet him when Fran suddenly shouted, "*Forward*! More *forward*!"

Ruthie startled, then realized that he was addressing the rider. She hadn't even glanced at him yet, but she looked now as he came down the long side of the arena towards them, and realized with a slight shock that it was Polo on a beautiful chestnut–coloured horse with a broad white stripe down his face, and four long white 'socks' reaching almost to the knees.

He wasn't doing very much, so Ruthie couldn't imagine what Fran had meant by 'more forward'. The horse was, after all, moving with a will, at a long–strided walk, with his head down and practically touching the ground. The reins were loose. This was riding? What a yawn.

She could see that Fran's attention was bound up in watching the horse again, so she watched in silence too, trying to imagine what was making him frown in so fiercely concentrated a manner.

"*Ja*, this is better. He begins to work a little," Fran said.

Work a little? thought Ruthie. He's not doing anything, he's just walking.

Ruthie watched the horse approaching down the long side. In a few seconds he would cross right in front of her. But Polo's stern and shuttered expression, the fixed and inward set of his gaze warned her off the little wave and chipper hello she'd been preparing. It was quite possible, she thought, that he didn't even see her. (He did.) So she kept still and said nothing. As he continued along, the horse still walking, the head still rhythmically bobbing in its extended downward position, as though it had lost something and was short–sightedly peering at the ground to find it, she grew a little impatient and bored.

"What's he looking for?" she joked to Fran.

"The horse?" Fran asked in surprise. "He seeks the ground, of course."

Now what the hell did that mean? He clearly wasn't kidding.

Fran peered at her. "*Ach*, you make the joke," he said with evident satisfaction at his perspicacity. "So you do not know about horses. You do not yourself ride?"

"Not only do I not ride, Fran," Ruthie said, "this is exactly the second time in my life that I have even *watched* someone riding close up. And in both cases the rider has been Polo.

"But what a difference–the last time I saw him ride he was in a stadium in front of hundreds of excited spectators, leaping over huge barriers at a terrific speed, whereas now..." she paused as she groped for something to say that would express her boredom politely.

"It is, as the well–known saying about dressage goes, like watching paint dry," Fran concluded for her with a wry and knowing smile.

"We–ell, since you yourself put it that way..."

"When you do not realize what you are looking at, it can seem quite dull. Perhaps I would surprise you if I said that you are observing two very remarkable things in this arena. First of all, this rider is performing the most important element in the formation and the schooling of a well–made jumper."

"But he's just walking around the arena with his reins all loose and the horse looks like he's falling asleep," protested Ruthie.

"*Nein!*" said Fran crisply. "The horse is not 'just walking', he is walking at a slightly faster pace than he wants to go. He goes *forward*, at a *working* walk, because the rider drives him so with his seat. This is the beginning of his schooling."

"So why is he 'seeking the ground', as you put it?"

"We say seeking the ground, but we mean that he looks for the contact with the rider. He wants it. But the rider teases him. He takes, just enough with the reins to give the appetite for contact. Then he gives, more than the horse expects, and each time he gives, the head goes lower, seeking always the contact." Fran pointed to the horse. "In this way he makes the horse go long and low to stretch out his back muscles, to warm him up and make him supple.

"And he makes him walk just a little faster than the horse would choose. Therefore the rider says to him, *I* am the master, *I* set the pace, we are going to work now. Look closely as they come toward us and pass. Watch the hand on the outside rein. He is now just starting to put him on the bit."

Ruthie watched carefully. The reins were taut to the mouth, and she could see the horse's head was a little higher. The neck seemed to arch up a bit.

"*Halbe–parade*! More *halbe–parade* in the corner!" Fran barked.

Ruthie had studied German, but was unfamiliar with this expression. "What does that mean? It sounds something like 'half–halt.'"

"*Ja*," said Fran. "This is what it means. The half–halt is the most important aid in all of riding. Watch his hand closely as he approaches the next corner."

Ruthie thought she might have noticed the muscles of Polo's forearm tensing a bit, but nothing more. "What did he do?"

"He squeezed on the rein, that is all, just a squeeze, as you would squeeze an orange. At the same time he drives with the seat and leg. And the horse has no choice, he must collect himself."

"Collect…?"

"He comes together. Three minutes ago, he was long and spread out. His weight was all in the front end. Look at him now, what do you see?"

"Oh, you're right. He seems more squished together, and his head is up and his neck is arched."

"This is because the rider's driving motion with the seat makes him bring his back end under and transfer his weight from the forehand to the back. Now he is light in the front, not pulling, and in the back, where resides the great power, he takes more weight. Thus he may launch himself for the jump, where the power is so important. Also, he makes himself balanced, and with the mouth he has full contact with the rider. He leans not into the bit, and altogether the rider has him, as we say, 'in his hands'. Now he is on the bit. Now he works."

"And he does this all because of these…half–halts?"

"Mainly, yes, and the other aids. The seat, the back and the legs command his direction, his speed, his bending, his stopping and starting."

"The *seat* stops him? He doesn't pull on the reins?" Ruthie asked.

"The seat and back and legs do most of the stopping, the reins should not do so much. Force is not necessary when the horse is in the rider's hands. But this is something only the advanced rider can do."

"Interesting," Ruthie murmured, her mind unconsciously at work kneading the scene before her into something conceptual, a critical dough compounded of external object, subjective image, symbol, and yeasty theme.

"But the half–halt is the rider talking to the horse," Fran went on, "the half–halt is 'pay attention', I am about to ask you to do something. Maybe I ask that you stop looking at that very fear-some waving flag, or that you bend into this corner without your shoulder falling in, or maybe I ask you to look sharp because we are going to jump a five–foot fence. It matters not.

"When the horse is frightened or unsure, the ears and the ten-sion of the body telegraph ahead that he will try to run away. The horse is a timid creature, he needs constantly the reassurance that he is safe. Partly the legs wrapped around him tell him this. Partly the half–halt, which says both 'I am in charge' and also 'I will pro-tect you'. Be not afraid. And similarly, whenever you ask the horse to do something, you must telegraph to him ahead, and the half–halt is the tool for this."

"Oh, he's finally trotting now," Ruthie said, pleased to have a little action to look at.

"Do you see the horse's ears?" asked Fran.

"Yes, they're twitching back and forth. Does that mean he's nervous?"

Fran chuckled. "On the contrary, it means he is saying to his rider, "I listen, I am paying attention", and he does this with every half–halt. Thus the two speak to each other in their private language. If the ears are pointed straight ahead, it means he pays attention only to what he sees, not to his rider. It means he is *thinking* about what he might do. Perhaps run away, perhaps jump to the side in fright.

"This independent thinking the rider may not allow. Of course, if he pricks the ears before a jump, this is natural and normal. He sees what is coming and he focuses on his job. In everything, however, the horse must be in complete submission to the will of the rider."

Seat, legs, hands, driving motion, control, tease, contact, private language, submission. Who knew riding was so sexy?

Fran was well into his theme. "Ideally, the horse is in something like a hypnotic condition. *This* is the control of the good rider, not the cruel force of the strong bit in the mouth. But ninety percent of riders, they have not the patience for this gentle formation, and so they depend on the equipment for control, and thus they ruin the mouths of the very good horses they have spent so much money to buy."

The horse was approaching down the long side at a vigorous trot. Ruthie noticed that Polo's legs were long on the horse's flanks, not bent at the knee jockey–style as he had been when jumping. She was impressed that Polo could sit so securely into such a bouncy–looking motion.

This time as he passed, Ruthie said indignantly, "Well, he may be paying attention, Fran, but he certainly doesn't like it. He's frothing at the mouth!"

Fran laughed out loud, rare for him. "Oh, that is very good,

Ruth. Frothing at the mouth." Ruthie rolled her eyes a bit as he lingered, the stereotypical pedant, over the hilarity of her false observation, and humbly waited for the explanation.

"Again it is the contrary," Fran explained with the mounting warmth of the didact in love with his subject. "The horse makes the cream in his mouth because he is *happy*, he is content. He plays with the bit. He chews it, like the child his biscuit. He makes more and more saliva as he plays, and thus the cream."

Creams because he's happy…Hello? Symbolism 101! Do these riders ever talk about the imagery of their sport? Would Polo laugh or would he get mad if I kidded him about this?

"If the horse comes back from the schooling, and he has made not the cream, but has a dry mouth, this is bad, this is when you know the horse is tense, or he has lost the feeling in the mouth through too much bad riding with the heavy hand. With such a horse there can no real enjoyment for rider or horse.

"This horse you see here has the exact amount of contact that he wishes. Your friend is a beautiful, sensitive, intuitive rider. He hurts the horse not at all. It is as if the reins are an elastic band. The hand of this rider feels to the milligram the weight he needs to keep the contact without ever hurting the delicate mouth. *Ach*, with these thoroughbreds it is a joy to work, they are so responsive."

Sensitive, intuitive. Ruthie wished she could turn off the spigot of her aesthetic imagination and simply accept what Fran was saying for what it was.

Suddenly the horse came from the trot to a dead stop in front of them. "Is he square?" asked Polo.

"Right hind back a bit," said Fran. Magically, it seemed to Ruthie a second later, the horse drew the misaligned hoof to line up with the other. What had Polo done? She hadn't seen him move a muscle, yet his seat or leg must have sent a signal. The horse was clearly in his thrall. And her earlier boredom had fallen completely away.

Then Polo and the horse went from the stop into a lovely, floating, cadenced canter and did circles, big ones and smaller ones, sometimes smaller circles spiraling into bigger ones and back again. He did these on the 'left hand' and on the 'right hand' as Fran provided a running commentary, explaining the purpose of each exercise, the muscle groups benefited, and the link to jumping skills.

Polo made the horse change the leading hoof in a kind of skipping motion on a diagonal across the arena–these were 'flying changes', Fran explained, and absolutely necessary for balance in the jumping arena as the horse followed the snaking course. He did dead stops from the canter, backed up, cantered collected, extended, did 'shoulder–in' at the trot, pirouhettes, again collected canter, extended trot, working canter. The hoof cadence notched up and down like heartbeats in a runner doing interval work. In a half hour Ruthie had learned a lot, as Fran waxed ever more expansive on the process.

She was actually sorry to see the schooling end. She felt it had been a bit like watching ballet. For the final few minutes Polo released the reins to complete looseness at the walk and the horse immediately relaxed into 'long and low'. Fran said, "The horse knows his work in the arena is done. This is his reward, and at the same time he stretches again the back muscles, just as the human athlete does after his training."

Polo walked the horse over to where they were standing. Fran took hold of the reins near the rings to each side of the mouth and played the bit back and forth. The horse tossed his head, clanked his teeth against the bit with agreeable cooperation, and viscous spume dripped copiously to the ground. Fran chuckled with pleasure.

The animal's body steamed gently into the arena's cool air. The pleasing aroma of oiled leather and clean warm horse, also a touch of clean warm Polo, swirled into Ruthie's sensory zone. She breathed deeply, closed her eyes, and was momentarily, dizzily, transported back more than twenty years to that other day of Polo and horses and her imagination...

Once is a random event. Twice is empirical evidence. Cause and effect. I can never watch him ride again. Not worth the wobbly knees and this feeling of warm ink rushing through the map of every neural pathway in my body. What would have happened if I hadn't said anything to my father after the horse show? What if I'd gone with my feelings, with all that pent–up adoration? I wanted him then, I want him now. When have I ever not wanted Polo...? And I think...I know he wanted me too. Then, of course, not now. But if I'd gotten him? What then? Oh sure, a trip to the moon on gossamer wings...for one delirious week, maybe. And then? A disaster of epic proportions.

Because it would have had to be all or nothing between us. It couldn't have been just a fling. And what kind of life can you have with someone in this world? Horses. What kind of life is horses? Isolated, cultish, meaningless to outsiders. No...purpose. No intellectual engagement with the world. I would have withered and died. Talk about your two solitudes. And yet Polo's so smart. A really first rate mind. And a mensch. He could have been successful in the real world. He could have done anything. Such a waste. And no children. What will he do when he can't ride anymore? I would have driven him crazy with all these thoughts. He would have wanted to kill me. You'd have to have a woman who's in horses too, and who understands, who doesn't judge. He's lucky to have Nathalie.

"Hey, Ruthie," Polo said with a relaxed smile, as he idly caressed the horse's neck. She was afraid to make eye contact, but noted that his colour was up and he had been sweating. It *was* work. She also saw that he had shed his austere and monkish air of urgent concentration. His eyes rested on her with lazy good humour, and he seemed altogether loose, refreshed and dreamily replete. *Omigod,* thought Ruthie, Polo has a *buzz* on.

"You know what, Ruthie, I can guess exactly what you're thinking right now," Polo said.

Please God, don't let him notice me blushing. "*Y–you can?*"

"Yeah, you're saying to yourself, that was the most boring half–hour of my life."

Ruthie laughed out loud, hoping he didn't hear the slightly hysterical tone of relief. "Au contraire, Polo. This has been a wonderful learning experience. Fran is a great teacher."

She felt rather than saw Fran's appreciative smile. She couldn't take her hungry gaze off the sweet languor of Polo's expression. She said, "It seems to have done you good. Is riding always such a stress reliever?"

Polo spanked the horse smartly on the neck, and Ruthie saw the sweat–darkened satin of the skin ripple swiftly in a delicate shiver.

"Not always. Depends on the horse. In fact, I didn't feel like riding today. Glad I did, though. When a horse puts out for you like this guy–yeah, it's a good trip."

Ruthie bit her lip, and looked for a diversion and somewhere else to put her eyes. "May I touch him?" She pointed at the horse's head.

"Sure. Scratch his nose, they like that."

Ruthie tentatively petted the moleskin–coated rubber of the gelding's nose, and smiled when he blew a huge, sighing puff of moist, oaty air into her face. "What's his name?"

"Robin's Song. Out of Rockin' Robin. That's the stallion that was cut."

"Oh, I see." And she repeated, under her breath, "Robin's Song. Robin's Song…"

Polo asked Fran, "So what do you think?"

"You tell me first. How feels he to you?"

Polo stroked the horse's neck, then moved his hand forward to cup an ear and pull gently up on it. "I love this guy. He's beautifully made. Someone took a lot of trouble bringing him along. An angel's mouth. Very responsive to the seat and lower back. Gorgeous trot, you can get in deep and stay there. You lay two ounces of your lower leg on, and he yields like a kitten. Gets in the rhythm and keeps it without making you nag. Didn't need spurs at all, never mind a whip."

Ruthie felt herself blushing and feigned a sudden interest in the jumping rails stored in the corner.

"I agree," said Fran. "He is not the super big mover for a Grand Prix, few thoroughbreds are, but no matter, his gaits are all regular, excellent even, and for an amateur dressage rider, yes, he would be ideal."

"It's funny, though. Michel said he could be a bit nappy. I didn't see a hint of it."

"Riding in an arena tells you but one third of the story for an event horse, *ja*? You must take him out," said Fran.

"Yeah, I was going to anyway. I think I'll have some fun with him, pop him over some of the jumps on the course, do the water, maybe part of the steeplechase."

"This girl, she was riding him in a full three–day event when the accident happened?" Fran asked.

"That's what I understand," said Polo.

"And before that she did only the horse trials?"

As they talked, Polo moved each leg in turn forward of the saddle flap while his hands shortened his stirrups by several holes on the leather straps. "I think so…ah, I see what you mean. You're thinking of the Roads and Tracks of the Three–Day?"

Fran nodded thoughtfully. "The nappy horse, I look first to the feet. In here is kind to the feet. If the problem is in the feet, the roads will tell you."

Polo clapped the chestnut's silky neck once more, and said, "Okay, partner, no more Mr. Nice Guy. We're going to find out if you have the right stuff on the battlefield." He picked up and shortened the reins. "Fran, I really appreciate you coming out to keep me honest. Thanks." Turning to the corner, he called out, "Ruthie, see you later." He picked up a posting trot and Ruthie rejoined Fran, her composure more or less restored, as he swept through the wide door at the far end of the arena.

As they watched Polo ride out, something tickled Ruthie's memory. "Fran, you said I would see two remarkable things here, and one would be the schooling. What was the other?"

"Oh yes," nodded Fran. "The other remarkable thing was to see an experienced jumper rider without so big the ego that he has no problem to ask a dressage instructor to observe and correct him, also who understands the importance of consecrating the time for these fundamentals over and over again. Such humility and respect for the art of dressage is rare in North America, I may tell you. In Europe, of course, it is a commonplace."

"Well, it's true. Polo never had a big ego." She was silent for a long moment.

"Fran," Ruthie then segued briskly into French, Fran's mother tongue, as a way to change the subject from horses completely, but still keep him comfortable. "Fran, I was wondering if I could talk to you a little more about yesterday's events. Polo and Roch and my brother and his wife and I are trying to work out what might have happened to this stable boy, because nobody seems to want to get the police involved. We've given ourselves until tomorrow. And–it seems that I've been assigned to talk to you–and I had hoped to your wife as well."

"To me you may speak, by all means. My wife is–well, perhaps it will not be necessary after we have spoken. We both wish only to cooperate, but she is fragile, as you no doubt have remarked. I try to spare her unpleasantness when I can. So–what is it you want to know?"

"Oh dear. Well, I guess the short answer to that question is–did you kill him–although I daresay a real detective wouldn't go about things so directly."

Fran chuckled smoothly. "Ruth, you are a most charming and intelligent lady, if you permit me to say so. And I am not one to beat around the bush, so let us dispense with the subtleties and strategies of the so–called 'real detective.'" He gestured toward a raised viewing gallery behind the interior long side of the arena. They climbed the short flight of steps and settled themselves on a bench.

Fran said, "This morning I listened very carefully to the responses of everyone when they were asked their whereabouts at the estimated time of the murder, which was late afternoon to early evening. It became clear to me that almost nobody has a real alibi for that time period. I had been worried that I might be the only one on whom suspicion might fall, that the others had waterproof alibis. But now I am convinced that even if you find who you think is the killer, you will never have the evidence or an eyewitness to prove it. This makes me feel freer to elaborate on my original story.

"Eva told you I returned home at my usual time. Her nervousness probably struck you as suspicious. You are right to be so. I returned home an hour later than usual. The reason? I was intent on finding this Liam and doing something to make him stop persecuting my wife. I had in mind to threaten that I would go to the police with what we knew of his vile activities"–

"Oh, so you know about his racist connections!" Ruthie cried.

"But of course. This was his vehicle for tormenting us. He seemed to know something troubling about everyone, I don't know how"–

Ruthie interrupted excitedly to tell Fran about the hole in the wall and the telephone.

"Ah, I see. But"—he shrugged—"this makes no sense for us. I never use the telephone there except perhaps to call to Eva to say I would prefer potatoes to cabbage for dinner. And in any case with Eva I speak German. No," he shook his head, "in our case our so-called secret was something he falsely inferred from our language and from his finding out somehow the birthplace of my wife."

"Which is"—

"Passau, Bavaria."

Ruthie sucked in her breath. "*Passau*! Oh, but that's where all those terrible things happened. That girl from Passau, Anna Rosmus, who had so much trouble finding out what happened, because nobody wanted to talk about it. She wrote a book, Hy read it, he was so impressed—oh, and some of that horrible hate literature Liam had, it came from there…"

"Ah! You have seen it!"

"Yes! Yes! Polo found a whole boxful of it under his bed. He brought it to my brother's house. It's there now. I don't understand"—

"It is simple, really. This idiot malcontent puts what he thinks is two and two together, and is convinced that we must be secret nazis waiting for our chance to do harm to the Jewish stable owner. He refuses to retreat from this craziness in spite of our frequent warnings. Finally my wife cannot take it any longer. She refuses to come to the barn. She has suffered her whole life because she resisted everything her town stood for. If you knew what happened to her"—his voice broke a little and he looked away.

Ruthie was distressed and alarmed. What she was hearing, coming from a determined and opinionated man, healthy and probably very fit in spite of his age, a protective and devoted husband furious at a senseless invasion of his and his wife's contented lives, was beginning to sound very much like an excellent motive for murder.

Fran continued, calmer and dignified. "I knew that Liam was working on the cross-country course. I set out on foot, as I did not wish my car to be seen in the area. Walking, it took about ten minutes to arrive at the course, and a further ten minutes to find the jump he was repairing. With wire, naturally. There was a roll of it in the wheelbarrow beside him, along with his other tools."

"And what did you say to him?" Ruthie asked, wide-eyed with suspense.

Fran smiled wryly. "Nothing. You may believe me or not, but I was close enough to see the wheelbarrow, yet still hidden by a screen of trees, when another person appeared, and immediately engaged the boy in an angry discourse concerning their own grievances with him."

"You don't wish to name this person?"

Fran sighed. "I am reluctant to tell you, because I did not see what happened for long. I was nervous about being discovered. I slipped away. And therefore I do not know if the person I saw was the killer, or was just angry with him, and then left, only to have a third person turn up after that. So if I give you a name, then I am implicating that person, *n'est-ce pas?*"

"I suppose so," Ruthie sighed, "but don't you think it looks a little suspicious if you don't give us a name? I mean, it's an awfully easy way to exculpate yourself without backing up your story, do you see what I mean?"

Fran was pensive for a long minute. "You are right, of course. I will tell you then, but I ask that you make no automatic assumptions. Because the problem is, this person, from the depth of the anger I saw, was as motivated as I was to see that boy disappear forever."

"Well, I can certainly promise for myself, Fran. I've been trying all along to see this thing from as many angles as possible," said Ruthie.

"It was Bridget who I saw, who was so angry, and so determined to intimidate Liam. He was insisting that the cross-country jumps at the Timberline three-day event were not of an official height. He reminded her that he had been there, working for the owner, Mr. Jones. He seemed to imply that the accident to the girl who died there had something to do with that, because Bridget had been the course designer for that event. She was furious at his intrusion into her affairs. But as well there was something that struck me very strangely. As a language student you may have some opinion. It may or may not have something to tell you about her guilt or innocence."

Ruthie cocked her head encouragingly.

"As you know, English is the language in which I am least expert. I speak it well enough, but my ear is not as attuned, shall we say, to the nuances. Liam was speaking with that very distinctive Irish accent of his. And yet, it was my strong impression that Bridget was speaking in a different voice, or rather in a different accent, than she normally does. Of course there are so many subtle variations in every language between regions, so perhaps I am mistaken, but you know, I could almost swear that her accent, normally very upper class, was distinctly more–how shall I say–*col bleu* perhaps? Working class?"

"That is actually quite fascinating," Ruthie breathed. Impulsively she added, "Look, Fran, do you think Eva might come with you up to my brother's house for a glass of sherry and a quiet hour of conversation later this afternoon, 5 p.m. perhaps? Your story is rather amazing, and if for no other reason, I would love for my brother to have a chance to actually speak to someone from Passau. He's a tremendous history buff, you see, and she would find herself in the most sympathetic company imaginable."

Fran's eyes widened as he considered this proposal. "Nothing would give me more pleasure, Ruth, than to spend a civilized hour with cosmopolitan and historically aware people. This is a sadly lacking component of our lives here in this little town–I do not complain, we are living the most enviable of lives–but still, at times one is nostalgic"–

Ruthie and Fran parted company outside the tack room. He exited to the parking lot and Ruthie wandered down the stable aisle, peeking in at the various horses over the stall doors, and reflecting on what Fran had just told her. He seemed very honest. Her tendency was to accept what he said at face value. But then that was the story of her life, wasn't it? Having been so sheltered and doted upon and cushioned against the colder realities, she saw the world–well, her personal world, anyway–as a friendly place.

For all she knew, Fran had just pitched a suavely constructed story to conceal his guilt. Because maybe Bridget had been there and argued with Liam, and maybe Fran had waited, and *he* was the putative 'third person'. And yet she did instinctively feel he had integrity. Oh dear, how was one to know?

Polo was right, she admitted to herself. The world was certainly full of creeps and hypocrites, she wasn't stupid enough *not* to know that–she just didn't happen to bump up against most of them. Polo probably did, it was a rough and tumble world he lived in, but he never brought those problems to their friendship. He was the protective type. Very manly, he probably felt, not to burden women with the seamier side of things. Very old–fashioned, really, considering the changes in gender relations over the years. But nice in a man, no matter what the feminists said.

At the very end of the corridor she could see a horse's head poking out, but she also noticed that the stall door was almost wide open. That wasn't right. She quickened her steps, but when she reached the door, she realized that someone was behind it. It was Guy, sitting on a low stool at the threshold, his head bent over, entering notes in columns on a steno pad.

"Oh, I didn't see you from down there," Ruthie said. "I saw the open door and thought the horse might just walk out."

"Th–that was n–nice of y–you."

"Oh well, not especially…oh, I see you're keeping a log. Is this the stallion who–I mean who"–she pointed to his mouth, and made a face.

"Y–yes, this is R–R–Rockin' R–Robin. I'mmmm k–keeping notes on his f–f–f–food intake. For an article."

Poor man, Ruthie thought compassionately. Manon told me. But he's fine on the telephone, she said, and almost normal in person with people he knows well. It's me, a stranger, bringing it out. No wonder he can't have a normal practice. Lucky he has this protective set–up. I'll just chatter away for a minute, then leave him alone.

"It was so shocking. Everyone is so happy that he's recovering so nicely. You know, I was talking to Manon about him. She mentioned that just by coincidence he was attacked on the day he was supposed to service her mare –– well, anyway, that's just a coincidence, of course, but then she said that the last time he was supposed to–um, visit her mare, her mare didn't ovulate or whatever the term is"–

"E–Estrus," Guy managed.

"Oh, thank you. Anyway, that sort of got me thinking. We're all into this kind of detective mode at the moment, and I thought to myself, is there any way I could approach this issue with the totally non–equine kind of background I have? And I said to myself, why not look at this from a kind of literary point of view–I teach literature, you see–so I asked myself what cutting a stallion's tongue might signify? In a symbolic way? So I'm thinking–tongue, tongue. Okay, in a human, it's language, language. Communication. Self-expression, you see."

Guy frowned and moved his mouth as if to speak. Ruthie hastened to continue on with her theme to spare him the need to comment.

"But a horse can't 'speak', can't 'express himself'. Or can he? Isn't it his function in life, in a way, to express himself by transferring his characteristics to a new generation? Does a stallion not 'speak' through his issue? I mean, symbolically? And then, just now I found out that this stallion's issue is called Robin's Song. *Song*. What is more self-expressively communicative than a song?

"So it seemed to reinforce my symbolism theory, if you see what I mean. So in fact it may be that the tongue actually represents the, um–well–penis. But who is going to have the nerve to cut a stallion's…well, you see the reason for the 'transference', as a psychiatrist might say."

Or did he see? Guy was looking at her as though she had dropped in from outer space and had green dreadlocks and three eyes. She had been babbling, she realized, in order to save him the trouble of conversation. Now she felt like an idiot. Wasn't he going to say anything at all?

Finally, Guy tried to go to work on a reply. "Th–th–th–thhhh"–

Ruthie couldn't bear it. "Oh, I know, it's so silly. I'm sorry to interrupt your work, you must think I'm the biggest pest"–

"Oh n–no, n–not at all." He smiled shyly, but, she couldn't help noting, a little fearfully too. "C–come b–back anytime."

"Thanks, Guy. Good luck with your article." She walked down the passage to the *resto* exit, feeling extremely foolish. He probably thinks I am completely loonie tunes. Passing the office, she noticed that it was locked and dark. So Roch still wasn't back. Hmm.

Hot, cranky and tired, Polo tucked up his stirrup irons, led the

Irish gelding into the barn, took off the bridle, put on a halter, and hooked him up to the cross ties. Jocelyne appeared silently beside the horse, as though she had been waiting for his return. Polo was about to comment on his ride when he saw her face, and the words died in his mouth. Her eyes were puffed and red, her mouth a thin sliver of woe. Gloom and misery radiated from her whole being. *Fuck!* What the hell had Michel said to her?

Head turned from him, she began to unbuckle the saddle girth with mechanical efficiency. "Joc," Polo said with embarrassment, "you don't have to"–

"I want to. Just don't talk to me." Before he could even think of what he would say if she let him, as she swung the saddle and underpad off and set them down against the stall door, she went on with heartrendingly contrived, brittle insouciance, "Oh, by the way, I was wrong about Thursday night. It was Wednesday night that I spent with Michel. Thursday I went with the kids from Ontario to a pub in Granby. You can check that with them if you want."

"Joc"–

"Just go away, Polo." She was already removing the ankle boots and bells. She'd prepared a bucket and was going to sponge down the saddle sweat. "*Please,*" she whispered as he hovered indecisively.

He sighed and turned, and saw Guy, sitting and writing outside the stallion's stall. He walked over. Guy looked up. "You rode R–Robin's Song."

"Sure did."

"He looks p–pretty wiped out."

"There's a good reason for that. He *is* pretty wiped out. And so am I," Polo added testily.

"What do you th–think?"

"I think I know what a love–hate relationship is. No more comment for now–at least not until I speak to the owner. But I have a question for you–did you vet the horse when he came over from England?"

"No. He p–passed in England."

"Hmm. Where can I find a pair of calipers?"

Guy raised his eyebrows in a wordless question, and started pointing to the small office at the end. At this movement his steno pad slid off his lap, and he dived to retrieve it. The tiny mishap seemed to fluster him. "Innnn R–Roch's office, d–down thhhere," he said.

Passing Jocelyne, Polo said, "Just leave him on the ties when you're finished, okay?"

She nodded stiffly. She had sponged down the sweat patches and was already fastening a light cotton scrim over him. Then she half ran down the corridor and out. Fleur was waiting for her and jumped up on her, whining, but she pushed the dog out of the way, and stumbled to her beat–up gray VW Gulf. Polo watched through a stall window as the car lurched out of the parking lot and roared off. He sighed. Like he needed this on his conscience today. What the *fuckfuckfuck* had Michel said to her?

CHAPTER TWENTY–ONE

"**D**OES IT HURT VERY MUCH, UNCLE ROCH?" GILLES ASKED timidly, gazing sympathetically at the ugly red welt high up on Roch's cheekbone. He would have a major black eye soon, probably a headache too, and Gilles would have liked to suggest stopping to find some ice to put on it or something.

No answer. Roch was either concentrating on his driving–much too fast for Gilles' comfort–or his thoughts were elsewhere, as who could blame him. Or, Gilles sighed in humble acknowledgement of the possibility, his uncle was so pissed off at him that he didn't trust himself for a civil response. The boy had never known Roch's default good humour to disappear for so long. And oh, how Gilles longed for a glimpse of the famous sunny smile that had illuminated what he now considered his sharply terminated youth. On the other hand, he freely admitted to himself, you'd have to be something of a simpleton to be cheery under the present circumstances.

Gilles clutched his backpack closer to his chest, and bleakly assessed the potential for an accident at this speed. On the plus side it wasn't raining. Traffic was light on the back roads from Knowlton.

And they were in a big, solid Chevrolet, not a wimpy little Japanese compact. He checked his seat belt for the hundredth time.

Well, at least he couldn't complain about his final meal, if that's what it turned out to be. Roch had taken him to lunch at the Pizza Hut on Taschereau Blvd, and he'd let him order whatever he wanted. Roch only had spaghetti. But Gilles had ordered the large all–dressed classic and a big Pepsi. And chocolate cake with ice cream for dessert. And eaten it all! Gilles hadn't realized how much the whole upsetting business had killed his appetite.

Roch had simply turned up at Gilles' home that morning. What a shock it had been to find him in the house when he got back from speaking to Father Pascal. Roch never came into the city except for horse business or family weddings and funerals. Gilles had opened the front door and immediately seen him down the short hallway, sitting at the kitchen table in urgent conversation with his mother. Both had turned to stare at him, *maman* so anxious and fearful it made his heart turn over, and Roch a scary–looking study in controlled anger.

It didn't take more than a few minutes to throw his things into a duffel bag. He was eager to go back. What he had to do now was nothing compared to his fantasies of being grilled by the police. Roch had obviously thought he was going to have to strong–arm him back to Saint Armand. But Gilles made it easy for everyone by explaining that Father Pascal had told him he had to make things right with his conscience and spill the beans anyway. So his uncle had naturally assumed he would spill the beans to *him*.

That's how he got the big lunch at Pizza Hut. Roch had waited patiently for him to finish eating, softening him up with talk about family stuff, with all those great memories of *les bons vieux temps*. Gilles went along, no problem. But he knew a good cop routine when he saw one. Did his uncle think he was stupid as well as rotten?

Sure enough, soon Roch started to crank up the guilt. Did he know how worried his family were about him, and oh, how it broke his heart to see Gilles' mother blaming herself for the sins of her poor, lost boy. Finally Roch began to ask the questions. But Gilles was prepared. All Gilles would say was that he hadn't killed Liam and he didn't know who did. He admitted there was more to tell, but that was all he was going to say about Liam to *Roch*. It hadn't been very pleasant to tell his uncle that he wanted to reveal what he knew to somebody else.

"Why Polo? Why not me, your own flesh and blood?"

Gilles didn't want to say that he was afraid of Roch's temper, and that he felt Polo would give him a fairer hearing. "I have to tell somebody I trust who isn't part of the stable, Uncle Roch."

"Why?" Roch's face with those unnervingly intense blue eyes homed in on him from across the table, but Gilles' hour with the priest had cleared his brain, and fueled him with a surprisingly calm resolve. He felt emboldened. He would stand his ground. The past twenty–four hours had aged him. He had never been so frightened in his life. But through the endless hours of waiting and brooding over the events that had brought him to this crossroads, the ex-perience had turned into a kind of pilgrim's progress. Along with remorse and repentance, the passage had delivered him up and on to a new plateau of emotional transparency and self–possession.

"Uncle Roch, I don't know who killed Liam. It could have been someone you know, someone you want to protect."

"You mean Michel…" Wincing at the withering ferocity of Roch's hushed voice, Gilles glanced quickly around at the neigh-bouring tables for reassurance. He could see veins cording up on Roch's forehead. But amazingly, the boy found himself certain that he wouldn't back down, even if his uncle got physical.

"Do you think I want it to be Michel?" Gilles whispered back hoarsely. "I love Michel, he's my cousin, I'm so proud of him." He swiped, unembarrassed, at his filling eyes. "But it could have been him. He hated Liam, and Liam was saying…things about him…" *O Seigneur*, here it came. He stiffened his spine.

"What? What was he saying?" Roch's voice stayed low, but Gilles noted with horror that his fists were actually balling up, and he was very thankful they were still sitting in a public place.

"I'm sorry, Uncle Roch. I want to speak to Polo first." He hoped he sounded implacable, but Gilles could hear the tremolo in his voice, and he held his breath while he watched the conflict playing itself out in Roch's face and body language. He wished he could have thought of a more diplomatic way. He didn't want Roch to be mad at Polo.

Roch seemed to understand there was nothing to be gained at the moment by further pressure. His big hands relaxed, though his laser glare never wavered from Gilles' face. He ended up by changing tack. "What about Benoit? Do you know where he is?"

"Oh," breathed Gilles in relief, "I don't mind telling you that. He has a girlfriend. It's off and on, but lately it seems to be on. She's a waitress in Knowlton. I'm pretty sure he would have gone to stay with her."

"Do you know where she lives?"

"Sort of."

Roch threw some money on the table and grabbed the bill. "Let's go."

As they pulled out of the parking lot, Roch began his interrogation. "Who did the office?"

"Benoit." He hesitated, and added, "I borrowed Marie-France's key on her lunch hour one day and had another one made, Uncle Roch. I'm sorry."

"And the stallion?"

Gilles became agitated, remembering the terrible scene. "I swear, I never knew that was supposed to be part of the plan. I don't think it was. Liam was a bad guy, but he really cared about the horses. I just can't see him doing that. And Benoit–he wouldn't have the nerve. He makes out like he's really tough, but he's kind of a baby underneath, you know?"

Roch sorted his thoughts for a few minutes, and Gilles struggled with his conscience. What hadn't materialized shouldn't matter, but he had to feel he'd emptied himself out on this side of the affair, as he intended to on the other side with Polo. "Uncle Roch, there was something else supposed to happen."

"What?" Roch's tone was gruff and contemptuous. Gilles felt himself close to tears again. Although he knew he was spiritually stronger, he felt helplessly emotional at every turn now. He hadn't known how much he loved his uncle until yesterday. He knew that whatever affection Roch had ever had for him was forfeited already. This would be the final nail in the coffin of their connection.

"You know the new dressage arena that Mr. Jacobson is building near his house?"

Roch nodded impatiently. "*Et alors?*"

"Liam was going to set it on fire," Gilles said glumly, hopelessly.

He stole a look at Roch's face, and read complete bewilderment. Roch said stupidly, "Hy's arena? On fire? Why the fuck would he do that?"

"It was his…mission."

Roch took his eyes off the road for two terrifying seconds as he raked Gilles' face. "Go on."

Gilles sighed and plunged in. "Liam belonged to this group. I tried to explain it to Father Pascal, but he already knew all about that kind of thing. It's a kind of club of guys who think they have to defend themselves against these enemies? Only the enemies aren't like soldiers or another country or anything, they're more like outsiders who live here, but don't really belong in our society. And they're rich and smart and have secret connections with each other. So they know how to take your stuff away from you, and have power over you. You know, like the Jews.

"For me it was the Jews just because I thought they're like Liam said, but for Benoit it was not only because they're Jews, but more because they took *le Centre* away from his family." He sighed deeply. "Father Pascal explained it all to me. Why it's wrong. And I don't know why it was so easy for Liam to get me going on the Jews. I don't even know any Jews. Except Mr. Jacobson. But he had me going. He definitely had me going."

Gilles looked bleakly out the window, as if the answer to Liam's powers might be found in the whipping procession of telephone poles they were passing at such intimidating speed. He felt Roch's eyes on him and reluctantly turned to face him.

Roch was staring at him with–incredulity, as it seemed to Gilles. As if his uncle were looking into his soul and not believing what he was seeing, it was that black. Gilles squirmed with a sense of bottomless shame. Stoically he soldiered on. "Liam said we had to show them who was boss, who was superior. He said we should burn down the dressage arena. Benoit thought that was a cool idea. I was really scared, but at least nobody would get hurt. Anyway,

Liam said I could just watch the fire. He said being a witness is as good as doing something, as long as you didn't blab afterward."

Roch's anger seemed to have ebbed a bit. Now he seemed more stunned and saddened than anything else. But he kept his eyes on the road, as he asked, his voice husky with frustration, "Gilles, did you have any idea what this crazy shit would mean for *Le Centre*? Or for your family? Didn't you even think about that?"

Gilles flushed. That word again. *Family*. The scope of his infidelity smote him so painfully it scared him. How many times could your heart squeeze up like this without doing some permanent damage? Again he felt those hot, ready tears glazing his eyes. "I–I don't know how it happened, Uncle Roch. I didn't think about anything. The way he talked–I don't know, it made me feel…important…"

"Important." Roch's voice held no expression at all. Or rather it was an expression that went so far beyond contempt, Gilles felt, that it was like the frequency only dogs can hear. For him, lowlife that he was, there was no expression in Roch's voice, but for people with character and standards, their ears would probably hurt just hearing him say that one word.

Polo returned the calipers to where he'd found them. He went back to the gelding on the crossties, checked him for a possible second sweat, found him reasonably dry, and put him back in his stall across from the stallion and Guy. Polo knew Guy had followed his examination of the horse's hooves with ardent curiosity, but for reasons Polo could not yet articulate to himself, felt quite sure it would be wrong to discuss his suspicions with him.

Polo went to the lockers to put away his chaps and spurs. Opening the door he saw his driver's coat hanging, and immediately recalled the bank draft to Bridget he'd stowed in the pocket. Impulsively he took it and walked back down to the stalls.

"Guy, have you seen Bridget this afternoon?"

"I think she's not f–feeling too well. She's p–probably sleeping."

"It's just that I happened to see this addressed to her when I was in the office before, and I was going to give it to her if I saw her." Polo watched Guy carefully as he held the envelope out to him. No

326

question about it, the sight of the cellophane window had unnerved him. His pen started to slip from his grasp and he fumbled quickly to retrieve it. More significant to Polo was that he was taking pains to disguise his surprise. Why should he, unless it was something Guy knew Bridget wouldn't want others, or perhaps even he himself in particular, to see?

"Oh–ah–I c–could t–t–take it to her, if you l–like."

"Thanks. Here."

Polo had no idea what purpose the bank draft had served in terms of unlocking secrets about Bridget, but Guy's reaction confirmed to him that he had been right not to discuss the gelding with him. Why, he didn't know. Yet.

They drove in silence to Knowlton. Gilles remembered that the girlfriend lived in a tiny apartment above a little bakery on the main street. They found it quickly because the main street was short, and because Roch spotted Benoit's Harley Davidson sticking out from behind the building. And Benoit, stripped to the waist, was working on it.

Later, when Gilles recalled having seen the wrench in Benoit's hand, he felt horrible. Roch was so pissed off it probably hadn't registered. Gilles should have run after him to back him up, or at least warn him. But instead, when Roch jerked to a stop and opened the car door, Gilles had slid as far down in his seat as he could. He hadn't wanted Benoit to see him.

Polo lingered under the blessedly powerful shower spray with his eyes closed until the water turned cold. Dry, cool, in clean clothes, he felt immeasurably restored. He brushed his thick damp hair until his scalp tingled. He cleaned his glasses. He took a cold coke and an Aero bar from the generous stockpile he kept in a box in the fridge. He settled himself on the sofa to zone out for a few minutes, savouring every little chocolate block as it melted on the tongue. Soon he would make some notes on the horse while the ride was still fresh in his mind. But first, but first…

There was no answer at the house. He hung up when the machine came on. He tried the barn. The stable boy was alone and didn't know where she was.

He called the house again, where she checked for messages more often. "Nath, give me a call. It's"–he glanced at his watch–"3:30. I'll be here til five. Then out. Back probably nine or ten. I'd–I really want to speak to you. Yesterday was…we shouldn't be doing this shit on the phone, you know? So just to say…*écoute*, I have to see this through, what's going on here, but I'm coming home Monday latest, and then–well, let's get somewhere on this, okay? Without… you know. And–wherever it is you're going tonight, drive carefully, okay? You can call me as late as you want tonight. Call, okay? And…for whatever it's still worth…I love you, Nath…"

"Does it hurt, Uncle Roch?" Gilles asked again now, a little louder.

"Not as much as Benoit's mouth will when they try to shove his front teeth back in," Roch growled. They turned into the unpaved ski condos road and drew up in front of Polo's.

Polo had barely replaced the telephone receiver, when someone rapped hard on the door. He crossed the room quickly, but a second knock came harder before he reached it. He opened the door and it was Gilles, a duffel bag at his feet, clutching a knapsack in one hand, and his other up and poised to pound again. They stared at each other, Gilles seeming as shocked as Polo at the encounter. Before Polo could say anything, his attention jerked to the sound of a car peeling rubber, and he saw Roch's chevvie taking off in a cloud of dust from the laneway.

The story poured out of the boy in a single torrent. He spoke so quickly it was difficult for Polo to follow, but he got the gist. When Gilles started to lag a bit from fatigue, Polo signalled for him to sit back and shut up. He got him a coke, which Gilles immediately and noisily gulped down. Then, pacing back and forth across the living room, Polo asked questions.

"Are you sure you weren't seen leaving the stable?"

"I didn't see anyone. It was so early."

"You didn't mention you took Fleur with you."

The boy was visibly startled. "How did you know I took her?"

"Someone saw her in the truck. And later at the stable, she recognized the dog. But she didn't see you."

"But I'm sure I didn't see anyone I know."

"You don't know her. It's Mr. Jacobson's sister. She just got there the night before."

"The Lexus in his driveway…"

"Yeah. So maybe she wasn't the only one. But let's say she was. So. You find him in the sand, you take off the stuff that would identify him, you wrap him in the paper, you take him to the *Clar–Mor* lot…a pretty good plan for the spur of the moment, Gilles. It was wrong of you to move the body in the first place, but it took guts to follow through."

Gilles blushed furiously. It was the first positive assessment of himself he'd heard in what seemed like an eternity, and he felt almost faint at being, as he saw it, hauled out of exile and reinstated in the small community he'd begun to hope might play an important role in his future.

"I–I was afraid it was Michel who did it, and I kind of panicked…"

Bon, so that was it. "Michel didn't do it, Gilles." Polo had to smile at the radiance of Gilles' expression, so much like his own when he first knew it was true.

"Are you–are you sure, Polo?" he gasped.

"Yeah. It's a long story, but his alibi is going to turn out rock solid," Polo said kindly.

"Oh jeez, Polo, that's *super*"–he jumped up and flung his arms around Polo in a kid's exuberant bear hug, euphoric at this unexpected and casual release from the gnawing torment of his worst fear. Conscious of the boy's chest trying to suppress a sob of relief, Polo felt his own arms clasp and tighten round him, and he thumped him reassuringly on the back. Then Gilles stepped back, puzzled. "But how do you know that, and Uncle Roch didn't?"

"I only found out this afternoon. Roch left this morning and nobody even knew where he went." Polo felt a little shy about the boy's artless gesture of affection. He'd hugged him back, though.

Gilles had merged, for a fleeting second, with Michel. It had felt good to have the power to give such instant animal comfort. But was it a good thing to have this kid hero-worshipping him or not? His gut tightened a bit. He didn't feel flattered. He was only conscious of a looming responsibility. Anyway...

"Okay Gilles, *on y va*. You cut off the ponytail..."

"...with the clippers from the toolbox–and I sort of scattered the hair around. It looked like horse hair."

This is not a stupid kid, Polo thought. He just needs educating. "I guess you threw away his sweatshirt and belt," Polo said, without much hope of contradiction.

Gilles grinned slyly. Without a word, he dragged the knapsack over to sit upright beside him, and opened it. He pulled out the sweatshirt and the belt, still sandy, unseen and untouched since he'd stowed them there. He laid them out on the coffee table. Polo threw him an approving smile, and Gilles beamed with rapture.

Polo gently smoothed out the Tufts sweatshirt and looked it over carefully. It told him nothing he didn't already know. Then he turned his attention to the belt. The leather part was ordinary, with no distinguishing marks. It was the heavy brass buckle that interested him, some kind of zodiac motif mounted on a captain's wheel–like circle with tubular fluted–edge spokes extending past the rim. He slid his fingers underneath it to pick it up. The only fingerprints that were likely to be there now would be Liam's and Gilles'. But wasn't there a slight possibility that the killer had touched it when burying the body? He decided to put it in a plastic bag. You never knew.

Polo looked up and saw Gilles yawning and rubbing his eyes. Deep bruised crescents were appearing below them, and his face was noticeably paler than when he'd arrived. Poor kid, Polo thought, he's completely wiped out from all the tension.

"I think we've covered enough for now, Gilles. Look, do you want me to take you back to your trailer"–he cut the question short as he saw Gilles' face crumple with fear. He clearly didn't want to be alone. You couldn't blame him.

"Or maybe to your uncle's house?" This produced a near–convulsion of recoil. He's really hurting, Polo thought. Roch must have laid into him pretty hard over this.

Gilles peeked shyly through the bedroom door at the two double beds. Polo sighed. Gilles looked up at him in hopeful, mute appeal. *Eh bien*, what the hell. Polo picked up Gilles' duffel bag and took it through. Gilles followed, tearful once more, this time with exhaustion and gratitude.

While Gilles was in the bathroom, Polo found a plastic bag, but before putting it to use, he studied the belt buckle, willing it to talk to him. Then, hearing the bed creak, he remembered something he had forgotten to ask Gilles before. He went into the bedroom.

"Gilles, one more thing."

"Mmm?" He was already under the covers, his sneakers and jeans in a little heap beside the bed. His lips were moistly relaxed, his tear-streaked face half-buried in the pillow, his eyes slowly closing. Polo sat on the opposite bed.

"Gilles, don't fall asleep yet. Listen, a fax was sent to the Jacobsons' house at four in the morning yesterday from the office."

"Not me. Not there then," he said thickly, struggling to keep his eyes open.

"It was a kind of cartoon. It was meant to scare the Jacobsons."

"Ohhh…Spider-Jew?"

"*Yes*. You know it? You saw it in the office?"

Gilles was semi-alert now. He raised himself up on his elbow. He was embarrassed too. "I–I forgot about that. I was supposed to send it. I mean, that was supposed to be my job. Liam said if I didn't do something easy like that, it was like not being part of the team." He kept talking through a huge yawn. "But just as I was going to send it, I thought about it and I decided not to. I was afraid someone would catch me. Anyway, there wasn't any fire, and then in the morning the–the other stuff happened, so I forgot about it. And also"–he looked guiltily at the floor–"I felt bad about Mr. Jacobson seeing it. I mean"–he gestured vaguely in the direction of the stable–"he's always very nice to me, you know…"

"So what did you do with it?"

"I left it in the office. I hid it before I went to the trailer for the night."

"*Where?*"

"In the filing cabinet." He had flopped back down on the pillow again.

"*Which one?*" *Tabarnouche*, this was like pulling teeth…

"The one beside Marie–France's desk." Gilles' eyes were closing again and his voice was clotted, fading.

"Which *drawer?*"

"The top one," Gilles mumbled. "In the first folder…Polo, can I…just sleep…for a few minutes? I'm so…" his voice trailed off as his face relaxed into the pillow. He was well and truly emptied out, and a faint smile played over his mouth as a delicious wave of sleep now carried him off beyond human command.

Polo sat on and watched the boy sinking out of consciousness. Gilles was small for his age anyway, and now in slack–muscled sleep looked about twelve years old. His silky dark hair, flopped forward onto his face, his eyelashes, fanned in dark wet clumps over the smudgy circles beneath, aroused a strong feeling of protectiveness in Polo. The kid looked so damn…vulnerable. And he *was* vulnerable, Polo thought angrily, because he was ignorant, and naïve.

This experience had clobbered him. Gilles was afraid of everyone now. But not of me, Polo mused. Gilles trusted him, otherwise he wouldn't have come to him with his story, otherwise he wouldn't have fallen asleep so fast. There was something so…sweet in knowing that. Looking down at the boy, he felt moved, he admitted that to himself. As he had when Gilles hugged him. As he had when he wished he had hugged Michel.

A kind of yearning, a weird form of homesickness, rose up in him like warm sap. Something is happening to me, he thought nervously. He was trying to be a detective, but it seemed that in adventures of this kind you couldn't pick and choose amongst your clues. Some might lead to the murderer, others…

If I had a son, and if he were in trouble and told me about it, and finally fell asleep because he knew his trouble was in good hands and he could let it go, I would be sitting here just like this, just sitting and watching over him, so no harm would come to him. If someone walked in here right now, and laid even a finger on this boy, I wouldn't stop to think, I would beat the shit out of him. If Nathalie knew I was sitting here like this, and feeling the way I'm feeling, she would hate me. If she doesn't already. For all the lost years. And she would be right to…

Polo considered life's ironies. Here he was, himself 'in flight from fatherhood', as Nathalie put it, for all this time, yet Michel had come to him with his problem instead of to his own father. And Gilles had chosen him instead of his parents or his uncle. It wasn't a coincidence. He had something special to give them, something they needed, something they knew they wouldn't find with Roch. He didn't feel he had done anything special. He had just been himself. He had never before imagined that just being who you were could be a *necessary* thing to another person.

But the two boys had given *him* something too. He had shared that story with Michel, willingly brought his buried shame to the altar of friendship. He had happily invited Gilles into his temporary home. And he had hugged him. These acts, trivial in the scheme of things, were not trivial to him. They had given him a feeling–joy– the purest kind you get from an unexpected gift, the one thing you wanted above all, but didn't know until you received it. Because it could only come as a gift. You couldn't will it or buy it. This gift, this–joy of connection–once would be a random thing. But it had happened twice in one day. That was a kind of evidence, wasn't it?

Was it their need that was the gift? He had to deal with this idea. Maybe not now. Was it too late? Where was Nathalie going tonight? And if she didn't call later, how would he know if she was safe? How did he even know if he would ever see her again? His heart galloped. Now there would be an irony...

Call, Nathalie. Please call. I am suddenly a little scared myself to be alone. And I am so ready to talk. I am so afraid it may be too late.

Polo leaned forward and listened to Gilles' deep, adenoidal breathing. He touched the smooth, pale cheek with a tentative finger. He caressed his hair, soft and fine as a baby's, and pushed it gently off his face. He closed the blinds, smoothed the covers, and neatly folded the jeans.

Polo stared at the belt buckle and thought about the unexpected collateral effects of the detective role he had undertaken with such naïve enthusiasm. What had he found out, objectively speaking? That Liam was a racist and his passing unworthy of regret or any emotion–apart from relief–in this small community. That Michel had solid values and was neither gay nor a killer. That Gilles was smarter and psychologically more complex than he would have believed. That Roch's devotion to Michel's career was more fanatically intense than he knew. That Jocelyne's obsession with Michel was even more consuming and unhealthy than he'd thought. That Guy and Bridget were hiding information that might or might not be relevant to the mystery. He still had no idea of who had killed Liam. He could hardly be said to have moved forward in terms of his mandate.

But subjectively, in his own relationships, this short sojourn in Saint Armand had sucked him into a maelstrom. The assault on the stallion and the invasion of the office now seemed thematically linked to his personal life, they seemed to have been the orchestrated prelude to, or prophecy of a general implosion in his once contained and well–defended emotional universe. He had assumed he would be married to Nathalie forever. Now Nathalie was poised to leave him. He had distanced himself from any involvement with dependents. Now two young men had trustingly placed themselves under his protection.

What he had thought was a rock–solid friendship with Ruthie, which had been nothing but a source of quiet pleasure for most of a lifetime, was softening, shifting, changing shape under his feet. Everything had shifted, with more turmoil to come when he met with Thea. Soon Thea would tell him something about Morrie that might weaken his connection with the whole Jacobson family, maybe even corrupt his perfect comradeship with Hy.

Finally there was Roch. Gilles had told him about Benoit, the fight, and about his anger at Gilles wanting to confide in Polo, not him. To add insult to injury, when he did see Roch at dinner in the *resto*, Polo was going to have to convey–in front of other people since the others had to know it too–the fact that Michel had a strong alibi for the time of the murder without revealing what it was. It was for Michel to choose his time and place for telling Roch about Claude.

So in the end Roch was going to feel the double sting of Polo being both his son's and his nephew's confidant on crucial matters. Polo was pretty sure he was witnessing the dissolution or at least the contamination of a cherished professional and personal friendship. The human, the psychological side of things in this case was becoming impossibly complex.

Polo acknowledged to himself that he had never felt so out of his depth in a situation. It had been flattering that Hy had demonstrated so much confidence in his judgment last night (was it really only less than twenty–four hours ago that they had sat in Hy's living room and so arrogantly assigned themselves such illegitimate autonomy?), but perhaps–even though it had piqued his *amour propre*–Ruthie's skeptical and withholding instinct had been the more intelligent reaction. She had that power still, to undermine his self–confidence with a word, with a gesture. Emotional claims were clouding his objectivity, he felt it. Had Ruthie unconsciously foreseen this outcome in some characteristically analytical recess of her mind?

It wasn't as if Ruthie only analyzed *other* people in order to find them wanting. Ruthie was admirably quick to perceive and articulate her own limitations, her own irrational impulses. She had backed down in a second from that fit of unprovoked hostility this morning. But he had reacted so stupidly and childishly to it. He grimaced, embarrassed at his petulant outburst. Overkill? No kidding. *Christi*, she could push his buttons when she got capricious like that.

But then, on the positive side, which was almost always the case, she was quick about human nature, other people's character, in general. Not in the jargon–y way that annoyed him so much when Nathalie expounded on the current theories she was learning. With Ruthie it came from someplace deep within. Maybe it was connected with all that reading. She had all her life loved thinking about people and what drove them and the nuances of what drove herself so much that knowledge now came to her through some organic process, by osmosis almost, unmediated by her intellect.

Did she know something he didn't about himself? She had looked at him rather oddly after he finished schooling the gelding. What was she thinking? What was she *ever* thinking, come to that? She was always a half step ahead of–or away from–him in the thinking department. It could be unsettling, unpredictable.

You wouldn't want to live with someone like that. Always that little thread of tension. Always that teasing note of challenge. That schoolteacher thing. *Polo has tremendous potential, but he could do better, if he only tried harder*...And yet, when it was missing for long from his life, he pined a bit for it, he needed it like...what the hell, it was a corny, lame analogy, but it happened to be true...like a horse looking for the contact with the bit. She could do that to him, Ruthie, put him on the bit, happy to be chewing on the bit...

This was what was bugging Nathalie. Nathalie knew–had always known–that it was something more–or something other–than friendship with Ruthie, and though he had attacked her for it in that awful phone call, he acknowledged to himself now that it was Nathalie's right to say so out loud. No wonder he'd been so angry. No wonder Nathalie was so frustrated and miserable. But what good was this insight if it led to a choice he couldn't bear to make? Would he have to cut Ruthie out of his life if he wanted to keep Nathalie? Never see Ruthie again? His heart contracted with pain. Impossible. *Impossible.* He loved Nathalie, but Ruthie was...

She's part of who I am. Maybe the best part. Don't make me choose, Nath...

But now, with Ruthie already in his thoughts, Polo wondered what, if anything, she had gleaned from Fran. Probably nothing of interest. The man was such an obsessive on his subject, it was hard to imagine him feeling passionately about anything else. And the one thing everyone agreed on was Liam's skill with, and respect for the horses. Fran had opportunity, Polo told himself, but certainly no conceivable motive. So it was safe to have let Ruthie pursue that line.

Wasn't it? He had left them alone in the arena. How did he know what motives Fran might or might not have? Fran was aging, but still a healthy, good-sized man, Ruthie wouldn't have a chance if Fran felt cornered and...

And hey, while I'm at it–punishing myself retroactively for responsibilities I fucked up on where Ruthie is concerned, that is–what the fuck was I thinking that day in St Lazare when she fainted from sunstroke, and then not more than an hour afterwards I actually let her drive home alone? Why am I thinking about that? Probably because later I was afraid that Morrie would hold me responsible for not looking after his princess properly. Because that was the only other time she ever saw me ride, so the two days are linked. Because I was so out of it from the shock of what Ankstrom said that I didn't think when I saw her, I just took her in my arms, I couldn't stop myself, and I kissed her, I'd waited seven years for that, it was like a dream, and I wouldn't have stopped there–because she wanted it too, I never hoped–but she did, and I would have...but thank God she fainted. She thinks I've forgotten. As if I ever...but it shouldn't have happened...I was ashamed, buried it. That day. That day. Everything goes back to it. And because I'm going to see Thea. She was there too. Thea knows something about that day, about Morrie and that day that I just know in my gut is going to rock me...

"Manon? Did Ruthie get back from the barn yet? Good... No, no, just wanted to know she was home safe. How's it going... good...yeah, making some progress, lots to tell...good, looking forward. Still at seven in the *resto...Bon. À tout à l'heure. Salut.*" *Merci, le bon Dieu.*

Using two eyeglass–cleaning tissues to avoid direct contact, Polo lifted up the buckle. He looked at it flat, then held it at different angles. The spokes of the wheel were rounded like thin cylinders. Holding the buckle vertically he turned it sideways and saw that the cylinders were open at the fluted ends. A large needle's eye diameter of hollowed–out space ran down each spoke of the buckle. Six of them. Slowly he revolved the buckle like a bicycle wheel with his eye fixed on the wheel from behind. He held it to the light of the reading lamp, and peered down dark tunnel after dark tunnel after dark tunnel after...whoa!

One of them was not a dark tunnel. It was a white tunnel.

He used the tiny little eyeglass repair screwdriver he was never without, and it worked a charm. Gently, gently, he poked and pulled against the inside of the cylinder. Little by little he coaxed the tightly rolled screw of paper to emerge from the tip of the tunnel. Finally he could pull it out with his fingers. His heart revved a bit as, taking exquisite care not to tear it, he unscrolled the single lined page torn from a very small notebook and laid it flat on the table.

The paper was covered with writing and numbers on both sides. Polo grabbed his notebook and started copying, so he could quickly put the fragile original into the plastic bag with the buckle.

On the side he was now looking at, there was a list of initials and phone numbers. The area codes were mostly Toronto and northern Ontario, Flesherton, probably, where his Heritage gang hung out. Easy to check. He copied them out.

Over now, very gently. Polo looked, and nearly gasped out loud. For there it was. Liam's hit list. He read: Michel–Claude!!! And a phone number in Montreal. Claude's, doubtless. Next was: Jocelyne–drugs!!! The phone number beside this was also a Montreal code. Her dealer? Then Fran/Eva–Passau!!! But no phone number. And finally, most intriguingly: Bridget–1–jump hght at Timbln /2–father!!!

Okay. Claude was dealt with. What about Jocelyne? He remembered their conversation in March. She had been telling him about Liam's hold on everyone. She said Liam had gone through her purse and found a few joints, and she had implied that that was all she had to be ashamed of. But she had been upset, she said, because Michel was fanatically opposed to drugs of any kind. She didn't want him to know. In fact, Polo now recalled, he'd never seen Joc smoking even a regular cigarette in front of fastidious Michel, though she had chain-smoked through that *resto* conversation with him.

So what if it was more than 'joints'? What if it was hard drugs? Cocaine was one of the drugs of choice in the horse world, amongst jumpers anyway. It was easy to come by. Jocelyne worked hard, and during the shows grooms were sometimes charged with inhuman hours and unremitting stress. It wouldn't surprise him if she were a user. Why should it? A lot of the riders were. The important thing was that Michel probably wouldn't fire her for marijuana–though he would read her the riot act–but he wouldn't hesitate for a second if it were coke.

And if Liam really had evidence for drug use against her, no wonder she was so upset about Michel blowing her cover for Thursday night. Michel had assumed she was doing him the favour. But if in fact she needed the alibi as much as he did, then it wasn't only humiliation Polo had seen in her face before, or might not have been. It might also have been fear that she wasn't protected herself. The pub thing with the other riders, that was probably true. But who goes to a pub before, say, 20h or 21h? That still gave her plenty of time. Time, motive and opportunity.

Fran and Eva. Passau. Where had he just heard that word? Was it a person's name? Or a place? He saw himself at the Jacobsons. Hy and Ruthie were murmuring together. They were discussing the box of hate material. That name Passau had definitely come up, but he forgot the context. Eva was German, Fran spoke German. Could they be in league with Liam in this Heritage Front business? No way. Well, if it were true, and it had already come out, Ruthie would have beaten down the door already to tell him. If not, he had no way of checking yet. But wouldn't it be just like Liam to make such a false assumption? Look how he'd completely missed the mark with Claude. Leave it to later. In any case, this was more Ruthie and Hy's department.

And speaking of false assumptions, was Liam off base on both his notations here for Bridget? The jump height at Timberland. If the height of the jump where Stephanie died had surpassed regulations and Bridget had supervised its construction or okayed the design, that would make pretty explosive testimony in a lawsuit. Bridget would be disgraced in the profession. But now look what else Liam had put down for Bridget. 'Father!!! Bridget's father had died in a hunting accident. Surely Liam must know that, it seemed to have been bruited about pretty thoroughly. Unless–was there something suspicious about the death? Or the life before the death? And what about the bank draft? Was that connected to a secret in England Liam knew about? Looking at the phone number, Polo's fingers literally twitched with curiosity.

The phone number wasn't an international code, though, as it should be for an English number. It was 613, so could be Ottawa or Kingston area. He copied everything down, exactly as Liam had, exclamation marks and all. Then with extreme delicacy he placed the paper in an envelope and sealed it into the plastic bag with the belt buckle.

Polo was wired. He was dying to get to work on this stuff. He looked at his watch and almost groaned with frustration. He couldn't stand Thea up. There was no other time to see her. And he probably owed it to the others to share this with them first. Patience, patience.

But he simply couldn't resist. He hadn't been able to speak to Bridget, but maybe that was a lucky break. Maybe if he knew whose number this was, he'd have the leverage he needed to shake information loose from her when he did see her.

He dialed the number. A friendly, public-savvy woman's voice answered. "Grassmere Island Club."

"May I–may I speak to Mr. Pendunnin, please," Polo said, his heart racing.

"I'm sorry, Mr. Pendunnin is busy with the dogs at this time of day."

"I see," said Polo, striving mightily to preserve a tone of laconic indifference. "When would be the best time to reach him?"

"Mid–morning, I should think. Or I could take a message and have him call you. Are you a member, sir?"

"No, actually. This is more or less a personal call. But I don't want to disturb him. Perhaps I'll write to him or fax. Can you give me your coordinates?"

He copied down the address–near Kingston–that she gave him and the fax number.

"That's very helpful. Tell me, if I were to drop a note to Mr. Pendunnin, what would be his correct–title? For my rolodex, you see."

"Oh, everyone knows who George is, and we don't stand on ceremony here, but if you want to be strictly accurate, I suppose you could just put 'George Pendunnin, Head Gamekeeper'…"

CHAPTER TWENTY–TWO

———————————————————

CLARICE JACOBSON LOOKED FORWARD TO HER EVENING WITH
Nathalie Poisson–no, Chouinard, she really must remember
this new fad, or *law* as it apparently now was, women keeping their
maiden names–with keen anticipation. Filomena had been given
the evening off, but before leaving had prepared hors d'oeuvres,
and a light collation of soup and salad, with fruit and homemade
cookies to follow.

Clarice could have organized dinner by herself, of course, and
would have enjoyed showing off her still–inventive culinary prow-
ess, but she was of an age to know that her day's energy had its
limitations. Today she had decided that her energy would be most
profitably devoted to exquisitely careful listening, and–hopefully–helping to salvage a marriage that anybody with a teaspoon of
insight could see was careening around amongst some very large
rocks.

As both the marriage–and, she feared, the rocks as well–would
not exist without her late husband's interference in Polo's life, Clarice felt motivated to lavish whatever empathy and common sense

she could muster on him and Nathalie. She loved Polo and had always felt only the greatest good will and affection for his young wife.

Of common sense Clarice was wont to say she had an elegant sufficiency, and it had served her well as a mother of two quite intelligent and ambitious children. Most of it had been deployed in her capacity as wife to her rough diamond of a husband. Morrie hadn't been an easy man to live with, but she had never been bored–and now she found she did miss him terribly. Clarice loathed self–pity and sentimentality in all its insidious forms, though, and had been valiant–or so she was told by her family and friends–in forging ahead with the hand life had dealt her.

A very *generous* hand, she reminded herself countless times a day. She considered herself a lucky person, a lucky mother. Although she could have wished her children's marriages to have lasted as long as her own, she saw them coping well, Hy of course already well launched into a stable second marriage (she had admired Marilyn, but she adored Manon), and Ruthie–well, seeing how competently she was already dealing with her loss, Clarice had no doubt that a happy second act awaited her daughter one day too.

And as tragic as Marvin's death had been, Clarice couldn't ignore the fact that it was the reason darling Ruthie and her granddaughters were back in Montreal. Poor Marvin–so clever and successful and dutiful, but just the teeniest bit of a prig and a bore, Clarice had always secretly thought, although no hint of such a mean–spirited judgment had ever wandered across the radar screen of Ruthie's gimlet sensibilities.

As for Clarice herself, she enjoyed robust good health, her cultural interests were diverse, she had the frequent company of four delightful, unspoiled grandchildren and–such a blessing, she never took it for granted, though she had been born to it–she had complete financial security.

Moreover, Clarice savoured the infinite pleasure of knowing that she had raised her children to be independent and productive citizens, a credit to their multiple communities and excellent parents themselves. What more could one ask in life? The rest–travel, *haute couture*, social life, community prestige–was gravy.

Clarice contemplated the evening's official agenda and its potential spinoffs, and as she did so, her eyes fell on the nearly empty old shoebox she had placed on the coffee table before her. The shoebox held the reason that Clarice had called Nathalie yesterday morning. Most of its contents–family photographs–had been given to Hy and Ruthie the previous evening, but there were a few items she hadn't shown them, or even mentioned. They were Polo's business, not her children's. She had unilaterally decided to let Nathalie be the messenger.

–Hello, Nathalie, this is Clarice Jacobson.

–Oh hi, Mrs. J. It's been such a long time.

–Yes, it has, dear. That's one of the reasons I'm calling.

–I feel bad that we only seem to have seen each other on formal occasions the last few years.

–Oh yes, I hardly count weddings, funerals and shivas as quality time with you.

–We'd love to have you come visit us soon. It's so hard to plan, though. Polo's schedule is so erratic. He's away now, in case it was him you wanted to speak to. Was there–something you wanted to ask me in the meantime, Mrs. J?

–I won't tease you, dear. As I say, I had another reason for calling. And it is you I wanted to speak to, not Polo. In fact I know from Hy that Polo's up that way for a while. What it's about is–well, I have been going through my things, all kinds of personal memorabilia, letters, and so forth that I haven't seen in years. I don't know if Polo told you, but I'm moving shortly. To a big condo with a nice view of both the river and the mountain. In Westmount Square.

–Yes, he did mention it. Will it be a difficult adjustment, do you think? You've been in your home for so many years.

–It's true, I have many happy memories stored under this roof. But life moves on. Don't feel sorry for me. I'm ready for the next stage.

–Well, I'm sure if anyone can make a success of it, it will be you. You're so organized and efficient.

–That's just it, you see. I do like things to be tidy. I don't like loose ends, and it would appear that I have found one that concerns you and Polo.

–Me and Polo…?

–Yes. So many mysteries attached to Polo's life, wouldn't you say? At last I have some answers. So satisfying even at this late date. Because I hate mysteries. Don't you?

–It's... rather strange you should say that just now, Mrs. J.–

–Really? Nathalie, are you all right? You sound a bit-muffled. Are you crying? Forgive me, that's so intrusive, but I just now had this sensation that there was a kind of strange coincidence in the timing of my call. Am I right?

–Well, you are, actually...It's just that lately I've been thinking that so much of Polo's life has always been so mysterious to me. But not to him. He thinks the way things were for him was just unconventional. He doesn't see it the way I do and–well, when I want to talk to him about it, he just doesn't, I mean he won't...

–But Nathalie, you happen to be right. Polo's life here was mysterious to all of us. Except Morrie, it seems. And now I know why. And I'd like to share it with you.

–I'm dying to find out anything that will make me understand Polo better. Things are rather...difficult between us right now. I'm desperate to know anything that will keep me motivated to keep trying to...well, go on like this...

–May I ask you a tremendously personal question, dear? I can hear the suffering in your voice.

–I wish someone would ask me a personal question. Polo never seems to want to...

–You've never had children, my dear, and I wondered–oh my dear child, I'm so sorry, I seem to have opened the floodgates on that one. I didn't mean to–shhh, shhh, now listen to me, Nathalie, you need a shoulder to do some of that crying on, and as it happens my shoulder has been available with no one to need it for some time. Won't you come to dinner tomorrow night–I dine rather early these days, if that would suit you–and see if together we can't find some missing pieces of this curious jigsaw puzzle called Polo?...Good...Around five, then.

"Wine? Beer? Liquor of some kind? Soft drink?" Clarice asked Nathalie as the younger woman settled herself on the sofa. "I like to have a little sherry myself before dinner, very old–fashioned, of course..."

"Some wine would be nice, thank you."

✤ ✤ ✤

"Beer? Wine? Diet Coke? I'm having a glass of sherry myself, very old–fashioned, of course…" Thea said to Polo, as he slid into the chair across the small dining area table from her.

"Beer's good."

"Molson?"

"Whatever you've got."

Thea set a glass and the bottle in front of him. She had made no effort to create a cocktails atmosphere. There was a bowl of pretzels on the table between them.

"Before we talk about the horse," Thea said, "I think you should know that I've been doing some sleuthing with that journalist, Sue Parker. She came for dinner last night, and she's coming back to-night. She's very keen to find out what you have to say about Robin's Song. She's building up rather an extensive file on 'hidden defect' horses brought over from England by Bridget and her partner. I think she's hoping Robin's Song will reinforce the emerging trend."

"Who exactly is this partner of Bridget's?" Polo asked. Maybe the partner was the source of the bank draft?

"Philip Fairclough. An aristocratic type. Married a minor Roy-al, so now he and his father, Lord Fairclough, are even more rari-fied mucky–mucks in the Royal enclosure, so to speak. Apparent-ly Bridget and Philip–he's known as Fig, don't ask me why–were neighbours all their lives and then rode together until she had her accident and came over here. He's still on the Three–Day circuit there. Quite the star, I understand."

"Neighbours," Polo murmured. To a lord? George Pendunnin, *gamekeeper*?

"So this Philip would have known Bridget's father."

"Yes, Bridget used to say they all hunted together quite a lot. He died in a hunting accident. The father, that is. Or so Bridget claims," Thea said drily.

Polo was startled. Did she already know what he had only min-utes ago discovered? "Why do you say 'claims'?" he asked quickly.

"Well," breathed Thea with high animation for her, "when Sue and I put our heads together, we came up with two extraordinarily interesting observations. Both of us had had the experience of being unable to make a long distance call from the telephone in the restaurant. Even with a calling card. It's blocked both incoming and outgoing, one can see why, as you'd have no controls.

"And yet I very distinctly remembered that in our Ottawa meeting of C–FES this past March, Marion Smy had made quite a production about being there in the restaurant when Bridget spoke to England and had the news of her father's death."

Polo's mind started racing with conjectures.

Thea went on, "And I remembered thinking, surely one would want some privacy for that kind of thing, one wouldn't want a whole lot of strangers around for that. Once I knew it was impossible for her to have had such a call, it became clear that it was a performance of some kind. To keep people from knowing something else, perhaps, or following up on rumours? Who knows?"

Or, thought Polo, to make sure no one discovered that her father was not only not dead, but working as a gamekeeper in a game club near Kingston? And Liam did just that, so that's a major motive.

"I've just found out something myself that could possibly get us further on this," he said.

Thea's eyes brightened. "Really?"

"Yeah. I'm thinking Sue might like to go out on assignment tomorrow morning. It would mean quite a lot of driving in one day, but it might be a crucial element in unraveling this murder."

"Does that mean you think it was Bridget who did it?"

"I'm not sure, but she's definitely in the running as a logical suspect. Bridget's a liar, she hated Liam, and I know that he had something on her she didn't want known. In terms of motive and opportunity, it seems reasonable. Especially now that a few other potential suspects have come up with strong alibis." He poured out the beer. "That is, assuming you aren't the killer yourself," he said, speaking amiably, but watching her face closely. "As I recall, your alibi wasn't exactly airtight."

Thea beamed with delight. "Polo, you really know the way to a gal's heart. It's been a long time since anyone paid me the honour of thinking I harboured such deep passions that I would actually kill someone." She placed her elbows on the table and cradled her face almost coquettishly in her palms. "And my motive would be…?"

Polo smiled sheepishly. "Haven't got a clue, Thea. Let's just say you're a lady of mysterious moods, and you had the opportunity." He sipped. "And we found out this morning that Liam worked at Timberline Farms where your daughter's accident happened. Is there a back story there we don't know about?"

"Did he really? Well, if there is a back story, I don't know it," Thea said, almost regretfully, Polo thought, "although you have no way of being sure that I'm telling the truth. I'm afraid you'll have to go with your intuitions for now." She smiled demurely. "Do I seem like the murdering type to you?"

"Not nearly as much as Bridget," Polo said lightly, "but who'd need detectives if there really were such a thing as a 'type'?"

"*Touché*. Well, it would be extremely gratifying for me if it *were* her," said Thea in low, feeling tones. "and if she spent the rest of her life in jail. I have a hunch that I'll never have satisfaction over the horse–in law, anyway…" Her eyes were suddenly veiled in the way familiar to Polo in his first weeks here.

Then she seemed to shake off the brief abstraction, and her eyes were clear and direct once more.

"Shall we do my horse now?" Thea asked briskly.

"Okay." Polo was relieved to see that she was taking an all–business approach to this. He had been afraid that grief might intrude. He poured more beer and sat back with the glass in hand. "Do you want the good news first?"

"Yes, why not."

"If you decide to sell the horse, I would look for a dressage rider. As an amateur dressage horse he would probably sell for anywhere from $25,000 to $40,000. He's got nice conformation, he's an absolutely beautiful mover for a thoroughbred, and he's well made, comfortable in his skin, as we say in French."

"Yes, Stephanie always got good marks on the dressage tests. But are you saying that's all he's good for?"

"Not at all. I think he might make a lovely hunter, maybe a jumper at the lower levels. What I can tell you, I think for sure, although obviously you'll want a vet's exam and X–rays to back this up, is that he won't stand up for long to a lot of high impact work.

His feet may go. That includes high jumping and Three–Day Eventing. It isn't the jumps in Three–Day that will stop him for now, it's the combination of the huge cross–country with the Roads and Tracks, and then having to do the stadium jumping the next day.

"Eventually he might not do the jumping either. Without drugs, I mean. With drugs, he could go on for years where they aren't prohibited, probably." Polo took a thirsty drag of the beer. "He could do horse trials, but probably not three–days. Which is fine for an amateur with no ambition, but if he's fit for only horse trials, it means he isn't worth much money."

"So his problem is a physical one. Navicular?" Thea asked pensively.

"I'd be guessing, but yeah, I think so. I put the calipers on every part of every hoof after a very tough ride. He's quite ouch–y on the exterior right fore, and slightly ouch–y on the left, and I'm sure it isn't a bruise. I didn't have time to *longe* him today, but I'm betting he'll be slightly 'off' even tomorrow in a tight circle."

"And would that account for him stopping, say, at a jump on the cross–country?"

"Not necessarily if he were revved and happy to gallop. I think there's another reason–or two–for the stopping."

Thea said nothing, but sipped at her straw–coloured sherry while her eyes encouraged him to continue.

"First of all, your daughter was using a Pelham bit on the horse. Why? That's a very strong, really quite punishing bit. I would only ever use it with an extremely aggressive horse that you can't bring off the gallop any other way. Or, well, It's just a guess, but I wouldn't be surprised if Bridget stopped riding because she was afraid. It happens after accidents sometimes. So she projects her fear on to her students, making them use hardware that's unnecessary for the horse they're riding.

"That's why I did the steeplechase. I put him into the gallop and let him run–flat out–no collection at all. Well, he sailed over the jumps–they're just low brush, and he knows it–and if a horse is going to run away, that's where he'd do it. But he hit his stride and kept it. I had no problem bringing him back even with the snaffle I was using. If anything, this is a horse who needs pushing, not pulling. So if your daughter was maybe a little afraid herself on the cross, and translated that into even a little added pressure on the mouth, well…"

Thea nodded. Her mouth was set, but she gave nothing away. "Go on."

"On top of that, the horse has been over-faced on the cross-country. Your horse," he swallowed some more beer and reached for a pretzel, "is so athletic that most stadium jumping up to, say, four and a half feet is a piece of cake to him. He could do it from a trot. And if he knocks down a rail, so what. It doesn't hurt him, and it doesn't scare him.

"The cross-country is different. These are heavy, fixed jumps. One bad knock, and a horse remembers. He'll start backing off if he's consistently over-faced with too high or too wide or too difficult approach-wise jumps. I'm no authority on three-day eventing, but in my opinion you have a Preliminary level horse with a great schooling base on him who's been pushed through to Intermediate much too fast. He's a prudent, self-protective horse. Athletic, as I said. But not a big heart. And, worst of all, he's dishonest under pressure."

"What is your definition of dishonest?" Thea asked. She had been listening with deep, concentrated interest.

"Most horses, when they're afraid they can't make a jump, you know it at least six strides out. Their bodies 'telegraph ahead', as Fran always says. You can just feel them sucking back. If you're sure they can do it, you drive them forward and try to get a good spot. But at least you know where you stand, and you're prepared for a runout or a stop.

"But what your guy did at one of the big jumps on the cross country–but remember, this is only after I worked him hard on the asphalt–was gallop forward right to the baseline of the jump with no indication he was even thinking of stopping. He jammed on the brakes at the last second, and to add insult to injury he bucked and twisted his body like a bronco to make sure that if the stop didn't get me off, the twist would."

Thea's eyebrows lifted. "He surely didn't get *you* off?"

Polo blushed a little and circled the base of his glass on the tabletop. "He came as close as any horse I've ridden in the last 20 years has. It was not a pretty picture out there, I can tell you." He added, soberly, "I'm betting that's what happened to your daughter."

"He was sold to me as an experienced Intermediate level horse, ready to go advanced, you know," Thea said quietly. "Not to mention as 100% sound."

"Well," Polo said evenly, "he isn't, on both counts." He sipped at his beer. "And I did it all–steeplechase, cross–country, the roads… he's definitely not an Intermediate level horse, and even if his feet hold up, if he doesn't go back down to Preliminary for at least a year with a patient and experienced rider, he never will be. Or at least not one you can count on."

"That's fraud, then."

Polo smiled. "This may seem like a peculiar time, Thea, but can I tell you a joke?"

Thea looked startled, but asked, "Is it relevant?"

"It is if you're thinking about suing Bridget."

"Go on, then."

"It's better with a real Yiddish accent, mine's awful, but–okay, there's this little old Jewish guy in Miami who puts on a fancy ship captain's hat with all the gold braid and stuff, and puffs out his chest, and says to his wife, 'so tell me, Sadie darlink, vot do you t'ink? Em I a captain?' Sadie looks at him for a minute, and says, 'You know, Abie darlink, by me you're a captain, and by you you're a captain, but by a captain you're not a captain…'"

Thea laughed. "So what you're saying is…"

"Yeah. By me it's fraud, and by you it's fraud, but by a judge it's going to be 'buyer beware.'"

Thea sighed. "I was afraid you'd say that. I take it that was a Morrie Jacobson joke."

"Yeah. He loved it. I heard him tell it a hundred times, and every time he killed himself laughing…"

"That was a side of him I didn't see on the one occasion he and I met," Thea said quietly.

Finally. It's Show time. Polo, you're two away…Polo, one away… Polo, you're on deck…okay, Polo, go on in…

"Talk, Thea. I'm listening."

✤ ✤ ✤

"It's the jokes I miss the most, I think," Clarice said, as she sipped at her straw-coloured sherry. Naturally I'd heard them all hundreds of times, but I always laughed. It was the way he told them, that borscht belt accent…"

"Polo loved them too," said Nathalie. She was holding her glass of red wine and circling the base with her finger. "He used to tell them to me. Of course his accent was just awful, but he got such a kick out of them."

She nibbled at an olive. "And okay, I thought the jokes were cute, but what always struck me as significant—and it's what I would tell him—was, here was this *p'tit gars* from St. Henri telling me these Catskill mountain-type Jewish jokes, and didn't he think that was a little…*different*, but when I'd say that, he'd just look at me as if it was *me* that was a little strange. I mean," she neatly deposited the pit on her little plate beside a cherry tomato stem, "that is just a perfect example of the kind of…denial he was–is–in about his life. And another thing I never understood was…"

It all came out in a torrent. Clarice nodded and listened very attentively (and with 'the third ear' she justly prided herself on) as Nathalie went on. She just talked and talked. Nathalie seemed to have many theories: about powerless mothers, feckless fathers, surrogate fathers living vicariously, and middle child syndrome.

"…not to be close to even *one* of his siblings? Out of that many? And not to *care* that he isn't? It's sad…"

Also about *anomie* and language confusion.

"…his message machine in the barn used to only be in English, can you imagine? He simply hadn't remembered there are horse people who may only speak French here…"

Also about parental and sibling rejection (more his of them than theirs of him), cultural heritage rejection, selective denial in general, intimacy issues…

"…Why does he always have to be away from me to worry about whether I'm safe or not? Why can't he stand it when women cry?"

…anger management issues…

"…just has *no* idea how much pent-up anger he's carrying around. Sometimes I think he'd like to hit me when I won't stop talking about his past…of course he never has, that really would have been the end...but why can't he face up to that...it's the father, obviously, he used to smack them around a lot–and I'm sure the mother too–his brother told me..."

...homophobia...

"...younger brother Jude is gay, and could really use some brotherly understanding, but Polo doesn't even want to know..."

...and –she gulped nervously at her wine, and her voice began to tremble slightly–above all, commitment issues ...

"Here's something that I find very ...symbolic–and kind of sad. Do you know what Polo loves to do more than anything? He loves to go out to western Canada and pick up these young thoroughbreds off the racetrack, the ones who aren't winning. You can get them here too, but out west they're cheaper, a dime a dozen in horse dollars. He'll bring back three or four–he has a fantastic flare for spotting potential–and then he just works on them for maybe up to a year, more if they need it.

"You never saw such loving patience. When he gets them, all they know how to do is run. He schools them and schools them, dressage, jumping, hunting, over water, in traffic, the works. Just the basics. He never pushes too hard. When he's finished they're confident, obedient, fit for advancing in anything a rider wants to do. And then he sells them for–I'm not kidding–at least ten times what he paid. You can't believe how hard it is for amateur riders to find a sound, made, well–adjusted horse with no fears or vices.

"But once they're sold, that's it. Just load them up, a slap on the rump, ship them out, no goodbye kisses, nothing. He never mentions them again, unless there's something a client wants to know. He doesn't know if they're treated right, or ridden well, or...anything.

"And this to me is so sad...that ever since Morrie sold Panjandrum, Polo has never had a horse of his own. I mean, Panjandrum wasn't really his, but he *was*, if you know what I mean...and so many times I would say about one of his finds, oh Polo, this one is too good to sell, why don't you keep him"–her voice broke–"...but never..."

This girl, Clarice thought, who is usually so quiet and even laconic in company, has been suffocating in a bell jar of emotional isolation for God knows how long. She's going to university, and she's easy prey for all these new fads and theories. She's–what do they say now–so politically correct. The odds are that her parents wouldn't exactly lose any sleep if the marriage broke up–they resisted it in the first place. And she lives in that dreadful, philistine horsy suburb, the back of beyond, tied down to their barn and Polo's business. Who does she have to talk to about this? Maybe no one at all. So let her talk.

But as any fool can see, for all her complaining and her theories and symbols, it's clear that she's still so madly in love with this boy (Polo would never be anything but a boy to Clarice) that she has to find some reason for his rejection of her, perceived or real. All this other stuff, his family background, the *anomie* and whatnot, she could deal with that if she thought he was totally committed to her.

But the commitment thing–well, she's not wrong to feel hurt about that. That's very real. What woman wouldn't feel rejected if her man won't commit to something so elemental as making a family. It's a Quebec thing, Clarice mused. All these poor boys from too–large families with their prematurely aged, overburdened mothers. Who'd want his wife to turn into that? The Quiet Revolution. Too liberating, maybe. Polo's surely not the only one. They don't even want to get married anymore, never mind children.

So she hurts and she needs to blame someone. Why not the Jacobsons? Or at least one of the Jacobsons?

"…and I wouldn't have minded about his feelings for Ruthie if he had only been honest with me. How can you spend an entire adolescence, constantly in the presence of a girl, a pretty girl, without having certain feelings?" Nathalie looked extremely uncomfortable, and she downed a sizable gulp of wine. "Mrs. J, can I be totally honest with you about something? There's just nobody else I can talk to about this."

"Are you going to ask me if Polo was ever in love with Ruthie?"

"Yes." And then Nathalie burst into a flood of tears.

Clarice reached over the coffee table to pat Nathalie comfortingly on the knee and offered her a tissue. (How prescient she had been to put a box of Kleenex handy.) She smoothed her skirt and cleared her throat, as she considered whether she should abridge and sugarcoat, or just 'let it all hang out', as the children put it (what a revolting expression), and see the chips fall where they might.

Honesty seemed to be what Nathalie wanted. Preparing to receive it, Nathalie was pouring herself a second glass of wine. She would no doubt have more at dinner, and Clarice made a mental note to insist that she take a cab to her parents and sleep in town there instead of driving back to St. Lazare, or even spend the night here at her house.

"Well," Clarice said as mildly and benignly as possible, "in my opinion, Polo and Ruthie were in love with each other almost from the day they met. But," she held up her hand to forestall Nathalie's questions or comments, "it was a child's version of love. It wasn't real, not in the way you love Polo now and the way I believe he loves you. I mean, we're not talking about Romeo and Juliet here, Nathalie. It wasn't sexual. Let me try to explain how it was between them and please, just without saying anything for a few minutes. Try the eggplant dip, dear. I made it myself."

Nathalie was looking down, biting her lip, and playing with the limp tissue. She seems like such a girl still, Clarice thought. Still no makeup (it's starting to be time for a touch of blush and lipstick at least!) and that same boring braid down the back (Clarice itched to whisk her off to Marc–André, who cut so divinely, to see what he could do with that wonderful thick straight brown mane of hers), she bites her nails, and yes, there's still that little bit of Bambi gawkiness when she's emotional, as if she doesn't quite know what to do with her hands and feet.

"Ruthie was a reader," Clarice began. "And is, of course. But in those days, still a child really, she didn't distinguish so well between fantasy and reality. She was so tremendously–impressionable, you see. She got into character with whoever was the hero or heroine of the current story. Well, as it happened, when Polo first started coming to the house, her great narrative passion was St. Exupéry's *Le Petit Prince*. You must have read it in school. It was quite funny, really."

–*Mummy, look.*
–*I'm looking. What is it, darling? Your book?*
–*No, mummy. Look at the cover. At the picture.*

–You mean the picture of The Little Prince?

–Yes. But don't you see who the little prince is?

–Oh darling, you mean he looks like Polo? Yes, I suppose he does in a way...

"And my dear, she just looked at me in this peculiar way, as if to say I didn't get it *at all*, and it dawned on me that she didn't think he *looked like* The Little Prince. She really thought he *was* the Little Prince." Clarice smiled faintly and shook her head at the still vivid memory of Ruthie's passionate, scornful eyes when it became clear to her that her mother didn't *understand*.

"Well, I suppose to Ruthie it must have seemed as if Polo had dropped into our house from another planet. No one ever offered her a more plausible explanation, that's for sure." Clarice held up her own beautifully manicured nails for inspection as she noticed Nathalie chewing nervously at the side of her thumb.

"And don't think for a minute that I didn't recognize the inherent dangers in that little scenario. It was one thing for her to fantasize about Heathcliff on the moors to her Cathy, but there was no actual Heathcliff in the house when she was reading *Wuthering Heights*, you see."

"Didn't you say something to Mr. J?" Nathalie's tears had dried. She was trying very hard to approach the subject in a kind of objective, historical spirit now, Clarice could see. Sweet, sweet girl. Her feelings too close to the surface, of course, and a bit naïve and unsophisticated in spite of her elite background, which made her vulnerable. But really a very honest, lovable, big–hearted sort of girl. The type a man wanted for the long haul.

Clarice sighed. This was going to be difficult to explain without segueing immediately to the shoebox, but intuition told her to plough on by the long route, and it would be better in the end. For, once she saw the contents of the shoebox, Nathalie wouldn't be able to take in another word that didn't bear directly upon it.

"Yes, I did, Nathalie. I told him that very night. But his reaction was not what I expected.

–She thinks Polo is a little prince?

–No, dear. She thinks he is a character from a famous French story–by St. Exupéry, called The Little Prince. *Here, here it is. Do you see the picture on the cover?*

–Oh my God, it's…him…

–Well, that's my point. Yes, I agree he does look a lot like Polo, but she's in some fantasy state where she thinks this fictional character is real. It's not healthy, Morrie. Morrie, are you listening to me?

"So what happened?" Nathalie was wide–eyed, riveted.

"Nothing very much, I'm afraid. It was a bit surreal. He seemed at a loss for words, unusual for him. Now I know why–but then… it was out of character for him to be so passive. In any case, he certainly didn't seem to think there was anything to worry about. There was no question of interfering with their friendship, Polo's and Ruthie's, he made that clear. I think I became convinced I was overreacting."

"So if Ruthie was living in a fantasy world, what about Polo?" Nathalie pressed. "No fantasies there, I'm sure. But you said he loved her too."

"Oh yes, he thought he was very cool and secretive about it, but his eyes were just locked on her whenever she was in the room. But you see, in his case it was fascination. I don't think he knew any little girls like Ruthie before. She was his…Other, as Sartre would say, or whoever invented that concept. And just as important, she was his teacher. She–how would I say–mediated, she helped to facilitate his entry into the world he had chosen, by giving him some important tools for survival there.

"Polo had a vocation. Horses–it seems a strange thing to have a vocation for. To me horses were a hobby, something you did for fun. But watching Polo over the years I came to understand it can be a very deep thing. That's something you can relate to very well, naturally. In the end I had to respect it. No priest ever took his calling so seriously. Of course it was a very selfish passion, unlike the priesthood.

"But his sense of–what?–consecration to that world was no less devout. He was totally absorbed in it. Everything he did was calculated to serve that passion, I think. And he needed and wanted good English to feel confident. He wasn't in school. How else would he have managed without Ruthie who was so coincidentally willing to pour herself into filling that need? So it was fascination and gratitude on Polo's side."

"And so you–just like that–stopped worrying that it might, you know, develop into something real?" Nathalie asked doubtfully.

Clarice smiled nostalgically. "I kept a sharp eye out, my dear, you can be sure. But not so they noticed." She took a single cashew nut. "And I found out that I could trust Polo–note that I say Polo, not Ruthie, I never knew from day to day what planet I would find that girl on–when it came to boundaries. He never transgressed a single one. That boy had the most exquisite sense, without it ever being spelled out, of what he was entitled to, and what not. It made it easy to include him when it suited, and not when it didn't. He wasn't envious of what the other children had, their possessions, their trips with us, none of that.

"So you see, he knew that anything other than friendship with Ruthie was a taboo kind of thing. He knew that even a single step out of line would end Morrie's patronage. He was never going to risk that. It would have shut him out of his idea of the Garden of Eden. No apple, no snake, could have seduced that young Adam. I came to see that very quickly. He's a practical sort of boy, Polo."

Clarice poured herself another half glass of sherry. "So in a way, because he put any such expectations out of his conscious mind, his feelings for Ruthie had no more reality than her foolish fantasies. And, since we're being honest, my dear, I will tell you that somehow I just knew–not that either Polo or I would ever have dreamed of discussing such matters–that he was sexually active elsewhere. And pretty early. That was reassuring in its own way too.

"When they grew up, all those airy–fairy feelings just…dissipated…disappeared. Or got sublimated into this lovely friendship they have now. So you see, Nathalie, you have nothing to worry about in that regard."

Nathalie murmured bitterly, "Disappeared? They were both pretty grown up when Ruthie came to the horse show in St Lazare that time. Nobody was worrying about transgressing boundaries then."

"Oh my," Clarice sighed. "Were you there when…? What bad luck."

"So you knew about that?" Nathalie said accusingly.

"Ruthie told me the next day. She was mortified. And terribly ashamed of herself. Honestly, Nathalie, I would say that was the exception that proved the rule. As I recall it was a very upsetting day for Polo. It was a kind of watershed in his career, no? Truly, my dear, it was the one and only time." She paused. Really, that was bad luck, her having been there. The poor child's face was so stricken, as though it were yesterday.

"Don't you think you should–let's see–look for closure and move on, as they say? It was so long ago, years before your real relationship with Polo began," Clarice chided gently. "Jealousy can eat you up, you know. It's never constructive. You may have good reasons for being unhappy, Nathalie, but don't blame Ruthie. Ruthie would never take what isn't hers, even if it were on offer. Which," she added emphatically, "it most certainly is *not*."

"I wish I could be of sure of that as you are."

"No one can be sure of honesty when it comes to other people. One can only answer completely for oneself. But when you love someone, unless there is direct evidence to the contrary, you would do well to act as though you are sure."

Nathalie was silent for a long moment and seemed to look inward. "You know, Mrs. J., the way you tell it, even though you seem to be praising Polo, it isn't a very flattering picture. It's as if everything he did was only to make sure he got what he wanted, to go on with his riding."

"When people are driven by a single passion in life," Clarice said slowly, "they can be difficult, as well as attractive. I mean difficult in the sense of seeming to be…detached emotionally, even to the people they love. They don't mean to be, but they're just so consumed by their work, or their art, or their vocation.

"If you realize that you need to have the electricity they tend to throw off, if that's what sparks your interest in life, then you have to make a conscious choice about how you're going to accept them. At least this is how I see it. You can say to yourself that they're selfish and unfeeling, and withdraw and feel hurt. Or you can love them *for* that passion, because a true passion, like real art, well, it's rare.

"Morrie had that kind of drive, but it came more from an immigrant's insecurity than a sense of vocation. Our early years together weren't easy. He was consumed with achieving his success. I also

felt neglected and exploited. I found that I only became truly rec-
onciled when his single–mindedness ran its course a bit and he had
the time and the maturity to re–order his priorities in life. I must
say that I was amply rewarded for the wait in the end."

"What happened in the end?" asked Nathalie.

"What always happens," said Clarice quietly. "He realized that
his passion and his success were empty vessels without the equally
important achievements of loving and being loved."

"Family," said Nathalie softly, "when you became a family." Her
eyes filled.

"Exactly, dear," said. Clarice.

"It's what I've been waiting for. But he hasn't re–ordered his priorities, as you put it. It's taking too long. I can't wait any more, Mrs.
J. I don't believe it's going to happen. And I can't live any more on
Polo's passion…" Nathalie said, her voice low and husky. Her eyes
were dark pools of sorrow, and Clarice's heart quickened with a
surge of maternal sympathy.

"There are limits to the most patient of loves, Nathalie. Timing
is everything in life. I have something to show you, something you
should have seen years ago. I hope it isn't too late to do some good."
Clarice reached for the shoebox.

CHAPTER TWENTY–THREE

"YOU WON THE GRAND PRIX, AND YOU KNEW YOU'D QUALIFIED for the Team," said Thea.

"Yeah," said Polo warily.

"You came out of the ring, and you were told my husband wanted to speak to you," she continued.

"Yeah." What was the point of all this lead–up, he wondered.

"And he said"–

"Thea, I don't want to be rude, but where is all this heading? You said this had to do with Morrie, and he wasn't there…"

"I'm trying to find out if Morrie had his facts straight, and if he did, why he felt he had to get involved himself. Is it true that my husband actually told you that it was you *personally* that he didn't want on the Team?"

"That depends on how you see the word 'personally', I guess. He said it was a question of the Team's 'cultural homogeneity'–that he didn't think I would 'fit in'. Actually," Polo smiled a bit grimly, "he seemed to imply that he was doing me a favour, saving me the discomfort of being the odd man out. Mind if I get another beer?"

Thea said nothing as Polo went to the fridge. He opened the bottle and poured out the beer, but didn't sit down at the table. He leaned against the kitchen counter and waited for her to go on.

"Why didn't you say anything back to him? You knew he had no right to make such a decision."

"I did tell him I didn't think the owner would agree to lend the horse to another rider…"

"Polo, you know what I mean. How could you let him get away with such an incredible insult?"

Polo stared into the beer. "It's the $64,000 question, isn't it," he said quietly. "I've asked myself maybe a million times how it was that I heard him saying it, and I didn't…" he stopped and considered how he could put it. "You know, if he'd said I wasn't a good enough rider, that I won by a fluke, I think–no, I know–I would have lost it. I would have punched him out or something–well, not really, but I would never have let it go without a fight.

"But it was so out of left field that at first I didn't even know what he was talking about. I mean," he laughed softly, "what the hell was 'cultural homogeneity'? I wasn't sure I understood either word, to be honest. 'Homogeneous' sort of clicked in after a second, but…cultural? What, my riding wasn't *artistic* enough?"

He shook his head and drank. Thea smiled faintly. "Then it kind of dawned on me in one of those slow movie double–takes. Hey, he means it's because I'm a *pepsi*. I was–stunned for a second. Couldn't believe it. It was the last thing in the world I would have expected as a reason."

"But even when you realized, you didn't lose your temper, or punch him out, or anything else…" said Thea.

"No, I didn't. I was young and naïve. And I guess–I guess I did what a lot of French-Canadians did in those days when an English Canadian with authority laid down the law on something. I assumed they had the right…actually, come to think of it, I'm sure I was the last French-Canadian in Canada to get the news that times had changed, but you know in horses we're always a long way behind the curve, it's a pretty isolated world. It's hard to believe it was only twenty–some years ago, eh?"

"Polo, did it ever occur to you that it wasn't really–or at least only–you he didn't want on the Team? That the cultural homogeneity thing wasn't only about you, but about Morrie too? You know, owners are very visible at the shows. There's a social component. Your owner wasn't exactly a social fit with the others."

Polo made a plosive sound of irritation. "Thea, I just don't have the patience for this, you really have to get to the bottom line here."

Thea nodded. She took a deep breath.

"Harold and I flew back to Toronto late that Sunday night. Monday morning at 7:30 a.m. I pulled the curtains open in the living room, and saw Morrie Jacobson sitting in his car at the curb. Or rather I saw a little man in a big Cadillac who appeared to be asleep at the wheel, parked outside our house. I only found out who he was when he rang the bell and introduced himself."

Polo felt his heart thudding hard and fast in a chest that suddenly seemed too small to contain it. "He–he drove overnight to Toronto?"

"Yes. He was wearing a tuxedo. You said he'd been at a wedding."

"That's right," Polo heard himself say. "I talked to him at about 11 p.m. I told him what happened. He didn't seem as interested or angry as I thought he would be. I remember that…it made me feel kind of sorry for myself…"

"*Kind of?* Polo, you really are…never mind, that's not important. Anyway, he rang the bell, I opened the door just a little bit, and he pushed it open, hard, and just walked in. It frightened me, of course. Harold was still upstairs, and even though Morrie wasn't a big man, it was obvious he was a very angry one."

Polo didn't trust himself to ask any questions. Let her tell it her way.

"He was very polite, though, in a Mafioso kind of way. 'I'm Morrie Jacobson,' he said, 'Polo Poisson's sponsor.' Then he said, very slowly and carefully, as if he were talking to someone who didn't speak English too well, and looking at me with the arrogance of someone who's–I don't know–at the time I actually wondered if he had a concealed weapon on him, his look was that fierce and scary, 'I understand there's been some kind of mix–up about Polo's eligibility for the Team. I'd like to straighten this out with your husband. So if you'd ask him to come down here, please, I'll have a private word with him.'"

Polo was transfixed. He couldn't have spoken even if he could have thought of anything to say. Thea no longer seemed aware of his presence, in any case. She stared blankly ahead of her, intent on memory.

"I must have gone upstairs to get Harold," she said, frowning at the gap in her recollection, "because the next thing I knew, Harold and Morrie were going into the study and they closed the door."

"So–you don't know what was said…" Polo said hoarsely.

"Oh yes, certainly I do," Thea said briskly. "There's an air–conditioning vent that connects with one in the upstairs hall. I've listened to many a conversation my husband assumed was private. So I heard it all pretty clearly, and I remember it well…"

–*I'll get right to the point, Ankstrom. Either that boy of mine is on the Team by tonight, or you'll be in the national news by the end of the week.*

–*How dare you walk into my home and threaten me!*

–*What does it matter how? I did dare is the point.*

–*You have nothing to say about decisions that are taken in the Team's interests. Get out of my house. Or I'll call the police.*

–*Call them. Go ahead. Think they're going to arrest a guy in a tuxedo that your wife let in to talk to you about fucking over Canada's best rider? And what if they did? I'll have a nap at the station while I wait for my lawyer. You don't want to mess with this lawyer I know, Ankstrom. He grew up on St. Urbain St. He's a barracuda. He eats Wasps like you for breakfast.*

–*It's in the boy's best interests. He's young, he'll have other chances.*

–*You creep, you don't get it. I'm not asking you, I'm telling you. Listen, I'm tired, I been driving all night. I only had one hour to do some due diligence on you, but I got enough to start making your life miserable. So don't pretend we're negotiating here. I'd really like to get home.*

–*Due diligence? What unbelievable arrogance. You don't know anything about me. And I'm sure none of your…people would either. We don't exactly move in the same circles, do we?*

–*Here's what I already know from a few of my Toronto buddies, Ankstrom. I know your so–called brokerage business where you spend maybe two hours a day rolling over your wife's relatives' treasury bills and Canada bonds because you're so fucking busy sucking up to your fancy horse pals pulls in enough money to put you in a semi–detached in Etobicoke, not in a Rosedale mansion. I know you're living off your wife's money. That's all I need to know. A man who lives off his wife is scum in my books, a nothing, a nobody. If he'll do that, he'll do anything. That's what I learned in one hour. You give me a few days, and I'll find the broads, the gambling, the little boys, whatever it is–because with guys like you, there's always something. I know the way you think. You think if you're tall and thin with blue eyes, and your people came from England, your shit doesn't smell. Your wife seems like a nice lady, Ankstrom. Classy, like mine. You think long and hard about what you got to lose. And then think about what this little Yid has to lose by fucking you over like you did my boy. I got nothing more to lose, nothing. If you don't give that boy what he earned, you bastard, I'll get you if it takes the rest of my life…*

Thea had gone quite pale, and a faint sheen of perspiration had raised a sickly glow on her cheeks and forehead. She pressed a hanky several times to her face, tucked it into her sleeve, sighed, folded her hands on the table and looked at the pretzels.

It's my move, thought Polo. He felt light–headed, his mind a blank. What she had said–and God knows what it had cost her to tell it like it was–that was Morrie. *Morrie.* She couldn't have made that stuff up in a million years. His heart raced. He leaned back harder into the support of the counter. He wished he were sitting down. He didn't even know how to start processing what he'd heard.

Nathalie was struggling to make sense of the photograph on the coffee table in front of her. Clarice had simply laid it there without comment, and she could feel the older woman's eyes on her as she looked at it. It was very old, she could see that from the sepia tones and the crackly lines, also from the much handled edges gone soft and clothlike to the touch.

At first she had automatically smiled because it was Polo in the picture, a rare childhood photo of Polo as a happy, curly–haired boy, sitting on a chunky, dun–coloured pony with a wildly bristling mane, smiling confidently into the camera's gaze. Then the impossibilities began to sink in, one by one, and she was finding it difficult to process what she was seeing. Clarice had moved from her chair to sit on the sofa quite close to her, almost as though she knew she might be needed for physical assistance at any moment.

This photograph, it's too old, Nathalie thought. Those bulky riding pants, they couldn't be…that smile, the teeth are perfect, but Polo had awful teeth, he wore braces for years…no glasses…who is that older boy standing beside him…not Hy, but a Jacobson, he could be Ruthie's twin brother…she felt a cold *frisson* down her back, and was frightened. Without comment, Clarice picked up the photo very gently and turned it over.

On one side there were a few lines written in–Hebrew? Yiddish? The writing was in real ink, quite faded. On the other, ball–penned more recently in English, were the words: 'Markus Jacobson, aged 11, with Morrie. May, 1931, Lodz, Poland. Our little prince.'

Nathalie looked at Clarice with shocked, questioning eyes. Clarice said quietly, "Morrie's brother. I never knew about him myself. Morrie left me a letter, explaining. It's so simple in the end. And"– she pointed to an envelope, still sealed–"one for Polo. It's for you to give to him. I'm not going to tell you not to read it first. You decide."

"What happened to him?" Nathalie's voice trembled as she picked up the slim envelope with only the word 'Polo' on it in strongly drawn capitals. She could feel the outline of a paperclip and a business–size card through the paper.

"He died. Not in the Holocaust, thank God. No, it was the kind of story that happened to all kinds of people in those days. Morrie couldn't stand what was happening in Europe and begged his parents to emigrate. This was the early thirties. But they wouldn't. He was only fifteen, but he left on his own. He somehow made it over to Canada before it got really difficult, almost impossible from about 1933 on. Immigration for Jews almost closed down entirely after that until after the war. Not Canada's finest hour, but that's another story. Morrie promised his brother he would send for him. Morrie was going to get rich and bring everyone over. That was his plan. Well, he got rich, but it was too late. Markus would never have been allowed in anyway. He was ill, tuberculosis probably. Lucky, when you consider what happened to the others."

"And he never told you about him?"

"There's two schools of thought on pain, dear," Clarice said sadly. "Some think it has to be shared at all costs. I think Morrie felt that if he ever started to talk about it he wouldn't be able to function. He would sink into a depression and never recover. The terrible guilt. The 'if onlys...' you see. I can't say he was wrong."

"So it was a complete secret–and then"–

"And then Polo fell into our lives, as if he'd been sent"–Clarice's voice broke, and she reached for a tissue–"you know, every time I think of Morrie walking into that room and seeing him with the picture of Hy in his hands, I just..."

Nathalie put a comforting arm around Clarice's shoulders. The two women sat in teary silence for a time.

Clarice finally drew a deep breath, wiped her eyes in two tidy strokes, and said, "It's a tremendously emotional subject for me, dear. I think I had better stick to the facts, or we'll never get anywhere."

She cleared her throat. "Nathalie, Morrie wrote these letters when he was pretty sure he was close to dying. I didn't even know *that*. I knew his heart wasn't strong, there had been episodes, but he kept from me what his doctor had told him, that there wasn't much time. In his letter to me, Morrie apologized for that and for...Polo. He... oh my, I thought I was going to be the strong one for you... just a minute, dear..."

Clarice blew her nose, and sat up very straight. "He felt very guilty towards the end–for exploiting Polo as he did. For taking advantage of Polo's love of horses. Morrie liked horses, but it would probably have been a passing thing if not for Polo. Morrie said it was irresistible, it was such an easy way to ...pretend, as though he'd been given this second chance...Markus had loved horses...it was a way of dealing with that gnawing grief...but he knew it was wrong, he knew he was using Polo."

Nathalie looked down at the sealed envelope. "I don't know what to do," she said in a small, fatigued voice. "What should I do?"

Still struggling with her own emotions, Clarice said, "It's not right for me to decide that for you. But what I think–if it were me–is that it would be unfair to burden him with this if you really intend to leave your marriage.

"I'm not one of those people who think the wishes of the dying always have to be respected, even if it means pain for the ones left behind. Morrie had his chance to make things right when he was alive. He couldn't face it. It was the only act of cowardice in his life. Morrie was a brave man. But he couldn't bear to hurt Polo. And he knew he couldn't deal with Polo rejecting him, hating him. Because he really loved Polo, you know. My belief is that it began as a way for Morrie to heal. But it ended in love for Polo. For who Polo really was.

"Life is for the living, Nathalie. What Polo doesn't find out won't hurt him. He can't modify the past, and if it's what made him what he is, knowing this won't change that. In my opinion he should only come to know this if he has you to work it through with. You'd need someone you love and who loves you to come out of this stronger than when you went in. I wouldn't want to be alone with this photograph if it was my ghost. Would you?"

"Are you all right, Thea?" Polo asked, as Thea emerged from the bathroom, her face and hairline still damp, and reseated herself at the table.

"I think so," she said in a slightly shaky, low voice. "That didn't work out quite as I had imagined it would," she said, smiling bravely, "I had assumed it would be me asking you if you were all right..."

"What happened there?" Polo was curious, but also relieved that Thea's sudden emotional breakdown had given him permission to put aside the shock and confusion of his own reaction. He had been so caught off guard by her tearful collapse that he hadn't even retreated in the usual nervous spasm of anxiety over a crying woman. He'd actually been calm and considerate–*appropriate*, Nathalie would have said.

"I think it's just that I never told anyone before," Thea said thoughtfully. "I've reviewed it to myself so many times, that's why I remembered it so vividly. Until now it was all about how shocking and coarse and even frightening it was to hear this angry man threatening my husband. The contempt, the gutter language, the complete disregard for civil behaviour, the naked aggression, it just floored me…"

"Thea, you have to understand, that was only one side of Morrie," Polo interrupted hastily. "It's true he was impulsive and emotional sometimes. But if you knew him"–

"Oh Polo, there's no need for you to defend him to me," Thea said. "Let me finish. What I was going to say was that in saying it out loud, telling you, I realized for the first time, I mean realized in my gut, not my head, that what he did was not only all those things. At the same time it was a truly, utterly magnificent action to take. And I was just suddenly overcome with this tremendous sense of shame."

"You've lost me, Thea. Why shame? Why magnificent?"

Thea drew a deep breath and took her hanky from her sleeve. "You know, I think I'll have another glass of sherry, if you wouldn't mind." Polo brought the bottle to the table and filled her glass. Then he sat down opposite and watched her face with nervous anticipation.

"Thank you." She took a deep swallow, and dabbed tidily at her eyes. "This morning, when you told me you knew nothing about what Morrie had done to change Harold's mind, everything I'd thought about that incident shifted in terms of how I saw it. I had convinced myself that that performance of Morrie's was a sort of bravado piece, something to impress you with. I found that idea very contemptible, and it coloured my perception of him as a person. Up until today, even though I had despised Harold for his treatment of you, I had actually felt sorry for him having to endure that barrage of abuse."

She sipped again. "But just now I saw it for what it really was. The words were the same, but they meant something quite different to me. Polo, I know Morrie wasn't your father, but what I heard that day was a father's rage against the man who had dared to hurt his son. It was a primitive act of revenge, not in the least bit Christian"– she smiled wryly at the obvious irony –"but so completely natural, so–so appropriate in the circumstances. And I felt ashamed because I knew in my heart that my daughter had been in danger of being hurt before she actually was, but I had done nothing. And I should have done for Stephanie exactly what Morrie did for you. I should have protected her against the self-interest of someone in so-called authority over–"

"Thea, you're wrong," Polo interrupted quickly, feeling strangely agitated. "This wasn't about Morrie's feelings for me. This was about his own self-respect, his sense of justice, his–he couldn't stand getting screwed, whether it was in business or"–

"Polo, you know a lot about horses, and I'd accept your word on anything you say about them, but you don't have children, and frankly, you don't know what you're talking about," Thea said scornfully. "What Morrie did wasn't about justice, it was about the instinct to protect someone he loved. He did it for love, and I don't know why that should upset"–she cut herself off, frowned, and looked toward Polo's right shoulder in surprise–"What are you doing?"

"What…?"

"Your hand…like a crossing guard…"

They both looked at Polo's right hand. *Merde.* With a small gasp of embarrassment he closed his splayed fingers into a fist, jerked it from the air and wrapped the fingers of his other hand around it to anchor it to the table.

"Sorry," he muttered. He could feel his face flaming and wished Thea gone in a puff of smoke and himself out of here, on a horse, on an endless cinder track, galloping away, just galloping, galloping forever away…

But here he was, and Thea hadn't budged, and was in fact staring at him with frank curiosity and compassion. He couldn't meet her gaze, and suddenly Polo felt Thea's words detonate a long dormant grenade of shame that was exploding in slow motion through his whole body.

Morrie, it's true. You were magnificent. You loved me. What's wrong with that? Why do I resist? What's wrong with her knowing that? This is shameful. It's an insult to your memory. This can't go on. Morrie, forgive me. I slept that night. I handed my problem over to you and I slept. You made things right and I never even asked how. I was a boy then. I was a boy in need of protection and I got it. Boys need protection. Men take risks.

Thea said sadly in her low, beautiful voice, "I am really very sorry, Polo, I had no business talking about your personal life so cavalierly. I seem to have gotten caught up in my own little drama. Forgive me."

Polo waved a vague dismissal of the need to apologize, and looked her in the eye. "Thanks for telling me about what Morrie did for me, Thea. Don't feel bad. There's nothing wrong in telling me I was loved. You're right. It was a father's instinct."

"It was the tuxedo, you see," Thea said softly. "He didn't stop to think. He didn't wonder about how he would look, or what might happen to him. The tuxedo just–got to me–that he didn't stop to think…"

I stopped to think when Andrea was beating the horse. And the horse almost died because of that. But just now when Gilles went to sleep I said to myself that if someone walked in here right now and laid even a finger on this boy, I wouldn't stop to think, I would beat the shit out of him…

"Thea, you're right about the whole thing. It was all for me. He loved me. If I have a problem with admitting that, it's mine, not yours. And–your daughter–I never really said…look, I didn't know her, but I'm sorrier than I can say for your loss."

He saw her eyes fill up, but again it didn't make him flinch in the usual way. In fact, to his amazement, he felt the urge to give comfort. He found his hand reaching across the table to circle her wrist and squeeze.

"It's been a strange few days, Thea. There's a ton of information coming at me. It's hard to take in. I just want to say that I appreciate what you've done for me. It took courage, and you stirred up a lot of pain for yourself doing it. And…two days ago I wouldn't have even realized that–or been able to say it."

Thea smiled through her tears. "Thank you," she whispered.

There was a sharp rap at the door. Thea jumped. "Oh my goodness," she said, looking at her watch, "I completely forgot about Sue."

Guy let himself in quietly and stood in the hallway listening for movement within the house. He heard nothing and closed the door. The faint click of the latch released a pang of foreboding in him. Reluctant, but knowing the coming confrontation with Bridget was inescapable and soonest begun, soonest ended, he walked slowly into the living room. Bridget sat at her cluttered desk, twirling a pen between the fingers of one raised hand, absorbed in a fanned display of maps, timetables, lists, and much-annotated columns of figures.

"Hullo," Guy said glumly.

Bridget registered his presence with a grunt, but did not look up.

"Are you feeling better, dear?"

"About what?" Bridget now looked up in apparent surprise at Guy's question.

"Your cold," Guy said. "You weren't feeling well. I told Polo you were sleeping. He wanted to speak to you."

Bridget snorted derisively. "You're an awfully good chap, Guy, but I do wonder how anyone can be so bloody simple. Did you really think I was sick?" She then put her hand to her chest, emitted a very authentic-sounding cough and croaked, "Oh I'm so sorry, Ma'am, I just couldn't do my essay, I'm just knackered from this horrid bronchitis, you see…"

"Very funny. But why did you pretend to be sick today?"

"That should be obvious. The blasted show committee is coming here tomorrow at noon, and Marion will have a hissy fit if I can't produce the budget and lists of volunteers and whatnot. I've been working like a good little Canadian beaver all afternoon and I'm just about there, although it won't look very pretty. And I wanted to get Thea off my back. The course isn't as ticketyboo as it should be either. And finally, if you must know, I needed an excuse not to be in the barn. I have no intention of being grilled by Polo over this Liam nonsense, and I certainly wasn't going to be around when he took Robin out. I'm furious that Thea asked Polo to ride him."

"Well, he is her horse, Bridget…"

"Gosh, Guy, whatever would I do without you to remind me of these details?"

Guy sighed again. He felt he really couldn't bear Bridget's sarcasm for another minute today.

"Bridget, please can we stop all this–this …playacting for a few minutes. I'm afraid I have to tell you a few things about what went on at the barn, as well as some other unpleasant truths, whether you want to hear them or not."

Bridget heard the fear in his voice, went very still and her eyes narrowed with concentration. "Go on, then. I'm listening."

And finally Guy knew that she really was listening, because she had dropped the posh accent and was speaking in her real, lower-middle class voice. This was a great relief, and he felt emboldened to share everything–almost everything–with her, and without his usual defensiveness.

Fifteen minutes later, having absorbed a full recital of Guy's concerns, and holding the bank draft in her hands, Bridget finally spoke. Guy's revelations had shaken her, but she was still in good command of her active intelligence.

"So Polo knows about the horse, and he knows about the cheques."

"Well, he only knows about this one, and he can't really know about the horse, he can only suspect."

"Yeah, but that'll set him thinking. He's too clever by half, that bloke. He'll tell Thea to get him X–rayed. He'll start asking around. He'll find out I talk a lot about going back and forth to England, but that I never actually do." Bridget frowned and played with the envelope, bouncing it from short to longer edge on the desktop.

"Okay," she said, "Now how long have you known about the horses?"

"I began to suspect when Stephanie told me she was having problems with him getting nappy after road workouts. I borrowed the portable X–ray machine from Ste. Hy, and that's how I found out. It's quite mild still, but it's in both horses."

"But why didn't you tell me?"

"Oh Bridget, I just couldn't. You were so thrilled with Rockin' Robin, and here was the proof in Robin's Song that he really was a great stallion–and it was such a lot of money involved. And it wasn't really bad. Navicular is such a funny thing. It can stay mild for ages. All he really needed was some bute before a hard workout. So that's what I did. I monitored it. Or at least, when I could…"

Guy's voice broke and he passed a trembling hand across his eyes.

"Ah, the light dawns. So that's why you were so upset when you were too sick to go with Stephanie to the Timberline Three-Day…"

"Oh please, Bridget, don't don't *don't* talk about that. I can't bear to think about it." Guy stifled a sob.

Bridget contemplated her friend. Her mind was swirling with the facts that were going to affect her life from here on, but she wasn't oblivious to the terrible strain Guy was suffering under. He needed a strong and consistent structure to his life to keep himself in emotional balance. She could almost see the foundations crumbling in his pale face, darting eyes and huddled frame. Was he going to crack up? Sad for him if he did, but more to the point, how much could she depend on his discretion where she was concerned from now on?

"Steady on, Guy. I won't mention it again." She frowned. "So then why didn't you give him bute before Polo rode him?"

"Well, I would have, except that Jocelyne happened to mention that Polo had asked Fran to do ground observation for him. I naturally assumed that he was only going to ride in the arena. And in the arena the horse is fine. How was I to know he was going out on the roads and the course afterward?"

Bridget digested this information. She said, "If Polo knows, then he'll tell the others. If that little journalist cretin gets hold of it, then I am well and truly fucked. It's the end of the line for me here. Wouldn't Mummy be amused."

Tears glittered momentarily in her topaz eyes. In husky, feeling tones, she added, "What I'm trying to understand is how this could be true. The horses passed in England."

"Oh Bridget," Guy cried, "Now you're the one who's being simple. Can't you see that it's Philip who's doing this to you? Can't you see that Philip is passing along horses that he knows are going to break down somewhere along the line? *You* know how superficial English vet checks are, but nobody *here* seems to. He just makes sure they're sound that day, or who knows, he may have a vet in league with him—that's not unheard of in this business—and off they go. And then it can be another year or two before the problems start."

"Fig would never do that to me," Bridget muttered, but she could feel her stomach churning.

Guy saw that the light was really dawning now for Bridget. Ten years, Guy thought, of my selfless devotion, and she takes me completely for granted, never considers what I've done for her, has no idea of the sacrifices, the friendship, the love I've given her, but she trusts that jerk in England, just because he's upper crust, because he's a star. "Did you really think he was your friend, Bridget? Did you really think it was anything more than the money?" Guy asked bitterly.

Bridget didn't respond. She couldn't. Suddenly she was adding up the ten years' worth of 'coincidences', the horses she'd sold who weren't competing any more, the too–high turnover of owners, the angry phone calls she'd so indignantly complained of to Guy. How many times had she mocked Guy for his *naïveté* and sentimentality, when all this time he'd kept track of the facts over there on his neatly organized desk and his beautifully archived files at the barn, while she'd been careless, lazy, disorganized, trusting…*oh Fig, you double–crossing little shit, you've been fucking me over for ten years, I should have known once would never be enough for a bastard like you…*

"Well," she whispered morosely, "I suppose I should be grateful for small mercies. At least Rockin' Robin didn't stand stud to Manon's mare."

Bridget had been staring hypnotically at the tumbling bank draft as she assimilated the widening implications of Fig's betrayal, but now she happened to look up at Guy and what she saw caused her mind to shut down momentarily, like a computer screen in a power surge. Then she rebooted. She took in the guilt in the eyes that were trying to escape hers but couldn't look away. She asked herself why this should be so. The answer came to her. He hadn't expected her to say that. He hadn't prepared himself for that mental connection. He was already on edge and frightened. The computer screen went blank again. Slowly, carefully she rebooted, and…

"Rockin' Robin…Guy…*oh my God*…it was you…*it was you*…"

Guy opened and closed his mouth once, twice, three times. But his throat remained stubbornly locked.

"You cut his tongue off," Bridget whispered, "so he'd have to stay in the barn… so he couldn't service the mare…"

Guy nodded and swallowed hard.

"And you knew it wasn't dangerous because you'd read about another case…and because you'd be right there to fix him up…"

Guy nodded sadly. Bridget stared at him, other memories surging to consciousness.

"And the time before…the mare didn't come into estrus–child's play for a vet to arrange with his little bag full of pills…"

He nodded again. These things were horrible to admit, but oddly enough, he felt a sweet surge of relief in the admission. He couldn't look at her. What would she do? Would she attack him physically? She might. That was okay. He wouldn't defend himself. Of course he'd lost her friendship forever. She would never understand that he'd done it for her.

"Good God! Who'd have thought you had the ba–the *nerve…*" Bridget's eyes were round and fascinated. Guy's shoulders hunched closer together, and he kept his gaze studiously lowered.

"Don't tell me you vandalized the office as well!" Bridget cried. Guy couldn't believe it, but he thought he heard a note of admiration as well as astonishment in her voice.

"Don't be ridiculous, Bridget," Guy said curtly, offended and hurt.

"Well, do admit, Guy, the word 'ridiculous' has acquired new depth of meaning in the last few minutes in this cozy little bungalow of ours."

Guy didn't know what to make of Bridget's inappropriately ironic take on this. Shouldn't she be sobbing or screaming or hitting…?

"Look at me, Guy," Bridget said. Her voice was strangely firm and steady.

He shook his head dumbly and kept staring at the floor.

"Either look at me, or I shall be forced to empty that bottle of Javel water under the sink into your aquarium." Guy gasped in alarm and leapt to his feet with fingers rigidly splayed in front of him.

"Thank you, luv. Now that I have your attention, do let's have a real heart to heart chat." Bridget got up and walked over to an armoire in the common area and opened it to reveal bottles, decanters and wineglasses. "What would you say to a spot of sherry? I think we could both use a little pick–me–up at this point, and somehow the thought of a cuppa just doesn't have a huge appeal. Call me old–fashioned, but at times like these only a sherry will do."

Guy felt dazed and disoriented, but he accepted the glass of amber liquor. Bridget shooed the chocolate retriever off the wing chair and settled herself in it. She sipped reflectively.

"Bridget," Guy ventured timidly, "why aren't you angry? You were so upset when it happened. You *love* him."

"Love," Bridget mused. "What, after all, is love in the end?" She sipped. "Ah, there really is nothing like a fine sherry to smooth the wrinkles out of a day." She set the glass down carefully on the wobbly end table. "You could say that I loved the stallion, Guy, but that was when I thought he was something it turns out he isn't. Rockin' Robin was going to be Bridget Pendunnin's ticket to success as a breeder. And I love Bridget Pendunnin quite a lot is what I love. Now it turns out he won't–can't–be. So the question is, do I still"– she sketched quotation marks in the air–" 'love' Rockin' Robin?" She paused and picked up her sherry glass. "I think not, on the whole."

Guy stared at Bridget and felt sick at heart. He would have understood, welcomed her anger. Or, better still, her grief. Yes, her *grief* was what he would have wanted above all. He had pictured himself comforting her, perhaps once again holding a wet cloth to her forehead as she lay sunk in mourning on the chesterfield. He had liked that part when she found out about the cut tongue, the nurturing part of that drama. That, and telling Manon, feeling the full weight of her attentiveness and admiration for his skill. It was rare that he was the cynosure of so many people's admiring attention. The stallion had needed him, Bridget had needed him, the stable people had needed him, and all that had felt good.

But this! This wasn't right. She was practically congratulating him for saving her embarrassment. Rockin' Robin was now damaged goods, so the stallion was suddenly nothing to her. Just like that. And Robin's Song too. That woman, Ruthie, what she'd said, God, she'd hit the nail on the head, what a scary moment that had been.

Guy's heart sank within him, and the damp, cold, familiar blanket of depression settled around his shoulders, weighing them down. All the terrible things he had done to protect her, because he had believed in the purity of her love for her horses, he had done all these things for an illusion, for a projection of his own need to be part of something greater than his lonely self. He had thought that they–he, Bridget, the horses–were a kind of… family. Oh, he knew what fun most people would make of the idea of a celibate man and woman calling themselves and their horses a family. But was it really so far–fetched any more? Was there only one way to be a family? Single mothers were a commonplace. Gays were having children. The world was changing.

There were no rules anymore. So why not? You had to make of life what you could with the limitations you were stuck with. He had felt very committed. He had finally found his niche. He'd thought Bridget felt the same, underneath the sarcasm and the teasing. Cutting that tongue–well, that was a crossing of the Rubicon, wasn't it? You wouldn't do such a thing for anything other than a greater love. Especially someone like himself, sworn to protect and serve animals in distress, not *cause* it. For it was a kind of symbolic child abuse, wasn't it? Done for Bridget. Otherwise–never, never, never! To protect her. And now to find that she didn't understand the first thing about love. How could he have been so deluded–

The telephone rang. Bridget picked up.

"Oh hello Marion, what a coincidence, I was just saying to Guy that I have everything you want for tomorrow's meeting… say again…Oh dear…surely not…but Marion…but Marion…no, but surely C–FES will stand behind you…oh dear…well, of course you can count on me…not a word…too awful for you…oh really? In what regard?…oh dear…look, Marion, I wonder if we couldn't continue this discussion in Ottawa…yes, I could be at your place in about four hours from now. Listen, can I call you back…only I think I may have to reconsider my own plans in the light of all this…stiff upper lip and all that, old thing…yes, yes, quite soon… just must think a bit…goodbye, dear."

Bridget replaced the receiver and stood up. "Well Guy, I'll tell you all about it while I pack."

"P–p–pack?"

"I can't stay. That journalist creature has the dope on Marion and the Taylor syndicate. Witnesses, affidavits, the whole bloody lot. Long story short, she's gone to the sponsors with it, and she's ready to publish the whole story if Marion doesn't resign. C–FES is throwing her to the wolves. She's out. She says my name came up a few times. Not looking too brilliant, dear chum. The show may not go on even with her resignation. At least not here. Cedar Meadows making a pitch, it seems. The Royal Dominion Bank pretty fed up with our team. Plan B time."

"B–b–but what about me?"

"You can come with me if you like." Bridget moved purposeful-ly to the hall closet and dragged a large suitcase out from its depths.

Guy's eyes swiveled round in panic as though to verify that his aquarium hadn't fallen through the floor at the very idea of his leaving. "How can I? How can I? You know I can't leave here." His voice was shrill with panic. "Where are you going after Ottawa? To Kingston?"

"Don't even say that word, you idiot," Bridget hissed. "That would be the last place I'd go." She lunged toward him and grabbed a handful of shirt. "Forget you ever heard about Kingston. Is that clear?"

Guy nodded dumbly. He felt a panic attack coming on. Shak-ing, he stood in the doorway and watched her fling clothes into the suitcase.

Without turning to look at him, Bridget said, " Guy, you've been a great pal. Don't think I don't appreciate what you've done. I would have liked to discuss the Liam thing with you, but somehow that all seems beside the point now. More important, I'm counting on you to look after Robin's Song."

"He belongs to Thea…"

Bridget turned and came very close to him. She kissed him gen-tly on the cheek and whispered softly in his ear, "I'm counting on you, *mon chum*. You're the only friend I have at the moment. You have to understand. I can't throw it back at Fig. He'll lie–he's done it before–and it'll only be the worse for me in the end. Those love-ly little cheques would stop coming if Fig's father thought I was making trouble for his darling boy. You're the only one I can trust, I realize that now. I've been a fool. I do love you, Guy darling, you know I do. I've been rotten to you, I admit it. I'm sorry, luv. Do say you'll keep Polo and Thea off my trail. Don't let sentimentality get in the way. Don't let me down. We'll be together again soon. Patience."

She looked long and hard into his eyes. She saw his eyes melting with trust and renewed loyalty. "There's a lamb stew in the fridge, pet. I made it especially for you."

She kissed him softly on the other cheek, and reviewed her performance in his spaniel eyes. *Oh yes, Budgie. Nicely done.* Then she turned back to her packing.

CHAPTER TWENTY-FOUR

"**I** COULD HAVE GIVEN YOU A NICE LAMB STEW," SAID CAROLINE to Ruthie across a glass tabletop on the patio outside the restaurant, "but I sent most of what I had over to Bridget's this afternoon. Guy loves it."

Ruthie wrinkled her nose. "Not stew anyway. It's too warm out. And Hy isn't allowed–too much fat. And"–shielding her eyes from the late day's sun boring in from the western horizon, she perused the menu with a slight frown–"lamb isn't Polo's favourite…maybe something lighter…"

"What about pizza?" Caroline said. "I can make you individual ones. Any toppings you like."

"Ooh, I like the sound of that. Who doesn't love pizza? Do you have feta cheese to mix with the mozzarella for me? And red onions? And tomato slices? And black olives?"

"*Mais oui.*"

"Great, and I know Hy will want just the veggies, and mushrooms, no olives, and easy on the cheese. Manon isn't coming, she's been on the go and playing hostess all day and she's zonked. And for Polo no veggies but lots of mushrooms and double pepperoni. But Roch–I don't know…"

"That's okay. I do. All–dressed with bacon and pineapple." Ruthie made a face, and Caroline laughed.

"With a nice green salad for everyone–and wine?"

"Oh, definitely salad. And wine. What's your house red?"

"*Pisse Dru.*"

Ruthie hesitated, knowing *Pisse Dru* was borderline for Hy, even just with pizza, but what the hell…She nodded. "I only asked because my brother is a little finicky about wines," she said, and closing the menu with an agreeable sense of accomplishment, added "but for myself, as my father used to say,"–this in English–"'I'm not a common sewer.'" Caroline laughed again, took the menu and headed back inside.

Ruthie looked at her watch. Early still. Dinner arrangements had taken less time than she had allowed for. She had decided that the four of them would sit out here on the flagstone terrace. What with that day's lessons having been cancelled, and the Saturday night dinner crowd from town tending to later arrival, they would have the place almost to themselves.

In the silence of her temporary solitude she gave herself over to the mellow gold of the receding day, the fragrance of mingled grass and horse, the view of rolling paddocks and the ruched silver surface of the pond below the well–proportioned sprawl of Hy and Manon's home and outbuildings. How strange, she thought, only this morning this open landscape made me afraid, and now it is filling me up with contentment. Yet nothing has really changed. Objectively, anyway. Maybe she had changed?

Because, she considered, this is the hour of day when I should be feeling down. It's almost sunset, time to get melancholy. But instead, for the first evening in ages, she felt–not happy exactly–but animated, open, friendly to the world, curious to know what was going to happen next in the bizarre chain of events that had begun only twenty–four hours ago. It was lovely, after two hours of intense discussion with Fran and Eva, to be sitting here by herself, drinking in this green and now peaceful landscape, and feeling her mind and sensibilities working at full throttle in the service of a task that had, blessedly, nothing to do with her own life.

For that, she mused, was the problem with the past two years. When illness and death overtook you, there was nothing to think about but yourself all day every day. Oh, of course you thought about the one who was ill, but it was never detached from yourself. His pain was your pain, his fear was your fear, his leaving the world was your guilt at remaining in it…Whereas now it was only the pain, the fear, the guilt of strangers she had to consider, and what good therapy it was turning out to be. And to think she had been so opposed to Polo and the others taking on this responsibility that she had almost gone back to Montreal and left them to their own devices.

If she had, she would have gone back to the cocoon of navel-gazing and inertia her bereavement had woven around her. Moving back to Montreal had used up the one curious burst of zest she had experienced after the *shiva*. Marvin's estate was easy to process–he had been organized in life, well organized for death–and, once physically settled in the practical lower Westmount town house she'd chosen for her transition period, there had been less in the way of tasks and responsibilities than she had predicted. The girls turned out to be more resourceful and resilient than she'd antici-pated. Time hung heavy on her hands. Ruthie knew she was lucky to have her mother available, as she'd lost contact with many of her old Montreal friends, but she was trying to be careful about tak-ing advantage of that. She wasn't ready to look for work–she knew she was finished with teaching, but not ready to think about what might replace it–and for the first time since she was a teenager, she felt purposeless, psychologically adrift.

Hy and Manon's invitation to spend time here had pulled her back from the lip of the slippery slide to full–blown depression. She was grateful for that, and now grateful too that she had decided to sign on to this–this equestrian crime task force She smiled at the concept. Detection by committee. How quintessentially Canadian that is, she thought with a smile.

And so, come to think, was the murder–committed offstage, in a sense, so as not to actually offend anyone's sensibilities. Quietly, discreetly, self–effacingly. Which was why it remained so stubborn-ly abstract. Why it had never touched her–or anyone else, as far as she could tell. Given what they now knew about Liam, in fact, his murder had even a quality of poetic justice about it, a punishment for his odious ideology. Or if not for that, for something equally horrid.

Ruthie knew it was unethical, but she almost hoped they didn't uncover the murderer. She was glad Liam was dead. And she was no longer afraid that Polo or any one of them was at risk. Whoever had killed Liam had been fulfilling a very specific and personal need–revenge possibly, or simply to shut him up. The murderer might run away if he or she knew discovery was imminent, but wouldn't kill again.

In any case her own hopes were irrelevant, since she hadn't been any help so far in discovering who the murderer was. Well, no, that wasn't true either. She had remembered the dog with the bandanna, and that might have led to some more clues. She looked forward to hearing what Polo had found out today. And of course to telling him about her encounters with Guy and Fran.

Guy. Ruthie revisited her strained and embarrassing one–sided conversation with Guy. She had felt foolish prattling on about the possible symbolic features of the attack on the stallion. Guy's look of amazement had mortified her. But now she thought of her analysis again, and really, looked at objectively, it didn't seem so absurd at all.

Obviously to literal–minded people, such a leap was bound to seem crazy. But symbolism existed for a reason. Even without being aware of it, people did act out their wishes and thoughts in symbolic ways. And come to think of it, had it been amazement on Guy's face because of the theory? Or amazement because she'd struck a nerve... Had he perhaps come to the same conclusion? And if so, in whose interest would it be for the stallion to stop producing issue? Hmm.

By far the most interesting result of the day's investigations had been the opportunity to hear Eva Briquemont's war story. Now that was something you usually only read about in books. Ruthie had read shelf loads of holocaust literature. But almost all of it had been about Jews, or by Jewish survivors. She knew there were many "righteous gentiles" in the world, but their stories had been peripheral to her education. Eva's was dramatic. Would Polo have the patience to hear it through? She would have to summarize for him. He wouldn't want to hear a long account about the romance with the Jewish music student, Eva's defiance of her family and friends, and the whole tortured narrative of the marriage, the camps, her survival, the boy's inevitable death...

For Polo the bottom line was going to be whether Fran had motive and opportunity to kill Liam. Unfortunately Eva's story supported such a view, at least in theory. That was the trouble with being a detective, though, Ruthie thought. In theory all kinds of things could be true, yet her intuition resisted any such notion. People who had faced the evils of Nazi Germany and come out the other side without devoting the rest of their lives to revenge were not suddenly going to become murderers forty years later. Fran and Eva believed in law and order. They were totally invested in preserving the secure and fulfilling life they had made here. They would have gone to the police before doing anything so drastic. No, Eva and Fran were the genuine articles–they were good people. Simply good, just as Liam was simply bad.

From this conclusion her thoughts wandered to the nature of good and evil in general, and how the one so often mysteriously flourished in the very soil fertilized to produce its opposite. And then she wondered, as she had so many times before, what *she* would have done if she had lived in an evil place like pre–war Passau...and as usual decided she would have gone along with everyone else. Because while she knew she was bold and principled and clever and honest and fair in the ideal, democratic greenhouse in which her glossy ideals had bloomed, she had never been tested. And deep in her heart she knew that with her back to the wall, heroism wasn't in her nature, or so she believed, and for the millionth time thanked God or Fate or History for never having had to find out for sure.

The faint sound of tires on gravel cut into her philosophical reverie. She looked at her watch. It was just on seven. She knew Hy would be walking over, and probably a little late, because when she left he had been still totally absorbed in discussing the war with Fran. Shading her eyes she looked left and down the exterior of the administration corridor to the parking lot. Two vehicles had pulled in at the same time. She recognized Polo's pickup truck, and the other was a somewhat battered–looking American sedan.

Ah, it was the elusive Roch getting out of the car. At last. She wondered how he had spent all this time. Social adrenaline flowed. What an interesting evening it would be hearing everyone's account of their day. She waited for the two men to greet each other and start walking over.

But something wasn't quite right. The body language of the two friends wasn't relaxed and trusting as it should be, but rather formal and stiff, and they were facing each other across too wide a space for friendship. She wished she could hear what they were saying. Polo was standing with his hands on his hips. He looked, even from this distance, extremely tense. Roch was gesturing as he spoke, first small, stabbing movements of the finger, then more arm involvement, more agitation. His voice rose, though she couldn't make out the words. Polo raised his hands in what seemed to be a signal to calm down.

And then, as Ruthie took concentrated note of Roch's confrontational stance, she stood up, suddenly quite alarmed. Something was terribly wrong. Then she gasped as she saw Polo turn, take off his glasses, and place them carefully on the fender of his truck. Before her conscious mind could bring the thought to the surface, she had understood what was the only possible reason for him doing this, and she felt her hands flying up to her face in shock and disbelief. Then the men disappeared from her line of vision. She immediately jumped up from the table, ran down to the parking lot and rounded the corner, her thoughts spinning in a centrifuge of fright and amazement.

They're going to fight! With their fists! O O O! They're fighting! They're fighting! Like boys in a schoolyard. Grown men! Friends! I don't believe this! Oh my God. Those sounds...grunting, like animals...they're really hitting hard. And the language! I never heard... where did Polo learn such... O I heard something crack, O stop, and in the face! What should I do? Oh my God, now they're rolling around on the ground, they're going to kill each other. O O O!

She had to do something "Stop it! *Stop it!* Polo! *Polo!*" Ruthie screamed. Did they hear her? She was close enough to see that Roch had a horrible welt high up on his cheek and there was blood all over Polo's mouth and chin. *Blood! O no, O no, O no! Oh God, don't let it be his beautiful teeth being knocked out. Three years of braces!*

"*Stop! Stop! Stop!*" she screamed, and without thinking grabbed at Roch's arm as he was drawing it back to strike. Growling like a bee–swarmed bear, Roch flung his fist out and up and it connected with Ruthie's stomach.

"Ohhh!!"

Instantly she was flat on the ground, the breath completely knocked out of her. The two men disengaged and staggered to their feet, breathing heavily.

"Ruthie!" cried Polo in horror, kneeling beside her.

"*Merde*," muttered Roch, hovering unsteadily a few feet away.

Disoriented, shocked, Ruthie tried to sit up. "Okay," she gasped, "I'm…okay."

"I've got you, ziess," Polo said, still breathing hard, supporting her back as she struggled, "don't try to get up yet, just relax and get your breath. Shit, I'm so sorry…" Even in her confusion, in a tiny back compartment of her mind Ruthie was registering the irony of being propped up–again–by Polo after an unexpected collapse.

Last time he held me up like this I was sitting on a hay bale and he looked so handsome in his white shirt and black show jacket. What a mess he is now…and here's an irony to savour, I'm breathless again too, but no chance of this turning into a romantic moment, that's for damn sure…

"Not…you…oh…Po…lo…teeth…blood…"

"Wha"–Polo swiped at his face –"oh, this?" He looked at the blood on his fingers, and smiled, wincing a bit. "Don't worry, just a lucky punch. Honest, just a nosebleed."

"Oh Polo…how… could…you…"

"Ssh, ssh, ssh, don't talk yet. Don't tense up, you'll be okay…" Ruthie felt Polo's hand squeeze reassuringly on her shoulder and she released herself into the security of the arm across her back. At once her stomach muscles relaxed and she felt better.

Roch had been shifting back and forth on his feet, striving for an air of normalcy, busily brushing dust off his sleeves and pants. Hearing her reproach Polo, though, he quickly abandoned his strategy of detachment. "Hey, Rut'ie, it's my fault. Don't be mad at

Polo. Hey, I'm sorry about"–he gestured in the general direction of her torso–"I, ah, I didn't know it was you *là*..."

"Are you okay, Ruthie?" Polo looked so unusual–she couldn't remember ever seeing him without his glasses on before–with his lower lip split and puffed up, his face smeared with blood from nose to chin–and both he and Roch so anxious and remorseful, Ruthie's anger melted into mere indignation.

"Better now. I can breathe. Just the wind knocked out."

Polo helped her to stand up. "So what the hell was that all about?" Ruthie demanded of the two men, brushing gravel dust off her hands and hair and then methodically attacking her linen pants and striped tee.

Polo shrugged, but said nothing as he tucked in his shirt, retrieved his glasses and flicked an over-to-you glance at Roch. Roch was penitential and embarrassed. He muttered, "I'm sorry, Rut'ie, it's not important, but it's between me and Polo."

Ruthie reverted to a teacher's exasperated censure. "I can't believe two grown men–two friends–can't find a more civilized way to deal with a problem." Roch reddened and looked appropriately sheepish. Immediately, with the same responsive concern she would have felt for an apologetic student, she added more kindly, "Well, you'd better get some ice on your face, Roch. That's a pretty ugly injury." She looked curiously at Polo. It really was nasty, and she was amazed that even a solid punch could do such damage.

Polo grinned at her assumption. Or started to, but stopped and cursed, delicately exploring his bloody lip with his tongue. "Ruthie, that wasn't me. Or at least mostly not me. Roch, tell her about your settling of accounts with Benoit"–

"I'm sure it's a hell of a story. Tell me too," said Hy, who had just rounded the corner.

"Should I put the pizzas in?" asked Caroline.

Hy and Ruthie looked at each other. "Um, maybe let's wait a few more minutes," said Ruthie. "I'm sure they won't be much longer."

"Okay. Just let me know when you're ready." Caroline poured wine for each of them and left the bottle on the table.

"What's keeping them?" Ruthie asked. "How much time does it take to wash up?"

"Nosebleeds take time. Also, I'd say they're taking the opportunity to clear the air on whatever the problem is," said Hy. "I hope so, anyway. Who needs the tension otherwise?"

"What do you think it is? Weren't they like really good friends?"

"Yeah, and I'm sure they still are. I just can't imagine what could be serious enough to warrant a fist fight."

"Hy, did you ever have a fist fight with a friend?"

"Are you kidding? Of course not. It would've been a *schande* for the neighbours when I was young. And at this age? No way."

"It's such a different culture…"

"Are you saying 'different' because you think Jews are physical wimps? Or no, wait, I'm betting it's because you're afraid the multiculturalists will get you for what you're really thinking–that our values are better."

"Maybe. At least in some respects. Would I be wrong? It doesn't mean I don't–care about individuals from that background. It doesn't mean I don't–you know–care about Polo as a person, or think I'm better than he is…"

"I know what you mean, *ziess*. It doesn't matter what you think. It's how you act that's important. You have nothing to be ashamed of."

"Are you happy here, Hy? Not with Manon, I know how well that's turned out. No, I mean, as happy here, in this actual place, as you'd imagined you'd be?"

"You mean, do I feel defensive about being Jewish here in a way I don't in Montreal?"

"Yes, exactly."

"Not until the calls started, and then getting involved in the show, and of course this latest crap. Up until then it was fine. But we're beginning to think about dividing our time more evenly with the city. I thought I could keep my personal life separate from politics, but you know, even if we settle this murder business, I can see the political thing is heating up again, and even if Mont Armand isn't *pur et dur* territory, it's going to get tense everywhere in Quebec. And yeah, if they work themselves up to a referendum or something, there's no question I'll feel better in the bunkers with the rest of the tribe."

"Definitely getting worse. For twenty marks: 'Separatism–is it good or bad for the Jews? Discuss.'"

"It's bad. Bad for the Jews, bad for all ethnics, bad for the economy, bad for them, if they could get past the emotions and see things rationally. End of discussion."

"A+."

Hy sipped at his wine. "*Pisse Dru*. Wow. That takes me back about thirty years. I remember when I first started dating I used to think it was so cool to order *Pisse Dru*." He paused and reflected a moment. "You know, I'm trying to think what could have started the fight. The only thing I can imagine Roch getting that worked up about is Michel. But what could Polo have done to Michel? Or would have?"

"I know," agreed Ruthie. "When we were talking this morning about who the killer could be and it seemed like Michel might have a motive, did you see Polo's face? He really likes Michel. So it can't be that."

Hy shrugged. "Well, they'll either tell us or they won't. Not our problem, I guess."

"So how are you doing otherwise, brother mine? It's been such a day, eh?"

"Don't ask."

"Did you get off the telephone even for a second?"

"Every time I put it down it rang again. Of course a lot of the calls were from Montreal about Bon–Gro, that pyramid scheme thing. Oy, what a mess that is."

"I bet you know half the people in it."

"At least. You know, I can't get over it, ziess. Now that it's been exposed publicly, it turns out the two American guys running it had a track record as long as your arm–fraud, jail time, bankruptcies in every state of the union practically. Unbelievable. On the public record. And these so–called smart businessmen. Did they check? No, they took the word of whoever got them into it. I can't get over it."

"When people want something badly, when they get greedy, it seems like they'll believe anything."

"It's always about short term gratification, always about forgetting the bigger picture."

"I think I read somewhere that that's supposed to be the definition of maturity–the ability to defer gratification."

"Sounds right. I guess I'm mature."

"So what am I? Chopped liver?"

Hy smiled. "No, you're mature too. We're the 'mature family'. *L'Chaim.*" They clinked glasses and laughed.

Ruthie shook her head and sipped. "So when we talk about it with them, I hope you're going to agree with me that Fran and Eva are off the hook for the murder."

"Yeah, of course I do. Wasn't that a fascinating story? No matter how much I learn about the war, it blows me away every time I hear about this kind of courage. And she seems like such a timid, ordinary woman. Who'd have thunk it?"

"I know." They sat in contemplative silence for a few minutes.

Hy said, "Oh, I almost forgot to tell you the big news. We won't be having the show here after all."

"What!"

"Yeah, I got a call from this guy March in Calgary, the president of the Federation, just before the Briquemonts came over. It's all very mysterious. Marion Smy has suddenly resigned. He seemed to imply that there was something not too kosher going on with her. He mentioned Sue Parker in a kind of oblique way. And something about Bridget missing deadlines. Anyway, bottom line, he's not happy, the sponsors aren't happy, the FEI isn't happy, so the meeting tomorrow is cancelled, and everything's up in the air. It looks like it might happen in Alberta. He'd already spoken to Roch."

Hy suddenly snapped his fingers and pointed to the place where Roch and Polo had fought. "Hey, you know what? Maybe that has something to do with the fight between him and Polo, or at least pissed him off enough to make a bigger deal out of some other reason. Losing the show would have to be pretty upsetting for him. The Desrochers will be all over him, they'll say it's a plot by the rest of Canada to screw Quebec or whatever."

"You don't sound upset about it," said Ruthie in mild surprise.

"I'm not," said Hy decisively. "I'm relieved. I thought it would be kind of a fun thing, a way of getting involved in the horse community and sharing a project with Manon, but to be honest, it's been nothing but a pain in the ass. I like Thea, she's really pulling her weight and more, but I can't stand some of the other Ottawa and Toronto people on the committee. They're total amateurs without a clue how to get things done, but so full of themselves. I feel like a complete schmuck sitting in at these meetings, which are totally useless, because they talk about all the stuff they're doing, but in the end they keep dumping the real work on my staff. That wasn't supposed to be part of the deal.

"More to the point, one or two of them are anti–Semitic–not the kind you can do anything about, you know what I mean–just that genteel undercurrent that's always there every time you have anything to do with them. I would have bailed out of any active involvement months ago if it weren't for Roch.

"Anyway, after everything that's happened in the last few days, who needs a horse show for excitement? All I'm looking forward to in the foreseeable future is some pizza and quiet."

"Amen to that. Where are they?"

"Polo, it's actually causing me pain watching you eat that pizza," Ruthie said. "I think you should go to the hospital for stitches–or you'll have a scar. And Roch, you have to keep the ice on your face longer. Twenty minutes on, twenty off." Roch obediently pressed the ice pack to his cheek.

"S'okay," muttered Polo as he shifted carefully in his seat be-fore leaning forward for another small bite. Ruthie in bossy teacher mode was the last thing he needed at the moment. The leaning part hurt his ribs, but if he sat up straight, he was sure to dribble sauce from a mouth that wasn't functioning very efficiently. Roch's care-ful upper body movements and laborious progress on his pizza told the same story.

Caroline had lit the candle in the hurricane lantern. It was dusk turning to night. Many of the tables around them were filling up. The tinkle of cutlery on plates, the scraping of chairs, the wink-ing glow of cigarettes, the wine bottles rustling in their icy nests, and the frequent bursts of soft laughter around them soothed and stroked away the day's tensions, nudging their meeting into the mood of a minor dinner party.

"So where is Gilles now?" Hy asked. He shook his head in won-der at the story Polo had relayed. "Who'd have thought the little pisher had it in him?"

"Sleeping. My condo." Polo shot a wary glance at Roch. No re-action. Good. It was over, then, like a sudden thunderstorm. It was too bad about the fight, but for Roch it had accomplished in two minutes what might never have been worked through in words. Polo asked himself if he was pissed off at being dragged into it, and the answer came back negative. He might not have felt that way two days ago, but today he understood. Polo knew Roch's strengths and limitations. He saw himself, after the day's revelations, as newly equipped to understand the full emotional force of a parent's pos-sessiveness. And on balance, he concluded, he would himself prefer a physical fight–with no one fighting dirty–over the continuing un-certainty and discomfort of unresolved issues.

Gilles choosing him as a confidant was hugely embarrassing for Roch, Polo had already grasped that before he saw Roch. Then the shock of losing the show to another site had to have been a total bummer. And his getting hold of Michel's alibi instead of Roch had been the final straw. Polo hadn't told Roch the important news, about Claude and the pregnancy, only that Michel had spoken to him. But it was one confidence too many. Now Polo could see that all that pent–up steam had been expended in the scuffle. Roch was himself again. And, Polo admitted to himself, the scuffle had even been a welcome personal release for this long day's accumulated stress.

"So Polo, what do you think of my theory about the stallion?" Ruthie demanded.

"Not crazy. Interesting. Definite possibilities." He chewed ten-tatively. "Sorry. Har' to tal' and ea' at same time."

Hy said, "Okay, don't talk. Just eat. I'll sum up. Okay, here goes, in no particular order. Liam is killed on the grounds and buried in the sand, either late afternoon or early evening. Almost everyone has a motive because he was listening to people's phone conversa-tions and snooping in their personal stuff. Almost everyone has the opportunity. But we can eliminate some people. First of all Michel because you say he left the stable mid–afternoon to go to Montreal to see a girl, Polo. How do you know that for sure, though?"

"Got phone number. Solid alibi. Trust me." Again Polo glanced over at Roch. But it was okay. Roch was happy. He was on his third glass of wine. The minute Polo had announced to Ruthie and Hy that Michel had been with a girl overnight in Montreal–he didn't elaborate–Roch's face had registered both happiness and relief. So Roch had wondered too, Polo had thought. All that bluster about Michel's hundreds of girlfriends, but he had really wondered…and now he was at peace. That was all he had cared about. He could have handled Michel killing Liam, but not the other.

Hy continued, "Okay, so Michel's clear on the murder. And we don't know yet who sent the fax, but we know where it came from, and we know Benoit did the office. And–ah–has paid a price for it, eh Roch?" Roch grinned, winced, and nodded emphatically. "And we still don't know about the stallion. As for all these crimes, Ruthie and Manon and I have decided to throw our vote of confidence behind Fran. We have no proof, but we believe he's innocent."

Polo and Roch looked inquiringly at each other, and nodded acquiescence.

"Now we come to the really interesting question of Bridget," Hy went on. And by the way, *chapeau*, hats off to you, Polo, for thinking of looking in that belt buckle. It certainly would never have occurred to me. I'm sure Congress can help us with those contact numbers, but that will have to wait til Monday. As for the other side of the paper"–

Ruthie jumped in. "Oh Bridget is definitely the one, in my opinion. All these lies you've told us about, Polo, and what's so interesting is that Fran's story backs it up. I mean, the accent changing while she's arguing with Liam, the father turning out to be a gamekeeper instead of upper class, the shady business stuff. My money's definitely on Bridget. I'm sure there's a fascinating story about the father. How are we going to get it, though?"

"Forgot to tell you." Polo had finally finished eating and was tenderly patting his mouth with his napkin. "Sue is getting the story. Or I hope she will. I thought she might go over to that island club tomorrow, but she was so pumped she decided to leave right after dinner, and stay overnight in Kingston. If she sees him first thing, she'll be back by early afternoon."

"Assuming he gives her a story. I wouldn't in his position," said Hy.

"Sue's pretty clever. She's a terrier type," said Polo. "What I'm thinking is that he won't want trouble in this job, and maybe he'll give her something so she'll go away and promise no more media attention. Also, if he thinks Bridget has already told us stuff, he may just think he's filling in the blanks."

"But Bridget hasn't told us stuff," Ruthie said.

Polo smiled as widely as he could. "Hey, Word Lady, listen up. I said if he thinks she's told us stuff…"

"Ooh," said Ruthie with wide eyes, "I say, Watson, the game's afoot!"

"What book is that?"

"Come on, cut me some slack, okay? Don't forget I put myself in peril to save you from a severe thrashing."

"What's a thrashing?"

"Hey, enough already, you two. Let's get back to our *moutons* here," grumbled Hy. "Okay, so we're on top of the Bridget situation as much as we can be, and we won't know more until tomorrow. What about Guy? I spoke to the vet school library, and nobody there noticed what time he left."

Roch said, "But why Guy? He was the only one Liam liked."

"And he's so–so–not the type somehow," said Ruthie. "He's like a scared rabbit."

"Look what timid little Eva did," said Hy quietly.

"Yes, but that was for love," Ruthie retorted. "I'll agree that for love of someone else people do extraordinary things. What is it, Polo?"

"What do you mean?"

"I don't know, you sort of looked funny when I said that."

"No, no, it's nothing. Go ahead…"

"Okay, so we don't rule out Guy, but who would he be trying to protect? Who does he love?" Ruthie asked.

"Well…Bridget, I guess," said Hy.

Roch snorted. "Love? Those two? The two of them, they're, ah, *spécial* that way. They don't do sex, neither him, neither her."

"Well, but they're close friends, aren't they?" asked Ruthie.

"Friends isn't love," declared Roch with finality.

"There can be love without sex," said Polo quietly. "There can be hopeless love. That seems to me as good a motive as protective love. And combined, both hopeless and protective–it makes a compelling motivation."

"For whom?" asked Ruthie.

"Jocelyne."

"She loves Michel?" asked Ruthie.

"Big time," said Polo. "And hopelessly, as I said, but always looking for that proof of her love that's finally going to win him. Plus the possibility that she needs to cover herself for drugs or some other secret Liam suspected. Don't forget, there's still a phone number we haven't investigated yet."

Roch waggled his hand in the air. "*C'est possible.*"

Hy said, "So, the committee's consensus is that the murderer is one of Bridget, Guy or Jocelyne. Polo, are you going to follow up on the phone number beside Jocelyn's name?" Polo nodded. Hy yawned. "Is there any 'good and welfare' before we adjourn? Because I've had it for today. And since we don't have to worry about the show committee meeting tomorrow, what do you say we reconvene for brunch on our deck at noon? I'll ask Thea too. We have bagels and lox in the freezer."

"Fairmount bagels, I trust?" asked Ruthie.

"Would I buy any other kind? Of course Fairmount."

Polo wondered, not for the first time, why Jews always answered a question with another question. But he didn't wonder it aloud. Because he was very tired. Once you asked them a question, they'd feel bound to give a proper answer, and, he sighed, who knew how long that could take?

CHAPTER TWENTY–FIVE

"**G**OOD NIGHT, HORSE PEOPLE. ROCH, KEEP ICING FOR A WHILE."

"Okay, Rut'ie. Salut."

"Bon soir, guys."

"'Night Hy, ziess.."

"Roch, I need to use the office phone for a few minutes."

"Okay. I'm just going to walk through the barn and do a final check."

Polo called the Montreal number beside Jocelyne's name. A young man answered. Polo said, "The word's out on your *affaire* with Jocelyne. I'm warning you to watch yourself."

"*Qui ça?*"

"Just a friend. She might be in trouble because of you. We know it's you who's getting the stuff for her."

"What are you talking about? There's nothing illegal. I just get it at wholesale for her."

"You're telling me the stuff is legal?"

"In Canada it is, yeah. Hey, who is this?"

Polo hung up.

Three minutes later Polo phoned the condo. Gilles picked up on the first ring. "I didn't wake you up? Good. Did you see my note?"

"Yeah. Thanks for letting me know. I made some eggs, and I'm watching TV. Oh, and I ate one of your Aero bars. Was that okay?"

"That's fine."

"Are you coming back now?"

"Soon. I want to check a few things. Gilles, the cartoon. Are you sure you put it in the top drawer of the filing cabinet beside M–F's desk, in the first folder?"

"I'm sure. Isn't–isn't it still there?"

"No. It's gone."

"What does that mean?"

"I'm trying to work it out. Anyway, I won't be long. Stay put."

"Okay." Gilles sounded relaxed and perfectly content. Polo heard a laugh track in the background.

Polo looked down the long corridor toward the round barn. No one. Roch must have checked the horses and left already. Then, from the end of the short corridor to his right, he heard Roch's voice, quiet, but strained with concern. "Polo, I have a problem here."

Polo joined him outside Robin's Song's stall. Roch was staring intently at the horse. Polo looked in, and almost immediately hissed with gloomy comprehension. The gelding was restless and apprehensive. Every few seconds he looked back at his flanks with big rolling eyes as if puzzled by what was going on inside them. Now and then he nipped at his sides, or lifted a back leg to kick at his belly. He was sweating, and shifting his weight back and forth at the hind end. The classic signs of colic. Polo and Roch exchanged a quick, speaking glance. Polo had looked forward to a hot bath to ease his aching muscles and sore ribs, followed by a well–deserved sleep. There was no hope now that Roch would be leaving the barn any time soon. And Polo knew he wasn't going to leave him alone with a sick horse.

"Did Michel ride him today?" asked Roch in a poor imitation of offhandedness, as he shut off the automatic water dispenser in the stall.

"No," Polo said guardedly, "I did, actually. Thea asked me to." At dinner, Polo had briefly sketched the outlines of Sue Parker's investigations into Bridget's horse import business, but without details. He hadn't told them about his own involvement because it hadn't seemed relevant.

Roch said nothing for a moment, but Polo was aware that he was relieved. Polo could see what it was that Roch was further wondering, but knew would be offensive to ask a colleague. So Polo added, "And yeah, I rode him pretty hard. Thea had some questions about his soundness she wanted answered, and I needed to pull out all the stops to test him."

Roch nodded as he knelt at the open door to inspect the meager scatterings of manure.

"Roch, I walked the last half mile home, and I swear he was dry when I put him away. He didn't take a drop of water before he was dry." Polo didn't even know why he was saying these things. If he and Roch hadn't fought, if he could take their mutual trust for granted, if this were happening two days ago in fact, he would never have felt bound to justify himself. Nor would it have crossed Roch's mind to doubt his professionalism.

Roch seemed to have come to the same conclusion. He stood up and unhooked the horse's halter from the division post. Gruffly, without looking at Polo, he said, "You didn't have to tell me that. I know this isn't your fault."

Polo took this as a pledge of renewed friendship and felt heartened by it, but only took the halter from Roch and said, "I better get him out and start walking him. He looks like he's going down any minute." The horse was starting to paw at his bedding and push his back end against the wall. He'd want to roll to relieve the pressure ballooning in his gut by rocking himself on the ground. It looked like an unusually fast–moving colic.

Roch went to call Guy and then to prepare a bran mash with some ground up bute, while Polo took the horse out to the parking lot and tried to get some momentum to his walk. Often that was enough to unkink the spasmodic gut and release the trapped gases. But it didn't look good. Robin's Song was in pain. He didn't want to move. He stopped to pass water and Polo's heart sank as, even in the moonlight, he could see that the urine was very dark. Soon there would be muscle tremors–he was already sweating freely and his gait was stiff and lethargic. The walking out wasn't going to work. Guy would have to give him a Banimine I–V or an injection of Dantrolene Sodium, or some other heavy duty muscle relaxant, it looked like.

By midnight, it was clear things weren't improving, even though Guy was doing everything and giving him everything he could. The horse's heart and breathing rates increased. They kept rubbing him down to keep him distracted, but nothing helped. Even with bute and the tranquillizers, the horse groaned and tried to throw himself down every few minutes. He was clearly in terrible pain. At some point they wouldn't be able to get him back up. If things had moved along at a slower pace, they might have made the decision to take him to St. Hyacinthe for surgery. But they soon knew he wouldn't survive the trip, even if they could get him to load into the van. And Guy was not equipped to operate at the stable.

Polo had called Gilles to let him know he had to stay on at the barn, that Robin's Song had colic. Gilles had been full of concern, and had said he would wait up for him. Like an understanding wife, Polo thought, pierced to the quick by the irony. And no, Gilles said, nobody had called the condo since Polo had left.

Now Polo asked Roch if they shouldn't call Thea. She had a right to know, if it wasn't going to get better. Ethically they ought to have already told her by now. But Roch was hesitant and Polo understood why. Emotional owners needed support, and took up time and energy you wanted to give to the horse. But Roch and Polo were pretty sure the horse was going to die, maybe within a few hours. There was no wiggle room on this. She had to know. They were both exhausted, but Roch looked physically ill over it. Polo felt for him. It was a nightmare for the owner or manager when a horse in his care died. Polo volunteered to call Thea. Roch accepted gratefully.

Thea hadn't been asleep. "When did it start?"

"Hard to say. Roch and I found him in some distress around nine, but he'd eaten his grain, so sometime after five, anyway. He hasn't passed any manure since dinner."

Thea didn't ask any more questions about the horse. She was her usual cool self. By now Polo wasn't surprised. Even after their intimate exchange of just a few hours before. She just couldn't open up for long. She needed the protection of emotional detachment to keep functioning normally. Polo didn't take it personally. He only wondered if she had always been that way, or if it was a survival mechanism adopted after her tragedy.

Then she said something that surprised him. "Polo, did you know that Bridget has run off?"

"What? No. What do you mean?"

"Marion Smy called me. Bridget is on her way there. Marion was furious. She practically accused me of being a traitor to horse sport in Canada by cooperating with Sue's inquiries. She told me the show is going to be held somewhere else, that it's all my fault, and that–again, my fault–she's had to resign as chairman."

"Actually, I knew the show was in trouble. Roch and Hy were both called by Ron March. But Thea, that doesn't seem very important at the moment. I really think you should come over."

"But Polo, why is Bridget going to Ottawa? Why? It can only mean one thing."

"I'm not sure I follow."

"Think, Polo. Bridget finds out the show is off, that it's because of Sue's investigations into Marion's conflict of interest with the Rob Taylor syndicate. That shouldn't be her problem. But after hearing about it, she suddenly ups and leaves. There's something very fishy there. I'm sure it's because she killed Liam, and she's afraid Sue or you and the others are on to her. On top of that she must realize you've told me Robin's Song isn't sound. She doesn't want to face the music on that either. And now my horse is suddenly sick?"

"Thea, I'm not sure you're getting the picture here. Your horse is actually in pretty serious trouble. I really think you should come over."

"Polo, I'm not sure you're getting the picture. Do you think the horse getting sick is just a coincidence? I'm telling you, Bridget is behind this."

"Thea, it's colic. How could Bridget have–look, Thea, just get over here and let's deal with the horse first, okay?"

"Polo, I would hate to have you think ill of me, but I'm no hypocrite. If the horse dies, it's sad, but he isn't much good to me alive, if I can't take Bridget to court over him. And I just don't believe this is a coincidence."

"*Calisse de crisse de tabernak*! Thea, are you coming or not?"

"I'm coming. But I'll need a few extra minutes. I was ready for bed. So I have to get dressed. And–I have to find something in my files."

"What?"

"A letter from my daughter."

Polo hung up with a sense of despair. He was weary, and sore all over. His lip throbbed. His ribs hurt with every normal breath he took. His nerves were frayed threadbare from the day's roller coaster of emotional highs and lows. But all of that was as nothing to the anguish of the last three hours, bearing what seemed like interminable witness to the cruel progress of the gelding's death by inches. A horse he'd just ridden, whose vigour and springing gaits still pulsed in the lingering sensory memory of his own body's nerves and muscles. They had done all that was humanly possible to save him, to no avail. Now they were watchers, not doers, the most refined form of torture to a horseman, and the animal was plunging further every minute into mindless terror and spiraling, unremitting pain.

At this point he would have welcomed the prospect of a typical owner. He would have welcomed the distraction of coping with someone in deeper torment than his own. Instead he was going to have to deal with single–minded, Bridget–obsessed Thea and these wild conspiracy theories of hers. This could turn out to be an intolerable additional burden. Why couldn't she forget all that shit for one goddam hour and spare a thought for her poor dumb brute of a horse in his final agony? And why in Christ's name should she be rummaging around in her files at such a moment to find some irrelevant old letter from her daughter?

Women. He'd never met a single one he fully understood. His eyes were grainy with exhaustion, and he pushed up his glasses to rub them with his raw, scraped knuckles, punishing his hands and his eyes at the same time. Fuck! In a way he hoped she didn't turn up before the end, if all she was going to do was crown the animal's suffering with her indifference.

Just die, you poor bastard, there's no hope. One good thing, Nathalie isn't here for this. It would tear her up. Where are you now,

Nath? I'd give anything to be holding you when this shit is finally over.

Slowly he made his way back along the corridor to the barn. The horse was down again, rocking his big, tight drum of a belly and groaning, and Roch and Guy weren't trying to get him up any more. The end was clearly near. Roch muttered something to Guy. Guy started to prepare a hypodermic with potassium chloride for a humane finish. When Thea arrived, they would ask her permission to use it.

Just then the door from the parking lot opened, and Jocelyne stepped into the pool of light over the entranceway. She was made up for an evening out. Seeing the cluster of men at the gelding's stall, she uttered a soft cry of dismay. She knew–by osmosis after all these years–that it was something bad. She ran to them. She gasped at the sight of Roch's battered face and black eye, and started to frame a comment, but then, hearing the horse's desperate lowing, sucked in her breath, and grew silent.

Without a word the men parted so she could see. Nobody felt like talking. She gulped and nodded. She had noted the I–V pole and had taken in the whole story without a single articulated word in her mind. At first there was nothing but sadness and unfeigned sympathy in her expression. She leaned down to stroke the sweat-drenched neck. It was a farewell. She stood up and made the sign of the cross. Then, after a further hushed moment Jocelyne seemed to remember something. Slowly her head came up and her face stiff-ened as she turned to scan the trio of haggard faces. Her narrowed eyes came to rest on Polo.

"You rode him too hard today. Guy, you saw the horse when he came back. He was exhausted." She sought Guy's eye, and Guy reddened as though she'd uttered an obscenity, but said nothing, turning back to the horse and pretending he hadn't heard her. Irri-tation and disgust flickered across Roch's drawn face, but he waited for Polo to answer.

"Jocelyne," said Polo very softly, a bolt of fury flashing through him, "I know you think you have reason to be pissed off at me, but if I were you, I'd be very, very careful what you say right now about that horse."

"And what's more," Jocelyne added heedlessly, with a chilly smirk and glittering eyes, "he was soaking wet with sweat when you put him in the stall."

Later Polo remembered he heard someone gasp at this deliberately incriminating lie or perhaps at what happened next. It might have been Guy, but then again it might have been Roch or even himself. He could never be sure, because the second after she said it his right hand had smacked her across the face so hard she actually spun a half-circle on her heels before staggering sideways into the stallion's stall door and falling down.

Feeling nothing in particular apart from the waning rage that had fuelled his action, Polo stared, puzzled, at his tingling palm. He heard the stallion whinnying. Then he heard swearing. He felt Roch push by him. He watched with dull attention as his friend knelt to assess the damage to the girl. Jocelyne was holding a hand to her face and keening harshly like a big, stricken bird. He looked around to find Guy physically shrinking back toward the end wall, his face a mask of uncomprehending shock. Still he felt nothing approaching regret. So he drew a deep, rib-punishing breath to stimulate his conscience, and waited patiently for the obligatory wave of shame and remorse. Strangely, though, all he could identify in the slow wash of returning consciousness was a weird sense of relief.

So this is what it took. But I finally did it. I hit a woman. I knew someday...but funny, I was sure it would be Nath... Jocelyne shouldn't have lied about me putting the horse away wet. If she'd said I'd murdered Liam...or was gay...or was stupid... I could have handled... but to say that...in front of people...that I would do that to a horse... deliberately endanger a horse...I wanted to really hurt her...even a woman...now I know for sure where the line is...

Roch was helping her up. She was whimpering and when she took her hand away from her face, Polo could see the angry red imprint of his hand. Roch tilted his head toward Polo, then back toward Jocelyne, and his eyes plainly signaled Polo to apologize. Polo nodded and cleared his throat. But the words, even a simple 'I'm sorry' stuck in his throat. The interesting thing was that he still wasn't the least bit sorry. In fact, what came out of his mouth was, "Joc, you owe me an apology. I shouldn't have hit you, but you deserved it, and if you were a man..."

"Polo! *Tabernouche*. Don't make things worse. Hey, it's not right, what you did, *hein*? This isn't a good time for splitting hairs. We got a dying horse here…" Roch passed a nervous hand over his scalp and swore. Cuffing Polo's arm, he murmured, "C'mon, fix it up, *vieux*. If this gets out…" his eyes darted reflexively around the barn, and finally Polo's dawdling conscience drew level with events.

Okay, then. A reconciliation gift for Roch. Fair was fair. Roch had already tendered his own olive branch hours before. "I'm sorry I hit you, Joc," Polo said coolly, making no attempt to hide his contempt. "It won't happen again." And it wouldn't. Not her, or any other woman. That he knew for a certainty.

As Roch, reassured, turned with finality back to the desperate struggle in the gelding's stall, Jocelyne shrugged sullenly and started down the long aisle towards the round barn and her pie–slice room. Polo followed her until he was out of Guy's and Roch's hearing range, and stopped.

"Hey!"

"What?" she muttered, halting too, but faced away from him.

"Who's the guy at 931–4236 in Montreal?"

Jocelyne turned and stared at him in amazement. The fading red blotch on her cheek suddenly blazed scarlet against the white of her face.

"How did you"–

"Why don't we just cut to the chase, Joc? What's legal here that isn't in the States? What kind of scam have you got going? How much did Liam know? Enough for you to kill him? Should I just take a wild guess and go to Michel with my suspicions? Or should I"–

"No! Stop! Don't go to Michel!"

"Okay, I won't. Yet. If you tell me about it. You know I could go to Michel with the lie you just told and that alone would be enough to"–

"Don't. Don't. I'm sorry. I'm sorry, okay? When you told Michel you knew he'd never–you know–with me, I was just so–so"–

Indignation, contempt, impatience–a boiling emotional stew twisted Polo's gut like a sympathetic colic. Too bad horses can't talk, he thought, and get out what's bugging them. But I can, and I've had it with that victim shtick. I've had it with the lot of them.

"You know, Joc, under normal circumstances, I'd feel sorry for you. I used to, in fact. But I don't any more. People who work with horses–they may be stupid, or obsessed, like you are, or corrupt, or blind to the corruption around them, or so desperate to win they can't have a civil relationship with other competitors– or any number of awful things. Above all, they may be cowards. Yeah, especially that. And you tend not to judge too harshly. You try not to, because we all know we're guilty of some rotten tendency ourselves, and we try to understand what's going on in the other person's life that makes him do lousy things.

"There're only two things that you can't, or shouldn't, forgive. That I can't forgive, anyway. One is horse abuse. The other is the kind of betrayal you just did back there. Blaming a professional horseman for deliberately putting a horse at risk. Something you know for a fact I would never do. And for what? To make your pathetic little ego feel better. I'll never forgive you for that."

Jocelyne covered her face with her hands and sobbed quietly. "Please don't tell Michel what I did, Polo. I would die if I couldn't be near him."

What she had just said aroused no pity in him. Instead, Polo was further repelled. And what he'd just said to her he hoped she understood wasn't rhetoric. It was a fact. She'd disqualified herself forever from inclusion in his wider sympathies. He'd found the limits of his tolerance, it seemed. He had nothing to say to reassure her. He hoped she understood that he'd go to Michel in a second if she didn't spill whatever it was she was hiding. And fast. The thought of the horse dying forty feet away was making him wild with frustration.

Jocelyne looked at Polo and quietly wiped away her tears, dragging runnels of mascara across her cheeks. She understood. She said, "It's not what you think, Polo. It isn't drugs. Or at least it's not the drugs you're thinking of. That guy in Montreal–he's a sales rep for a pharmaceutical company. His girlfriend rides in Hudson. The company he works for–Progentex–they make this allergy pill–Allerprieve. His girlfriend was using it for her allergies to hay–you know how it's a big problem for riders, allergies. Then she found out there's something in the pill that takes away your appetite. She started losing weight. So, you know, the word got around, and you know the girl riders on the circuit, they"–

"Bottom line it, Joc. Where do you come in?"

"You can get it without a prescription here, but it hasn't passed the FDA in the States yet. I get a whole bunch of it here from this guy, wholesale, and I sell it to the girl riders in the States. They pay a lot. I give the guy a kickback. That's the whole story, Polo, it's no big deal."

"Liam thought it was something else. Coke. He said he'd go to Michel with it, didn't he? That's a good motive for murder."

Jocelyne looked at him with what seemed like spontaneous astonishment. "Me? Kill someone over allergy pills?" She laughed mirthlessly. "You must think I'm stupider and crazier than"–she shook her head in wonderment, then continued quietly, "Listen, Polo, I don't have much going on in my life except Michel. That part's true, and I–I've done some stupid things because of that. But"–she twisted a strand of hair that had come loose from her ponytail –"I would never let it go that far.

"Yeah, Liam thought he could blackmail me, but he got it all wrong. Just like he got the part about Michel being gay wrong." She looked up at him boldly, as the old defiance flashed momentarily before subsiding once more into resigned humility. "If worse came to worse, I'd have told Michel about the pills. But Michel wouldn't have got rid of me just for that." She sighed. "I'm glad to get that off my chest, to tell you the truth."

She looked down and fresh tears spilled down her face in clownish black streaks. "Polo, I know you don't believe me, and I know you'll never be my friend again, but I just want to say anyway that I'm really sorry for what I said about you."

"Good night, Joc."

"*Salut…salut…*" Joc whispered sadly to the empty space where Polo had been standing.

Thea shuddered and nodded to Guy. The needle plunged and within seconds the racked body relaxed and stilled to immobility. They had all been holding their breath without knowing it, and the air came out of them as a collective sigh. Nobody spoke for a long minute.

Roch tried to frame a consoling sentence, but Thea patted his shoulder and shook her head. "Not necessary, Roch. I've had it easy. Only five minutes of this horror. You poor men, you're exhausted, just look at you all." She cocked her head, and added, "On top of whatever else you've been up to. I know my horse isn't completely responsible for the wear and tear I'm seeing."

Roch and Polo exchanged a look of mutual revulsion for Thea's ironic distance from events. There was no question of either one of them telling her about their fight. Roch mumbled something inaudible about walking into a door, and Polo pretended he hadn't heard as he gently covered the horse with a turnout sheet. Thea took the rebuff with grace.

"So now what?" she asked, glancing discreetly into the stall and away.

Guy cleared his throat. "In the m–morning. Th–they'll come for h–himmmm." He looked at the floor as he spoke. Roch and Polo instinctively looked away from Thea, hoping she wouldn't ask who 'they' was.

"By 'they', I assume you mean the people who will take him to Saint Hyacinthe? To the veterinary hospital?" she inquired sweetly but pointedly.

Roch and Polo turned to her in surprise, but it was Guy she was staring at with inexplicable fierceness. He was agitated, and to Polo seemed even frightened by her question.

"Why the hospital, Thea?" Polo asked quietly. But even as he asked he knew the answer. He just had to hear her say it. Guy knew why too, Polo could see. He was pale and obviously miserable, longing to escape Thea's gaze. Poor guy, thought Polo. He's like a pinned butterfly. But why should he care one way or another, unless–

"Because," Thea said with suave authority, "the vet hospital is where they do autopsies." Roch took a step toward her and opened his mouth to speak, but Thea's eyes didn't move from Guy's face as she went on, "Roch, please don't bother to explain to me that it was colic, and there's no need for an autopsy. I am convinced that there is a need."

"Thea," Polo said, "I've seen a lot of colics over the years. This was unusually quick, but it was definitely colic. There's no way Bridget could have planned it."

"If that's the case, Polo," Thea said softly, "then why does Guy look so worried? Why should he care if there's an autopsy, if you're all so convinced it was colic?"

Polo turned to Guy and then flicked an uneasy glance at Roch. Both of them could see that Guy was struggling to contain his anxiety. His hand fluttered up to wipe sweat from his forehead.

"What the hell is going on?" demanded Roch, looking from face to face. No one spoke. Thea's lips set in a hard line, and her light gray eyes blazed with purpose.

Then Guy finally broke eye contact with her, and, as though he had come to some sad but definitive decision, sighed heavily. He knelt swiftly and began packing up his medical bag. In silence they all watched as he dismantled the I–V apparatus. Finally he stood up, equipment in hand, and muttered, "You must d–do as you see f–fit, Thea." Without a further comment or glance at anyone, he strode quickly down the aisle and out of the barn.

His lids drooped, but Gilles' glazed eyes were still resolutely fastened on the TV screen when Polo opened the door to the condo. The boy looked up at him with a smile of undisguised relief.

"I didn't want to go to bed 'til you came back," he said. "Is Robin's Song okay now?"

"The horse died, Gilles."

"Oh, no," the boy whispered.

"Yeah."

"I'm really sorry, Polo."

"Yeah. Thanks."

"Polo?" Gilles said softly.

"Yeah?"

"What happened to your–I mean, did you–were you in a fight with–someone?"

"It's not important now, Gilles."

"No, I mean–if it was Uncle Roch–I mean, then I think maybe it was my fault, and–and"–

"Gilles, listen. It was with Roch, but it wasn't your fault. And it's finished. We're still friends."

"Oh. That's good. Poor Uncle Roch. He has so much on his

mind, and now the horse…"

"Yeah. Anyway,"–Polo gestured to the bedroom–"you might as well go to sleep. I came to tell you I have to talk to Thea and then Guy before I turn in. Are you okay on your own?"

He nodded. "But you're coming back eventually, aren't you?" Gilles tried to appear nonchalant, and failed.

"Yeah. I promise."

"Good. Polo?"

"Yeah?"

"You look awfully tired."

"Yeah. I know. *Salut*, Gilles."

"Wait!"

"What?"

Gilles had dashed to the refrigerator.

"Here. Take this." Gilles thrust an Aero bar at him. "In case you get hungry…"

"Thanks, kid."

Polo knew it was just the fatigue and his nerves and missing Nathalie, but the sweet spontaneity of Gilles' gesture unmanned him. As the chocolate bar passed from the boy's hand to his, Polo felt a prickling in his eyes, and his throat closed up. He managed a weak smile and squeezed Gilles' shoulder. Gilles blushed with pride.

"*Salut.*"

"*Salut.*"

✤ ✤ ✤

"I made coffee, Polo."

"Coffee would be good."

Thea poured him a full mug and set it down before him.

"Thanks." He gulped greedily, and grimaced as the hot liquid insulted his cracked lip. Then he said, "Okay, Thea. Why the autopsy?"

Thea sat opposite Polo and pulled some folded pages from her handbag. "This is a letter Stephanie sent me from school two years ago." She laid it on the table and lovingly smoothed it flat. "Her letters are all I have now. I wish they'd found her journal."

"They?"

"I mean after the accident. The people at Timberline got her tack box, her riding gear and clothes together for me, as well as her purse and documents and so forth, but they should have found her journal. Stephanie was very disciplined about keeping it–she used it mostly as a log of her training and competing history, and she never travelled without it. She'd keep it in her tack box at the shows because she locked it at night and it was safe there."

"Could someone have taken it deliberately?"

"But who? And why?"

"Well, for an obvious starter, Liam worked at Timberline. And why? Because he liked knowing people's secrets. It was his way of getting power over others."

Thea frowned and considered this possibility. "He certainly never tried to blackmail me, or approached me in any way, and I can't imagine what he'd have found of interest in her activities." She shrugged, and went back to smoothing out the letter. "Whoever took it, I doubt I'll ever get it back."

"Anyway, sorry to sidetrack you, you were about to tell me why you wanted a post mortem."

"Right. Polo, do you remember I told you that Stephanie's research had to do with cattle?"

"Yeah. Growth hormones. You said some pharmaceutical company was funding it."

"Yes, that's right," said Thea with pleased surprise. "You really listen when people talk to you, Polo. That's a rare quality in a man."

"My wife probably wouldn't agree with you," Polo blurted out without thinking. He felt himself blushing. Fatigue was making him indiscreet. "I mean," he added hastily, "she'd say sometimes there's listening to what people say they mean, as opposed to listening to what they really mean. But yes, I do remember what people say. I was illiterate up to my teens, and it was the only way to store important information."

"Oh. That must have been a very painful handicap for someone as intelligent as you," Thea said.

"Yeah, it was…" He shifted in his seat. "Actually, I don't even know why I told you that."

"It's nothing to be ashamed of. I imagine, though, that you're not given to much in the way of personal revelation as a rule." Polo acknowledged this with a vague hand gesture and a sudden interest in the design on his coffee mug. He really had not meant to wander off track like that.

Thea said quietly, "Perhaps we've both come to see that confession really is good for the soul. I don't mind admitting that talking to you earlier was–well, good therapy for me. I've needed to talk about my guilt feelings for a long time, but I was too proud to go to a professional, and there was nobody else I could…well, anyway, let's just say I'm glad you were there for me." She remained composed as she spoke, but, Polo noted, her hand kept on mechanically caressing her daughter's letter.

"Confession has certainly been the big theme today," Polo said. "And yeah, it's been good"–he couldn't bring himself to say therapy –"it's been good for me too," he finished lamely. He looked at his watch and sighed.

"I'm sorry," Thea said. "I know it's late, and you're tired. Okay, here's the thing. In this letter Stephanie was telling me about a conversation she'd had with Bridget at a horse show. They were talking about Dick Francis novels, which they both enjoyed, and Bridget had mentioned that colic was a great way to murder a horse, but you could never be sure a horse would get it and if he did, whether he would die from it. Okay, now listen carefully to this part.

'…so I said to her, I could kill a horse and nobody would ever know it wasn't colic unless they did an autopsy. She was all ears, of course, so I told her about what my prof, who's a murder mystery freak, told a bunch of us. This product I'm working on–Rumenex–well, it's made with a drug–Monensin–that's used as a growth promoter in cattle, but also as an agent to kill parasites in chickens. So listen to this. With about 12 grams of this stuff you could kill an average horse! Of course, if you wanted to be sure of knocking him off you would give him a big dose, maybe 100 grams, you could just mix it in with his grain. It gives all the exact symptoms of colic–sweats, going down and rolling, black urine, muscle weakness, tremors, etc, and the important thing is, the horse always dies in the end.

What he actually dies of is heart failure because the drug attacks the muscles, and the heart is a muscle–you probably knew that. The drug kills off cells in the heart. Most people don't ask for post mortems when their horse dies of colic. In the post mortem you would see the pale white streaks throughout the muscles of the hind limbs and the heart, and that's what would give the murderer away. Isn't that creepy?'

Thea paused here and looked at Polo. He didn't know what to say, but his fatigue fell away, and he felt as though his heart was suddenly pumping an extra litre or two of blood.

'Ostie. I would have sworn it was colic but it just went so damn fast. Creepy is about the right word with this woman. First she brings Morrie back from the grave, now it's the dead daughter, and both times I can't believe what I'm hearing...and yet it all makes perfect sense...

What were the odds of stepping on two land mines set by the same person in a single day? But he had to say something... "Thea, is it possible that Bridget could actually get hold of this stuff?"

"Don't you remember something else I told you about her research?"

And he suddenly did. "Guy," he said slowly, "Guy was working on it with her."

"Exactly. Now listen to this. Listen to how she ends it–

'But you know, mom, I felt kind of bad after I told Bridget, because really it was just to show off how much stuff I'm learning, and even though it was just Bridget, I don't think it was very ethical of me to be blabbing this kind of information. I mean, what if it got into the wrong hands?'"

CHAPTER TWENTY-SIX

POLO PARKED HIS TRUCK ON A GRASS VERGE, FAR ENOUGH away to announce his arrival on his own terms. Guy's truck was there in front of the bungalow. Bridget's Toyota Corolla wasn't. Clouds obscured the moon. The darkness surrounding the isolated house was almost absolute. Few lights were on inside. He could see a fluorescent ceiling fixture through the drawn half-curtains of the kitchen window to the rear of the house. Apart from that, there was only the feeble glow from one table lamp in the living room, and a luminous blue light across the hall.

There was a garage, or shed, to the side and back, not attached to the house. Polo advanced cautiously towards it, on the alert for sudden barking. They were horse people, so there had to be a dog. But it might not be the watchdog type. Bridget was English. She would have a Labrador. With Labradors, you never knew—some were viciously territorial, others were complete wimps. He gripped his flashlight more firmly and listened for barking or scrabbling at the door. Nothing.

The door to the shed wasn't locked. It creaked a bit, not alarmingly, but again he waited for the dog. Again, nothing. Inside,

415

he flicked on his flashlight and let it roam. There didn't seem to be much here. Winter tires, old garden tools, an ancient, rust–streaked stove, plastic gas containers, a small generator. And there, in plain sight against the far wall, was what he'd hoped to find only after a tedious search, if at all, the dirty, worn out Aer Lingus duffel bag that he knew at once must be Liam's. It wasn't even zipped up. He pulled the handles apart and shone his flashlight on the contents. Clothes, heaped like a pile of dirty laundry, thrown inside in haste. A Ziploc bag with a few documents–a passport, a cheap, fake leather wallet.

He looked through everything. About fifty dollars, a Zellers card, a video club card. Nothing handwritten or personal. The duffel bag was only half–full. The rest of the space would have contained the hate literature in the box. So either Guy didn't know about the material or he hadn't had time to look for it. Or–Polo couldn't discount any theory at this point–Guy had wanted it to be found back at the barn.

Why hadn't Guy taken any trouble to conceal this incriminating evidence? Was it a kind of fatalism? Was it like, 'okay, if you knew enough to look here, I can't be bothered to escape because you already know I did it' kind of thing? Or would he have the *hutzpah* to say ' I have no idea how those things got there. Someone must be trying to frame me'. Or–or–Polo tried to anticipate other explanations so he wouldn't be thrown when he confronted Guy.

Liam could have left it there himself for some reason. Bridget could have put it there after she killed Liam, if she killed him. Her sudden departure was suspicious. Why was he assuming it was Guy, just because he had looked guilty about the horse when Thea demanded a post–mortem? *Merde*. He was going to have to rely on Guy telling the truth. In fact, so far he'd had to rely on everyone telling the truth.

He shone the light on his watch. Pretty funny, when you thought about it. Two in the morning, he'd been on the go since eight the previous morning, he was ninety–nine percent certain he was about to talk to a murderer, and in spite of what looked like conclusive evidence, he had no real leverage to bring to bear, nothing that would bring Guy–or Bridget–to justice in a court of law.

Wordlessly, and with no sign of surprise or fear, Guy ushered Polo into the hall. Polo dumped the duffel bag on the floor between them. Guy glanced at it and nodded.

"*Bon,*" he said lightly, looking Polo squarely in the eye, "I wondered what had kept you so long. But it's clear you haven't been idle."

With the bag as his opening gambit, Polo had assumed he would have the advantage in the confrontation. He was taken aback by Guy's calm self-possession, and he was sure it showed. Not a good beginning. But it wasn't only Guy's apparent detachment that was so weird, it was–hey, it was–

"Guy! You're not stuttering," he exclaimed.

Guy blushed a bit and smiled. "You noticed," he murmured.

Noticed. Even after a few short sentences, the change in Guy's speech pattern made a stunning impression on Polo. In the scheme of things it shouldn't be such a big deal whether a man stuttered or didn't, but somehow Guy's unanticipated fluency turned him into a different person altogether. He even looked different–less geeky, more manly. As though Guy had an identical twin who'd been adopted out to more confidence-inspiring parents. It was unsettling, even disturbing. Polo felt–he struggled to explain his anger–duped, defrauded somehow.

Polo said, "So was the stuttering an act too? I mean, you and Bridget. She did the accents, you did the special effects?"

Now Guy was on the defensive, embarrassed. "You've found out something about Bridget..."

"I know all kinds of things now, but first things first."

"*Eh bien,* come in and sit down, then." Guy led the way into the living room and nudged the brown Labrador in the wing chair. Yawning, indifferent to the newcomer, the dog heaved himself down to the carpet and padded over to his floor cushion against the wall. Before sitting down, Polo set the duffel bag on the floor in plain view of both of them. Guy opened the liquor cabinet.

"I could use a drink. What about you? We –I have Scotch, vodka, rye–what else–oh, gin, of course."

"Scotch."

Polo watched intently as Guy chose and lifted, measured and poured with the familiarity and assurance of the frequent urban host. This too struck him as bizarre, but he was mainly concerned to see that Guy didn't slip anything into his drink. Just to be sure, when Guy set the glasses down on the coffee table between them, Polo leaned over and with deliberate candour switched the glasses around. He picked up the one intended for Guy and sipped, then replaced it on the table. It was the quickest and most direct way to cut off Guy's charade of this being a casual collegial schmooz.

"Oh, now really, Polo, surely you don't think..."

"The stuttering, Guy."

Guy sipped and sighed. "I wasn't born stuttering, you know. Even after it started, in adolescence, it was only when I was nervous, or afraid, or with new people. I'm fine when I feel comfortable with people, or on the phone, or giving a prepared lecture, for example. And I wasn't always afraid of my own shadow either. I was a pretty normal kid up to the age of twelve. Decent parents, nice home, the best schools, all that sort of thing. After that—well, it doesn't matter why, but my life got–difficult, let's say, and I lost my confidence. Nothing so dramatic as an assumed identity, I assure you."

"It seems a strange moment to get it back. Your confidence, that is. When you consider that you're under suspicion for murder, and that's just for openers."

"Yes, I can see that it looks peculiar. It's Bridget leaving, I think. She scared me, I don't mind admitting it. I'm not a very brave person, and I'm used to having her run interference for me. She's so much stronger than me, but that was all right. I've felt quite protected all these years. I surprised myself tonight. When Thea said that, about wanting an autopsy on the horse, I thought it was the end. I thought, this is it, first I am going to crack up, and then I am going to end up in prison. Then I said to myself, no I'm not, I'm not going to prison, I'd kill myself first.

"And that was a kind of epiphany. I realized that that is true. I *would* kill myself first. It was a very liberating thought. I realized I had a *choice*. And then I became very calm and very relaxed. And I felt strangely–free... So you see, that was it. The minute I gave up thinking of other people as my–judges, I guess,–I got my self back. I mean, the self I left behind before–the difficulties."

"Very inspiring," Polo said dryly. "But I'll have to take your word on this, won't I? Because the other explanation, that you and

Bridget were a tag team, and you've decided you can't be bothered to go solo now that she's split, seems just as plausible to me. But–okay, so you've miraculously recovered your confidence and the power of normal communication. Now what? Are you going to come clean?"

Guy shrugged and smiled. "Look, as I understand it, you've given yourselves until tomorrow to find out who did it. Otherwise you're going to feel you have to go to the police. Let me offer an alternative. I'll tell you what you want to know. You'll have unequivocal reassurance that Liam deserved to die. After that, I'll get my affairs in order and clear out. I'm no serial killer. I'm not a danger to society. I'm making this offer because I have a phobia about being locked up. Even the thought of going in for questioning"–Guy shuddered delicately, and sipped.

"Anyway, apart from my fears, I find I'm dying to talk to someone intelligent about all this. Between you and me, the horse world isn't exactly a greenhouse for the production of Rhodes scholars. But you knew that, didn't you? So be flattered. If confession is good for the soul, and I've come round to the belief that it is, then an intelligent confessor is *de rigeur*." Guy pulled deeply at his drink and said, "You looked startled when I said that. Does that sound stupid to you, doing something for your soul's benefit?"

"Not a bit. It's just that you're about the fifth person today who's told me this. It's a little weird, that's all. As for letting the matter drop–well, that's a toughie. I know Liam was a creep and probably did deserve to die, but if the police happened to trace him here and questioned us, I'd be morally bound to tell what I know. Or at least what you choose to tell me."

Guy shrugged again and looked at Polo with the weary air suggesting a more profound and comprehensive understanding of life. "You say that with such touching conviction. As though your moral compass is so inalterably fixed in matters of right and wrong, it could never lose its sense of direction."

"It's not so much murdering Liam. It's the horse abuse–and horse murder–that gets to me. I can't see where I'd have much of a moral struggle in betraying you about that." As Polo said the words, an image of the gelding groaning in agony rose before his eyes, and he gripped his glass with force. "Although, ironically enough, you probably wouldn't have to serve jail time for it. But maybe we could dispense with the philosophy of life stuff and get on with your story."

"Fine," said Guy softly. "Point taken about the horses. I was pretty impressed with your–ah–dialogue with Jocelyne on the subject of horse abuse. Just remember the words 'moral struggle' when I get to the surprise ending about Liam, that loathsome creature. When I get to the part about Liam's fascination with *you*–and your past. Because I'm banking on that part to win you over in the negotiations."

Polo leaned forward. "What do you mean? We hardly met. I came to drop some construction bids off for Hy one day in March. I didn't spend more than three minutes with Liam that day, and since I've been here for the show and Hy's arena I haven't spoken ten words to him directly."

Guy said archly, "Well, apparently that first three minutes was enough to fire up his animosity. Oho, just look at you now. It's as I suspected. You're very objective, very high and mighty when you think this is all about Liam's relationships with the regular stable people. You didn't know Liam had it in for you too."

Polo seethed with curiosity and apprehension. But Guy had made it clear that he was going to wait until the end to reveal whatever this was about. Shrewd. There was probably nothing to it. It was a ploy to keep him at bay, to make sure Polo heard him out. Polo forced himself to sit back quietly, and appear composed. He took a deep, burning pull at the scotch, and felt it go to work on his balled–up, now–empty gut. Probably not a good thing to be drinking on an empty stomach. He remembered the Aero bar Gilles had given him and fished it out of his windbreaker pocket. He stared at it. Gilles, Thea, Ruthie, Roch, Hy, Michel–they seemed light years away, miniature dolls in different rooms of a cutaway plywood playhouse.

Noticing the chocolate bar, Guy exclaimed, "You're hungry, of course. I can do better than that if you like. I've some lamb stew from the *resto* that Bridget thinks I believe she made, if you want."

"Never mind. This'll do." He tore open the wrapper. "Before we get to Liam, let's talk about the horses."

420

"Robin's Song, you mean."

"No. Horses. Plural."

Guy raised his eyebrows in a mute question.

"I mean the stallion, of course. You did him, didn't you?" Polo broke off a block of chocolate and let it melt on his tongue while he watched Guy shift uncomfortably in his chair.

"When I said I wanted to confess, it was Liam I wanted to tell you about. The horses are a different matter altogether. The horses are between Bridget and me."

"But you can't separate the stallion from what happened between you and Liam."

Guy crossed his arms and hugged his meagre chest. He said, "I told you I don't want to talk about the horses," but his tone was muted, as though he were registering futile disapproval of a motion that had passed unanimously around a committee table.

Polo said, "Ruthie told me she shared a theory with you. Some literary deduction. Symbols about communication and stud service. I forget the details. At first she thought it was foolish, but when she mentioned it to you, you got nervous. I didn't think it was foolish the way she explained it, though."

Guy turned his glass in his hands, watching the play of light from the table lamp turn the liquor different shades of gold.

Polo went on. "Once I knew the gelding wasn't a hundred percent sound–and I know you realized that, I saw you watching me with the calipers, and you saw the horse's reaction–I began to wonder about the stallion. If the stallion was unsound as well. But it never occurred to me to put *you* together with that. Of course, I was still working on the assumption that you were committed to serving animal well–being at that point"–

Guy didn't take the bait. He refused to meet Polo's gaze, looked down into the amber fluid and waited.

"Here's when it came to me. Gilles was the one who found the body and drove it to Montreal. He told me that this afternoon. That was when he confessed to being part of Liam's little hate group cell. He told me about the fire Liam was going to set at the Jacobsons'. But I'm sure you know all about that, yes?" Guy nodded curtly. "He also told me that he was supposed to send a particularly nasty anti–Semitic cartoon to the Jacobsons' house from the office. It was Benoit's job to trash the office and spray the separatist slogans. You following so far? Or am I telling you stuff you already know?"

"I knew about the office. I knew about the proposed fire."

"You left your files unlocked. That was your–not job, I guess–your gesture of trust in Liam. Am I right? If you didn't, I have a feeling they'd have been trashed good and proper. I think Liam liked the idea of everyone being subservient to his authority, and proving it."

"I wasn't part of his cell, as you put it. Never that," Guy said scornfully.

"No, but you knew a lot, so you had to expose yourself, just a teeny bit, to give Liam that extra little thrill, the power of the–the mafia Don or whatever."

"He liked to tell me things."

"Oh, I just bet. But we'll come back to that. Let's finish with the stallion. So Gilles is supposed to send that fax. But he gets cold feet. Instead of sending it, he panics and hides it in the first place he sees. In your files, which are of course conveniently open.

"So after dinner tonight I go and look for the cartoon. By now they're locked again, but I know M–F has a duplicate key in her drawer, and Roch has given me office keys, so I open M–F's desk and then the files. It wasn't there. So that cartoon was taken out of your files and sent to the Jacobsons. But who else knew to look there to get it and send it? Who but you would have been rooting around in your files? The fact that it wasn't there meant that you yourself found the cartoon and you had to be the one who sent it. And then got rid of it to make sure no one saw it in your files by accident. If you were thinking more cleverly, by the way, you would have replaced it in your files, so you could say someone was trying to incriminate you. That's the trouble with spontaneous gestures.

"But it was sent at 4:17 a.m. What the hell were you doing in the office at that hour? There could be only one reason. You had come to cut the stallion, early enough in the morning that no one else would be there, late enough that the stallion wouldn't have to wait too long to be seen to. You also wanted to see the kind of job Benoit had done, and to make sure he had left your files untouched.

You found the cartoon that Gilles had stashed, and I'm thinking you said to yourself, hey, why not complicate things. You had buried Liam in the sand. Or at the very least you knew he was buried there. The plan was to have him discovered on the Monday. By that time it would be hard to establish the time of death.

"You left the hate material under Liam's bed so it would be discovered. If I hadn't found it, you would have 'discovered' it yourself. You wanted Liam identified with the material so when we looked at the time printed on the fax, we would assume it must have been Liam who sent it and therefore it had to be Liam who did the stallion. Then you'd be off the hook for the horse for sure. At the very least you meant to tangle up our thinking and complicate the process. And it worked, you know. We did get tangled up in our thinking. How'm I doing so far?" He popped another square of chocolate in his mouth. He must be striking home runs, or Guy would have stopped him.

Guy didn't crumble. "I'm agog with admiration for your imaginative powers," he said. "I can't complain, can I, since I specifically said I was looking to talk to someone intelligent."

"You did the stallion. And when you did, you thought it would be a one–off with little risk–who'd have figured a vet as both attacker and healer? You didn't count on having to get rid of the gelding later on. A much riskier proposition, but by then you were too invested in protecting Bridget to back away from it. But you're not actually going to say it out loud, are you–that you did it. You're willing to confess to people murders, but not to horse abuse. *Chapeau*, you still have a sense of scale in your moral priorities. But I don't know how hiding the horse stuff is so good for your soul and all that."

"It was Liam I was prepared to talk about."

"Did you kill him?"

"Isn't it obvious?"

"A little too obvious. Like your stuttering mysteriously disappearing."

Guy smiled wryly. "This isn't the usual interrogation technique, trying to stop someone from confessing. Why don't you want it to be me who killed Liam?"

"It's not what I want. It's what is in fact true. It could have been

Bridget. It's one of you, anyway. And you could be eager to confess to it to keep us off her trail. You seemed very keen for me to find the bag in the shed. So far today I've heard nothing but stories about people going to extraordinary lengths to protect those they love. You could be protecting Bridget. She had motive and opportunity."

"But so did I, and so did others," said Guy, spreading his hands in a gesture of helplessness. "Even you did."

"I had opportunity, but no motive."

"You seem very sure about that," said Guy.

"I am. I didn't know Liam. Tell me about your own motives," said Polo, as he put the rest of the chocolate in his mouth and sat back to listen.

Guy rose with his empty glass and went to the liquor cabinet. He poured and waved the bottle at Polo inquiringly. Polo shook his head. Guy settled himself in his chair, clasped his hands around the glass in his lap, and launched himself into his narrative.

"My life was perfect here at *Le Centre*–or as perfect as my life was ever going to get. Bridget and I may have seemed like an odd couple from the outside, but we got on very well. We complement-ed each other. No married couple could have been more content, I believe. We were both–fugitives, in a way, from our respective pasts, and we understood each other. I'd assumed life would go on forever the way it was–before Liam arrived on the scene.

"From the day he got here, everything started to change. I be-lieve in good and evil. And he was almost completely evil. He only knew about hatred. Hatred and personal power. Except for the horses. I have to say he loved the horses. And it was because of that one spot of goodness that I misread his character. When he first came there was a coincidental run of problems–a colic, a horse cast in his stall, two bowed tendons, a hoof abscess, a bad skin infection, that sort of thing–and he was a fantastic help. He really would have made a great veterinarian. If he'd had the educational opportuni-ties, it's what he would have been. Anyway, because of that, because of seeing so much of his normal side, I was pretty friendly to him, and we spent a fair amount of time together.

"Liam hadn't had a lot of friendship in his life. Any, really. He locked onto me like a space capsule docking into port. At first it was flattering, but then, as he started to talk about his–interests, his mission, all that craziness, I became quite horrified.

"You're naturally wondering why I didn't express my repugnance to him. Here's why. Liam worked at Timberline Farm in Ontario before he came here. I'm sure you remember that Timberline is where Stephanie Ankstrom was killed in a Three Day Event. Did you know that she was my friend? From Thea? I thought so. Well, it was Liam who was made to collect all her belongings so they could be returned to Thea. And he did. Only he kept back something."

"Ah. Her journal," Polo said.

"Oh God, how did you–oh, of course, Thea…"

"She only mentioned it an hour ago, when we spoke after we left the barn. She feels rotten about it going missing."

"Well, as you have probably already deduced, there was stuff about me in that journal, very personal, private information I never told anyone but Stephanie."

"About your–difficulties…"

"Yes."

"So he was blackmailing you."

"On the contrary. He was most sympathetic. Empathetic, I mean. He was thrilled to be a friend of someone as–how should I say–*wounded* as himself. He'd had similar experiences in Ireland. He thought we were soul mates. I was terrified of rejecting him after he told me these things, for fear that he would expose me–or worse. By that time I knew he was mentally unbalanced. I knew he was the type to be far more punitive to a friend who turned on him than he would be with those he perceived as enemies from the start. He didn't want money or favours or sex. He wanted friendship, a break from his loneliness. So I played along until I could figure out what to do.

"It wasn't long before he began confiding the most appalling things to me. He just talked and talked and talked. People who stutter are used to listening. And people talking to them don't expect a lot of feedback. They take your silence for interest and think they're doing you a favour doing all the talking themselves He showed me his disgusting collection of hate material. He started boasting about all the things he knew about everyone at the barn. I have no idea how he managed to find out such personal information, but it frightened me, I can tell you."

"It's quite simple, really. He made a hole in the wall of his bedroom and listened to people's phone calls."

"Ah. That straightforward, was it?"

"And he got almost everything wrong, by the way. He heard things and made false assumptions. But you didn't know that, so when he started talking about Bridget's secrets you knew you had to act, right?"

"Right. At that point I knew that my little world might come tumbling down if I didn't do something."

"Was it the problem with the jump at Timberline that would screw up her political future in C–FES or the secret about her father that was the final straw?"

Guy gasped. "How could you possibly know about Bridget's father?" He added quickly, "I mean, what exactly do you know?"

"That he's alive, not dead. That he's no aristocrat. That in fact he's a gamekeeper at a private hunting club near Kingston."

Guy stared and swallowed. "How? How?"

"Liam kept notes, along with phone numbers, didn't you suspect that he must have?"

"Of course I did, but I searched through his belongings and his room, and I couldn't find anything. I found Stephanie's journal, thank God, and destroyed it, but no other personal material."

"It was well hidden, but I found it."

Guy was unnerved, Polo could see. That felt good. "What was the big deal about the father being working class? Who cares, here anyway, what class you come from?"

"Oh, it wasn't just the class thing. It was a bit more complicated than that. But it isn't important for you to know what the secrets were."

"But I want to know. Of course if you won't tell me, I suppose I could always write to Lord Fairclough–or the son. Her partner."

Guy sighed heavily. "No, don't do that. Do you know anything about Bridget's partner, Philip Fairclough?"

"That would be Fig?"

"Yes. Fig." The distaste, even hatred in Guy's voice was palpable, Polo noted. "They grew up together, riding together, all very cozy, except for the one minor detail that Bridget's father was Philip's father's gamekeeper. The Pendunnins lived on the estate. Hired help, though of course to Bridget that didn't quite sink in for some time. Horses can be a great leveler up to a point.

"Bridget's mother was a fiery Irish beauty who loved hunting–Bridget has her hair and eyes, and because she hated her mother, she hated the Irish. Her father was a decent, boring man who didn't ride, while Lord Fairclough was rich, bold, a dashing horseman, etc, etc–well, fill in the blanks."

"I see. The mother has an affair with the lord of the manor–you know, Guy, I don't read novels, I just read the blurbs on the back when my plane is delayed, but this is beginning to sound a lot like the books with quilted covers you see in airports."

"It was, actually. Very Harlequin Romance. Yes, the mother has an affair with Lord Fairclough, and then has Bridget. Bridget's real father is Lord Fairclough. All three adults know this, but Fig and Bridget don't. So when her half brother rapes her"–

"Fig rapes her?" Polo was now fascinated in spite of his determination to stay aloof from the sordid details.

"Yes. And they were observed by a stable lad. Stable lads don't normally jeopardize their jobs by reporting their boss's bad personal behaviour to authorities, but this lad had a serious grievance against Bridget–she never made clear to me what it stemmed from–so he doubtless thought she deserved it, but then he doubled down on his knowledge, and went to Fig's father with the news that Fig and Bridget were sexually involved. Lord Fairclough freaked out, naturally, and had Bridget shipped over here with the promise of continuing financial support to make sure she'd stay put in Canada."

"So Bridget is predisposed to panic and over-react when yet *another* stable boy threatens to turn her life upside down" –

"Indeed."

"And that would also explain the cheque! And the elaborate charade about the so–called frequent but actually bogus trips to England."

"Very quick of you. We knew the cheque would get you thinking."

"Yes. So when *does* she find out?"

"Only recently. Her father–I mean George Pendunnin–has a drinking problem. It's usually under control, but sometimes he gets careless. He had a bad episode and made a terrible mistake. Lord Fairclough had a shooting party. Pendunnin let some game stay uncollected on the ground too long. Did you know that it's extremely dangerous to leave any dead game on the ground? Botulism. It seeps into the ground and gets picked up by the live birds. He'd gotten drunk and lost track of time. An infected live bird was then shot in the twenty–four hours it would have to live after infection, cooked and served to Lord Fairclough's hunting guests. One of them got botulism poisoning and nearly died. Pendunnin was fired, of course, but threatened to reveal the dark family secret.

"So Fairclough did exactly what he had done for Bridget– shipped him off to the colonies, so to speak. He got him this position at the Grassmere Club, a very hotsy–totsy club in the Thousand Islands, only sixteen members, a half million a year in fees to shoot an unlimited number of birds. They swoop down in their private planes. Ninety days in a row a year, seven days a week, only eight guns allowed at a time. Captains of industry kind of thing. Very low profile. Very festive for the lucky few. Anyway, once here, George finally told Bridget the whole story. She made sure everyone thought he was dead to take him off the riding community's radar screen. I daresay Liam overheard her speaking to him in Kingston."

"So now," said Polo, "both of you knew that Liam definitely had to die to protect yourselves and George as well, this no doubt being his last kick at the career can. There was no way Liam could be trusted to keep that secret. And if Fig got wind the secret was out he'd blow her off. Her horse importing career would be finished."

"Right. Liam was intending to take off after setting the fire, and I said I would help him, take him to the bus depot and so forth. It was a perfect opportunity because everyone hated him anyway, they'd assume he'd run off and nobody would look for him. I advised him to tell Benoit that he'd gotten 'the push' from some unspecified authority. That way, Benoit wouldn't be resentful at being left to hold the fort. In fact he'd feel empowered. That would also keep everyone mixed up. Not that they would care why he left. Good riddance, they'd say. Instead, well…I left the box of hate literature under his bed, and brought his other stuff here. If the police were to find it, I would have expressed the utmost astonishment that it was there. I don't go into that shed for weeks on end."

"So I still don't know if it was you or Bridget that killed him."

"It's probably better that way, don't you think? It justifies your not going to the police. If you were really sure, you'd have quite a 'moral struggle' about keeping it to yourself. This way, if you went to the police with 'it could be him or her', you know damn well that they'd be obliged to turn the whole stable upside down checking out every possibility. They wouldn't stop at who you consider the obvious suspects. They'd think Hy had a motive–the anti-Semitism. You know it wasn't Hy, and you're sure it wasn't Fran or Michel or Jocelyne or Roch, so it would be pretty depressing to see their lives turned upside down for nothing, *n'est-ce pas*?"

"I'm fairly certain it was you, Guy," Polo said.

"How so?"

"Because up until a few days ago you were a man dedicated to helping animals in distress. You were a good vet. All of a sudden you find no difficulty in brutally mutilating one horse and killing another. My reasoning is that once you've murdered a human being you have a whole different perspective on the world. You're damaged goods, Guy. The slippery slope, I think it's called. You killed a person because it seemed necessary to save yourself and someone you loved from exposure, and once you'd crossed that line, when it became necessary to take the horses out of commission to shore up Bridget's reputation in the horse world, well, what the hell… "

So far I've gone with my instincts on everyone else, and I know I was right about the others. It was Guy, it was Guy, and I'm never going to be able to prove it. And he's right about the police. The publicity would kill Le Centre's business. Hy will get sick over it. And they'd turn the place upside down for nothing. Because they'll never prove it was Guy, either. Fuck.

Guy asked with breezy curiosity, "Just for the record, what makes you so sure I killed Robin's Song just because I didn't want an autopsy?"

"Rumenex."

Guy jumped a bit. "God! Stephanie again…"

429

"Yeah. In a letter to her mom. It's been an interesting day that way. All kinds of voices from the grave."

"Then I guess one more won't hurt," Guy said bitterly, "the one that Liam dug up from your own personal little cemetery. Your own teeny little headstone. Maybe it will give new depth of meaning to your theory about 'damaged goods.'"

Polo felt a frisson down his back. What could Liam possibly, *possibly* have found out about him? And why would he want to?

Guy sneered and said, "You look a little uptight, Polo. Are you wondering how anyone as pure as you could be harbouring something in his past that a creep like Liam could exploit?"

"No. What I was wondering was why Liam would bother spending all that energy on someone he met for three minutes."

"Oh, that's easy. During those three minutes you made two mistakes. First of all you made fun of him—you asked him if he was a vet because he was wearing the Tufts sweatshirt. You hurt his feelings, Polo. You mocked his fantasy, his unattainable dream."

"Oh, for Christ's sake"–

"But secondly, and more important, you said you were a friend of the stable owner."

"*Et alors?*"

"Hy Jacobson is a Jew. If you're a friend of his, you're an enemy of Liam's. Well, don't look at me like that. I didn't make the rules up. I'm just telling you how Liam saw it."

"And what did he find out about me?"

"Regrettably–for him that is–no one in the horse world that he had contact with had a bad word to say about you. But Liam was the determined sort, pragmatic and not at all lazy. If not you, then was there a relation–say a girlfriend or wife? Oh yes, indeed there was, and guess what? The wife's parents are fairly prominent people in political circles. Any breath of scandal might do some serious damage there. Hmm, says our Liam…"

Nathalie. Even her name linked to that slimeball, Liam, it was intolerable, he–the fishhook in the gut was back, tugging upward, and pain, sharp and sudden, had him pressing a hand hard against his gut.

"Yes," said Guy, savouring his moment, "you have to give our Liam points for ingenuity. How, you're wondering, did he get his information? Remember that after he met you he went to all the spring shows to help out with Michel's students' horses. He only had to hang out with people from your era for a while at every show. It's the same people year after year, decade after decade. He knew the drill for getting information. Just casual conversation, and plenty of it. Gossip is one of the favoured drugs of choice for horse people, as you know. Fills all that down time between classes.

"'Polo Poisson? God, yes. He's a legend. Wife? Oh sure. Nathalie. Cute gal, quite a bit younger than him, I seem to remember. Yeah, they were a hot couple. She must be what, about thirty–five now? Girlfriends? Oh, ask Twinkle over there, they used to hang out at the shows when Twinkle was grooming for Marty Braide'... and so forth. Getting the picture?"

"Nathalie never did a thing in her life that anyone could use against her," said Polo tightly, leaning forward and fighting the instinct to grab Guy and shake the mockery out of him. He could feel his fists balling up. He willed his chest muscles to relax. They were making his ribs hurt, but he was glad of the physical distraction.

"Your wife's parents are, apparently, practicing Catholics," Guy went on smoothly. "Quaint in this day and age in Quebec, but you never know, religion may some day be back in fashion here, and then they'll be on the cutting edge."

"Guy, where the fuck are you going with this? Is this about *religion*?"

"Sort of. Liam had given up religion, but he'd grown up Catholic himself. Some of it still resonated, I guess, because he always felt instinctively repelled by the idea of *abortion*. And I guess he knew that any practicing Catholics in Quebec political circles would be pretty upset for all kinds of reasons if they knew that their future son–in–law had made their daughter have an *abortion*."

Le verglas. Black ice. Not a patch, but an unending sheet that covered the whole goddam road and just went on and on. Polo felt like he was clutching the wheel of his truck, skidding, skidding, and he couldn't get a foothold. Any minute he would skate off the road, and flip, over and over. A balloon of nausea swelled under his heart.

His voice was low and hoarse. He felt it thrumming with tension. "Nathalie never had an abortion, Guy. Liam got it wrong, just like he got almost everything else wrong. She had a miscarriage once"–

"No, Polo, I don't think he did get it wrong this time. Too many details. Apparently Nathalie needed help in finding someone who would do it. How would a nice girl from Outremont know where to look for an abortionist? But this Twinkle girl was a worldly type who did know. And so it was that Nathalie found herself in the hands of the famous Dr. Werzberger, much in the news for years, if you recall, abortion rights crusader, and saviour of damsels in distress. This was the icing on the cake for Liam, of course, that it should be the swarthy, beetle–browed, beaky–nosed Jew, of all people, who did the shameful deed, the very model for that ridiculous cartoon"–

Polo felt sweat breaking out on his forehead. The telephone call yesterday. What was it that she had said? What was it?

'Why can't we ever talk about what happened back then?'

"That's enough, Guy. Don't say another word about my wife, or I'm going to have to do something to stop you." He felt the outline of his flashlight in his pocket. He pictured himself smashing Liam's greasy head with it, but no, it would have to be Guy's head, and at the thought his pulse quickened as he imagined the thrilling crunch of the collapsing skull, the fountain of blood and bone and brain flying up and out...

'Polo, come home for a day. Not to sell horses, not to buy them, not to wheel and deal. Just to talk. Please. Please. One whole day. It's not much to ask.'

Polo forgot where he was. Nathalie's tearful voice roared in his brain. His right hand gripped the flashlight and his left crept under his glasses and covered his eyes. He squeezed them tight, but it didn't help, he was remembering...remembering...

'There's something–something I want to tell you–finally–tell you– it would mean so much to finally–finally...'

"Excuse me a minute, Polo."

Polo opened his eyes to see that Guy had suddenly risen and walked across the corridor toward the blue light. Dazed, Polo followed his progress and realized that it was a nightlight softly illuminating a huge aquarium. Guy now very slowly reached into the water and drew something out. With a triumphant smile, he walked back to the living room. Polo saw that he was holding a fishnet with a long handle.

"Look!" Guy exclaimed cheerfully. "I've got him. This hawkfish was terrorizing my whole tank. He'd already killed one poor little defenseless shrimp, and he thought he was so clever–every time I came near him with the net, he just scooted away. So I just left the net there with some bait and decided to be patient–and look, he took the bait, and I've got him! I'll just go and flush the little bugger down the toilet. Be right back."

I told you I have something to tell you, but you didn't ask what. 'Cuz you don't want to know, do you, chou? You don't want to know… Cuz you don't want to know, do you…don't want to know…don't want–

"You don't look too good, Polo. Have I told you something you didn't know?" Polo looked up to see Guy standing over him and staring at him with mournful eyes. "You know, I believe I have. Do you realize that if the police knew this, they'd figure that you in fact did have a motive as well as an opportunity for murdering Liam? Why do you think I left the bag out for you to find? Your finger-prints are on that duffel bag's handles now. Not to mention on the plastic bag and the wallet."

Guy sighed and shook his head in mock disappointment. "All this running around playing justice–seeking detective–what a great cover for a murderer. That's what they'd think. Maybe you'd like to reconsider your pretentious little thesis about damaged goods and moral struggles and killing and the slippery slope"–

Polo felt a rush of blood to the head, and heard a sound come out of his chest–savage, atavistic–he didn't know was possible for a modern human being to make as he launched himself at Guy. Guy screamed as he collapsed backwards under Polo's weight. As soon as he hit the floor, he curled up in the fetal position with both hands clamped over his face and head. Polo straddled him and drew his fist back to strike. But he hesitated, because Guy was pleading for mercy in a voice Polo had never heard from him be-fore, a tinny, child's voice, "No, p–p–please, sir, oh p–p–please, sir, nnnno, please, d–don't, d–d–d–don't do that…"

Snarling with loathing and contempt and pity–for Guy or for Liam or himself, he couldn't have said–Polo stood over his miserable, shrunken prey for a long minute with his fist raised, wrestling with a passionate desire to strike and strike and strike until his strength gave out.

Long minutes passed, or seemed to. Finally, panting, sobbing, depleted and ashamed, he lowered his arm, and stepped back. He considered what he might do to dissipate the ebbing, but still punishing waves of rage. Smash Guy's fucking aquarium? No. He had to get out of here. He picked up Liam's duffel bag and flung it blindly across the living room. It struck the big Lab, cowering on his floor cushion. The dog yodeled sharply in pained shock, and scrabbled furiously across the floor into the kitchen with his tail tucked between his legs. Polo made a child's noise of disgust at himself and lunged for the door.

 He didn't remember driving back to his condo. The next thing he knew he was leaning over a sleeping Gilles to make sure the boy was breathing–why?–and after that...falling, falling onto a pillow and into the void's welcoming embrace.

CHAPTER TWENTY–SEVEN

IN HIS DREAM HE WAS HAVING Sunday brunch at the Jacobsons. He was at the house in Westmount, and the mahogany sideboard was crowded with the kind of things that the Jacobsons loved–scrambled eggs, smoked salmon, black olives, sliced onions, tomatoes, that very exotic smoke–flavoured chopped eggplant thing Clarice made. And bagels, of course, poppy seed and sesame, a dozen of each, still hot in their brown paper bags, that Morrie picked up from Fairmount Bagels after he'd bought his Sunday New York Times.

But at the same time he knew he was dreaming, because he was aware that he was still lying in bed in the Saint Armand condo. He was suspended between sleep and waking–a very cool feeling. He was on the floating island, the no–man's–land where you could reframe and manipulate your dream like a movie director. Now, for example, he had reset the brunch on the deck of Hy's house in Saint Armand. The sideboard was pine and it was 1992, but even though the waking part of him knew Morrie was dead, the dreaming part invited him to stay in the scene. And he knew it was still brunch in the dream because he could actually smell the bagels and the fresh coffee, and he could hear the voices. The anglophone characters were speaking in French, but his sleeping director benignly allowed what his waking mind noted as a departure from authenticity.

He heard a male voice, then the clatter of cutlery, the fridge door opening and closing, then a woman's voice...he drifted away...he drifted back...something so familiar about the woman's voice...not Ruthie Jacobson, though...and the smell of the bagels and the coffee, so real...

Groggy, stiff and sore, uncomprehending, Polo stood in the bedroom doorway and thought, 'I'm still dreaming. There is my smiling wife standing beside the table pouring coffee for another man'. But of course he knew he was awake. It was just that his mind, like unmittened fingers adjusting tire chains in a blizzard, was stubbornly numb, fumbling at its task in clumsy slow motion, unable to process his visual intake.

"'Morning, Polo," said Nathalie a little warily, setting the coffee-pot back on its burner. "We were just about to wake you."

"Hi, Polo," said Gilles. "Are you okay? I tried to wait up last night, but..."

"Nathalie. Gilles."

What is Nathalie doing here? Why is Gilles acting like it's the most normal thing in the world to be sitting there having breakfast with Nathalie? I don't feel right.

Nathalie was staring at him with concern. "Polo, you really look awful. Did you sleep in those clothes? Are you sick? You're so pale. Do you have a fever?"

He looked down. Why hadn't he undressed when he got back? He frowned, trying to remember the sequence of events of the previous night. Was he ill? Because he felt so spacey. "No. No. I don't know. I'm just–Nathalie, when did you–why didn't you phone last night?"

"I'm sorry. I should have. But I was–otherwise engaged until too late. I was going to call this morning. And then when I woke up, I decided to just come here. I just got in the car and drove. Except," she gestured at the bag on the counter, "I stopped at Fairmount for bagels."

"These are great," piped Gilles enthusiastically, licking jam from his fingers. "I didn't know what bagels tasted like when they're fresh."

Polo's mental spark plugs were damp, but his cognitive motor was at last turning over, revving a bit. He had to speak to Nathalie alone. He caught her eye and they both looked meaningfully at Gilles. Gilles got the message instantly. He said, "Um, you know what? I think I should go over to the barn after breakfast and help Uncle Roch with stuff."

"Good plan," Polo said immediately, and not altogether kindly. "I'm sure there's lots to do."

Boy, thought Gilles, a little hurt, talk about getting the bum's rush. *Salut la visite.* Forget the 'after breakfast' part. Gilles gazed yearningly at his coffee and unfinished bagel and sighed. He glanced at Nathalie, and then at Polo. Their eyes were locked and they seemed already oblivious to his presence. Sexually charged static swirled around the room. Polo looked very strange to Gilles, very sombre and remote. And the way he was looking at his wife– Gilles felt the hair on his arm stirring. He shivered. Never mind the bagel. He was suddenly only too happy to leave those two alone.

Polo had thought that the reviving pleasures of a hot shower and shave and clean clothes would snap him out of whatever it was that was dragging him down, but he still felt the same disturbing disconnect from reality when he came to the table twenty minutes later.

"Feeling better?"

"Yeah. Yeah, I'm fine." Nathalie set down a glass of juice and poured his coffee.

"Thanks."

She eyed him sharply. He looked older, drained, as though he were just on the mend, recuperating from some horrible bug, something swift and viral. Dwelling on his appearance or making any further comment would be unconstructive and worrying, she decided. But it was a little frightening. Polo was never sick. She sat down opposite him and wrapped her hands around her own coffee mug.

"So Gilles filled me in on everything," she said to him briskly, but sympathetically, the determined hostess to the diffident guest.

"The murder, the stallion, the colic–it's horrible."

"Yeah. It's been a bad trip."

"And he told me about you and Roch. Good thing he warned me, because you still look a little scary." She made sure to smile as she said this. Not to sound judgmental.

Polo touched his lip. The cut was healing all right, but it was ugly. He was thankful he didn't have to explain it. And that was also strange. He'd been dying to see her, dying to talk to her for two long days. But she'd caught him off guard. She'd shocked him, and he felt–ambushed a little. One shock too many. She should have warned him she was coming.

He downed the juice in one swallow. Immediately he felt a promising little rush, like a mini-transfusion. Good. He drank some coffee. It was hot and strong, and that felt good too. Maybe it was just fatigue. Maybe he hadn't gotten enough sleep. He willed himself to feel normal. He asked himself how he would feel if he had to ride a horse. Joke. No way.

Nathalie put a split bagel with cream cheese and a jar of jam in front of him. He shook his head.

"I'm not hungry."

"You should eat something."

"Later."

"Try to eat just a little."

"Later."

"I got the bagels for you specially."

He said something inaudible.

"What did you say?"

"Nothing."

"No, you said something. Tell me."

"I said, don't do the Jewish mother thing."

"Ohh…"

"You asked."

"That's true," she said quietly. She looked down into her coffee, and colour bloomed up her throat into her cheeks.

This is great, you schmuck. Perfect. Way to go, asshole. Great opener.

"You know," Nathalie said neutrally, "I have never understood that joke. I never had a problem with Jewish mothers. I was with

438

one last night, in fact. She's quite wise. I don't know why they get dumped on. But maybe by the 'Jewish mother thing' you're referring to the old stereotype about them making their children feel guilty. I'm sorry if I make you feel guilty. Maybe you'd rather no one ever mentioned that they did something for you–so you don't ever have to feel you owe them anything."

"Oh, I'm sure you must be right, you've taken courses in this stuff."

Putz. Ditch the sarcasm. Say you're sorry. Stop whatever the hell it is you're doing to her.

"S'rry," he muttered.

The colour in her cheeks deepened, but Nathalie said nothing, and seemed prepared to say nothing for a good long time.

"You were with Clarice last night."

"Yes."

"I should have guessed."

"How?"

"Ruthie said she thought the Duchess had a date with a man because she told Jenny and Aviva not to come to dinner. You said you were going to see an old friend of mine. I should have put it together. I don't suppose you're going to tell me why."

"I am, but not yet."

Polo shrugged. "Yeah, well, God forbid you should feel you owe me any explanation," he said. "God forbid you should feel you have to tell me where you're going for a whole fucking day and night."

Calvaire. What the hell was it with him? Here she was, here was his fucking *chance* with her, and he was completely blowing it. If only he could shake this damn–cloud, this fog. Two more minutes of this and she would walk out.

Nathalie looked down at her coffee and shifted the mug back and forth. "Polo. I–look, I know I should have called you…"

"I thought I'd never see you again."

He'd meant it as a statement, but it came bursting out like the rasping, frightened cry of a lost kid, finally claimed by his mother in the mall's security office.

He scraped his chair back, stood, and jammed his hands in his pockets. "Ah, *merde*," he muttered, looking down at the table. "I didn't mean to do that."

Nathalie didn't look at him. She was playing with a napkin, folding it into ever-smaller squares. If Polo hadn't looked away in self-disgust, if he'd been looking at his wife, he would have seen her face registering first surprise, then wonder, then discreet, cautious joy. She said softly, still intent on the napkin, "Do you think, if I were going to walk away–do you really think I would just–do it–like that–after all these years?"

"I don't know," he said truculently. "Why not? You're pretty fed up, you made that clear when we spoke on the phone. You're tired of making all the moves. I wouldn't blame you." He yanked open the fridge, saw the Aero bars, felt a little nauseous, closed his eyes, and let the cold air caress his face. Maybe he did have a fever. He closed the door. But he didn't turn back to look at her.

"Polo, I know why you're mad. That phone call the other day–listen, it was more than a little over the top, and I feel stupid about it. I can't believe I got drunk and called you. Now that I know what was going on here, I realize I should have waited 'til you got home and"–

Fuck! He smacked his hand hard on the fridge, and he sensed her startled little jump. There was no way he could let her do this again. Ever. Take the blame, give him an easy out. This was it, didn't she see? It was the story of their lives. She got mad, or sad or bad, always for a good reason. He sulked and verbally abused her or walked out for a day–or a week. She was afraid he'd leave for good, or maybe hit her, or–whatever. So she apologized. *Fuck*! He was flooded with angry love for her. He turned to face her.

"Nath. Don't do that. *Don't do that!*"

"What? *What shouldn't I do?*" She had both hands up on her face, and there it was, just as he'd known it would be, that–look–that–scared look–

"Don't let me get away with this shit. Don't let me–use you–use your goodness to–don't"–he threw his hands up in the air and let them fall–"Nath, you have to stand up to me. *Don't let me do what he did!*"

"He...?"

"My *father*, for Christ's sake. My *father*! He scared her. She was so *scared*. All the time. She was so scared he'd leave her with all those brats, so she just–caved in–every time–and it didn't matter, sometimes he just smacked her–or us–for the hell of it…I'd lie in bed at night and hear her crying…hear her crying…"

He felt lightheaded suddenly and thought he might faint. He leaned against the refrigerator and closed his eyes. He heard her little cry of compassion or maybe fear, heard her chair rub across the floor and then she was there beside him, but he opened his eyes in time, and luckily he had her by the wrist before her hand could reach up to touch his face. He shook his head and whispered hoarsely, "Don't. Don't touch me. I have to keep talking…"

The dizziness ebbed, and he closed his eyes, still holding her wrist. "I'm okay," he whispered. "Go sit down." And she did.

"Nath, listen to me. This is important. You didn't know what was going on here. You don't–listen, you have nothing to apologize for. I don't even know where to start, but that's as good a place as any. You have nothing to apologize for. You've never had…It's me that has to…it's me, Nath…I've…so much has happened in the last two days…I hear us–in my head–that phone call–and I'm saying to myself, was that me talking? Was that me thinking that it's *you* that's the problem because you actually had to get drunk to let me know that having a kid is more important than my fucking ego? Was that prick who wouldn't let his own wife tell him about *his* baggage that she's been carrying all these years–was that prick really me?

"Because I've changed since that call. I know, I know, men say that all the time, don't they? Guys who beat up on their wives, guys who drink, do drugs. They say 'baby, give me another chance because I've changed' when they're scared their woman is going to leave for good. Men'll say anything not to be left. I know that. Maybe you think that's what's happening here. I hope not. I'm babbling a bit. But it's true, Nath. This isn't a con. I have changed.

"Things have happened here. I've had to talk to so many people because of the kid who got killed–and listen, Nath–there's so much I want to tell you, but–but maybe you didn't come to hear me tell you stuff. Maybe you came because it's like you just said, you'd do it in person, not just walk away. I mean, break up. So if that's why you're here, tell me right away. Stop me right now, because once I get going spilling my guts to you, I don't think I could stop even if I wanted to."

Nathalie had been sitting very straight, statue–still with big eyes that never left Polo's face. The knuckles on her hands gripping the mug were white. She said, her voice a little shaky, "To be perfectly honest, I had no plan. I have something to tell you, but it's contingent–on what I was going to hear. I came to listen more than talk. I have a bottom line now where our marriage is concerned, but you already know that. What you've already said–what you've just said–it's so different from–it's like a new language–I hardly know what to say."

"Start by telling me I still have a chance with you."

Nathalie's eyes welled up. "Oh Polo, when did you ever *not* have a chance with me?"

"Nath, I know what it is you came to tell me. It's a story from the past that I should have figured out, but I didn't want to know. So go ahead. It's time we put the secrets from the past on the table."

Nathalie looked shocked and a little fearful. "But you couldn't possibly know what I was going to tell you. Clarice and I only talked about it for the first time last night. No one else knows."

Polo remembered riding the bombproof ponies stables prudently provided for beginner clients. He was too good for them by his second lesson, and he would pound his heels furiously into their big, furry bellies to make them break out of a walk. But they were on automatic pilot, no matter what you did. They didn't even feel your heels drumming away. Clip. Clop. Clip. Clop. This was his brain at this moment, a bombproof pony.

"What are you talking about, Nath? Why would you want to discuss your abortion with Clarice Jacobson?"

Nathalie stared at him as though he were deranged. The colour drained out of her face, and her lips fell apart. Polo's pulse raced.

"That wasn't what I was going to tell you," she whispered. "I mean, not today. Not until I knew whether–Never mind. It was something else I was going to tell you. About you. *About you.* Not about me. Who told you about the abortion? How did you know?"

Clip. Clop. Clip. Clop. Giddyup. Giddyup. The English word–giddy–that's a good word. My brain is plodding and my heart is galloping. I think I need to get out of here.

"Will you take a walk with me, Nath?" He glanced around the

condo. The walls of the tiny space seemed to press inward. "I think I need some fresh air."

"It's so beautiful here, Polo." They were standing on top of a hill with views of the cross–country course and steeplechase. "Didn't you ever consider the Townships when you were looking for land?"

"It is beautiful. I love it here. But I think I didn't want to be too near Roch's turf. It's hard to maintain a friendship when you're competing for slim pickings. And St. Lazare is closer to the airport."

"Should we sit for a while, Polo? You look a little–you don't look well, you know."

They settled down on a flat rock and looked out in silence for a few minutes. Polo took off his glasses and rubbed his face and eyes. "I'm whacked, Nath. It's not the flu or anything. It's all mental. Overload. I've been telling you about it for an hour, and I don't even know if I got in half the details. There was so much. I thought I was doing okay yesterday up to dinner, but then there was the fight with Roch, then the gelding, and hitting Jocelyne, and then Guy…"

"Polo, I'm sorrier than I can say that you found out that way."

"Why didn't you tell me when it happened?" His throat closed over the words.

"*Comment?*"

"Why"–he cleared his throat and breathed deep. "Why didn't you tell me back then?"

Nathalie reached for a stick and picked at the earth in front of the rock. "You know why," she said softly.

"Tell me anyway."

"If I'd gone on with the pregnancy, you would have left me. The next best scenario was to tell you I was pregnant but was thinking of an abortion, and have you immediately try to talk me out of it. But that wasn't going to happen. That was the problem. I knew you'd agree to it, encourage me. Then I'd not only hate myself, I'd hate you too. This way"–

"I wouldn't have left you if you decided to have the baby."

"Not right away, maybe. But you know it would have killed us as a couple. You were afraid. What child needs a father who feels trapped and shows it? Sooner or later we would have split, and I didn't want a child under those circumstances."

"I should have been with you when you went for it, at least. You shouldn't have had to go through it alone."

"I was ashamed of what I was doing. Having you with me would have made it worse–the shame. It wasn't as if it was a rape, or a deformed fetus, or that I was too poor. It was a healthy, viable pregnancy. What kind of relationship could we have had after that if you'd shared in the planning and–execution…? Sooner or later, it would have come between us. This way I didn't have to resent you. I made the decision myself, and I have only myself to blame.

"Why do you think I was so patient for so long about starting a family? It was important to me that the next time, you really want it to happen. I could never go through that again, me wanting it, you sucking back. Anyway for years I didn't feel I deserved another chance. When I did feel I deserved one, I realized that the other part–you wanting it–just wasn't happening, likely never would."

Polo studied his thumbs, which were cleaning his glasses with the edge of his shirt. Nathalie made little random pokes at the ground with her stick.

"So"–he cleared his throat after a long minute's silence–"even though I didn't know about the abortion, you had it for me. I as good as made you do it."

"No."

"Yes. You were like a soldier who knows what the campaign strategy is without having to ask. You did the triage. You chose me over that baby."

Nathalie's voice was thick with anguish. "Don't do this, Polo. I can't bear it. I loved you so much. I knew I would lose you. I was young. I didn't realize–I thought I could walk away from it and forget and we'd start again"–

"It's kind of funny, you know. You should have seen me last night, so pompous and righteous and rational, telling Guy he was damaged goods, lecturing him all about the slippery slope, and then, when he very reasonably pointed out that I was a killer my-self, I went ballistic. I'm no better than he is–where human beings are concerned, anyway."

"You are *not* a killer."

"I am in spirit. If I were the kind of man I should have been, if I were the kind of man you knew would take his responsibilities seriously–a man, in other words, not a cowardly boy, you wouldn't have felt you had to do that to keep me."

Nathalie was now stabbing hard at the ground. A little crater was forming between her feet. "Do you hate me for it, Polo?"

"*Hate* you?" he echoed in wonder. "I could never hate you, Nath. You're the only woman I ever met I could picture waking up with every day for the rest of my life."

He too had been gazing out at the landscape, but now he turned to look at her profile. Really look. She had dropped the stick and was hugging her knees and staring blindly at the rock face of Saint Armand. Polo had known her face in all its subtle variations since she was a nine–year old girl. Now he saw fine lines around her eyes he hadn't noticed before as she squinted into the late morning sun. She had never seemed more desirable to him. What smote him, though, was her expression. Not sad. It was way beyond sad. She looked–bereft. And–he ached with shame–so alone in her grief. The solitude of her long sorrow tipped his full heart to overflowing for her. He hadn't touched her once since she arrived, but now his arms reached out and pulled her to him.

"I love you, Nath. More than I can say. I would give anything to have known then what I know today." She moaned and buried her face in his shoulder, and he felt the sobs begin. "Dearest girl," he murmured, "I want to tell you something important, okay?" He bent to kiss her hair, and confided to its lemony fragrance, "I have it in me to be a good father. That's what I found out this weekend. And I want that before it's too late. I want us to have a child. Children. When I thought you weren't coming back, and I had missed all these years of us being a real family, and I was going to end up alone, a failure, a nobody, I got very, very scared. I can't bring back the years. I can't undo our mistake. I can't promise I'll be the greatest husband and father of all time. I can only promise I'll be there a hundred per cent, giving it my best shot. Nath, I've only ever been half there for you, and you've always known it. I may not be the man you deserve, but from now on I can give you the best of what I am. If you'll let me."

He pulled her closer, tighter, ignoring the pain in his ribs. She was weeping with complete abandon now, in great, racking, noisy convulsions, and he didn't have the slightest impulse to run away. It was the complete opposite. He only wanted to comfort and protect her. He pulled her on to his lap and folded her into the hollow of his body. He sheltered her in his arms, and rocked her like a child. He stroked her hair. He purled soft nursery noises into her ear to soothe her. He found her hand and caressed the bitten-down nails. Tenderly he kissed her salty wet cheeks and eyelids, over and over again.

And in this way, oblivious to everything else, he attended her passage through the storm. He would have been her safe harbour all day if he had to. At some point as he waited, the heavy cloud in his brain dissipated, and he began to feel physically well and strong. Mentally he felt–at peace? Yes, and that was good, but he distinguished another sensation too–something unfamiliar, unanticipated, but glorious, actually. He felt–normal...

Hands linked, they walked slowly back to the condo. Polo was thinking about what a lucky man he was, when suddenly he thought of Guy, alone in that isolated house, and he remembered those mournful eyes staring into his. He tried to shake the image off–he wanted to wallow in the unalloyed pleasure of his own windfall, but–

"Nath, I can't get Guy out of my mind."

"You're still angry at him. That's natural"–

"No. It's not that. I'm actually a little–Nath, I can't remember–I mean, I remember I went for him when he said–you know–about me being a killer too, but that's all. I seem to remember leaving the house without doing anything to him, but not the drive home. The next thing I remember is checking Gilles back at the condo–crazy–to see if he was, like, breathing, and I'm wondering"–

"You think you may have gone back and hit Guy? Hurt him and then blocked it out?"

"I–it's weird–I just can't remember. I was out of my mind with rage..."

"You would have. Remembered, I mean. You probably just don't want to think about what he said."

"Yeah..."

They walked on.

"He's the saddest, loneliest guy I ever met, *chérie*."

"There are a lot of lonely people in the world," she said softly, and laced her fingers with his, squeezing tight.

"Not like him, Nath. He's…human wreckage…a lost soul."

Nathalie sat beside Polo on the sofa, as Clarice had done with her, and she laid the photograph gently on the coffee table in front of him. She expected to wait a full minute for his reaction. But Polo leaned over to see it closely and knew instantly.

"This isn't me," he said flatly. "It looks like me–but it isn't. Who is it?"

"How did you know so fast? He looks exactly like you."

"I never sat on that pony."

"Turn it over."

Polo read the inscription, and now it took a little more time.

Clip. Clop. Clip. Clop.

Then he turned it back to the picture and took a good look at the older boy. Morrie. Then back to the other side.

Clipclop. Clipclop.Clipclop.

"Morrie's brother."

"Yes. He died young. In Poland. Morrie had thought he would bring him over here one day, but it never happened."

clipclopclipclopclipclop

"I was the pretend brother. The knock–off."

"Yes. He always meant to tell you, but he was afraid you'd hate him for it."

"Me? Hate Morrie?"

"Well, it's a serious thing he did. He–kind of bought you from your parents, didn't he?"

Polo smiled wryly after he considered what she had said for a moment. Then he said, "Let me tell you a joke."

"A Morrie joke?"

"Yeah. I'll give you the short version. 'Okay, so this St Urbain type, this crude street guy asks this very proper Westmount lady, would you sleep with me just once for a million bucks? And she hesitates and says, well, a million dollars, I could buy a lot with a million dollars, so yes, I guess I would sleep with you once for a million dollars. So then the guy says, would you sleep with me for a hundred bucks? So she gets all huffy and says, what do you think I am? And the guy says, oh I know what you are, we're just haggling over the price…'"

"Any other time, I'd laugh. But jeez, Polo, that's a pretty harsh comment on your parents…"

"Is it? Nath, all the money in the world can't buy something that isn't for sale at any price."

"Whoa! That's not being fair to your mother anyway, Polo."

Polo shrugged. "It's not a judgment on her character. Circumstances took away her leverage. She had too many children. The temptation was too great. I honestly don't blame her." He paused and smiled a little sadly. "It was my being 'bought' that gave her some independence, ironically enough. Things improved between her and my father when I left, you know. That *Clar-Mor* material she got every month–she knew she could support herself if he walked out. I think he started treating her with respect when I left."

"And as for Morrie"–he took a deep breath and carefully picked up the photograph. He stared intently at the smiling boy on the pony–"How can I blame him for trying? He'd lost his family. Love makes you selfish. Losing someone you love–a broken heart–you want to mend it. It's natural. It's human. You take what's at hand."

"I'm glad you don't hate him. It's a shame he never told you so he could know it too before he died."

"No, it's better this way. Telling me would have changed things. I don't think I could have accepted his generosity if I'd known where it was coming from. Ignorance was really bliss in my case."

"He loved you, you know. I mean, not because he loved his brother. He loved *you*."

Polo flashed on Morrie in his tuxedo. He said softly, "Oh, I know that, *chérie*. That was another thing I found out this weekend."

"There's a letter, too, Polo. Clarice said it wouldn't be wrong for me to read it first, but in the end I decided not to." She took the sealed envelope from her purse and handed it to him.

Polo looked at it, turned it over and back again. He looked at his name, nothing else, printed large on the outside: POLO. He ran his finger over the outline of the card and the paper clip on the right hand top of the envelope. He suddenly felt quite nervous, reluctant to know more than he already did. He made himself slide his thumb under the edge of the flap. The telephone rang, and he jumped. He looked at Nathalie with raised eyebrows. Did she mind? Go ahead, she signaled.

Gilles clutched the phone so hard his hand and ear hurt, and his teeth chattered so hard he could barely speak. "P–Polo? I'mmmm at Guy's–I'm –I'm –I think he's dead–I can't–I can't–okay…okay…I'm breathing…no, no, I didn't touch anything–I just came and I saw–he was supposed to look after the stallion like he always does since–but he never showed–his line was busy–and Uncle Roch told me to feed the stallion–but I don't know–I mean, how?–the tongue–and Uncle Roch has so much to do, so I thought –okay…okay…I'm breathing…Oh Polo, did you kill him? I mean, you looked so weird this morning–oh *crisse de crisse*–he looks like Liam–can you come?–o good o good o good–no, I'm not touching anything–can you hurry? I'm–I'm so…okay…okay…I'm breathing…okay…okay…"

CHAPTER TWENTY-EIGHT

G UY LAY DEAD ON THE FLOOR, ALMOST EXACTLY WHERE POLO had left him eight hours before. Polo could see that Guy was dead in the two seconds he had before Gilles launched himself, blubbering with relief, into his arms. Heart racing, he concentrated on the absolute necessity of getting Gilles to calm down. He gave the boy a swift hug, then sat him down at the kitchen table, out of sight of the body. He strode to the liquor cabinet and poured a shot of scotch into a glass. He thrust it at Gilles. "Drink this first. Then we'll talk."

Gilles took it with trembling hands, swallowed it all down in a gulp and grimaced. Slowly the colour came back to his face and he stopped shaking.

"Are you okay?" Polo asked.

"I think so."

"Is that how you found him?"

"I didn't touch anything, I swear," said Gilles. "He was just… there…and all I could think was that you said you were going to see him last night, and…" he choked up and put the glass down and looked miserably at the floor.

Polo wanted desperately to say what Gilles was waiting to hear– 'don't be stupid, kid, of course I didn't kill him.' But the words stuck in his throat, because the last thing he remembered was standing over Guy with his fist poised to strike. Yesterday he would have answered, 'don't be stupid, kid, there's no way I *could* or *would* kill him, or anyone'… That was something he could never say again. Adrenaline surged. He couldn't answer Gilles' question until he examined the body.

"Just sit there for a minute, Gilles. Just breathe and try to let your muscles relax. You're not in any trouble here, okay?"

"Okay."

Holding his breath, heart pounding, Polo bent down over Guy and checked for blood under the head or bruises on his face or neck. Nothing. Nothing. Nothing. *Merci, le bon Dieu.* And he crossed himself for the first time since–he couldn't remember.

Guy looked peaceful in death, in spite of the half open eyes with their wooden stare and the waxy laminate of his skin. He was curled loosely on his side as if he'd decided to take a nap on the floor. One hand was half hidden under a chair. In it was something white. Polo gently pushed the chair aside. Guy held a legal size envelope in his hand. And beside that hand, revealed now that the chair had been moved, was the empty syringe. Polo's eyes traveled up Guy's arm, and there the entry point was, marked by a drop of dried blood, on the inside of the elbow. He sighed with relief–and profound sadness.

Polo slid the envelope carefully out from under the curled fingers. It was sealed. There was one word marked on it: POLO. Through the paper at the right hand top he could feel the outline of a business card and a paper clip. Polo felt disoriented. A little wave of panic swept through him. *Why was Guy holding Morrie's letter? How the fuck…?*

"Polo?" Gilles' voice quavered with the strain of waiting for the answer to his question. Instinctively Polo folded the envelope and shoved it in his back pocket.

"I'm here, Gilles. And I didn't kill him."

Muffled sobbing.

"Gilles, I need you to be brave and help me to deal with this, okay?"

452

The sobbing choked off abruptly and Gilles was beside him, wiping his nose with his sleeve and blinking rapidly.

"Gilles, first you have to know that Guy wasn't murdered by anyone–he killed himself." Polo pointed to the empty syringe on the floor. Gilles gasped.

"But why?" Gilles asked, baffled. Then, when Polo didn't reply at once, he said softly, "Oh, is it because–Polo, was it *Guy* who killed Liam?"

"It looks that way, but listen, Gilles, we can't talk about that now. I don't want to telephone from here, because I don't know who will answer or who'll be around if Roch answers. So here's what you have to do. Take the truck and drive to the barn. Find Roch and get him to his office or somewhere private. Tell him what you found, tell him I'm here. Then you stay at the barn and Roch and I will deal with what needs to be done." He paused and added, "Gilles, you're going to have to talk to the police, you know."

Gilles nodded and bit his lip.

"Not just about this. About Liam too. You understand? Your fingerprints are on the buckle."

Gilles nodded again and made for the door.

"Oh, yeah, and Gilles"–

"Yeah?"

"Ask Jocelyne to show you how to feed the stallion. You have to learn to do this stuff, you know, if you're going to make a go of it in stable life."

Gilles coloured up and stood taller, squaring his shoulders. He said firmly, "I *am* going to learn, Polo. Uncle Roch is going to be happy he asked me to come here."

As soon as Gilles left Polo took a deep breath and opened the envelope. There was a single sheet of paper, neatly written in small, but legible script.

Polo, I'll be dead when you read this. I told you tonight that I'd made a kind of breakthrough, that I'd decided I wasn't going to live my life in fear any more. I believed it. But then when I thought you meant to hurt me–justifiably, in retrospect, as I shouldn't have trifled with your obviously deep feelings for your wife–I think we both understood from my reaction that I was never going to escape the "difficulties" of my adolescence. I am not brave enough to face the challenge of a lifetime spent in fear and self-loathing. And so I have made another kind of breakthrough, you might say.

Consider this my confession–not only to you, but to the police or anyone else you choose to show it to. I killed Liam because he was a threat to my privacy and because he was a danger to Bridget and her father. I cut the stallion to prevent him from doing stud service until I could think of a more permanent solution. I killed Robin's Song to prevent Thea from finding out about his navicular syndrome and ruining Bridget's import business. I feel great remorse about the horses, but not about Liam. It was his intention to start with fires and vandalism, but eventually to move on to killing his "enemies." He told me this, and I have no reason to doubt it would have happened. The world is well rid of him.

I bequeath my aquarium and my savings (see marked folders on desk) and any reef literature he wants of mine to Matt Graham from Aqua-Tech (see card attached) who helped me create my system. I know he will reconstruct it and keep it going, and in my own weird way, I feel I will be leaving something of myself to continue on. Secondly, I told you that I destroyed Stephanie's journal, but I didn't. It's in my bedroom, under my pillow. Please give it to Thea with my hope that she will find solace in it. I loved Stephanie, and I failed her. Finally, Harley is in the garage. Harley is an easy keeper. Maybe Gilles would take him on? I notice he likes dogs and is good with them. I have nothing else of importance–do what you think best with my books and other possessions.

Don't blame yourself for this, Polo. Even if you hadn't been so sharp about figuring things out, I am pretty sure this would have happened sooner or later, once Bridget left. I was okay with her around. It was the being alone. That isn't living.

Guy Gilbert

p.s. Dr. Forget at Saint Hyacinthe should be consulted for any questions regarding care of the stallion.

Ruthie put down the telephone. "It's rather mysterious. Polo and Roch can't come for brunch, but they want us to be here all together later so they can explain everything. He said he couldn't be precise about the time, but he'll call when he knows. He said to go ahead and eat without them. Oh, and Nathalie is here. She'll come over later too."

They trooped outside and took places at the prettily laid out table. Manon poured each a mimosa of champagne and peach juice.

"Too bad," said Hy. "He's missing out on the Fairmount bagels, which I happen to know are one of his all time favourite things. He didn't mention Nathalie was coming up."

"I have the impression it was a surprise for him too. He sounded a little tense. I hope they're not fighting. They're such a good couple, basically."

Thea said, "I have to admit I'm very curious to meet the wife. What's she like?"

"Nice. Sweet," said Hy promptly. "Quiet, though. Kind of background-y, if you know what I mean."

"Uncomplicated," added Ruthie decisively. "And undemanding. That's what Polo likes about her. He's not into–oh, you know. Nuances. Layers. Introspection. Relationship analysis. All that touchy–feely stuff."

"She's pretty bright, though," said Hy. "She's just not assertive."

"Not like–ahem–some women we know, eh brother dear?"

"Oy! Let's not get started on the Jewish wife thing," Hy said in mock alarm. "So what's the deal? Do we have a murderer?"

"I hope so. He sounded very serious. He wouldn't have told us to wait around for him if he had nothing, would he?"

"Let's not forget Sue Parker," said Thea. "Even if Polo didn't find out anything, she may have."

The telephone rang. Manon ran in to answer.

A few minutes later she returned to the table. "Talk of the devil. That was Sue. And I'm afraid she's had bad luck. Bridget's father wouldn't talk to her, and in fact had her thrown out of the club grounds. She said she has no more time to spend on this, and she's continuing on to Toronto to work on the Palm Beach story. She says she wants–how did she say–'first dibs' if we find the murderer."

"In that case," sighed Ruthie, reaching for a bagel, "it all depends on Polo…"

It was getting late, almost dark, when Polo and Nathalie arrived at the condo for the night. They had agreed it was too late to go home. And the police had wanted Polo handy for another day.

"You never got to read Morrie's letter," said Nathalie, as she switched on the lamps.

"I just want to decompress a bit first. Big day." Polo didn't want to admit his reluctance to face up to Morrie's final words. He didn't want to find out a single new thing today...

"Are you hungry yet?" Nathalie asked.

"Now that you mention it, I'm starving."

"What about some scrambled eggs and those bagels finally? They're probably a little stale by now, but they'll still be good toasted."

"Eggs are good. And it would be a privilege to eat a bagel that you got for me 'specially' at Fairmount." Polo said. Nathalie stiffened and looked at him guardedly.

He grinned and kissed her lightly on the forehead. "I wasn't being sarcastic. I mean it. That was nice of you."

Nathalie moved around the tiny kitchen organizing their meal. "Polo, what would you have done if Guy hadn't...you know...I mean, would you have called in the police anyway, knowing they'd grill everyone, even you?"

Polo took a beer from the fridge and twisted off the cap. "I honestly don't know." He stood frowning for a moment, staring into space. "That wasn't an off-the-cuff answer. I mean, I've thought about it and thought about it and that was my conclusion. I honestly don't know. Whatever I did would have come from some spontaneous impulse at the last minute. Want a beer?"

She shook her head. "It's not a nice thing to say, but we were lucky."

"No kidding." He took a long pull at the beer. "Did you see how relieved Roch was when the police promised they'd keep it quiet? They were pretty good about it."

"And weren't you impressed with how manly and cooperative Gilles acted with them?"

"Yeah, I think the kid's going to make it here. Roch was proud of him. He invited him to stay at his house 'til he felt okay by himself in the trailer. Lucky for him, since there was no goddam way he was staying here tonight."

Two pairs of eyes flicked toward the bedroom, then met and held. Nathalie blushed like a schoolgirl. Polo's heart, mind and flesh quickened in unison to the thrill of her implied invitation.

"Um–how are your ribs?" Nathalie asked demurely, intently focused on the eggs she was whipping in a pyrex bowl.

"I just took some Tylenol. Extra–strength. Three."

"*Three.* Ohhh…then soon you shouldn't be feeling much pain at all."

"I'm counting on it."

"Because," she stopped whipping the eggs, looked him in the eye and said, with a note of soft, but candid challenge, "I would never want to hurt you…holding you too close, I mean."

Polo immediately set his beer on the counter. He took her face in his hands and kissed her tenderly on the lips. He said gravely, "You can only ever hurt me by letting me go, Nathalie, not from holding me. I want to be held–as close as you want." Then he took the bowl from her hands and put it down beside the beer, adding lightly, "And by a strange coincidence, speaking of holding and being held, I find I'm suddenly not nearly as hungry as I thought I was."

As he led her toward the bedroom, Nathalie said, with a philosophic sigh, "I guess it was the destiny of those bagels to get stale."

"Better them than us."

"Polo, I can't make this kitchen any cleaner. I'm dying of curiosity. You must have read that letter five times. What did Morrie *say*?" She slid into the chair beside the sofa.

Polo handed her the letter, but his expression told her nothing. He looked more than a little stunned, she thought, as he leaned back and stared at the card he was holding with both hands.

Polo, if you're reading this, I'm dead, maybe for a few years, since I know Clarice wouldn't be looking in that shoebox until she decided to move. I knew she would eventually, because I made her promise she wouldn't sit around in that big house being a professional widow and worrying about burglars and crazies.

Anyway, I hope this finds you and Nathalie and your family well. I say 'your family' in the sense of a wish, because as of this writing, you're married quite a while and so far no kids. This troubles me, because it makes me wonder if that's partly my fault. Clarice has probably told you already, but the boy in the photo was my brother Markus. You look at him, you got the picture. I always said you were smarter than my own kids (which I know I shouldn't be putting on paper, but never mind, I know it's safe with you), so by now you figured everything out.

I always used to say I never jerked you around, and that was true where the horses were concerned, and I think in this respect you have to admit I'm not like most of the people I ever met in horse sport. But I did jerk you around big time where your life was concerned, and for this I hereby apologize. I know I gave you lots of material things, and I'm glad you ended up with nice teeth and good glasses and saw the doctors you needed to see and all that, and I can't be sorry about the horses. You have a God given talent, like no one else I ever saw in that sport, and believe me, I knew what I was looking at. That part was good.

But the other part, taking you away from your family, as the years went by, it started to weigh very heavy on my conscience. But I didn't know what to do. Then Ruthie came home from that horse show in St Lazare and she asked if you were her brother. That was a terrible shock, I have to tell you. I thought my secret was out and it scared the hell out of me. I hit my own daughter. I never hit a woman in my life, before or since, so you can imagine how I felt. Then she as good as told me she was in love with you. That was another shock. Don't get the wrong idea about that. Don't think it was I didn't consider you being good enough for Ruthie. You were more than good enough. But it would have been like her being with a brother. I never thought of you two as being anything except like a brother and a sister. So I went a little crazy. I hope you understand.

And that's why I lost my heart for horses. That and what those fuckers tried to do, keeping you off the team. And that's why we sort of lost touch in the later years. I couldn't pretend anymore. After Ruthie told me that, I realized Markus was really dead, and you were you, not him. I mean, I'm not stupid, I always knew you were you, but it was still mixed up somehow and gave me a lot of comfort til Ruthie told me that.

Anyway, I stand by what I always told you. A man should marry someone from his own background. Marriage is hard enough. So that's what I'm getting at. Maybe you don't know what is your real background anymore. Maybe what I did confused you, and it screwed up your life a little. I apologize for that. I hope the good stuff balanced out the other part.

Nathalie's a good girl. You should be happy, and you should have children. It doesn't matter what else you'll ever do in your life, nothing beats children, even when they make you tear your hair out, which thank God mine never did.

So now you're wondering about the card. This guy on the card from BNA Trust–or whoever he gave my file to if he isn't there anymore–he's got some news for you. Remember I gave you half the money from Hamish? You did the right thing with it, with the land and the investments. But just in case something happened to you, or you couldn't work, or whatever, I wanted that your kids should be secure, and they shouldn't feel that all the goodies only come from one side of the family. That's an unhealthy thing for kids in my opinion.

I know Nathalie's going to inherit a big chunk, but what if she left you or she died? I know, I know, I'm morbid. So sue me. I was right to be, though. Look, I'm dead! (Joke!) I don't have to tell you after all the years you spent with us, security for Jews is the big thing, right? So this guy at BNA, he has the portfolio from the other half of the money from Hamish. The account number is on the other side of the card. They have a (sealed) copy of this letter, and if Clarice didn't give it to you, they would have eventually.

The money isn't for you, except for emergencies, like brain surgery in the States, (God forbid). It's for your kids, especially for their education or to set up a business or something. If they want to go to Harvard, they should. Harvard costs an arm and a leg. But you got enough arms and legs for an octopus in that portfolio by now so don't sweat it.

So that's the deal. If you don't have kids (I forgot to mention, adopted counts), the money eventually goes to charities. But I'm hoping they're not going to get it, if you take my meaning (don't worry, they got plenty from me already). Also, I'd feel very bad if you weren't going to have kids, but read this and had them for the money! But to be

100% honest, I wouldn't care even if you had the kids for the money, because once you had them, you'd be glad.

There's probably quite a lot of money there by now. That makes me happy. Like I told you after the Royal, when I told you I was selling Hamish, I want you should have a good life, Polo, and never be beholden to some of those schmucks in that business. Don't get proud about accepting this, either. Like I said, it's for your kids, and for kids you take all the lucky breaks you can get.

Well, that's about it, 'yingele' (that's Yiddish for young one–I know, I know, but that's how I like to remember you). I hate schmaltz, but you know what I think of you. I was proud to be associated with you. You were always a good boy, with a strong character, and in my humble opinion, you would be a great dad. Like they say in Fiddler on the Roof, *a blessing on your head. Best regards to Nathalie. I forgot to mention that I think she will be a great mother.*

Morrie

Nathalie handed the letter back, and Polo folded it and tucked it back in its envelope. "Wow," she said awkwardly, and wiped discreetly under her eyes.

"Nath, I don't think I can talk about this yet. Do you mind?"

"Of course not. It's too huge."

Polo didn't speak. He kept staring at the card.

Nathalie searched for a neutral topic. A book with a bright green cover on the table beside her caught her eye. She picked it up.

"*Faux Amis*? What kind of dictionary is that?"

"It's words that seem the same in English and French but sometimes have a different meaning. You know, like deception in English and *deception* in French."

Nathalie opened the cover. "Oh," she said with prim disappointment.

"What?"

"There's an inscription from Ruthie."

"Yeah, it was a birthday gift or something. What did she say? It's so long ago."

"It says, 'Here is a book about false friends, from one true friend to another. Polo, you are special/*tu es spécial* (see p. 668–joke! but not my friendship for you for ever and ever), love, Ruthie."

Polo looked at Nathalie, and saw how it still was for her where Ruthie was concerned. Enough already. This had to end.

"Nath, put the book down and come and sit beside me."

She sat beside him, and he pulled her in close to him. "Okay. Let's do Ruthie. I'll tell you whatever you want to know. You have to really understand two things, though. Ruthie will always be my friend, no matter what, is one, and two is, I love you, Nath, only you. Whatever was between Ruthie and me that was more than friendship, that's finished. You read the letter. In her heart Ruthie knew I belonged to her father in a special way. The one time we forgot that, I think we both felt very ashamed without exactly understanding why. I know I did. Now I know why.

"Ruthie was good for me, Nath. She was the first girl I ever met who knew her own worth, and acted like it. She was the first girl I ever met who had respect from her father for her good mind and her opinions. It was because of Ruthie that I found out girls could be real women–sexy and fun, and still be a man's equal in every way. Ruthie stood up to me when I deserved it, Nath, and that was good for me. She educated me in more ways than one. She set standards. I'm finally going to start meeting them. With you. She paved the way for us to be happy. And that's the story on Ruthie.

"So don't be jealous of her, Nath. Be her friend. It would make me very happy. Don't forget, when we have kids, she'll be their Auntie Ruthie. Soon it won't be just us any more. When we have a kid. It'll be lots of other people who have a stake in our lives. My *maman*, your parents, my brothers and sisters. Your sister. And the Jacobsons. If we want to be really happy, we have to think about fitting everyone into the picture in a good way."

Nathalie sighed. "Polo, how did you get to be so smart about people without taking courses?"

"I have horse sense. I had to. It was the only alternative to going to school…"

Three months later, when she was absolutely sure, Nathalie told Polo her good news. He was ecstatic, but immediately fearful that having sex would damage the embryo. Nathalie was persuasive in her reassurances. Some days later, while they were contentedly cuddling after a particularly rapturous hour of lovemaking, Nathalie said drowsily,

"I loved Michel and Claude's wedding, didn't you? It was amazing, the way the inside of Hy's dressage arena got turned into that huge white tent."

"It helps when you're in the *shmatta* business. That was a good speech Roch gave, welcoming her into the family. He even seemed to mean it."

"Oh, I think Claude has him wrapped around her little finger. She's a terrific girl. I love her self-confidence."

"A plain Jane like that would have to have self-confidence walking around with Michel."

"You know what? I think she's used to his looks. I think she loves him for what he is inside. And what's funny is that I don't see her as plain anymore. She's so full of personality and energy, and that big, friendly smile–I always think of her as pretty now."

"They're good together. It's going to work."

"It was nice of the Jacobsons to give them such a great party."

"Yeah. Nath, I was happy to see you and Ruthie having fun together."

"I always liked her, you know. I just didn't *like* it that I liked her."

Neither spoke for a moment. Then Nathalie murmured, "You're thinking about riding a horse, aren't you?"

"How did you know?"

"You're doing half halts on my bum."

"Clever wife, do you have any idea how cool it is for a guy like me to have a woman who on top of her other great qualities knows when her bum is getting half–halted? *Je t'adore.* Listen, Nath, you know that little black three year old with the off–centre white star I got in Alberta last year?"

"Mm. Nice gaits."

"Yeah, but he's got something special. It's more than just gaits."

"What?"

"It's his personality. He's got heart, and he's honest, and so willing to learn, with this kind of quiet peppiness to him. And there's such a calm, well–adjusted look in his eyes. I just like him, I guess."

"Polo, you're sounding a little schmaltzy about a horse. This isn't you."

"I'm going to keep him, Nath."

"Oh Polo, that's lovely. It's time you had a horse of your own. Except that black one is so small, he's barely fifteen hands."

"He's not for me. He's for our son. I'm going to put a ton of time into him. He'll be the best-made horse in the world, and he'll take good care of Marc while he's learning to ride."

"Son? Marc? Excuse me, have I been in a coma for seven months?"

"It's going to be a boy, Nath. We have to call him Marc."

"For Morrie's Markus?"

"Yes. And also for Marcus Aurelius."

"Who's Marcus Aurelius?"

"A Roman emperor–and a great writer."

"Why an emper–oh right, I almost forgot…*Napoléon*!"

Polo smiled and hugged her. He ran the fingers of his right hand through the shaggy thatch of hair that Clarice's *coiffeur* (to Polo's delighted surprise) had cropped and styled for her. His left hand drew her fingers to his lips. He kissed them, silently noting and approving her newly grown and polished nails. Then he sighed with gratitude for the sweet perfection of his life.

"Yeah. It's a Poisson family tradition."

THE END

CPSIA information can be obtained at www.ICGtesting.com
Printed in the USA
LVOW12s2021250116

472172LV00002B/350/P